"Waitin' for me like a good squaw, darlin'?" Colt drawled.

"Why did you bother coming at all if you can't tolerate me?" Sam shot back.

"It was expected of me," Colt rejoined lamely. "What kind of man could neglect a beautiful bride on her wedding night?"

"The kind that never wanted a bride in the first place."

"Just so you understand that I don't intend to honor your heathenish rites," Colt reminded her sternly. "You're my squaw, nothin' more."

"It's no more than I expected from a blackhearted skunk."

Above the blanket Sam had pulled up to shield her nude form, her shoulders gleamed like antique gold in the dim glow of the fire burning in the center of the tipi. Colt's eyes glinted wickedly as he dropped to his knees and stripped away the thin covering with one fluid motion, tossing it aside.

"Damnation, you're beautiful!" he muttered. "Maybe a saint could resist such outlandish temptation, darlin', but as you well know, I'm no saint...."

CONNIE MASON

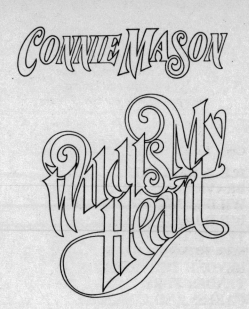

Wild is My Heart

This one is for my husband,
Jerry, because of his love
of westerns and because
he's put up with me for 39 years.

A LEISURE BOOK®

June 1999

Published by

Dorchester Publishing Co., Inc.
276 Fifth Avenue
New York, NY 10001

ISBN 0-8439-4605-9

The name "Leisure Books" and the stylized "L" with design are trademarks of Dorchester Publishing Co., Inc.

Printed in the United States of America.

Chapter One

It's comin', Sam. Listen. Do you hear the poundin' hooves?"

"Pull your hat down over your eyes, Will, do you want to be recognized?"

"Are you certain we're doin' the right thing, Sam?"

"Hellfire and damnation, we've gone over this before, Will. Now hush up and draw your kerchief up over your nose."

Adjusting the twin Colt revolvers that rested in a snug leather holster girdling slim hips, Sam jammed the disreputable felt hat over shiny black hair until nothing but piercing violet eyes peered above a red and blue kerchief.

Will followed Sam's example, beads of nervous sweat dotting his forehead. "What if the money ain't on the stage?" he asked uneasily.

1

"It will be," Sam replied. "Just remember to stay in the background and follow orders. I've already told you we'll take only what we need. No more, no less. Keep your guns on the driver and guard; they're the most dangerous and likely to cause trouble. Let me do the talking and under no circumstances are you to fire your weapon anywhere but in the air."

"But, Sam," Will protested, "what if they—"

"You heard me, Will, no killing," Sam emphasized. "Get ready, the stage is rounding the bend."

Sam had spent hours finding the perfect spot to hold up the stage, finally settling on a deserted stretch of road ten miles south of Karlsburg where the road wound between wooded hills before curving down into the valley. The flat, arid plain farther south offered little in the way of concealment, but this spot provided ample protection.

Behind a stand of tall oaks the two youthful bandits waited for the stagecoach from San Antonio carrying an undisclosed amount of gold destined for Calvin Logan's bank in Karlsburg.

A streak of lightning flashed across the threatening sky, and Sam cursed the luck that brought a storm on this day of all days. But perhaps, Sam reflected, the rain would work to their advantage, turning the road into a quagmire of mud and making tracking impossible. A clap of thunder rolling in from the west matched the thunder of horses hooves pounding on the dirt-packed, rutted road.

Suddenly it was time. Digging booted heels into the flanks of their mounts, Will and Sam rode fearlessly onto the road, firing warning shots in the air just as the stage came hurtling around the bend.

"Christ! That sounds like gunfire!"

Steve "Colt" Colter uncoiled his long buckskin-clad legs and leaped to the window of the rattling stagecoach. Seated across from him, a heavily pregnant woman clapped a fluttering hand to her chest and would have swooned if her husband, a shopowner returning from a visit to San Antonio, hadn't chided, "Pull yourself together, Annie, it's only thunder."

"Thunder, hell," muttered Colt, palming one of the Colts riding low on his hips. He'd heard pistol shots far too often not to recognize them now. The sounds even disturbed his sleep sometimes and invaded his dreams. No matter where he went they pursued him. It had been that way ever since he ran off at seventeen to help General Zachary Taylor's army defeat the Mexicans in the war of 1846.

Another volley of shots set off a new violent reaction in the pregnant Annie, who began wailing at the top of her lungs and flailing her arms in the air.

"Christ! Keep her quiet, will you?" Colt growled, slanting her husband a quelling look. Another passenger, a drummer from San Antonio, pulled out a small revolver and peered cautiously out the opposite window.

How could he have let this happen? Colt asked himself disgustedly. The trip from San Antonio to Karlsburg had thus far been without incident and so boring he had ridden frequently beside the driver on his high perch. But when rain threatened he had climbed inside the relative comfort of the rambling coach to snatch a much needed nap. After all, he was a paying customer.

Colt had been traveling constantly since leaving north Texas over a week ago on his way to Karlsburg, stopping briefly at San Antonio where he conferred with Captain Rip Ford about his next assignment before boarding the stage for Karlsburg. Captain Ford had suggested he ride the stage rather than his own mount, which was tied behind the vehicle, because of the large amount of gold being delivered to Karlsburg. Protecting the gold shipment wasn't exactly Colt's assignment in the German settlement, but as long as he was going there, Captain Ford hinted, he might as well take on the chore.

Suddenly the coach screeched to a halt, sending the occupants flying. "Harry!" Annie cried out, clutching at her husband. "Is it Indians? Oh, God, we're all going to be killed!"

Before Colt could untangle himself from the crush of bodies pressed against and atop him, the door flung open and a gruff voice ordered, "Get out!"

Colt cursed the luck that had caught him off guard; for climbing in out of the rain was a mistake that could cost him his life. If he lived through it, he'd never make the same mistake again.

"My . . . my wife is pregnant," Harry said in a strangled voice. "Don't hurt her."

Violet eyes narrowed on the rounded middle of the half-fainting woman. "Do as I say and no one will get hurt." Sam waved a six-shooter menacingly,

4

and Harry scurried out of the coach, half-carrying, half-dragging his nearly paralyzed wife.

"Be careful, you idiot!" growled Sam, to Colt's surprise. "Don't let her fall." In all his years of knocking around, Colt had never encountered a thoughtful outlaw before.

Sensing the bandit's preoccupation, Colt made a lunge for his gun. But he had miscalculated the man's concentration. "Try it and you're history," Sam ground out. "Toss your gunbelt to the ground."

Colt froze, raising tawny gold eyes to stare into pools of incredible violet. Cursing, he complied, dropping his guns into the dirt outside the stagecoach.

"Step out real slow like."

The low timbre of the bandit's voice grated on Colt's nerves, and for the space of a heartbeat he considered defying the man who appeared to be no more than a lad. But even a cold-hearted bastard like himself couldn't be so unfeeling as to endanger the lives of others, especially a pregnant woman. Years of being a loner, of fighting for his very existence, had changed Colt from a happy-go-lucky youth into a hardened and cynical drifter, but every so often a spark of decency proved he wasn't entirely without redemption.

Gingerly Colt stepped from the coach, followed by the drummer, whose jerky motions revealed his fear. Colt's sharp eyes took in the situation with one sweeping glance. Until now he hadn't been aware of the second bandit still astride his mount holding the driver at bay with a Winchester rifle. A snort of disgust left Colt's lips, for the second bandit, though brawnier than the first, looked nearly as young.

Could these two youths be the fierce desperadoes who had been terrorizing the citizens of Karlsburg? The same bandits Captain Ford had sent him to dispatch after a desperate plea from the mayor and townspeople? If these two sorry-looking specimens were an example of the rest of the gang, Colt reflected, his job should be fairly simple. And you could bet your ass he'd not be caught napping again.

"Throw down the strongbox," rasped Will, pointing his Winchester at the driver.

"It . . . it's too heavy," the man protested, unwilling to give up his precious cargo so easily.

Will started to dismount in order to help, but Sam's curt order stopped him in his tracks. "No!" Violet eyes studied the four people assembled outside the stage, finally settling on Colt. "You! Help him."

The gun waved dangerously before his nose, and Colt would have lunged for it if the pregnant Annie hadn't been standing beside him. A stray bullet might easily find its mark in her soft flesh. For himself, he'd taken chances far more dangerous than facing down a pair of stagecoach robbers barely out of diapers. Gritting his teeth, he whirled and climbed atop the coach to join the driver. Together they hefted the heavy metal chest and tossed it to the ground.

"Climb down, both of you," Sam ordered.

Once the two men stood beside the others, Will dismounted, gathered their weapons, and flung them into the dense brush beside the road. A pelting rain began to fall and a loud roar of thunder brought a wail from Annie's bloodless lips.

"Get her inside out of the rain," Sam said, motioning to Harry with the muzzle of the Colt. Harry hesitated only a moment before lifting Annie inside the coach, where she sagged against the seat, sobbing softly. Sam hated putting a pregnant woman through all this, but it couldn't be helped.

Will approached the strongbox, kicking at the padlock that protected its contents. "How in the hell did ya know we was carryin' gold?" asked the grizzled driver. Tobacco-stained teeth, scraggly gray beard, and sun-browned, leatherlike skin attested to his many years of experience.

"I have my ways," growled Sam.

Suddenly the Winchester exploded in Will's hand and the lock on the strongbox shattered. Immediately he was on his knees flinging the lid open, revealing a score or more of heavy sacks neatly stacked inside.

"You know what to do," Sam told Will, fearing to turn his eyes from the man whose aura of reckless disdain prompted caution. While Will stashed sacks of gold coins in his saddlebags, Sam studied Colt from beneath thick, black lashes. He was the kind of man who stood out easily in any crowd. Tall and slim, he moved with an inbred self-assurance. His eyes were deep and tawny, and flashing with fury. There was a brooding quality about him that projected power and ruthlessness.

His skin was taut and bronze, but weathered by the Texas sun and wind and etched by tiny lines around his eyes and mouth. A magnificent mane of tawny sun-streaked hair swept away from his temples and fell below the collar of his buckskin jacket in back. Those distinctive, golden eyes were framed by startlingly luxurious dark lashes and brows. His mouth was full to the point of sensuality.

He was large but lean, with wide shoulders, a strong chest, and big hands. He had the look and stance of a gunslinger or drifter whose livelihood depended on his wits and his gun. Sam prayed the day would never come when they would face each other on equal terms.

'It's done, Sam," Will called, jerking Sam to attention.

Sam. Colt silently filed the name in his brain.

"Vamoose out of here, Will," Sam ordered.

"But, Sam—"

"Go! Don't argue, just leave. I'll be right behind you. You know the plan."

Reluctantly, Will mounted, swung his horse around, and dug his heels in the animal's sleek flanks, sparing a fleeting, silent glance in Sam's direction before riding off into the wooded hills. Colt was confident his mustang, Thunder, was faster than the nag under Will and could easily overtake them.

Still covering Colt with the six-shooter, Sam slowly backed up to where Colt's horse was tethered behind the stage with a leading line, loosed the reins, and delivered a hearty slap to his rump, sending him flying into the woods with a snort of protest. Then he leaped astride his own mount, wheeled, and pounded after Will and the purloined gold.

One corner of Colt's full lips curved upwards in a sneer as he watched Sam ride off. While the other men scrabbled in the brush for their weapons, Colt puckered his mouth and loosed a piercing whistle that brought Thunder to his side as if by magic. Someone handed him his gunbelt seconds before he hurtled into the saddle and kneed Thunder forward.

"Find those sons of bitches, mister," the driver rasped, shooting a stream of dirty brown tobacco juice into the wet ground. "Mr. Logan will have my hide if the gold don't arrive. I'm too old to find another job."

Sam heard the shrill whistle but thought little of it, too consumed with the need to follow Will to safety. At least Will had a good start, Sam thought, bending low to escape the wind-driven branches lashing out at horse and rider. The rain was coming down faster now, but Sam kept the grueling pace, certain that the tawny-eyed man would find a way to follow. He did not appear the kind who gave up easily.

Trailing closer behind than Sam realized, Colt drew his Winchester from the saddle holster and rested it on his lap. With the back of one hand he swiped the rain from his eyes and peered into the gloom ahead. Thunder's sturdy legs stretched out to their limit and Colt knew he couldn't be far behind the bandit.

Then suddenly Colt spied the rider several yards ahead, head bent low over his horse's damp neck. "We've got them now, Thunder," Colt laughed, relishing the chase.

Sam heard Colt's mocking laughter and realized with a plummeting heart that he was closing in. The first shot Colt squeezed off whizzed harmlessly past Sam's head. Panicking, Sam grew incautious, straightening up and turning to peer over a shoulder. Colt's carefully aimed second shot sent the bandit hurtling to the ground. Shooting the enemy was something Colt did well.

He'd returned home from the war with the smell of gunpowder in his nose and fighting in his blood. Still, he would have been happy on the family ranch if he hadn't found both his parents dead in an Indian raid, his twelve-year-old sister missing, and the homestead north of San Antonio a pile of ashes and rubble. For two years he'd searched for Laura but failed to find the tribe of Comanches that had stolen her. After that he knocked around Texas hiring out his gun, bounty hunting, and killing Indians, whom he hated with a passion. Then a few weeks ago he'd met an old acquaintance from the Mexican War, Captain Rip Ford of the Texas Rangers.

Restless, trained for nothing but using his gun, and proficient in his trade, Colt had found Rip in a small border town noted for fierce brawls, pliant prostitutes, and violent killings. He was familiar with the Rangers from his Mexican War days when they fought valiently alongside the army. Not only did those revered and fearless men carry messages, they trail-blazed routes for the army to follow and scouted enemy positions. They ruthlessly gunned down the enemy but refused to be controlled by the army, whose generals called them "lawless men."

So relentless were the Texas Rangers that the Mexicans believed them to be only half civilized. It was no wonder they'd earned the name "Los Tejanos Diablos," the Texas devils. The Mexican War made them famous; their deeds became legends. Yet they were disbanded after the war and were not called back into force until just this year, 1858. Colt met Captain Ford shortly after the Rangers were recalled to handle the desperate Indian situation. It took little persuasion to talk a footloose, cynical, bored, and hardened Colt into signing on for a six-month enlistment.

Approaching the fallen bandit cautiously, Colt dismounted, his gun ready in case of a trap. But he could see at a glance that Sam was beyond pretense. Blood stained his jacket and seeped into the ground beneath him. He was lying on his stomach, his face in the mud, and Colt carelessly flipped him over with the toe of his boot. He looked dead, but Colt, wanting to be damn certain, bent an ear to Sam's chest.

"Christ!" He reared up as if shot, tearing the hat from Sam's head with one hand while exploring the bandit's chest with the other. A rich abundance of thick, black hair spilled from beneath the battered felt hat and fanned out in wet strands on the mud. "I've shot a goddamn woman!"

When Colt put his ear to Sam's chest, soft breasts pillowed his cheek. He'd had intimate knowledge of too many women, enjoyed their naked charms far too often not to recognize Sam's femininity. He cursed himself roundly for not realizing immediately that the youthful bandit was a woman. Those huge violet eyes fringed with long, thick lashes should have been a dead giveaway. He had let some whoring bitch make a damn fool of him. "Colt" Colter, a man feared for his swift trigger finger and quick temper, had been tricked by a female barely out of her teens, by the look of her.

Suddenly the sight of blood gushing from the gaping wound jolted Colt into action. She was alive—and, strangely, he didn't want this woman to die. For some unaccountable reason her courage and daring intrigued him. Ripping the kerchief from her face, he opened her shirt and pressed the kerchief to the wound just inches above her left breast. Any lower and she would be dead now. A low moan escaped her lips as he stood above her, studying her delicate features.

Sam opened her eyes to find a dark figure standing silhouetted against the storm-lit sky, his stetson pulled low on his forehead. His shirt was unbuttoned down his dark chest, and his tight buckskin trousers molded thickly muscled thighs. One word escaped her parched lips as he bent to lift her from the wet ground. "Will?"

"I don't know who Will is, lady, unless he's your pardner," Colt ground out. "But you're both in a heap of trouble."

"Wh . . . where are you taking me?" she asked shakily.

"I don't know. How far to Karlsburg?"

"Ten miles." The way she said it made it seem like hundreds, so weak was her voice. Colt doubted she'd withstand the long ride to town, bleeding as she was.

"Then we'd best get goin'. You need a doctor. Pronto." She gasped in agony and paled when he swung her into his arms.

"Take me home," Sam begged, her violet eyes hazy with pain. "Please take me home." Large tears rolled down her cheeks.

"Jail is the only place you're goin', lady," Colt insisted, deliberately hardening his heart. He had knocked around too long to be moved by a woman's tears. Yet the suffering of this woman touched him in a way he'd never thought possible. Was he getting soft in his old age?

"Not jail," Sam gasped, shuddering at the thought. How strange, she reflected dazedly, but when she'd planned this holdup she'd never considered that either she or Will might end up hurt—or in jail.

"Christ! If you don't get help soon, lady, you'll bleed to death and then it won't matter where I take you," Colt muttered.

"Home," Sam repeated weakly, slowly slipping into a world of darkness.

"Where is home?" Colt heard himself asking. What in the hell had gotten into him? he chided himself, allowing a woman to interfere with his job. Captain Ford's orders were to get the Crowder gang out of Karlsburg, not to cater to the whims of an outlaw. Yet he wasn't entirely convinced this woman was a part of the gang he'd been sent to investigate. Perhaps this holdup was an isolated incident having nothing to do with the Crowders. He certainly intended to find out. But regardless, the girl and her accomplice belonged behind bars, and it was his job to see that they got there.

"Five miles due west," Sam faltered, mustering the remnants of her strength. "Circle H Ranch . . . on . . . on the creek. Please take . . ."

Whatever she started to say died in her throat as her head lolled sideways onto Colt's broad chest. Spitting out a stream of expletives, Colt lifted her atop Thunder while he carefully mounted behind her. If they were but five miles from her home, her horse would eventually make its own way back. Setting Thunder in a westerly direction, Colt concentrated on the wounded woman in his arms, alarmed by the copious amount of blood seeping through the makeshift bandage he had applied. She'd be damn lucky to reach home alive, he thought, kneeing Thunder into a faster gait.

Reaching behind him, Colt retrieved his raingear and spread it over him and the girl, who had begun to shiver from shock and exposure. "I don't know why you did this, lady." Colt shook his head disgustedly. "Or why your boyfriend left you and took off with the money. But if you live, you've got a hell of a lot of explainin' to do. And somehow I don't think the townspeople of Karlsburg will understand your need to rob stagecoaches or terrorize pregnant women."

The ranch looked deserted when Colt rode into the yard. Only a few scraggly chickens greeted their arrival. No cowboys were about performing their duties, and from the looks of things, none had been employed in some time. He wondered what or who he'd find in the house. Did the girl have parents? Or a guardian? If so, they were certainly lax in exercising their authority.

The house was the usual log structure one expected to see in this section of Texas but much larger than most. Colt reckoned that at one time this spread must have been quite prosperous. But now everything looked badly neglected and in need of repair. The outside of the house was peeling, and large chunks of mud caulking had disintegrated into fine dust.

Colt dismounted awkwardly, still supporting Sam's unconscious form, and carefully negotiated the three steps to the wide front porch. Kicking the door open, he entered the house and found himself facing the business end of an old-fashioned muzzle-loading shotgun held in the trembling hands of an aging Mexican.

"What have you done to Senorita Samantha?" the old man demanded.

Samantha. So that was her name. "Your Senorita Samantha has been wounded. Did you know she held up the stagecoach along with an accomplice? A large amount of gold intended for the bank in Karlsburg is missin'."

"Madre mia! I never thought she would go so far."

"Who are you?" Colt asked.

"Sanchez. I am the only one left on the Circle H."

"Well, Sanchez, if you have fond feelin's for this young bandit, put down that gun and show me where to take her and I'll attempt to save her life. She's already lost more blood than she can spare."

The weapon in Sanchez's hands wavered, then shifted to point to a hallway, leading, Colt assumed, to the bedrooms. "First door on the right, Senor. What can I do to help?"

"Have you ever taken out a bullet, Sanchez?" Colt threw over his shoulder as he carried Sam inside the obviously feminine room and placed her in the center of the bed.

"Many times, Senor," Sanchez allowed, "but not since I have grown too old and crippled to hold a knife." He followed Colt into the bedroom and held his hands out for inspection. Besides being misshapen by arthritis, they were shaking so badly it was obvious he would be of little help.

"Then bring boilin' water. Plenty of it. And a basin, and towels, whiskey and soap. I shot her, so I reckon it's up to me to save her."

"You shot Senorita Sam?" Sanchez gasped, swinging the gun around to point it at Colt.

"Put that damn thing down and follow orders. If you kill me, who will remove the bullet? There's no time to go to Karlsburg for a doctor. The water, Sanchez, hurry. And don't forget a needle and thread."

Coming to a decision, Sanchez leaned the gun against the door, nodded to Colt, and scurried out the door in the shuffling gait of a man in pain. Immediately Colt turned his attention to the mud-splattered girl lying pale and motionless on the bed.

First Colt removed her oversize jacket which had no doubt been meant to disguise her feminine curves. Moving his hands to the buttons on her checkered shirt, he carefully peeled the blood-soaked garment from her shoulders, earning a groan from her bloodless lips as he raised her to slide her arms out. The sight that met his tawny eyes turned them to glittering golden slits.

He had thought her a half-formed schoolgirl, but her generously proportioned breasts crowned by dusty rose nipples were hardly childlike. Samantha, or Sam as she was called, obviously was a woman full grown. One fully responsible for the crime she had just committed. Despite the familiar tightening in his loins, Colt deliberately turned his eyes away from those tempting forbidden fruits and concentrated instead on her wound.

Lifting the blood-encrusted kerchief he had used to stanch the blood, Colt saw at a glance that the bullet was still embedded in her chest. He'd hoped it had gone cleanly through, leaving a neat hole, but that hadn't been the case. The bullet had to come out, and there was no one to do it but him.

"What are you doing?" Sanchez had just reentered the room with a stack of towels, soap, whiskey, and a basin. "You've removed Senorita Sam's clothes." His voice held a strong hint of reproach and his face was filled with indignation.

"Christ, Sanchez, I can't take the bullet out with her clothes in the way. Either do it yourself or let me do what has to be done."

Muttering in Spanish beneath his breath, Sanchez shambled out of the room, returning moments later with a kettle of boiling water. Colt retrieved a long, slim knife from his boot, dropped it in the basin, and poured the boiling water over it. He let it sit a few minutes and then carefully removed it and plunged his hands into the water, scrubbing vigorously with the bar of lye soap. He had seen too many men die of infection in the war to discount cleanliness when it came to open wounds. He didn't want to touch Sam's pristine flesh with filthy hands and dirty fingernails. Then, to Sanchez's surprise, he poured whiskey over the knife, his hands, and the wound in Sam's chest. She jerked violently but did not awaken.

"What can I do, Senor?"

"She's goin' to start thrashin' around when I probe for the bullet," Colt said. "You can help by holdin' her down."

"*Si*," Sanchez nodded grimly. "Senorita Sam is very brave, she will live."

"She's also very foolish," Colt muttered darkly. "If you're ready, I'll begin."

His hand steady on the knife, Colt started the delicate operation as he probed ruthlessly into Sam's tender flesh. Deep in unconsciousness, Sam felt the pain and reacted violently. But Sanchez was ready, his gnarled hands somehow finding the strength to hold her narrow shoulders pinned to the bed. Her head thrashed from side to side, and she screamed once, twice, then went still.

"Is she dead?" Sanchez asked fearfully.

"No, but she's in shock," Colt noted, wiping at the beads of sweat gathered on his forehead.

"Have you found the bullet, Senor?"

"No, dammit. Can you wipe away some of this sweat, Sanchez? I can barely see what I'm doin'."

No longer needed for the previous task Colt had set for him, Sanchez complied.

"There it is, I found it!" Colt shouted, elated as the tip of his knife scraped against the metal ball. "It's lodged against the breastbone."

Carefully, his hands shaking with the strain, Colt pried the bullet out of the wound. When it was visible to the eye, he used his fingers to lift it free, dropping it in the basin.

"It's done." Colt sagged wearily, staring at the gaping hole in Sam's chest.

She looked so innocent lying there. Innocent and

vulnerable. He had probably saved her life, yet duty dictated he must turn her over to the sheriff in Karlsburg once she was well enough to travel. Perhaps it would have been kinder to let her die. Well, it was done. He had only to finish up and watch carefully for infection. The next thirty-six hours would be crucial.

Reaching for the whiskey, Colt poured a liberal dose into the wound, then took up needle and thread and made a few clumsy stitches to hold the edges together. He finished by preparing a thick bandage and holding it in place with strips of cloth wound about Sam's chest.

"Bring more water, Sanchez," Colt directed tiredly. "I need to get her cleaned up."

"Where did you learn to do that, Senor?" Sanchez asked, gesturing toward Sam's neatly bandaged chest.

"When you've bummed around as long as I have you learn many things," Colt said wryly, not wanting to go into details. The truth was that one of his duties in the Mexican War had been assisting the surgeon. After the war ended he'd considered studying medicine until he found his parents brutally murdered and his sister missing. That incident had changed the fabric of his entire life.

Once Sanchez had refilled the basin and left to prepare a broth from the squirrel he had shot that morning, Colt set to work cleaning Sam's mud-splattered body. The first thing he did was remove her boots and pants. Tawny eyes widened appreciatively as he bared long, slender thighs, shapely calves, and trim ankles. But what really drew his attention was the jet black forest crowning the vee between her legs. Judging from her ample proportions, Colt assumed her to be over eighteen. He couldn't help wondering about her accomplice and if they were lovers. He'd ask Sanchez about it later, but unless Sam was isolated from civilization, her body was too lush, too developed for her to be an untouched virgin. Perhaps he . . .

"Don't even think it," Colt muttered aloud, mentally chiding himself for his erotic thoughts about the female bandit he had unknowingly shot and nearly killed. He had a job to do, a town to defend, an oath to uphold. Colt was astute enough to realize this woman meant trouble, and in any event she'd soon be behind bars where she belonged. Once she revealed where her partner had gone with the money, he'd turn them both over to the sheriff. The sooner he was rid of the treacherous little beauty, the better he'd like it. Colt sensed in her a threat—a threat to his independence, his freedom, his very existence.

Shaking his tawny head to rid himself of thoughts that could only bring him woe, Colt set his mouth in grim lines and began bathing Sam's face and body. So beautiful, he thought distractedly when her face was shiny clean.

The tangled mass of black hair was long and straight, accentuating high cheekbones and golden skin. The contrast of tan skin and ebony hair was startling. It surprised Colt that her flesh was golden all over, not just where her exposed parts had been kissed by the sun. She had a lovely mouth, full-lipped and red—enticing enough to make him want to taste the sweet nectar within. With firm resolve and a tiny bit of reluctance, Colt pulled the sheet over Sam's clean body and left the room. There was much he wanted to know about the wounded girl lying in the bed. Information only Sanchez could supply.

Chapter Two

Her name is Samantha Howard," Sanchez revealed grudgingly. If this gringo meant harm to either Senorita Sam or Will, he would volunteer nothing substantial. "She is twenty years old."

"Where are her parents?"

"Dead."

"A guardian?"

"No one. Her father was killed by the Crowder gang six months ago. Her mother died long before that."

"Does no one else live here on the ranch?"

"There's no one left but me and W— just me," Sanchez amended. "Who are you, Senor? Why did you shoot Senorita Sam? She is a good girl."

Colt snorted derisively. "I hadn't the slightest inklin' the bandit I shot was a woman," Colt defended stoutly. "She robbed the stagecoach and I went after her. My name is Colt . . . Andrews," he improvised, choosing the last name he had used during the years he drifted from place to place. Somehow, using his real name had seemed an insult to his parents. "I'm a Texas Ranger. I was ridin' the stage from San Antonio when a holdup occurred. Two bandits escaped with a considerable amount of gold. Imagine my shock when the one I shot turned out to be a woman! What do you know about her pardner? I'm almost certain the one that got away was male."

"Nothing, Senor, I know nothing," Sanchez returned quickly. Almost too quickly. "Senorita Sam told me nothing. She knew I would disapprove."

"Did she have a . . . friend who might have talked her into this dang fool idea? Whatever possessed her to pull a dangerous and foolhardy stunt like that?"

"You'll have to ask Senorita Sam," Sanchez insisted staunchly, clamping his mouth shut. "It's not for me to say." Fiercely loyal, Sanchez refused to say a word against the young woman he had known since her birth. There were even things Senorita Sam didn't know about herself. Things he had promised Senor Howard he would never divulge. "What do you intend to do with her?"

"As soon as she's recovered—if she recovers," Colt added ominously—"I intend to learn the identity of her pardner and recover the gold. They'll both be turned over to the sheriff in Karlsburg."

"No, Senor Colt, I beg you. Not that. Senorita Sam could be sent to prison. Or worse, if Sheriff Bauer has his way. He is one mean hombre."

"She should have thought of that before she tried

anythin' so reckless." Colt scowled, wondering what
the old Mexican had meant by his last remark about
Sheriff Bauer. "What made her do such a thing?"

Sanchez knew exactly why Sam robbed the stage
but held firm to his resolve to divulge nothing to this
fierce Texas devil. "I am an old man, Senor, and the
years have taught me to mind my own business."

Snorting in disgust, Colt replied, "You're doin'
Sam no favor by remainin' mute. No matter. One
way or another I will have the truth—and the
gold. I'm hungry, Sanchez, rustle me up some
grub."

Twenty-four hours later Samantha returned to the
world of the living. Surprisingly, her wound remained infection-free, and, though still gravely ill,
she had not suffered extensively from fever.

Huge violet eyes reacted slowly to the relentless
stab of sunlight upon weighted lids, and with difficulty Sam clawed her way through layers of suffocating cotton into stark reality. She blinked repeatedly
until the mist before her eyes cleared and a rather
startling image came into focus.

Lounging against the doorframe, hands laced
across his flat, buckskin-clad stomach, one long leg
crossed in front of the other, a tall, slim man stood
looking directly at her. His thick hair was sun-
streaked tawny gold. His nose was straight and bold,
his mouth full and sensual. In one lazy motion he
pushed himself away from the door, gliding to her
bedside with catlike grace and a hip-rolling stride.
At close range his golden brown eyes appeared
liquid and shiny. For some reason this intriguing
stranger looked vaguely familiar. Was he a friend of

Will's? And what was he doing in her bedroom? Had he named himself the devil, Sam wouldn't have been shocked, for an aura of something dark and mysterious surrounded him.

A sudden untoward movement sent shards of agonizing pain knifing across her upper body. She struggled to sit up, unaware that her motions caused the sheet to drop around her waist, baring breasts the color of rich cream tipped with dusty coral.

"Hellfire and damnation, I hurt," Sam moaned, tears springing to those incredible violet eyes. Colt felt as if he could lose himself in their mysterious velvet depths forever. "What happened? Who are you?"

"Don't you remember?" Colt asked cautiously. No answer, just a wide, innocent stare that completely unnerved him. "Lay back, you've been wounded." With gentleness rare in a man of his calling, he pressed her back against the pillow. "You're a mighty sick gal and damn lucky to be alive."

Glancing down to locate the cause of her terrible pain, Sam gasped in mortification to find herself naked from the waist up except for a bandage covering her upper chest. Groping clumsily beneath the sheet, she discovered her entire body was likewise unclothed. A deep red traveled slowly up her neck to the roots of her hair. "What have you done to me? Where is Will?" She pulled the sheet up to rest beneath her chin.

"Who is Will?" Colt asked with deceptive calm.

"Will is . . ." Suddenly Sam's eyes flew open and her mouth clamped shut.

"You may as well tell me, Sam, I'll find out sooner or later."

"Now I remember!" Sam cried, appalled by what her memory had dredged up. "Hellfire and damnation, you shot me! Who are you and what are you doing in my house?"

"I saved your life, Miss Samantha Howard, you should thank me." His use of her full name made Sam aware that he knew more about her than she would have liked.

"Thank you? You could have killed me," she spat.

"Where is your pardner?" Colt asked angrily. "Where did he take the gold?"

"Why should you care?"

"My name is Colt Andrews. I'm a Texas Ranger. Mayor Mohler of Karlsburg wired Cap'n Ford for help with the Crowder gang. Seems like they're terrorizin' the town and disruptin' business. I was on my way there by stage when the holdup occurred. Are you and your pardner mixed up with Crowders?" Colt really didn't believe that, but one never knew. Looks were often deceiving.

"N . . . no! They killed my father! How could you think such a thing?"

"Perhaps you'd like to explain."

"Vamoose, Ranger, can't you see I'm hurting? Haven't you done me enough harm?"

An unaccustomed twinge of guilt contorted Colt's rugged features. He had seen so much suffering during the war he had become immune to it. "Okay, Miss Howard, I'll let you rest—for now. Sooner or later you'll be well enough to pay for your crime." He turned to leave.

"Wait!"

26

Colt halted but did not turn.

"Who took care of me? Sanchez lacks the ability to remove a bullet. Did he bring the doctor from town?"

"No time." Colt smiled with lazy amusement, swiveling to face her. "I took care of it. As well as your . . . other needs."

"You . . . you are a doctor?"

"Hardly."

"You undressed me!" It was more an accusation than a question.

"I wasn't aware you had a maid to perform those duties."

"How dare you!"

"Would you rather I let you die?"

Closing her eyes, Sam swallowed convulsively, weakness and outrage driving her back to the edge of darkness. The thought that this ruthless man had seen her completely unclothed, indeed had actually undressed her, sent her spinning away into shock. She managed to hiss one word before blackness claimed her. "Bastard!"

The next time Sam awoke, Sanchez was sitting beside the bed holding a bowl of steaming broth. "You must try to eat something, Senorita Sam," the old man urged. "You need to keep up your strength if you wish to get well."

"Why?" Sam complained bitterly. "So that beanheaded lawman can put me behind bars?"

"You did a very foolish thing. You and Will could have gotten yourselves killed. You risked much, Senorita Sam. Where is your brother?"

"I . . . I was desperate, Sanchez," Sam admitted,

choking on a sob. "It would have worked if that Ranger hadn't been riding the stage. Of all the rotten luck! But at least Will got away. Did you tell the Ranger about Will?"

"No, Senorita Sam, I wouldn't do that. And if Will has any sense he'll stay away. Senor Colt is one smart hombre." He tried to spoon hot liquid into Sam's mouth.

"I'm really not hungry, Sanchez," she said listlessly.

"I'll take over, Sanchez." Colt's deep, resonant tones had a quality that under other circumstances would have thrilled Sam.

The old man took note of the implacable look on Colt's face, nodded somewhat reluctantly, and handed him the bowl and spoon. Then the old man shuffled from the room with a resigned sigh.

"How are you feelin'?" Colt asked, taking the chair Sanchez had vacated.

"Like hell," Sam grumbled peevishly.

"You have a nasty mouth for a young woman. A simple answer would do. Even a 'much obliged' would be appreciated, considering I saved your life."

"What are you going to do with me?" Sam asked between swallows of broth.

"Take you to Karlsburg and turn you over to the sheriff as soon as you're well enough," Colt stated with cool indifference.

"Sheriff Bauer?"

"If that's the sheriff's name, then I reckon he's the one."

A shudder rippled over Sam's flesh. "Enough,"

she said, pushing the spoon away from her mouth. She couldn't swallow another bite until a more pressing need was satisfied. Yet she was too embarrassed to ask this cynical stranger for the help she required. Instead, her face grew red and she began to squirm uncomfortably beneath the sheet.

Noting her discomfort, Colt knew intuitively what bothered her. Not one to mince words, he asked, "Would you like the chamberpot?"

"Oh, God," Sam groaned, horrified by his blunt language. "Send in Sanchez."

"Who do you think did this for you these last few days?" Colt asked, amusement coloring his words.

"Oh, God," she groaned again, covering her flaming face with the sheet. "Just leave it beside the bed and get out of here."

"Are you certain you're strong enough to—"

"Yes! Yes!" Her voice quivered with barely concealed rage. What a thoroughly despicable, arrogant man. "Bastard," she hissed, giving emphasis to her thoughts.

"Call me that one more time, Sam, and you'll find what a bastard I can be. So far I've treated you with more respect than you deserve, considerin' the serious nature of your crime. But you're sorely tryin' my patience." He placed the chamberpot beside the bed with a resounding bang. "Are you *certain* you can manage?"

"Just vamoose," came her muffled reply from beneath the sheet.

Later, Sam had to suffer Colt's ministrations once again when he returned to change her bandage. Tears rolled down her pale cheeks when he callously pulled the sheet down, exposing her breasts. But he seemed not to notice her acute embarrassment as he swiftly and efficiently peeled off the blood-soaked bandage and replaced it with another. If Sam hadn't kept her eyes tightly shut the whole time, she would have noticed that Colt wasn't as unaffected as she supposed. His hands shook with the effort of controlling the urge to linger on the provocative rise of velvet skin. His breath shuddered unevenly through his body, keeping time with the erotic pounding in his chest.

"There, it's done," Colt sighed, turning away with an effort that taxed his steely control.

Sam said nothing, peeping through lowered lashes while he gathered up the soiled bandages. His next words sent her wits scattering. "Would you like a bath? You haven't had one since the one I gave you after I removed the bullet."

"You . . ." squeaked Sam, the words dying in her throat.

"I think you're well enough to do it yourself this time," Colt continued complacently. "I'll have Sanchez bring in hot water. In the meantime, I'm ridin' to Karlsburg. I should have reported in two days ago. Mayor Mohler will be expectin' me. I reckon there's no need to remind you not to leave this bed. I'll find you no matter where you vamoose to. There's no one to help you. It's obvious your lover isn't comin' back. He has the money, that's all a man like that wants."

"My . . . my lover?" stuttered Sam, thoroughly confused.

"Perhaps I'm being presumptuous, but you never

did explain your relationship to your accomplice." Colt waited, dark brows raised inquiringly, but when Sam refused to acknowledge his taunt, he snorted derisively. "As I said before, your *lover* isn't coming back for you." He strode purposefully toward the door.

"Wait! What day is this?"

"If this is some trick—"

"No, please, just tell me the day and date."

"Tuesday, May 5, 1858."

"And the time?"

"Just past noon."

"Then there's still time."

The words were spoken so low that Colt had to strain to hear them. He started to ask Sam to explain but thought better of it, deciding he hadn't gotten a straight answer from her yet, so why expect one now? Shrugging, he left the room.

Colt had been gone about fifteen minutes and Sam had just finished an awkward bedbath and pulled on a voluminous white nightgown Sanchez removed from her bureau at her direction when the door to her bedroom burst open.

"Sam! Thank God! I thought that lop-eared jackass killed you. Who is he?"

"Will!" Sam cried, joy suffusing her drawn features. "Where have you been? Where is the gold?"

"It's safe, Sis. But first tell me what happened. Are you hurt badly? I heard the shot but daren't turn back."

Will Howard was a big, strapping lad for his fourteen years. With little education save for what

31

Sam was able to instill, at times he seemed immature for his age. After his father's death he seemed to depend on Sam to the point of surrendering his own independence. Though Sam could not see it, Sanchez did, and worried over the boy's lack. Some boys were men at fourteen, but if Will did not have a strong male to guide him, his own masculinity would surely suffer.

"Thank the good Lord you didn't turn back," Sam replied, glad that Will showed sense enough to follow orders. She should never have involved him in this wild scheme in the first place. "If you did, we'd *both* be in a heap of trouble. It was damn rotten luck that a Texas Ranger was riding the stage that day."

"Texas Ranger! You mean the man who shot you is a Texas Ranger? Where did he go? I watched the house until I saw him ride off."

"His name is Colt Andrews. He went to Karlsburg to talk to Sheriff Bauer and Mayor Mohler. He intends to turn me in as soon as I'm well enough."

"Sam, no, he can't do that! I won't let him."

"There's nothing you can do, Will."

"I'll give back the gold!"

"No! If you do that, everything we've done will have been for nothing. I'm a woman, Will, they'll be lenient with me. But even if they put me in jail, you'll have the means now to continue without me."

"How badly are you hurt? I'll take you with me and we'll hide in the hills where no one can find us."

Sam shook her head. "You don't know Colt Andrews. He'd not rest till he found me. Besides, I'm far too weak to be traipsing through the countryside. The bullet caught me in the chest. Colt removed it and I'm healing nicely, but it will be days before I'm able to leave this bed."

"Tell me what to do, Sam," Will said worriedly. "Today is the last day."

Colt cursed the luck that made Thunder throw a shoe barely out of sight of the house. Now he'd have to walk him back and ride Sam's mount into town. Perhaps Sanchez could put on a new shoe while he was in Karlsburg. Leading Thunder into the stable, Colt was surprised to see a strange horse in one of the stalls calmly munching hay. Upon closer inspection, Colt recognized the horse as belonging to the second bandit and cursed roundly. Evidently the bastard was just waiting for him to leave before coming for Sam. Then he chuckled. Thunder had done him a favor by throwing a shoe. He'd have both of them now.

Moving with the stealth of a cougar, Colt entered the house through the back door, pausing outside Sam's bedroom. The door stood ajar and Colt could hear every word spoken by the couple he assumed to be lovers as well as partners in crime.

"Tell me what to do, Sam. Today is the last day."

"Where is the gold, Will?" Colt smiled nastily. It *was* the second bandit, just as he suspected.

"It's hidden beneath a loose board under the bed in that old line shack in the north pasture," Will revealed, proud of his cunning. "That's where I've been stayin'. Did I do all right, Sam?" It was obvious that Sam's approval meant a lot to him, and she gave it unstintingly.

"You did just fine, Will," Sam praised. "A sister couldn't ask any more of her brother. Pop would be proud of you. It's up to you now to carry on."

"Not without you, Sam. I'll think of somethin'. I won't let that blasted lawman turn you in."

His ear cocked toward the voices, Colt's heart leaped in his chest. Brother! Sam's partner was her kid brother. And if the unformed quality of his voice was any indication, younger by several years. But he didn't wait around to hear any more. He had to retrieve the gold before Will returned to the line shack. He wouldn't bother with the youngster now, for he knew exactly where to find him when he wanted him. Besides, he was just a lad. The full responsibility of the crime lay fully on Sam's head. Leaving Thunder in the stable, he saddled Sam's mount and kneed him forward.

The gold was exactly where Will described. Colt located the shack easily and pried up the loose board beneath the cot. There were ten bags, each containing about three hundred dollars in twenty-dollar gold pieces. Three thousand dollars in all. Colt placed them carefully in his saddlebags, then left after putting everything back in place. He was gone a full ten minutes before Will arrived.

Will was close to tears when he returned to the ranch. It nearly killed him to tell Sam the gold was gone. How could anyone know? How could he be so inept? He had failed his beloved sister and all was lost.

Sam took the news stoically. Only one person could be behind this. That damn Ranger. The Mexicans were right. Texas Rangers *were* half-man, half-devil. Then a terrible thought assailed her. If Colt Andrews knew where to find the gold, he also knew about Will. She had to protect her brother no matter what the consequences.

"He knows, Will. Colt knows about you. Quickly, get Sanchez." Will scurried to obey.

"You wanted me, Senorita Sam?" Sanchez asked when he stood before the bed, a frown worrying his wrinkled brow.

"I know I can trust you, Sanchez," Sam began, searching for words. "Colt knows about Will. That heartless bastard will think nothing of sending a mere boy to prison. I want you to take Will away from here. You have relatives in Laredo, don't you?"

"Si, Senorita, a daughter and six grandchildren."

"Take Will to Laredo, Sanchez. Now, today, this minute! I have some money in the house. Enough to buy supplies for the trip. Just steer clear of Karlsburg."

To Will's credit, he resisted violently. "No, Sam, I won't go. I won't leave you to face the law alone when we both were responsible for what happened."

"It was my plan, Will, my idea. You merely lent your help to my dimwitted scheme. If I remember correctly, you were against it from the beginning. If you don't want to spend years in prison, you'll do as I say."

"How long do I have to stay away?" Will asked, resigned to his exile when threatened with imprisonment.

"Until the Ranger is gone. Make a new life for yourself in Laredo," Sam advised. "Forget the ranch, we've already lost it. I . . . I should have married Vern Logan, then the land would still be yours."

"It would be Vern Logan's," spat Will contemptuously. "We both know you wouldn't be happy with him. Come with us, Sam. Somehow we'll make it. We'll take it easy and—"

Sam shook her head regretfully. "No, Will, I'd only be a burden to you. You know I wouldn't last a day in this heat. Besides, Colt won't be so anxious to trail you if I remained behind. Now give me a hug and get out of here." Her violet eyes grew misty with unshed tears.

"I'll be back, Sam," Will promised, his young face contorted in agony. "When all this blows over, I'll be back. No matter where you are I'll find you." His words hung in the air long after he was gone.

Chapter Three

The settlement of Karlsburg lay in the green depths of a valley in the heart of the Texas hill country. Rugged granite outcroppings showed on the bare crests of hills, glowing dull red in the face of cliffs above the timber growth of the valley floor. Colt followed a deep stream along the valley into town, amazed at the sight of farmhouses constructed of stone with loopholes built to permit rifle fire against Indians.

Founded in the 1840s by German immigrants, Karlsburg was a clannish, thoroughly German town. The granite and limestone outcroppings in the encircling hills suggested a permanency reflected in the thick-walled limestone houses, mellowed to amber by the sun. Colt knew little of this German community except that the people were a tenacious lot who continued on even after the Comanche reduced their numbers considerably in 1846. In 1847 an epidemic took 150 of their remaining 600 settlers. In that year their leader negotiated a tenuous peace with the Comanche. And now they were threatened by the Crowder gang.

When Fort Martin Scott was established on Baron's Creek, it furnished not only protection but a ready cash market for their produce. A general store was opened and the colony prospered. The surrounding area was rich in fish and game, the valleys fertile, and the heavily wooded hills provided ample wood and building stone.

Riding down the wide main street with buildings crowded close to the road, Colt easily located the jail and sheriff's office. Several sour-faced townspeople followed his progress, some with fear in their eyes until they realized he meant them no harm. Then they went about their business.

Colt reined in before the jail, dismounted, wrapped the reins around the railing, and aimed his steps toward the boardwalk that lined both sides of the dirt street. Suddenly the door swung open and out stepped a sturdy, square-built man sporting a deputy's badge on his broad chest. He eyed Colt suspiciously before growling in thickly accented German, "Karlsburg don't like strangers, mister. State your business."

"My business is with the sheriff," Colt stated in a lazy drawl that set apart a native-born Texan from all the others.

"I'm Deputy Lender, Sheriff Bauer is . . . er . . . busy," the man said, slanting a nervous glance over his shoulder. "If you want the sheriff, come back later."

Something in the deputy's manner did not set right with Colt. By now, sniffing out trouble was second nature to him. "I'll wait," Colt replied with cool authority.

A prickling sensation at the back of his neck and a vague feeling of unease kept him from going on to other business until the sheriff was free to see him. During all his years of fending for himself, he had developed a sixth sense where danger was concerned. It wasn't infallible, but he learned to heed its warning. Therefore he wasn't unprepared when a feminine scream and a series of low moans came from somewhere inside the building housing the jail.

"What's that?" Colt asked sharply, his right hand hovering above the six-shooter riding on his hip.

"I didn't hear nothin'," Lender growled in his guttural accent.

A woman's terror-stricken voice filtering through the thick walls proclaimed him a liar. "Please, have mercy."

Colt didn't wait around to question Lender further but sprinted past the sluggish man and burst through the door straight into a scene that set his blood to boiling.

A man, obviously Sheriff Bauer, was struggling with a woman in one of the two small cells at the rear of the large room. He was grossly obese, his huge frame straddling the small woman beneath him. Her clothes lay in tatters about her small form, and Colt saw at a glance that the determined sheriff had already unfastened his trousers in preparation for his assault. Colt's temper exploded.

"Sheriff Bauer! Take your hands off that woman!"

His voice was low and menacing yet charged with quiet authority, demanding instant obedience.

Pinning the helpless woman to the narrow cot with his considerable bulk, Bauer swiveled, his face mottled with rage. "Gott in himmel, who are you? I told Lender to keep everyone out while I interrogate the prisoner."

"Aren't you usin' the wrong word?" Colt spat contemptuously. "Don't you mean rape? Are all women prisoners subjected to your personal brand of justice?"

"What's it to you, stranger? I'm sheriff here. If you don't want to end up in the other cell, get the hell out of here and keep goin'. We don't like strangers in Karlsburg."

"So the deputy told me," Colt sneered, obviously unimpressed.

"Ja, I told him you were . . . busy," interjected Lender, all but groveling before his superior. "But he wouldn't listen."

"Vamoose, Lender, and take that nosy son-of-a-bitch with you."

"No, please," a timid voice begged. "Don't leave me with him. Help me."

Colt's tawny eyes blazed with barely suppressed rage as they settled on the woman still struggling beneath Bauer's sweating body. He reckoned now was as good a time as any to reveal his identity. With cool deliberation he reached in his pocket, removed the Ranger badge, and pinned it to his chest. Lender's mouth flopped open and his eyes bulged grotesquely.

"My name is Colt . . . Andrews." Colt's voice boomed with authority. "I'm a Texas Ranger and as ornery a son-of-a-bitch as you'll ever meet. Move off the woman. You've got some tall explainin' to do."

Reluctantly levering his body off the woman, Bauer bent Colt an assessing glance. "Did you come in answer to Mayor Mohler's plea?"

"That's right."

"Where's the others?"

"Others?"

"Ja. You don't expect to face a gang of desperadoes by yourself, do you?" Bauer's nasty laugh set Colt's teeth on edge.

"I'm accustomed to workin' alone," Colt said, slicing him an affronted look. The truth was he had a partner, Jim Blake, waiting in San Antonio for word to join him. Colt had chosen to arrive in Karlsburg alone and evaluate the situation before sending for Jim. "I'm still waitin' for your explanation. Do you rape all female prisoners?"

"Frau Scheuer is no virgin," whined Bauer obsequiously, as if that explained his vile conduct.

"Why is she in jail?"

"The woman killed her husband. I've been . . . interrogating her, but she refuses to confess."

"I told you it was an accident," the woman sobbed, plucking the thin blanket from the cot and draping it around her tattered clothing.

"Likely story," sniffed Bauer haughtily. "Herr Scheuer was a respected businessman."

"What happened, ma'am?" Colt asked kindly.

The woman looked to be somewhat over forty, still trim and pretty with lovely gray eyes. Before she had covered her ill-clad form, Colt noted vivid purple and orange bruises on nearly every part of exposed flesh. Some looked to be several days old, and Colt wondered if Mrs. Scheuer had been in jail long enough for Bauer to abuse her more than once.

"My name is Ida Scheuer," the battered woman began hesitantly. "I didn't mean to kill my husband, it was an accident." She began to sob, and Colt reached out clumsily to pat her shoulder.

"Go on, Mrs. Scheuer."

"Herman was a brutal man. Our two sons left home because they couldn't stand the beatings. After they left, Herman was even meaner than before, blaming me for their leaving. It's true I encouraged them, but they had no life at home." She paused to catch her breath.

"Herman directed his anger toward me, and during the last few months he beat me nearly every day," Ida continued. "Two nights ago he deliberately found fault with his meal and began beating me with a thick switch he kept for just that purpose. Suddenly I couldn't take it any more. I grabbed an iron skillet from the stove intending to deflect some of his blows. He lunged at me just as I swung the skillet up to protect my face. I hit him, not hard enough to kill him, but the blow knocked him to the floor, and as he fell he hit his head against a sharp edge on the corner of the stove. I ran for the sheriff, and when my husband was pronounced dead, he put me in jail."

"She'll stay here until the judge comes to town," Bauer insisted stubbornly. "I'm only doin' my job. The people of Karlsburg pay me to protect them."

"What about the Crowder gang?" Colt taunted. "You've done damn little where they're concerned.

So little, in fact, that the mayor felt compelled to seek help from the Texas Rangers."

"It will take an army to chase those outlaws from our town," Bauer complained. "I wish you luck, Andrews, but don't expect miracles. The gang seems to like our town and keeps comin' back."

"Where are you and your deputy when they shoot up the town?"

"Holed up in my office. Gott in himmel, I'm not stupid."

Snorting in disgust, Colt turned to Ida. "Is this the first time Sheriff Bauer has assaulted you, ma'am?" He perceived Ida Bauer as a decent woman who had been abused by her husband for years. She shouldn't have to endure more of the same cruel treatment from a lawman.

Ida lowered her head and whispered, "No, he . . . he raped me last night. So did his deputy."

Colt's tawny eyes stabbed with relentless fury into Sheriff Bauer. "I want Mrs. Scheuer released immediately." His voice exploded with menace.

"Now see here, Andrews, the woman is a murderess. You got no business comin' here and tellin' me what to do."

"I'm makin' it my business. It sounds like a case of self-defense to me. I *strongly* suggest you set Mrs. Scheuer free." His words were calmly spoken, but the threat implicit.

"What if I don't?" Bauer defied.

"Then I'll leave and let you handle the Crowder gang by yourself. It wouldn't be long before you find yourself without a job. Or maybe the Crowders would save the town trouble and eliminate you."

"Get out of here," Bauer growled to Ida and gesturing toward the door. "The Texas Ranger says you're not guilty."

Ida didn't need a second invitation. Sailing past the sheriff, she scurried out the door, pausing briefly. "Thank you, Ranger Andrews. If there's ever anything I can do for you, you can find me in Scheuer's Grocery. I'll be running my husband's store from now on." Then she was gone.

"I hope you're satisfied, Andrews," Bauer grumbled crossly. "What in the hell did you want with me in the first place? It's Mayor Mohler you should be dealin' with."

Colt's original purpose in visiting the sheriff was to hand over the holdup money and make arrangements to house Sam and her brother until they could be brought to trial. But something strange had happened to him on the ride into town. A hard kernel in his heart began to dissolve, allowing an unaccustomed emotion to take its place. An emotion so raw, so unwelcome, it defied definition. Sam was but a child playing a dangerous game. He could remember her now, lying on the wet ground with a hole in her chest that he had put there. Then in his mind's eye he saw her lovely body nude beneath his hot gaze, and her spitting fire at him like a declawed tigress who hadn't the strength to hurt him. God, she was magnificent!

By the time Colt had reached Karlsburg he was so confused he was undecided exactly what to do with Sam and Will. But now, after seeing with his own eyes what would happen to Sam if left to the tender mercies of Sheriff Bauer and his deputy, he knew he couldn't condemn her to a life in hell no matter how guilty she was. Something desperate had driven her to attempt that foolish robbery and he fully intended to find out what it was.

But at least he could rid himself of the money from the holdup. He dropped the bulging sacks on the desk, leaving Sheriff Bauer and Deputy Lender gaping in disbelief. "Turn it over to Mr. Logan," Colt said tersely. "It's the stolen gold shipment from the stage robbery."

"You caught the thieves?"

Colt hesitated only briefly. "No, they got away. Be thankful I recovered the gold. Now that that's settled, tell me where to find Mayor Mohler."

"His office is in city hall, at the west edge of town. If he isn't there you'll find him across the street in the Palace Saloon."

Colt nodded, turned on his heel, and left.

"Watch that man, Lender," Bauer muttered darkly. "No one's gonna take over my town. No Texas Ranger will tell me how to do my job. See to it that he concentrates on the Crowders and leaves me alone."

Dealing with Sheriff Bauer left a bad taste in Colt's mouth. Instead of turning toward city hall he headed across the street to the Palace Saloon. He needed a whiskey to wash away the bitter dregs of Bauer's cruel brand of justice. He'd come up against men like Bauer before, but most were on the opposite side of the law.

Few customers patronized the saloon this time of day. Though it seemed much later, a glance at his pocket watch told Colt it was only four o'clock. One man leaned against the long, polished bar, four others were seated around a back table playing poker, and another occupied a table close to where Colt stood at the bar, an attractive bar girl draped over the man's lap. No one paid heed to Colt as he bellied up to the bar and ordered a whiskey, bolted it down, then asked for another. He was about to carry it to a table when the bartender's sharp eyes noted the badge. "You one of them Texas Rangers Mayor Mohler and the town council been expecting?"

"Colt Andrews," Colt said, extending his hand.

"Damn glad to meet you. I'm Dirk Faulkner. Things been a mite hectic around here since the Crowders came to town."

"You own the saloon, Mr. Faulkner?"

"Naw, I only work here. The boss don't usually come down till the action starts."

"I understand the mayor often comes here in the afternoon. Is he around?"

"Not yet," Dirk replied, "but if he's on schedule he'll show up soon. Enjoy your drink while you're waiting."

"Much obliged, I will," Colt smiled, carrying his drink to the nearest table.

He was glad for the respite. He had some hard thinking to do concerning Samantha Howard, for he had no earthly idea what to do with the little spitfire. She was like no woman he'd ever known before. Beautiful, brave, foolish, feisty, exasperating, and thoroughly enchanting. And she could cuss with the best of them. Their all too brief conversations had left him with the unexplained need to know her better, to find out what drove her to such dangerous adventures as robbery. Colt's mind was so consumed with Sam he thought his imagination was working overtime when he heard the man at the next table mention her name.

"I'm gonna call on Samantha Howard tomorrow, Molly," the man was saying, the sly look on his face leaving an uncomfortable feeling in Colt's chest.

"Why do you keep chasin' that snooty bitch, Vern?" Molly pouted. "She's turned your marriage proposal down so many times you'd be wise to forget her."

"This time is different," Vern bragged, smiling deviously. "At five o'clock she'll lose that damn ranch she's so proud of. With no roof over her head, no visible means of support and a young brother to raise, she'll be grateful to me for rescuin' her. Once the bitch is mine she'll be sorry she turned me down all those times."

Vern Logan, banker Calvin Logan's son, Colt surmised as he sipped his whiskey and listened.

"A year ago Sam's daddy borrowed money from the bank to buy cattle," Vern explained. "Shortly afterwards Indians stole the herd and old man Howard got himself killed by the Crowder gang on one of their rampages through town. Daddy gave Samantha six months to repay the loan or lose the ranch. Time runs out today at five o'clock."

"What do you want with an old ranch anyway?" Molly asked, wrinkling her nose.

"Daddy learned from influential friends in San Antonio that the railroad is plannin' a route that crosses the northern section of the Circle H Ranch. He's been able to buy up most of the land the railroad intends to build on except for the Circle H. Old Man Howard refused to sell to Daddy. That's why Daddy was so eager to loan him money. Too bad about them Indians stealin' his cows. Him gettin' killed later was another stroke of bad luck." Colt thought the tone of Logan's voice indicated little if any remorse as well as hinting that he knew more than he was willing to divulge about the affair.

"Vern, honey," Molly enthused, "sellin' railroad rights to all those properties will earn your daddy a fortune."

"I'm an only son, Molly. One day it will all belong to me. I'm tellin' you this in strict confidence, you understand," Vern said, fixing Molly with a baleful glare.

"You can trust me," Molly huffed indignantly. "But I don't understand why you want Samantha Howard when you'll soon own her land whether she's your wife or not."

"Samantha is beautiful, smart, and will make me a good wife once she's tamed," Vern replied. "Besides, I always did have a yen for her. She's much too independent and wears outlandish clothes, but I'll soon have her eatin' out of my hand. Once she's ridden a few times and broken to the whip, she'll make a proper banker's wife. Daddy insists I marry soon and he favors Samantha. He says with her as my wife our children will have some backbone." Vern snorted. "The old coot thinks he can run my life."

"What about me?" Molly asked petulantly.

"Nothing will change between us, honey," Vern cajoled with smooth words. "We both know I can't marry you. Daddy will disinherit me for sure. But that doesn't mean we can't still make each other happy."

"Howdy, Vern, what are you doin' here at this time of day?"

Colt pretended disinterest as a man entered the saloon and sauntered over to where Vern sat with his blond floozy.

"Howdy, Keno," Vern greeted in a friendly manner. "Daddy's not feelin' well today so I'm in charge at the bank."

"Don't 'pear like you're workin' too hard to me," Keno guffawed.

"Klaus Spindler is handlin' things for a spell. I needed a little time off to . . . uh . . . wet my whistle." He patted Molly's posterior affectionately and winked at Keno. "What good is bein' the boss's son if you can't take time off when you want it? 'Sides, it's nearly closin' time and Klaus is perfectly capable of handlin' business." They shared a laugh, then Keno moved off to join the poker game in progress at the back of the room.

"As long as you don't have to hurry back, we could go upstairs to my room," Molly invited.

Vern licked his lips hungrily. His father kept him so damn busy lately he'd had little time to devote to Molly. An afternoon's romp in bed was just what he needed to top off a perfect day.

Colt watched in disgust as Vern followed Molly up the stairs, fondling her generous bottom while she giggled and slapped ineffectually at his hand. Neither one had paid him the slightest attention nor noted the badge on his chest.

What Colt had overheard explained why Sam needed money badly enough to steal. It was ironic that she should choose to steal gold belonging to the very man who was planning on seizing everything she held dear. Suddenly an idea began to form in the back of his brain. An idea so bizarre he nearly abandoned it. Driven by impulse and the desire to thwart the Logans' nefarious plans, he pulled out his watch and noted that it was exactly five o'clock. Too late to redeem Sam's note, but perhaps not too late to keep the Logans from taking advantage of a helpless woman, and so long as Vern remained in Molly's bed, Colt felt certain his plan would succeed. Deliberately he removed the badge from his shirt.

"I'm interested in buyin' land suitable for farmin' or ranchin'," Colt told the young bank clerk sitting behind the cluttered desk.

"You've come to the right place, sir," the man said importantly. "We've had several foreclosures recently and some are still available." He went on to list five parcels of land, none of them the Circle H.

"Hmmm . . ." mused Colt, "none of them seem exactly what I had in mind. Vern Logan is a good friend of mine," he lied, "and informed me only moments ago that somethin' might be available north of the city."

"You're a friend of Herr Vern, you say? I don't recall seeing you before. You're a stranger in town, aren't you, Herr . . . Herr . . ."

"Colter, Steven Colter. I met the Logans in San Antonio. I just spoke to Vern over at the Palace Saloon but he . . . er . . . had his hands full at the moment and couldn't leave. He said to talk to his assistant. Are you Klaus Spindler?"

"Ja, I'm Klaus Spindler," Klaus acknowledged, puffing out his chest. "And now that you mention it, I do recall hearing that the Howard ranch became available at five o'clock this afternoon. Miss Howard never showed up to pay the note due. But I'm surprised Herr Vern suggested it. I thought . . . well, never mind, obviously I was wrong."

"The property sounds perfect for my needs. If it's for sale I'd like to buy it. How much is it?"

"I see no problem if Herr Calvin agrees. The note is for three thousand dollars. Come back tomorrow, Herr Colter, and either Herr Vern or Herr Calvin will handle the sale for you."

"That won't do," Colt replied evenly. "I want it done now."

"But . . . but . . ." sputtered Spindler. "We close in less than an hour. I couldn't possibly . . . not without Herr Calvin's approval. Not even Herr Vern does anything without his daddy's approval."

"Was I wrong to assume you are in charge, Mr. Spindler? Are you too inexperienced to draw up the papers without help?" Colt used his most condescending tone and it appeared to produce the required results.

"No!" Spindler said huffily. "I'm a trusted employee. I've worked in this bank for over five years. There's nothing I don't know about procedures." He knew that wasn't entirely true, but close enough.

Sometimes Klaus felt more like an errand boy than head clerk. The Logans, especially Calvin, kept him woefully uninformed about most of their secretive dealings.

"Then you'll draw up the papers?" Colt prodded.

"I . . . I . . . This will require some time, and as I mentioned before we close promptly at six o'clock."

"A hundred-dollar bonus is yours if you accommodate me before closing," Colt replied, pleased to note the covetous gleam in Spindler's pale blue eyes.

"That's very generous, Herr Colter, but—"

"Two hundred, Mr. Spindler. Cash."

Klaus' eyes bulged greedily. Two hundred dollars! Except in the bank vault he'd never handled that much money at one time. It would give him the freedom he only dared dream about. He could leave Karlsburg, flee the straightlaced atmosphere of his father's house and the homely bride chosen for him.

"I always did want to see New Orleans," Klaus mused wistfully, unaware he had spoken aloud.

"A fine place to visit, Mr. Spindler." Colt smiled knowingly. "Or settle, if one has a mind to. Two hundred dollars will go a long way toward establishin' yourself, if that's your wish."

"I assume you have the money, Herr Colter?" Spindler asked cautiously.

"I have a letter of credit for five thousand dollars drawn on the San Antonio Bank," Colt said. "More than enough to purchase the Circle H. The remainder can be deposited in an account in my name."

The money represented the amount Colt had received for the sale of his father's homestead. His daily needs were modest and he had saved most of his earnings over the past twelve years. Bounty hunting had proved most rewarding, and Colt's savings had accumulated faster than he could spend them. A firm believer in being prepared, he usually carried the letter of credit wherever he went, though it represented only a portion of the monies deposited under his name in San Antonio.

"I'll have you out of here long before six o'clock." Spindler grinned, feeling more carefree than he had in years.

True to his word, it was fifteen minutes before six when Colt signed two copies of the transfer papers and accepted the deed to 20,000 acres of prime land. The rest of his money was safe in the bank, and Klaus Spindler had two hundred dollars in his pocket. Before he left, Colt penned a brief statement giving Samantha and Will Howard authority to live on the ranch until he saw fit to claim it on some future date. The note was clipped to the transfer document and left in a conspicuous place on the elder Logan's desk.

A few minutes after six Vern Logan staggered out of the saloon, having overindulged in both whiskey and sex. He knew he should have returned to the bank before closing, but Molly's soft flesh proved too tempting to leave so soon. Besides, he knew Klaus to be capable of handling whatever mundane transactions might have occurred during the past hour. But to salve his conscience, he walked past the bank and checked the doors to make certain they were locked before heading home.

* * *

It was dark when Colt returned to the ranch. His meeting with Mayor Mohler had taken longer than he had anticipated. But he felt he now had a factual account of the Crowders' assault on Karlsburg. During the past six months they had inflicted untold damage and killed several innocent people, including Sam's father. Many shop owners were paying the outlaws to leave them alone, and ranchers in the area found themselves minus their herds when the Crowders rode their way. Ten men in all made up the gang, most of them related. They delighted in terrorizing the town and had left the saloons in shambles too many times to count. The bank had been robbed once, but evidently banker Logan had struck up some kind of bargain with their leader for he'd not been bothered since.

Riding directly to the stables, Colt wondered where Sanchez was as he rubbed the horse down and put fresh hay in the stall. His own mustang was exactly where he had left him earlier that day. He didn't tarry to find out whether Sanchez had replaced the thrown shoe but went directly to the house.

It was pitch black inside. In fact, it appeared so deserted Colt's first thought was that somehow Sam had mustered sufficient strength to leave bed and flee, thinking he meant to turn her over to the sheriff. Of course, he had intended to do exactly that until he met the despicable man.

"Christ!" Colt cursed, bumping his shin in the dark. He struck a match, located a lamp, and waited until the dim glow lighted his way. Automatically his steps led him to Sam's room, a helpless feeling grinding his gut at the thought of facing an empty bed.

A muffled sob sharpened his wits and made him aware that he was not alone. As he transferred the lamp to his left hand, his right hovered close to his six-shooter. The door stood slightly ajar and he carefully nudged it open with his booted toe. Sam lay in the center of the bed, quietly sobbing. She blinked at the sudden blaze of light and stared warily at Colt, waiting for him to explode once he learned about Will.

Discovering Sam in bed where he had left her hours earlier gave Colt an unexpected jolt of pleasure that surprised as well as nettled him. No woman had ever caused him the anguish Sam had. Nor made him angrier. He had no idea what to do with her. That's why he had left instructions allowing her to continue living on the ranch, for Colt was astute enough to realize that this was not the time to tell her he was the new owner of the Circle H. Somehow he doubted she would understand. Yet he couldn't deny the vast sense of relief he felt upon finding she hadn't left. What in the hell was the matter with him? He was in the midst of an assignment dealing with vicious outlaws and needed no distractions, certainly none like the feisty Samantha Howard.

"Where is Sanchez?" Colt asked, setting the lamp on the nightstand. "Why is it so dark in here? Have you eaten?"

"Sanchez is gone," Sam replied cautiously. "He left shortly after you did."

"You've been alone all this time? Damn that man! When he returns I'll—"

"He's not coming back."

"I don't believe that," scoffed Colt. "The man is devoted to you. Why would he leave?"

Abruptly Sam changed the subject. "How long do I have before you take me to jail?"

Taken aback by her bluntness, Colt said slowly, "I haven't decided. Though you might be interested to know I turned in the gold you stole. Mr. Logan should have it tomorrow."

"So it *was* you," Sam accused bitterly. "How did you know where it was?"

"It doesn't matter. Reckon by now you know I found out Will is your young brother. I found out where he hid the gold, and since I'm a lawman and the robbery occurred under my nose, so to speak, I felt it my duty to retrieve it and turn it over to the sheriff. He'll see it gets to the bank."

"Don't be so sure," Sam muttered disparagingly.

"Ah, yes, I see what you mean," Colt readily concurred. "The man's character leaves much to be desired. By the way, your brother may as well show himself, now that I know where he's hidin'."

One corner of Sam's mouth quirked upward in a satisfied smirk. "Will has gone where you won't find him. Someplace where you can't hurt him."

"What makes you think I'd harm a half-grown boy?" Colt countered.

"You shot a woman, why should a young boy stop you?"

"Christ! Must you keep throwin' that in my face? You took a calculated risk and lost. Did you send Will away with Sanchez?" he asked astutely.

"I suppose there's no harm in admitting it. By now they're long gone."

"You could have trusted me to do the right thing by the lad," Colt defended. "Contrary to what you believe, I don't harm children."

"It's too late," Sam said wearily.

Noting the pinched look around her mouth and the paleness beneath the natural golden hue of her skin, Colt decided to drop the subject for the time being. What's done was done. Besides, he had no time to go after the boy. It was up to God and Sanchez to keep him safe for Sam.

"Have you eaten?"

"Not since morning. I'm not very hungry."

"I'll fix us somethin'."

Twenty minutes later Colt pulled up a table beside the bed and shared with Sam a makeshift meal of beans, bacon, biscuits, and canned peaches. He was pleased to note she ate ravenously, consuming nearly as much as he did. Afterwards, he cleaned up and prepared to change Sam's bandage.

"I'll help you remove your nightgown," Colt said with a mischievous grin as he moved the lamp closer to the bed.

"My bandage doesn't need changing," Sam refuted, stirring uncomfortably beneath his probing tawny eyes. Why did he make her feel like this? she wondered distractedly. Those strange golden brown eyes of his made her experience things she knew nothing about. She hated him, of course. Because of him she and Will had lost the ranch. She wished she'd never heard of a Texas Ranger named Colt Andrews. She'd rather tangle with a rattlesnake.

"I'll be the judge of that," Colt said, his fingertips playing with the drawstring at the neck of her voluminous white nightgown.

Sam assumed a stoic facade as she felt cool air fan her flesh. Carefully Colt raised her to a sitting position and lowered the gown to her waist. Lack of strength made Sam pliable to his wishes and she submitted ungraciously to his ministrations, noting on the fringe of awareness the gentleness of his touch. When his hands lingered overlong on the rise of soft flesh, Sam inhaled sharply, drawing a reaction from Colt she was unprepared to deal with.

"You have beautiful breasts," he shocked her by saying. "About as perfect as I've ever seen."

"Why, you lowdown skunk! How dare you," Sam gasped, groping futilely for her nightgown. "It's bad enough I have to submit to your clumsy doctoring, but I don't have to listen to your crude remarks. After this I'll change my own bandage. In any event, I'm healing nicely and need no more of your vile attentions."

"I fear you're right," Colt sighed with a hint of regret. "I'm a better doctor than I gave myself credit for. You're comin' along fine."

Mesmerized, he watched as Sam shoved her arms into her nightgown and primly retied the drawstring beneath her chin. Slowly his eyes slid upwards to linger on her lips, struggling to resist an emotion completely foreign to him. Suddenly some force stronger than the life coursing through him made him want to kiss her, the need so urgent it bordered on pain.

Sam saw the look in Colt's tawny eyes change from teasing interest to hot, molten desire, and could not turn away from it, nor did she want to. She felt the soft fullness of his mouth cover hers, moving slowly and sensuously, his tongue gently probing to part her lips. The feeling was so exquisite Sam was too stunned to resist. Against her will her mouth opened and his bold tongue slipped easily inside, teasing, cajoling, taking, until she threw caution to the wind and kissed him back, with all thought, all reason, falling away. He continued to kiss her in ways she could never have imagined.

When his hands moved to her breasts, stroking the soft mounds and stimulating her nipples through her nightgown with his thumbs, Sam suddenly came to her senses. With a start she realized something was happening between them that shouldn't be. She might be a prisoner, but that didn't give him the right to use her for his own pleasure. Breathless from his kiss, reeling from shock over her unprecedented response, Sam pulled free and struggled within the circle of Colt's arms.

Regaining his wits, Colt reared back, staring at Sam with something akin to horror. What in the hell was the matter with him? He had no business involving himself in a situation that could adversely affect his performance in the line of duty. He had no experience with women like Samantha Howard. For all her daring and courage, she was innocent of the type of games he usually played with the opposite sex. Sex and gratification with no commitments was the code he lived by. His kind abhorred permanence and involvements that tied them down and interfered with their wild ways. Not once did Colt delve deeply into his reasons for buying the Circle H Ranch. He assumed it was to keep skunks like Vern

Chapter Four

You're a strange and complicated man, Colt Andrews," Sam mused as Colt stared at her warily. You're hard as nails, yet I've never felt a more tender touch when you dressed my wound. First you shoot me, then save my life just so you can send me to prison. Everything about you is a contradiction.

"Who are you really? Are you a hardbitten Texas Ranger or a caring man beneath that rough exterior? I sense in you a loneliness, a yearning, a need for . . . for . . ."

"Don't try to analyze me, darlin'," Colt drawled lazily, stunned by Sam's astute summation of his character, "for you'll find me lackin'." How could this mere slip of a girl he hardly knew strip away the layers of carefully built reserve and unbare his soul so thoroughly? No man or woman alive had ventured past his tough veneer, and he wasn't certain he liked the feeling.

Sam accepted Colt's statement at face value. Besides, it mattered little what made Colt tick. What concerned her were his plans for her future—if she had one.

"Get some sleep," Colt said gruffly. "Tomorrow you can get out of bed and move around some. I'm takin' you into town real soon. My assignment is to rid the town of the Crowders, and I can't do it playin' nursemaid to a lady outlaw with no more sense than a rabbit dumb enough to get snared."

"I expected as much," Sam said with a defeated sigh. "I was right, you are a—"

". . . Heartless bastard who'd shoot a woman, then send her to jail," Colt finished, an amused smile crinkling the lines around his eyes. "I'll try to live up to your high regard."

"You have already exceeded my expectations," Sam retorted. "Will I be allowed to take a few of my belongings with me?"

"Take anythin', darlin', as long as you can stuff it in a saddlebag. Goodnight, Sam."

Bewildered, Sam stared at Colt's departing back. After acting like a no-account polecat he did something so totally out of character it left her stunned. If only things had turned out differently. If Ranger Colt Andrews hadn't been on that stagecoach she'd still have her ranch and Will wouldn't be halfway to Loredo. Sam felt no remorse over stealing from Calvin Logan. If he hadn't foreclosed on Pop's loan she wouldn't be in this fix now.

Of course, she could have married Vern Logan and lived a comfortable life as a banker's wife. Perhaps she might have persuaded the elder Logan not to call in the loan and she and Vern could have lived here until Will reached his majority and took over his inheritance. But she didn't love Vern. Though he was nice enough to her, something deep inside told her he couldn't be trusted. Months ago she'd learned about the woman he kept at the Palace Saloon, and that hardly endeared him to her. No, marrying Vern Logan was not the answer, Sam reflected, sighing wearily as she turned over, trimmed the wick on the lamp, and finally drifted off to sleep.

Pacing restlessly in the bedroom across the hall, Colt was not so lucky. It rankled to think that this woman, a young, inexperienced one at that, could penetrate the carefully constructed wall shielding his emotions—a barrier that had taken years to erect. He had racked his brain trying to decide what to do with Sam. Since Sanchez and her foolish brother bolted, he couldn't leave her on the ranch by herself. The Crowders might get wind of it and pay her a surprise visit. Or an Indian raiding party might come down out of the hills and attack the house. Yet placing her in Sheriff Bauer's jail was completely out of the question now that he knew what would happen to her under the man's dubious care.

Taking Sam to San Antonio was an alternative Colt considered. He knew Sheriff Cole well enough to know he wouldn't harm Sam. But he had no time for a trip to San Antonio, nor the inclination to see Sam behind bars. She was just a silly little girl struggling to hang on to a ranch for the sake of her young brother and had chosen the wrong way to go about it. True, he was a Texas Ranger sworn to uphold the law, but Rangers were notorious for bending the law to fit their own purposes. The best thing to do, in Colt's estimation, was find a suitable place for Sam to stay where she would be properly cared for.

Sam found she could easily manage her own dressing when she arose the next morning. Disdaining the accepted woman's garb she considered too frivolous for ranch work, she donned tight buckskin trousers much like Colt wore and a plaid shirt. A pair of sturdy boots completed the outfit. Pop preferred her in dresses, but she had neither time nor inclination for fancy fripperies. Actually, Sam had no idea how seductive she looked with the tight pants hugging her round little bottom and long sleek thighs. In keeping with her no-nonsense mode of dress, she braided her long hair in a fat plait that hung down her back.

Though dressing had taxed her meager strength, Sam found it easier than she had expected. Four days in bed allowed sufficient time for recuperation, and she was able to move around with surprisingly little discomfort. Say what you want about Colt Andrews, he *was* a good doctor. As well as a complete enigma. Sam seriously doubted that any woman or man alive knew him well enough to judge his character. Something inside him forswore intimacy. A shield of iron surrounded him, a will of steel governed him, and a relentless seeking drove him. Sam pitied anyone who tangled with Colt Andrews.

Colt was already gone when Sam left her bedroom. The remnants of a makeshift breakfast still were on the kitchen table, and Sam picked listlessly at the leftovers, not really hungry. Vaguely she wondered where Colt had disappeared to so early and decided it really didn't matter. He'd be back, and all too soon she'd be sitting behind bars. The thought was so terrifying she sat down in the nearest chair as a twinge of pain lanced through her body. Perhaps for the first time she truly realized the terrible consequences her recklessness had earned.

A knock on the door at first brought no answer from Sam, so enmeshed was she in the agonizing thought of endless years in prison stretching before her. It was the voice that finally raised a response from her.

"Samantha! Are you in there? It's Vern, Vern Logan."

Calvin Logan approached his bank at the ungodly hour of seven a.m. The bank didn't open until nine, but he liked to spend an undisturbed time on private business before opening the doors himself each morning. Vern knew some of what was going on, but Klaus Spindler was entirely in the dark about the railroad and the inordinate number of foreclosures Calvin had acquired. Sickness had confined Calvin to his bed the past two days and he had more business than usual to catch up on. He hoped Vern hadn't messed up things too badly in his absence.

Though Vern was his only son, he was not overly bright where business was concerned. He also had a propensity for hard liquor, gambling, and whores. It was all right to indulge, Calvin allowed, but one had to keep a clear head if one wanted to succeed. That's why Calvin relentlessly goaded Vern into choosing a wife. He'd even helped Vern along by foreclosing on the Howard ranch, hoping to force the willful but extremely desirable Samantha Howard into marriage.

Of course, Calvin had an ulterior motive. The railroad people would soon arrive to buy the right-of-way for land on which to build their railroad. As of five o'clock last night he had added the Howard property to his list of holdings, all of which were located along the right-of-way. Calvin's goal was to be the richest man in the state of Texas. There were still a few holdouts who refused to sell their land, but the Crowder gang was slowly changing their minds. Striking a deal with those lawless outcasts had been the smartest move he'd ever made. Costly, but smart.

When Calvin sat down at his desk, the first thing he saw was the sale papers completed the night before by Klaus Spindler assigning the Howard land to a Mr. Steven Colter, and he promptly flew into a rage. He cursed Klaus, cursed the illness that kept him confined to bed, but most of all he cursed Vern for not being here to prevent Klaus from making such a muddle of things. Who in the hell was Steven Colter? He asked his poor, unsuspecting clerk that very question when he arrived an hour later.

"I . . . I never saw the man before," replied Klaus, cowering beneath his employer's scathing rage. "But he's a friend of your son's. Or at least he said he was. He was looking for property, and since the Circle H became available at five o'clock last night I saw no reason not to mention it. Mr. Colter expressed interest and decided it would be perfect for his needs. He wanted the papers drawn up immediately and I . . . I complied," Klaus said, carefully excluding any mention of the bonus he received. "I had the bank's best interest at heart."

"You addlepated idiot!" Logan raged. "How could you do this without consultin' me? Where was Vern?"

"Herr Vern . . . er . . . stepped out for a time," Klaus flushed. "He told me to handle things in his absence and close up if he wasn't back in time. I was only following orders. The bank forecloses and sells property all the time."

"Not this property!" Calvin thundered, a vein in his temple throbbing dangerously as his face turned a mottled purple. "Where can I find Mr. Colter? Perhaps all isn't lost yet."

"I . . . I don't know," stuttered Klaus. "I got the impression he was leaving town immediately because he left instructions allowing Miss Howard and her brother to remain on the ranch until he appeared to take possession."

"Dammit, you're fired, Spindler! Gather up your things and clear out of here."

"That's fine with me, Herr Logan. I only came back this morning to tell you I quit. I'm leaving for New Orleans on the ten o'clock stage."

Without a backward glance he spun on his heel and marched out the door, grateful to Herr Colter for giving him the opportunity to strike out on his own.

Vern Logan fared no better in his father's treatment. Standing meekly before the raging man, he was alternately cursed, condemned, and disinherited. His only chance to atone for his irresponsible behavior, according to the elder Logan, was to settle down with a good wife and give him a grandchild. Until that child rested in Calvin's arms his money would go to a cousin in Chicago. Calvin expressed his intention to alter his will immediately to include those conditions.

Vern knew his father meant to follow through with his threat. Many times in the past Calvin had threatened to cut Vern off without a cent if he didn't mend his ways, give up gambling and whoring, take a greater interest in his job, and get married. Vern suffered his father's rampage in silence. When the older man finally exhausted himself, he suggested Vern might partially redeem himself by persuading Samantha Howard to become his wife. With her property gone she might be more amenable to Vern's suit.

Vern was thoroughly puzzled as to the identity of the new owner of the Circle H Ranch. To the best of his knowledge, he knew no one named Steven Colter. Obviously the man was a charlatan and wanted the property for the same reason his father did, else why would he lie about their being acquainted? If it weren't for Steven Colter, he would still be in his father's good graces. He hated the man without knowing him.

Samantha knew the reason for Vern Logan's early morning visit without being told. No doubt he wanted to inform her that she had to leave the ranch. She already knew that. Colt had irrevocably altered her life the moment he interfered with her plans to rob the stage.

"Can you hear me, Samantha? I know you're in there."

"I'm coming," Sam replied with a small sigh of resignation as she levered herself out of her chair.

"What kept you?" Vern asked after Sam let him inside. He eyed her unfeminine garb with obvious distaste.

"It's early," Sam replied with a hint of reproval.

"I know, and I apologize. But I had to see you. It's been weeks since I've seen you and I've been hankerin' to talk to you."

"Just two weeks." Sam knew exactly when she had seen Vern last. He was the one who had told her about the gold shipment.

"Seems longer." He moved closer, and automatically Sam retreated. "You know why I'm here, don't you?"

"I reckon," Sam said shortly. "You've come to tell me the ranch no longer belongs to me and Will. I know the date and that your father foreclosed last night."

"Daddy is a businessman, Samantha, you can't fault him for callin' in the note. You know there was absolutely no hope of your repayin' your father's loan."

"I'll leave tomorrow," Sam said.

"Where will you go?"

"I . . . have a place to stay," Sam hedged. No need to elaborate, he'd find out soon enough that she had lodging in the town jail.

"Marry me, Samantha. I'll provide everythin' you'll ever need, and your brother will always have a home with us."

"Can you give me back my property?"

"You know that's impossible."

"Why? Surely it's within your power." Sam knew that marriage between them was out of the question, with a jail sentence hanging over her, but she couldn't resist the urge to test him.

"The ranch was sold shortly after five o'clock last night."

Sam paled, groping for a chair. The shock of learning that someone else owned the land her father had fought the Indians for, combined with a lingering weakness from her wound, left her thoroughly shaken.

Instantly contrite, Vern dropped to his knees before her. "I'm sorry, Samantha, I didn't mean to tell you this way, or even for this to happen. It was Daddy's intent to keep the property and present it to us as a weddin' gift. A quirk of fate took it out of our hands. Both Daddy and I were out of the bank when a Mr. Steven Colter came in near closin' time and expressed an interest in the ranch. That idiot of a clerk sold it to him without consultin' either of us. Mr. Colter is now the new owner of the Circle H."

"Steven Colter," repeated Sam woodenly. The name sounded strangely familiar.

"Do you know him?" Vern asked sharply.

"N . . . no, I'm sure I don't. It's just . . ." She faltered, choking on a sob.

"Samantha, are you ill?" Vern asked with mock concern. "You're so pale."

"I . . . need time to digest all this, Vern," Sam replied, feeling weaker by the minute.

"Where is Will?" Vern asked, suddenly aware that

they were alone. "Come to think on it, I didn't see that Mex Sanchez around when I rode in."

"They . . . went hunting," Sam improvised, "but I expect them back soon."

Realizing they were alone, Vern rose and pulled Sam from the chair into the circle of his arms. "You didn't answer me, Samantha. Will you marry me? It's time you gave up your hoydenish ways, dressed like a woman, and thought about motherhood. You want children, don't you?" he asked slyly.

"I . . . of course, but . . ."

"Then it's settled. I'll make the arrangements and we'll marry one week from today. Daddy will be ecstatic."

"Sam isn't free to marry."

Vern whirled. A dark, powerfully built stranger lounged in the doorway, a sardonic smile curving the corners of his full lips. "Who in the hell are you, mister?"

Suddenly he spotted the distinctive badge that Colt had pinned on his chest when he recognized Vern Logan's voice coming from inside the house.

"Ranger Colt Andrews," Colt volunteered, uncoiling his lanky length and ambling into the room with the sleek aggressiveness of a cougar.

"Do I know you?" Vern asked, his light blue eyes narrowed thoughtfully. "Seems like I recollect you from somewhere. The name's Vern Logan."

"We've not met formally, but you might have seen me in town yesterday," Colt informed him. Then he turned tawny eyes on Sam, his next words bringing a gasp of dismay bubbling from her lips. "You were sleepin' so soundly when I got out of bed this

mornin', darlin', I didn't want to disturb you."
Deliberately he made it sound as if they had occupied the same bed.

"What's this man to you, Samantha?" Vern demanded angrily. "I can't believe you'd sink so low when I offered you respectability and marriage. Are you lovers? I thought we had an understandin'."

"Vern, it's not what you think," Sam tried to explain, slanting a venomous glance in Colt's direction. "Colt is—"

"Is what? He made it perfectly clear what he's doin' here."

"Colt is here to take me to j—"

"Explainin' won't help, Sam," Colt warned.

"Forget Ranger Andrews, Samantha," Vern snapped, his voice ripe with disgust. "Because I love you I'm willin' to swallow my pride and forgive your . . . er . . . indiscretion. Maybe I'm loco but I still want to marry you."

Vern was so anxious to be reinstated in his father's good graces that he was willing to take damaged goods. Besides, no other woman excited him like Samantha Howard. Not even Molly whose body gave him so much pleasure.

"'Pears like you didn't hear me the first time, Mr. Logan," Colt repeated with calm deliberation. "Miss Howard isn't free to marry. I've already staked my claim."

"How can that be? Two weeks ago Samantha didn't even know you existed."

"She does now." Colt grinned with wicked delight.

"I'd like to hear what Samantha has to say about

this," Vern insisted. He wasn't about to give up so easily. A lot rode on Samantha's answer. There wasn't another woman in Karlsburg to compare with her, and he desperately needed a wife to please his daddy and earn back his inheritance. His eyes settled disconcertedly on Sam's pale face.

"I . . . I'm sorry, Vern, but I can't marry you," she repeated. "I've refused your offer before and must do so again."

"Because of this man?" He nodded toward Colt.

"You could say that," flushed Sam, hating the knowing smirk on Colt's rugged face.

"Is he offerin' marriage?"

"I . . . no. It's not . . ."

"You got your answer, Mr. Logan, I suggest you hightail it out of here," Colt prodded.

"Is there nothin' I can do or say to change your mind, Samantha?" Vern asked tightly. "I know I can offer you more than a man whose gun is his fortune."

"You're wastin' your breath, Logan," Colt sneered, well aware of the banker's scurrilous character. He would make Sam a lousy husband. He was shallow, deceitful, selfish, and a liar to boot. Sam deserved better.

"You'll be sorry, Samantha," Vern bit out nastily. "If you should change your mind you know where to find me." Turning on his heel, he slammed out of the house.

"Are you all right?" Colt asked, concern coloring his words. Sam was deathly pale and looked on the verge of collapse.

"Why did you make it sound as if . . . as if we

73

were . . . intimate?" Sam accused, stifling a sob. "You're a shiftless, no good, worthless no-account, Colt Andrews!"

"I figured I was doin' you a favor," Colt said sourly. "You could do better than Vern Logan. And didn't I warn you about your nasty mouth? Cussin' is not ladylike."

"I'm no lady, as you pointed out before," Sam ground out defiantly. "Why didn't you come right out and tell him you're taking me to jail?"

"'Cause I'm not."

"What! What did you say?" His shocking words sent Sam reeling.

"Sam, I know why you held up the stage. You needed the money to keep the bank from foreclosin'. Why didn't you tell me that in the beginnin'?"

"Would it have made a difference?"

"You know I'm a lawman. What you did was illegal."

"But you just said you weren't taking me to jail."

"That's right. Not now, anyway," Colt acknowledged. "I tangled with Sheriff Bauer while in town yesterday and I wouldn't put a dog in his keepin'. You're not a hardened criminal, Sam, I can't do that to you. And I don't have time to take you to San Antonio."

"What does all this mean?"

"Do you know Ida Scheuer?"

Sam nodded. "Her husband owns the grocery."

"I rode into town this mornin' to ask if you could stay with her till my job is finished in Karlsburg."

"I couldn't," Sam demurred. "I know her husband and he—"

"He's dead," Colt revealed, "and Ida is runnin' the store by herself. She'd be glad for the company and help, if you've a mind to once you're well."

"I didn't know about her husband. I didn't like him, but neither did I wish him dead. What happened?"

"I'll let Ida tell you. If you're up to it we'll leave tomorrow."

"It doesn't change a thing, does it?" Sam asked slowly. "In the end I'll go to prison, so I don't reckon it matters where I stay. I no longer have a home. Mr. Steven Colter is the new owner of the Circle H, whoever he might be."

"Don't you own any dresses?" Colt asked, deliberately changing the subject. The sight of her in tight pants was provocatively distracting. He could imagine the attention and disapproval she would generate in a town like Karlsburg.

"Certainly, but I prefer pants. I enjoy the freedom."

"I readily admit your round little bottom is encitin', darlin', but aren't you afraid of attractin' unwanted attention in town?"

"Don't be crude," Sam scolded, "and don't call me darling. The townspeople are accustomed to seeing me wearing pants."

She rose somewhat unsteadily to her feet. Her first hours out of bed were more exhausting than she would have thought. Now she needed some time alone to mourn the loss of the ranch and ponder her uncertain future. She must have been weaker than she thought, for her wobbly knees buckled and she swayed dangerously. Flexing his sleek muscles, Colt scooped her into his arms.

"Christ, you're a lot of trouble," he muttered, his slight burden hampering him not at all as he made his way to her bedroom. "You weigh hardly nothin' at all."

"I'm sorry," she whispered as Colt held her suspended in his arms. "I usually don't act like this, but you must admit I have sufficient reason."

"Can I help you undress, darlin'?" he teased mischievously.

"I can manage. Put me down."

"I was sure you could."

They stared at one another for several tense minutes, sparks leaping between them and igniting some hidden place within Sam while a foreign emotion Colt never knew existed reached out to touch his heart. Neither recognized or acknowledged it.

Sam was the first to break the spell. "Colt, please put me down, I'd like to rest."

"Sam, I'm damn sorry about the ranch," he said after putting her on her feet.

"I'll bet."

"I mean it. I know it means a lot to you. But you have to understand the awkward position I'm in. You've committed a crime, I'm a lawman."

"You could forget it and let me go."

"Go where?"

"I . . . don't know. Anywhere. I don't want to go to prison."

She looked so appealing, so vulnerable and so damn beautiful, prison was the last place Colt wished to see Samantha Howard. "Would you marry Logan if you were free to do so?"

A thoughtful pause ensued. "I . . . don't think so."

"If you weren't such a damn innocent I'd—"

"You'd what?"

"Do this." His head dipped to capture her lips.

Her mouth was incredibly soft and sweet. He kissed the full lower lip, tasting, savoring, while his hand shaped the supple curve of her bottom. Slow pleasure replaced anger as the source of Sam's passion and she experienced true arousal for the first time in her life.

The tantalizing play of Colt's mouth only heightened her desire. Now his lips were brushing wildfire over her eyelids, jawline, and throat, before returning to cling gently to her eager mouth. She was swallowing a moan when she felt his tongue touch her lower lip, then her teeth, until it grazed the tip of her tongue. Her mouth opened wider to allow him to plunder at will. Her heart beat furiously, and she wanted the kiss to go on forever. But it was not to be. Abruptly Colt broke contact.

"What you need is a firm hand on the reins to tame and master you, a real man in the saddle," Colt growled, placing her on the bed and lowering himself atop her quivering form.

"You're no different than any other woman in your position. Admit it, you'd do anythin' to keep from goin' to jail. Even beddin' me. Are you really as innocent as you pretend? Have you bedded Vern Logan?"

"Why you rotten, ornery, braying jackass!" Sam cried. "If and when I want a man it won't be someone as arrogant and lowdown mean as you.

Why don't you just take me to jail and get it over with? I can't stand this waiting. My ranch is gone, my brother forced to run away, nothing matters anymore."

"Darlin', I could easily be persuaded to forget about the holdup," Colt said, his voice a husky purr.

With the evidence of his desire pressing against her stomach, Sam knew exactly what he meant. The question was, did she want freedom badly enough to allow him use of her body? It was a question that, thankfully, she didn't need to answer as Colt's weight suddenly left her body.

"Christ, what in the hell is wrong with me?" he chided himself, tunneling long fingers through sun-bronzed hair. "Forget I said that. Forget everythin' I just said. I never forced myself on an innocent woman before and I don't aim to now. I've been around whores and cowpokes so long I've forgotten how to act with a decent woman. Go on, get some rest. I'll wake you in time for supper."

Too stunned to speak, Sam stared at Colt's departing back. Never would she understand that man. He was ruggedly handsome yet dangerously wicked. Things he said and did shocked her, then he confused matters by turning around and contradicting everything. He was tough as nails, hardbitten, unscrupulous, and thoroughly disreputable. The perfect description of a Texas Ranger—a breed apart, feared by red man and white man alike. Yet . . . yet she sensed in him an odd gentleness, a crack in the thick shell surrounding his true self. What would it take to find the real person inside? Why did she even care? Eventually exhaustion claimed her and she slid uneasily into slumber.

While Sam slept, Colt paced, torn apart by conflicting emotions. He was a man not easily led from his chosen path. Life had dealt him many blows, but a will of steel and strength of character provided the means to survive situations that would have felled lesser men in his profession. Danger lurked around every corner, and the slightest deviation or distraction could cost him his life. Samantha Howard was definitely a distraction he could not afford.

Chapter Five

Sam missed the ranch dreadfully. She missed the freedom, the pride of ownership, the space to do and be what she pleased. Not that Ida Scheuer wasn't the kindest soul alive. Ida regarded Colt as something of a hero and would have agreed to anything he asked, but she truly liked Sam and a warm friendship developed. Ida knew only what Colt had told her—that Sam needed a place to stay since foreclosure had forced her off her property. She also had been informed that Sam had recently sustained some kind of injury but not its nature.

In return for room and board Sam offered to work in the store. The one thing Ida insisted upon that Sam didn't like was that she wear a dress while working in the store. Ida considered pants an unlikely outfit for a young woman as comely as Sam.

Staring pensively out the window of the cheerful

room she now called home, Sam recalled vividly the ride into town that day over two weeks ago. After what had nearly happened in her bedroom, Colt had been subdued to the point of surliness. The next morning, after a silent breakfast, Sam had packed her saddlebags with some of her belongings and wandered around outside waiting for Colt to close up the house. It was the only home she had ever known, and tears flowed down her cheeks at the thought of it being occupied by anyone but a Howard.

Colt either did not notice or did not care as he saddled their horses and helped her mount. He felt somewhat guilty not telling Sam that he was the new owner of the Circle H, but things between them were too tense right now for confidences. Besides, he knew she would insist on staying on even if she would be alone and unprotected.

They rode in silence for a time until Colt said, "I know the ride into town can't be too comfortable for you so we'll take it slow and easy."

"Don't worry over me. I can keep up. Are you sure Ida Scheuer won't mind a boarder?"

"I told you yesterday I already talked to her. She's lookin' forward to havin' you."

"Will you stay there too?"

"No. I spoke to the bartender at the Palace Saloon and he said the owner often lets rooms. The owner was out of town but will be back today. I'll inquire if he has any rooms available."

"You mean she."

"What?"

"The owner of the Palace Saloon is a woman. Her

name is Dolly Douglas. She bought it from the previous owner over a year ago. I'm sure she'd be happy to accommodate you," Sam said suggestively.

"Dolly Douglas? Blond, blue eyes, late twenties?"

"You . . . you know her?"

"Damn right I do." Colt grinned with devilish delight. "Me and Dolly go back a long ways. Well, I'll be hanged," he said, shoving his hat back on his tawny mane. "Last I heard she went to California to strike it rich. If she owns the saloon she must have hit pay dirt. Wonder what brought her to Karlsburg?"

"I'm sure I don't know," Sam returned with a hint of sarcasm. "You'll have to ask Miss Douglas. You two will have a lot of . . . catching up to do."

After that the conversation had lagged until they reached town. Just as Colt had predicted, Ida welcomed her warmly, got her settled in the room she now occupied, and allowed her a few days rest before acquainting her with the store. Before long Sam settled down to a daily routine. Though she tried to deny it, some devil inside her made her wish she could have witnessed Colt's reunion with the infamous Dolly.

After leaving Sam with Ida, Colt continued on to the Palace Saloon, his thoughts taking him back several years to the small Texas border town of Nocogdoches. He had met Dolly Douglas in the Outpost Saloon where she worked as hostess, and their mutual attraction soon evolved into a comfortable relationship that provided not only sexual gratification but good companionship as well. But their association died of natural causes when Colt's restlessness took him off in another direction. When he returned months later he learned Dolly had gone to California to make her fortune.

Their reunion was all Sam had imagined, and more. Colt found Dolly in the nearly deserted saloon giving instructions to the bartender about the night's festivities. She had changed little during the years, Colt thought warmly. Still blond, all the curves in the right places, still lovely, looking not a day older than when he had seen her five years ago. As if sensing his presence, Dolly slowly turned in Colt's direction. She searched his face for the space of a heartbeat, then squealed in delight.

"Colt! By God, you're a sight for sore eyes! I reckoned if I sat in one place long enough you'd show up." Slowly, provocatively, she walked to within inches of him, then hurled herself into his open arms.

"You're lookin' mighty spruce, Dolly." Colt grinned cheekily as he hugged her tight.

"And you're still a handsome devil," Dolly twinkled in return. "As well as somewhat of a rogue, if memory serves. How many hearts have you broken since I saw you last?"

"Who's countin'?" Colt shrugged with exaggerated casualness. "'Sides, none were as pleasin' as you."

"Sit down, honey," Dolly said, leading him to a table at the back of the room. "Let me buy you a drink while we catch up on old times." She motioned to the bartender. "What brings you to a dump like Karlsburg?"

"I might ask the same of you. The last I heard you were in California makin' your fortune. What happened, did you run out of men?"

Instead of taking offense, Dolly laughed raucously.

"Still the same old Colt. Would you believe I got married?" The news seemed to stun Colt and he choked on his drink, bringing on another round of laughter.

"The poor bastard up and died after he struck it rich in the gold mines. I hightailed it back to Texas with more money than I thought existed. I heard about the Palace from a friend, liked what I saw, and bought it. Now it's your turn. What's occupied your time since we parted five years ago? We had some good times, didn't we, honey?" she sighed wistfully.

"The best," Colt agreed. "But nothin' so excitin' happened to me. I bummed around Texas for a while, tried my hand at bounty huntin', fought Indians, and finally turned lawman. Cap'n Ford recruited me for the Texas Rangers."

"Lawman! You?" guffawed Dolly, her eyes sliding to the badge adorning Colt's broad chest. "You've come in answer to Mayor Mohler's plea? You're here because of the Crowder gang?"

"I'm here to preserve the peace and keep the gang from killin' off the ranchers and stealin' their cattle."

"They're mean, Colt, real mean," Dolly emphasized. "They shot up my saloon twice. Gunned down innocent men, too. A few right here in my saloon—ranchers and townspeople who did nothing to provoke them except be in the wrong place at the wrong time. I hope you got plenty of backup if or when they return."

"There's just me."

"Are you loco? You don't stand a chance alone."

"What about the sheriff and his deputy? Or the townspeople, for that matter. Won't they help defend the town? Cap'n Ford was countin' on their cooperation."

"The sheriff and his deputy are cowardly bastards and the townspeople are afraid of their own shadows. They're good people, Colt, who don't believe in violence. Their peaceful ways earned them respect from the Indians and a tenuous treaty. I'd say you're pretty much on your own where the Crowders are concerned."

"The mayor hinted as much," Colt mused thoughtfully. "I won't know what I'm up against till the Crowders come visitin'. In the meantime I need a place to stay. The bartender said you had rooms for rent."

"There's only one vacant right now, Colt, and it's yours for as long as you need it."

"Much obliged, Dolly. Just point me in the right direction. Would a bath be an outrageous request at this time of day?"

"I'll see to it," Dolly nodded, her voice ripe with promise. "And I'll be up later to scrub your back." Smoky blue meshed with tawny gold, provoking a wealth of fond memories.

"Suit yourself, Dolly," Colt responded, his tone telling her it was entirely her choice. "But you'll find I haven't changed. Nothin' is forever with me. If you can live with that, then I'd be obliged to have you scrub my back."

Dolly's keen disappointment didn't show in her carefully composed features. "We're two of a kind, honey. I was married for a year and hated it. I'm rich enough now to pick and choose my lovers. I'm discriminating and only take men to my bed who attract me. I hire girls to satisfy customers who come here for female companionship. Till you showed up there's few in Karlsburg who've captured my fancy. We were damn good together once, and I'd like to recapture what we had for as long as you're around."

"How can I refuse on those terms?" Colt grinned wolfishly.

Sam had been in town over two weeks when two things happened almost simultaneously. Vern Logan came to call on her, and the Crowder gang rode into town.

It was just past noon when Vern showed up at Ida's house. Cagily he timed his visit to coincide with the exact time Sam left the store to eat lunch and relax a few minutes before relieving Ida. Sam's first thought was that he had been spying on her.

As Sam's friendship with the older woman grew, Ida told her the details of her husband's death and her arrest for his murder. Sam wasn't too surprised to learn that Colt had been directly responsible for saving Ida from rape and getting her released. Just another inconsistency in his somewhat flawed character. What was he—devil or angel? Why couldn't she forget the exasperating man? She hadn't seen him except from afar since they'd arrived in Karlsburg. For some reason he seemed to be ignoring her as if she were as insignificant as a wart on a toad. But Sam was willing to bet her soul that Colt hadn't forgotten she had robbed the stage.

Sam was more than a little surprised to see Vern Logan at the door. She had expected never to see him again after Colt had deliberately misled him to believe the worst about her.

"Do you have a few minutes, Samantha?" Vern asked. He was still not ready to give up on her, especially since Molly had told him Colt and Miss Dolly were thicker than fleas on a hound dog. "It's important I talk to you."

"I . . . suppose," Sam allowed grudgingly. "But I'm due back at the store soon. Let's sit on the porch," she suggested, unwilling to be alone in the house with him. "What did you want to see me about?"

"First let me say how nice you look in that dress, Samantha. You look like a real lady." Sam flushed but said nothing. "I came to apologize. I should have realized nothin' happened between you and that Ranger. I was too angry to think straight. I don't know why he said what he did. You're not like that. I still want you for my wife."

"What made you change your mind?" Sam asked.

"I know you haven't seen Andrews since you left the ranch," Vern replied. "And I have it on good authority that him and Miss Dolly have become quite close. You understand what I mean, don't you?" Silence. "They're lovers, Samantha. I can't put it any plainer than that. One thing does bother me, though. What was he doin' at your place?"

"I . . . I was out riding and my horse threw me. Colt happened along and helped me back home," Sam fabricated. "I don't know why he said what he did. The man must have a perverse sense of humor.

What him and Miss Douglas do is no concern of mine." If that were true, why did it hurt so much? Sam wondered glumly. It was no more than she expected from him.

Vern searched Sam's face. He still couldn't shake the feeling that something was going on between Andrews and Samantha. Her explanation of their meeting sounded pretty far-fetched. But Sam had appeared so unmoved by the fact that Andrews and Miss Dolly were lovers that he was inclined now to believe her. Besides, the man did save the bank's gold the day of the robbery and couldn't have been at Sam's house for any length of time. Of greater concern to Vern was the fact that his father had kept his word and disowned him. Vern saw the new will and was told that until he proved himself responsible, it would stand. Hopefully, marrying Samantha would be his first step toward earning his father's trust.

"What's your answer, Samantha?" Vern asked impatiently. "Will you marry me?"

"I told you before, Vern, that I don't love you. I . . . can't marry you."

"I won't give up, Samantha. I'll ask over and over until I wear you down. I . . . I love you," he lied. Though he didn't actually love her he wanted her in his bed. She excited him more than any woman he had ever known.

"I have to go, Vern." Sam stood up. "Ida is expecting me."

"Wait, Samantha, there's something else."

Somewhat vexed by his persistent badgering, Sam frowned. "What is it?"

"Earlier today I was goin' over the papers transferrin' your ranch to Mr. Colter and came across this note. I'd forgotten about it till now."

"What does it say?"

"Here, read it yourself." Vern handed the note to Sam, who quickly scanned the brief contents, then stared at Vern, hope flickering in her breast.

"Mr. Colter says I can remain on the ranch until he claims it!" she exclaimed. "Did he indicate when that might be?"

"No one has seen the elusive Mr. Colter. He waltzed in and out of town without anyone knowin' what he looks like. The only one who can identify him is Klaus Spindler, the clerk who completed the deal, and he's in New Orleans."

"Mr. Colter might not show up for a long time."

"That's entirely possible. Who can say what he has in mind? It's downright peculiar how all this came about."

"I appreciate you telling me this, Vern. Now I really do have to go."

Sam took her time walking back to the store. Vern had given her much to think about. As much as she liked Ida, she hated living in town and wearing dresses every day. If Mr. Colter wanted her to continue living on the ranch in his absence, then why shouldn't she? Surely Colt wouldn't object as long as she promised not to run away. Where would she go anyway? Perhaps he had changed his mind about taking her to jail in San Antonio. He hadn't mentioned it in some time, and the feeling persisted that he really didn't want to see her behind bars. Evidently Dolly Douglas was taking up all his spare time—that's why he hadn't been around to see her. Well, Vern's surprising disclosure put a different picture on things and she needed to see Colt without delay. By the time Sam reached the store she had made up her mind to beard the lion in his den.

Toward the middle of the long afternoon Ida noticed Sam's preoccupation and wondered if she was feeling ill. She appeared to be recovering from her injury nicely, but one never knew. She could be driving herself too hard.

"Sam, business is slow right now, why don't you take the rest of the day off," Ida suggested kindly. "I'll close up and be home around seven. You look like you could use a long nap."

"I am tired," Sam admitted. She hated lying to the kindhearted woman but she knew Ida would try to dissuade her from doing something shocking. "If you're certain—"

"Absolutely, dear, you run along. I'll see you at home later."

Sam directed her steps up the street toward Ida's house but turned into the Palace Saloon instead of taking her usual route home. She was relieved to find the main room nearly deserted at this time of day. Few of the bargirls were in attendance; several men were scattered around but most paid her little heed. She was pleased to note that Dolly was nowhere in sight.

"Can I help you, miss?" Though Dirk hadn't personally met Sam, he knew her by sight from her trips into town with her father. He was more than a little shocked to see her in the Palace, although he needn't have been. More than once he'd heard the beautiful girl described as being headstrong and somewhat unconventional. Her father's death was a tragedy that shouldn't have happened.

"Is Mr. Andrews in his room?" Sam asked with more confidence than she felt.

"He was out earlier but I believe he's in now," Dirk replied, scarcely able to contain his curiosity.

Sam directed her gaze to the stairs and the several doors visible along the open balcony. "Which room?"

Dirk hesitated for the space of a moment. Sam's unorthodox request startled him. Well-bred young ladies didn't visit men's room. But it was obvious this young woman defied convention. He couldn't help but admire her spunk. She neither offered lame excuses nor apologized for her brazen behavior. Yet there was no denying she was a lady, albeit a somewhat bold one. Besides, it was none of his business if the girl chose to damage her reputation.

"Room three."

"Much obliged." Turning, Sam mounted the stairs, refusing to be undone by curious onlookers.

It took a long time for Colt to answer the door. When he did, Sam was dismayed to find he wasn't alone. Dolly Douglas stood in the middle of the room looking charmingly flustered in a revealing robe of clinging blue satin.

"Sam!" Colt gasped, stunned. "Christ! What are you doin' here?"

Sam's violet eyes slid to Dolly, then back to Colt's partially clad form. It was obvious she had interrupted more than friendly chit-chat. Colt was naked to the waist, his gleaming torso intimidating in the small room. He was very muscular with a honed, lean kind of strength. Sam couldn't help but admire his sun-bronzed chest or the curling patterns of tawny fur narrowing to a thin, fine line disappearing into the waistband of his buckskin trousers. Virility and power oozed from every pore, and Sam made a supreme effort to concentrate on her mission.

"I . . . I need to speak to you—privately." Her eyes slid to Dolly, who appeared vastly amused by the intrusion.

Colt knew it must be important to bring Sam to the Palace looking for him. He had deliberately kept his distance from her these past weeks hoping to exercise her from his mind and heart. Yet somehow, even when he made love to Dolly, Sam's face had a way of intruding into his most intimate moments. He didn't have time to analyze the feelings she evoked in him, and wasn't entirely certain he wanted to.

Turning to Dolly, he said, "Do you mind? We'll . . . talk another time."

Dolly raised a slim eyebrow, slanting Sam an assessing look. "Sure, honey, I got things to do anyway." She pulled her robe about her and sailed past Sam and through the door.

"Come in, Sam." After a moment's hesitation, Sam stepped inside. She stiffened when Colt closed the door behind her but did not protest.

"This better be important, darlin', to be riskin' your reputation over."

Sam flushed. "I think it is. I want to return to the ranch," she said, tilting her chin at a defiant angle.

"I just learned from Vern that the new owner offered to let me live on the Circle H until he claimed the property."

"Christ!" Colt cursed. He'd forgotten about that damn note. He'd written it before he knew both Will and Sanchez had skedaddled. "No!"

"Why? I won't run away, if that's what you're worried about. You can still put me in jail anytime you please."

"Aren't you unhappy with Ida? I thought—"

"It's not that. Ida is a dear and I truly like her, but—"

"It's out of the question, Sam."

"Hellfire and damnation! Haven't you punished me enough? Why can't you allow me this small concession?" A tiny sob caught in her throat, and Colt's heart did a flip-flop.

"This has nothin' to do with punishment. Where are your brains? I'm thinkin' of your safety."

Dismay followed by disbelief marched across Sam's face. Colt Andrews struck her as a man with little or no compassion and even less conscience. Why should he care what happened to her? "Why, Colt?" she couldn't help but ask. "Why should you care?"

"Do you want me to be brutally honest?" Suppressing a shudder of apprehension, Sam nodded. "You intrigue me, darlin'," Colt drawled, grinning wickedly. "I've thought of nothin' but makin' love to you since the day I discovered you were a female."

Sam inhaled sharply, Colt's admission shocking her. Obviously women were a challenge to a man like Colt whose experience was wide and varied.

His kisses had been sheer bliss to someone as inexperienced as herself, and she was glad she hadn't succumbed, though her willpower was sorely tested whenever those tawny eyes settled on her—like now.

"I admire your honesty, Colt," Sam conceded, color staining her cheeks, "but it hardly solves my problem."

"No, but it sure as hell complicates mine," he muttered, moving closer. "You can't begin to realize how badly I want you, how I've deliberately put space between us these past two weeks. You're dangerous, Samantha Howard. I sense it every time I'm near you. You're a threat to me. Every instinct tells me to turn and run, yet something deeper in me wants to do this—"

Before his lips crashed down on hers that roguish smile appeared again, transforming his rugged face into a mask of pure masculine aggression. He kissed her with a fury that surprised even him. Sam felt a pleasant numbness creeping through her body. Heat seemed to radiate from deep inside her until she warmed and tingled all over. She felt fevered. She ached. A throbbing began deep in her core.

His lips slid across her cheek to her ear where he tasted its sweetness, flicking his tongue in and out with a deftness that left her gasping for breath. She knew she should resist—knew exactly what he meant to do to her.

"Please let me go," Sam begged, struggling unsuccessfully against the splendid passion overwhelming her senses.

"I don't think you mean that, darlin'."

"Hellfire and damnation but you're a bullheaded varmint! I didn't come here to . . . to bed you."

"You've thought about it," Colt ventured wickedly. "I dare you to tell me differently."

"You . . . you . . . braying jackass!" Doubling her fists, she pushed ineffectively against his bare chest.

Daring to look into his eyes, Sam saw a smiling warmth there, sign of an emotion she least expected. He stood towering over her, tall and bronzed, and the tense silence was made even more pregnant by the drumming of her heart. Her lips parted, her breath grew labored as Colt's hands slid down to her hips, pulling her fiercely close, with a violence that made her cry out. He tasted the hot sweetness of her mouth, his kiss stirring something volatile in both of them. Time shuddered to a halt.

The awakening pleasure deep within her was fertile with the promise of fulfillment. Strong warm fingers expertly loosened and discarded her clothing as Sam watched in mute fascination, eyes half-closed, panting breathlessly. She was mesmerized by the glistening bronze of his body as he lifted her in his arms and carried her to the bed. The heat of his kisses flooded her senses until a raging desire destroyed the last of her will and scattered her self-control. Colt sensed her capitulation and rejoiced.

"You want me," Colt murmured huskily. "I can feel you tremblin', darlin'. Every silken inch of your luscious flesh is quiverin'. You're on fire for me." All Colt could think about was to have her long golden legs wrapped around him and her violet eyes liquid with desire.

Sam could not deny she wanted Colt. Her purpose in coming to Colt's room scattered like ashes before the wind as his strong arms enclosed her, his open mouth settling over hers with maddening insistence. She found herself moaning softly beneath the brute force of his need and his expert touch. Suddenly she burned for him, a totally foreign feeling, as she was rendered incapable of speech or thought or anything but the hot liquid melting in her core, his to do with as he pleased.

Encouraged by the unexpected passion he found simmering beneath the surface, Colt's hand cupped a swollen breast, fondled it, went down to touch her thigh.

Sam groaned. His fingers felt like live coals on her satin skin. Her traitorous body wanted to arch up, to seek what he offered with no quarter asked. The male musky scent of him came to her, and the scent excited her; enticed her; repulsed her.

One questing finger sought out her tender flesh, teasing it to fullness, torturing it until she gasped and writhed against his palm. Emboldened by her response, the finger plunged into her moist, hot depths. Sam cried out in delicious agony, her passion sparking his. Suddenly the brief limit of his control expired when Sam cried out, "Colt!" The ache to have him inside her reached a fevered pitch.

"I know what you want, darlin'," Colt answered her silent plea, "'cause I want it just as badly. But if you're the virgin I think you are, the first time will hurt. There's no holdin' back now, Sam, I'm beyond that point. I'll give you the most pleasure I'm capable of if you relax and go with your feelin's."

The ache he had aroused within her demanded immediate easing, but he would not grant her that. Instead he stoked the delicious agony with his tongue, hands, and voice. The intimate touch of his tongue on her nipple sent Sam soaring. When he took the swelling bud into his mouth and gently sucked, she nearly shot off the bed. He moved to the other nipple with the same delicious torment, and a hot flame flooded her body.

Sam cried out in deprivation as suddenly his warmth left her. But before she could voice her protest he was back, without the restriction of clothing between them. Then he was looming above her, his eyes scorching her with blazing intensity as slowly he lowered himself into her. Sam stiffened against the intrusion. "Relax, darlin'." Exhaling softly, Sam heeded his words, trusting him. The moment he felt her muscles relax, he thrust sharply forward, severing the membrane. Sam's response was a cry of pain and a shudder.

"I'm all the way in, darlin'," Colt exulted as he felt himself being squeezed by her tightness. "Christ, you feel good!" The splendor of the feeling severely taxed his control. He could feel his shaft pulsing wildly as he slid further and further into the moist depths of the most welcoming place he had ever entered. His heart soared as he sensed her answering passion, so alive, so vibrant that it almost shattered his steely reserve.

Sam gasped from the hugeness of his shaft. She had never imagined that anything so huge would fit and feel so good inside her. Once the initial pain subsided, she thrilled to the pleasure he was creating within her. She wanted to move wildly beneath him, seek the ecstasy he promised as swiftly as possible. As he sensed her impatience, a chuckle rumbled from Colt's throat.

"Pace yourself, darlin'. Don't get greedy. Let it come naturally, don't hurry it. Let the emotion carry you—risin', fallin', buildin' till you reach that jumpin' off place. Don't be afraid, I'll be there to catch you."

His body moved with masterly expertise as he pumped rhythmically against hers. Deliberately he withdrew when he felt her coming to the brink of explosion, then entered her again as soon as the fire abated. Then he thrust deeply in unbroken tempo until almost driven to the point of no return. But somehow he gathered the remnants of his self-control and withdrew again, until their boiling passion cooled.

When he entered her again, her body screamed for release and her thighs clamped tightly together lest he try to escape her, holding him in place and squeezing. A lusty roar escaped his throat as his hot seed spurted into her receptive body. Sam's own climax brought a scream to her lips as she exploded in a million tiny fragments. For a long time they clung together as if suspended in time, neither of them willing to break the spell, and both afraid of what lay ahead. The sweet taste of passion turned to bitter reality all too soon.

Colt stared at Sam with sheer incredulity at what she had done to him. Why did this slip of a woman have the power to make him forget everything except the promise of her sweet lips and tempting body? His every physical sense urged him to claim and hold this offering of something rare and valuable, but his mind resisted. He had fought too long against entanglements, seen many a good man ruined by a woman to allow it to happen to him. He valued his freedom far too much to fall under the spell of a spitfire named Samantha Howard.

"What happens now, Colt?" Sam asked softly.

"You're better than I imagined, darlin'," he murmured, his words like a slap in the face to Sam's pride. She had hoped for something tender and loving after what they had just shared. "You're the damnedest hellion in bed I've ever had, and," he laughed with devilish delight, "as wild and untamed as the Texas prairie. I could grow addicted to that kind of lovin'."

The look he gave her was magically stirring and tantalizingly sensual. "If I didn't know better I'd swear you were experienced. But the blood on the sheet is proof that I just took your maidenhead."

Startled, Sam looked down and saw the red splotch beneath her thighs. A deep crimson spread up her neck to her cheeks.

"Don't blush, darlin'. I appreciate your offerin' though I usually don't mess with virgins. They're too much trouble and demand things I'm unwillin' to give."

Sam snorted. "I take that to mean you won't consider my request to move back to the ranch."

Colt's eyes narrowed dangerously. "Did you come here intendin' to seduce me into givin' in to you?" he asked, his voice laced with contempt. "If you did, you sacrificed your innocence for nothin'."

"The only seducer in this room is a cantankerous billy goat who thinks with that thing hanging between his legs," Sam sputtered angrily.

Colt's scowl disintegrated as he broke into raucous laughter.

"What are you laughing about, you cross-eyed rattlesnake?"

"Your language hasn't improved any, has it?" Colt said, leering at her heaving breasts. "I reckon I'll have to find a way to shut you up."

"I don't—" The words died in her throat as Colt seized her open mouth and the magic began anew. It didn't end until the last sigh, the final moan, was wrung from her.

Colt still slept soundly when Sam slipped from his bed. Glancing at Colt's pocket watch lying on the dresser, she was shocked to discover it was six o'clock. She had been in his room over three hours! Gathering her scattered clothing, she hastily dressed, noting that the sun was a red ball low in the western horizon. She hoped to reach home before Ida arrived and asked a lot of uncomfortable questions. She couldn't help pausing for one last looked at Colt, thinking how innocent and young he looked with his ruffled tawny hair falling across his forehead. Yet she knew him to be anything but innocent. He was a devil—a womanizer with a heart as cold as stone. She found him utterly without morals or conscience. She didn't expect marriage from him—and he didn't offer. But the least he could do was let her live on the ranch until the new owner showed up.

A kind of hopelessness settled over her when she thought of how easily and totally she had surrendered to Colt's seduction. Why? she wondered bleakly. Why hadn't she resisted? Why had she allowed him to capture her senses so thoroughly and seduce her so effortlessly? A part of her heart which she kept guardedly locked held the answer to those questions. But she dare not turn the key and confront the truth. Fully dressed now, she tore her eyes from Colt's magnificent body and left the room.

As she stepped into the corridor, the sound of boisterous laughter could be heard from below, and the terrible realization struck her that the saloon was now crowded with customers. She hadn't meant to stay so long in Colt's room, but she seemed to have had little control over what happened that afternoon. Taking a deep breath, she prepared to descend the stairs with as much aplomb as she could muster.

"Miss Howard."

A groan of despair slipped past Sam's teeth when she whirled to find Dolly Douglas standing behind her.

"I began to think you'd remain in Colt's room all night."

Sam flushed. "You spied on me," she accused.

"There's not much going on here that I don't know about." Dolly shrugged carelessly. "If you're interested, there's a private stairway at the end of the hall. To preserve your reputation as well as mine, I suggest you leave as unobtrusively as possible."

"Why should it make any difference to you?" Sam asked curiously.

"Idle talk could ruin my business. It wouldn't do for the townspeople to learn that an innocent girl was seduced in one of my upstairs rooms."

"You don't know that!" denied Sam, incensed.

"I know Colt," Dolly said bluntly. "You were in his room for over three hours. He's not the man for you, Miss Howard."

"I suppose he's just right for you," Sam returned shortly.

"Colt and I understand one another. We go back a long way. We're both takers. We take what we want and give nothing in return, except, perhaps, pleasure. Could you live with that? Would you want a man under those circumstances?"

"There's nothing I want from Colt," Sam refuted resentfully. "You're welcome to him."

"If you knew Colt like I do, you'd know his goal in life is to steer clear of commitments. All his life he's done his best to avoid women who expect more than he's willing to give. Until today virgins were off limits. You're an exception."

Stunned by Dolly's frank words, Sam could only stare at her.

"I'd advise you to forget Colt," Dolly continued. "You're dangerous to him, and I'm too fond of Colt to see him hurt."

"I'm no danger to Colt, Miss Douglas," Sam contended huffily. "He's yours if you want him. Now if you don't mind, I really do have to leave. Much obliged for showing me another way out."

"He'll break your heart, Miss Howard."

Gathering her scattered pride, Sam all but ran down the stairs and into the alley behind the Palace, Dolly's words lending wings to her feet. Her hand was on the doorknob of Ida's house when she heard the shots.

Chapter Six

Dolly barged into Colt's room the moment Sam disappeared down the narrow staircase. She snorted in disgust at the sight of Colt's nude body sprawled across the rumpled bed. She lit a lamp and Colt bolted up, immediately reaching out for Sam, only to encounter emptiness where her small, enticing form had lain beside him.

"She's gone," Dolly said, controlling the anger boiling below the surface. "Are you loco?"

"Don't preach, Dolly."

"For a man who goes out of his way to avoid virgins, you've gotten yourself into one helluva fix. If you're not careful you'll find yourself biting off more than you can chew."

"I know what I'm doin'," Colt growled crossly.

"I doubt that. How could you seduce an innocent like Miss Howard?" Dolly challenged.

"How do you know she is innocent?"

"I'm not blind. There's blood on the sheets. Virgins usually bleed the first time."

"Christ!"

"Are you prepared to pay the consequences, Colt?"

"Sam made no demands, and I offered her nothing," Colt revealed sullenly. How could one black-haired wildcat disrupt his life so thoroughly?

"What if you just put a baby in her belly?"

"I didn't—that is—Christ, Dolly, I didn't think of that."

"Men seldom do," Dolly muttered with a hint of sarcasm. "Women like me have learned to deal with such things and know how to protect ourselves. But Samantha Howard isn't likely to know about such things. If she's pregnant she'll expect marriage, Colt."

"No woman will trap me like that," Colt insisted defiantly.

"What will you do if she *is* carrying your child?"

Fate saved Colt from searching his heart for an answer when the sound of shots and thundering hooves sent him racing into his clothes. A slow, mirthless smile tilted the corners of his mouth upwards. "'Pears like I'm fixin' to meet the Crowders."

The shouts, laughter, and shots continued unabated, seeming to intensify beneath Colt's window. Evidently the Crowder gang was about to invade the Palace Saloon. Her eyes wide with fear, Dolly fled from the room.

Colt's face bore a grim reminder of the reason for his being in Karlsburg as he fastened the badge to his buckskin shirt and strapped his gunbelt sporting

105

twin six-shooters below his waist. He carried a bowie knife, too, in a scabbard strapped to his boot. There was an amazing quietness about him and a confidence few men possessed. Before leaving his room he pulled his hat low on his forehead and tightened the strings.

Sam froze, her hand hovering on the doorknob. The shots and sounds of violence coming from town could mean only one thing. The Crowders had returned! Damnation! How she hated those bastards! They had killed Pop in cold blood. She knew it sounded crazy, but it seemed as if they had known exactly what they were doing when they shot Pop. They had no reason to want him dead. They were lowdown mean, and the thought that Colt would be facing them alone put fear in her heart. He could be wounded—or killed—and not one person in Karlsburg would come to his defense.

Not only did the townsmen have an aversion to taking up arms, but they feared reprisal from the gang if they defended themselves. The majority of the German residents were peace-loving farmers who abhorred violence. Colt was on his own against the Crowders. Captain Ford was a fool to expect one man to defend a town against a gang of outlaws who delighted in killing innocent men. Well, never let it be said that Sam Howard was a coward. If Colt needed help, he'd damn well get it.

Determination as well as fear for Colt drove Sam as she turned the knob and rushed inside the house. She recalled having seen a shotgun above the mantel and she headed in that direction. It was only a single-shot, but Pop had taught her to load and shoot as fast as any man.

Sam needed a chair to reach the gun, and then she began a frantic search for ammunition.

"Sam! Did you know the Crowders are—what are you doing?" Ida couldn't believe her eyes. Sam was racing around and going through drawers like a dose of salts.

"Damnation, Ida, where's the ammunition?"

"What do you intend to do? The Crowders are in town, it's too dangerous to leave the house."

"I know. Where do you keep the bullets?"

"Didn't you hear me, Sam? The Crowders—"

"Hellfire and damnation, I don't have time! I have to help Colt. Are you going to give me the ammunition or do I tear the house apart looking for it?"

"If I know Colt, he won't appreciate you butting in. You could get yourself killed," Ida warned, growing desperate.

"Someone has to help. Please, Ida, the ammunition. You can scold me later. Do you want to see Colt dead?"

"You care that much?"

"Yes! Yes, dammit, I care! Please, Ida, if you have any feelings for Colt you'll give me the bullets."

"I'm as crazy as you are," muttered Ida, flinging out her arms in mute appeal. "They're in my bedroom, hidden beneath the mattress. God help us all."

Colt stepped onto the balcony that overlooked the barroom, surveying the destruction below through slitted eyes. Ten men stood in the center of the saloon shooting at bottles lined up behind the bar. Men and women were crouching behind over-turned tables and the bar. Ducking low behind the bar, Dirk Faulkner wistfully eyed the shotgun resting against the mirror. But to reach it he'd have to expose himself. Brave he might be, but a fool he wasn't.

A stray bullet shattered the light above Colt's head and he ducked as particles of glass rained down on him. His mouth tightened into a thin white line. His tawny eyes as cold and empty as death, Colt prepared to face the Crowders, his superb muscles taut, his face hardened into a ruthless mask.

The twin Colts riding his hips slid into his hands with flawless precision. In a matter of seconds he had metamorphosed into a cool, calculating fighting machine geared for survival. The only alternative was death and he wasn't quite ready for that. Extending himself to his full six-foot-four, Colt surveyed the scene below, his eyes trained on the outlaws raising a ruckus in the saloon. To capture their attention he picked out one man at random and squeezed off a shot, catching the man in the shoulder. He could easily have killed the man, but that wasn't his way. He hoped he wouldn't be sorry later for sparing his life.

When one of their own fell at their feet, the gang ceased shooting abruptly. "What the hell!" All eyes lifted to the balcony where Colt stood, supremely confident, knees flexed, one gun smoking, both aimed into the group staring up at him.

"Drop your guns!" Colt bit out. His voice was low, imposing, and deadly.

"Who are you?" A barrel-chested man stepped

forward and spat a wad of tobacco juice on the floor, his small eyes narrowed to ruthless slits. A dirty stubble darkened his cheeks and chin, and his ferocious grin revealed uneven, yellowed teeth. He was big, unkempt and filthy, and looked as if he ate children for breakfast.

Colt's eyes swept briefly over each man, settling on the one, obviously the leader, who challenged him. "The name's Andrews. Ranger Andrews."

"Ranger! You mean like in Texas Ranger?"

"I don't like this, Lyle," one of the outlaws complained, elbowing Lyle in the ribs. "I ain't tanglin' with no Texas Ranger."

"Don't get all riled up, Dusty. You don't know doodle-de-squat. Ain't but one man up there and ten of us down here," Lyle scoffed. "I ain't about to let no Texas Ranger scare me."

A truly evil smile curving his thick lips, Lyle shouted up to Colt, "You alone, Rangerman?"

"Just me and my six-shooters, Crowder. Are you hankerin' to test my aim? You can leave peaceable like or carried out feet first, it's your choice."

"We ain't the scarin' kind, Ranger. A nod from me and you're history," Lyle warned. "There's at least ten guns down here to your two."

"I got eleven rounds left, so several of you will eat dirt before I die. You'll be the first, Crowder."

"Ain't he a riot, boys?" Lyle crowed. "Brave words from a man facin' sure death."

"I don't rightly know, Lyle," Dusty hesitated nervously. "I've heard said the Rangers take care of their own."

"Listen up, Crowder," Colt bellowed from above. "If you kill me you'll have the whole dang troop

109

breathin' down your necks. There isn't a place in this part of the country where you'll be safe from them."

Lyle licked his dry lips, intuitively sensing he was rapidly losing control of his en, but uncertain as to how to remedy it. Should he shoot first and take his chances with the Rangers? "You talk big, Ranger," he drawled, "but there ain't nobody backin' you up. You're either stupid or loco to think you can win. Me and the boys got this town sewed up. Ain't nobody gonna spoil our fun."

"You're wrong, you murdering skunk!" a voice from behind them challenged. "He's got me, and I can shoot as well as any man."

Lyle spun on his heel, laughing raucously when he spied Sam pointing a shotgun in his direction. "Shit! A female—a half-growed one at that."

"I load fast, shoot straight, and can hit a gnat's ass at ten paces," Sam countered with unwavering resolve.

"Christ!" Colt exploded. What in the hell was she doing here? "Vamoose, Sam! I can handle this."

"I'm staying, Colt," Sam called back. "If they kill you they'll have to kill me too 'cause I aim to come out shooting."

"I ain't killin' no woman," another of the outlaws said.

"And I ain't killin' no goddamn Ranger," Dusty added, backing away. One by one the others followed suit, leaving Lyle alone to face Colt's six-shooters. Experience had taught them to fear Rangers, the word synonymous with reprisal and death. It was said the Rangers always got their man, more often than not bringing them in draped over the rear of a horse.

Hatred drew Lyle's brow into a fierce scowl. Backing down before the very same townspeople he had been terrorizing was damn humiliating and an insult he wouldn't soon forget. He suffered no guilt over killing women and he'd just as soon shoot a Texas Ranger as look at him. Hell, killing was killing, what difference did it make who it was? But without his men behind him his hands were tied.

"Take your wounded man and vamoose out of town," Colt advised, still seething over Sam's unwelcome interference. How could she deliberately place herself in danger when she saw he had things well in hand?

Lyle glanced down to where his cousin Barney lay bleeding on the saloon floor. "Help him up, Dusty," he growled. "We're leavin'—for now. But you ain't seen the last of us, Ranger. Nobody runs the Crowders outta town." He shook his fist at Colt to give emphasis to his words. "We ain't quits yet."

"I'll face you whenever or wherever you say," Colt stated quietly. His eyes never wavered as the outlaws trooped out, dragging their injured comrade with them. No one inside moved until the sound of pounding hooves disappeared into the distance. All eyes turned to Colt, who calmly shoved his sixshooters back in the leather.

Then all hell broke loose. "You did it! By God, you did it!" Dolly crowed, rushing up the stairs from her office behind the bar where she had sought refuge when the fracas began. Dolly's most prized possession was the money in the safe. Like a mother hen protecting her nest, she had sat behind her desk with a revolver in each hand. The first man to step through the door would have been blown to kingdom come.

The last time the outlaws rode into town they had wreaked such havoc on the Palace that she had to close down for a month until repairs could be made. It nearly ruined her. The fact that this time the Crowder gang had been driven off was so astounding that Dolly threw herself exuberantly into Colt's arms. She rained kisses over his face and neck, caring little who might be watching, for Colt had just performed a miracle. She clung to him adoringly, preventing him from bounding down the stairs and shaking the living daylights out of Sam.

Sam watched from below, the gun sagging in her hands. Now that the danger was over, her knees buckled and only the wall kept her from falling. During the actual confrontation a surge of adrenaline had made her oblivious to all but the need to save Colt from what she thought was sure death. She never questioned her motives, just reacted spontaneously to the danger, knowing she didn't want Colt dead. It mattered little that her foolish act of bravery went unrewarded, or that Colt had reacted unfavorably to her interference. At least he was alive and might not be if she hadn't shown up when she did.

Sam watched as Dolly and Colt embraced, his response to her kisses fueling her jealousy. She could not tear her eyes from the loving couple until Colt looked down and spied her. From across the space separating them their eyes met and held. For a long silent moment they stared at each other through an invisible wall of an emotion neither could name. For a second it seemed as if Colt would shake himself free from Dolly's arms and race down the stairs to her, but the moment was lost when the room erupted into a frenzy. Cheering men flew up the narrow stairs to offer congratulations, and then Colt was lost to her. Choking on a sob, Sam whirled on her heel and quietly left the Palace.

"Sam, dear God, what happened over there?" Ida asked in an agony of apprehension after waiting on the porch for Sam's return, wringing her hands and pacing. "I was so worried."

"The Crowders left town."

"I know that much, I heard them ride off," Ida replied. "What happened? What did Colt say when he saw you? I'll bet he could skin you alive for interfering in such a dangerous situation."

"You could say that," Sam allowed, smiling mirthlessly. "I did help him, though, I know I did."

"Did he tell you that?"

"N . . . no, but the Crowders would have killed him if I hadn't showed up. The least Colt could do was offer a smidgen of gratitude."

"I take it he didn't appreciate your help."

"I . . . I didn't wait around long enough to find out," Sam admitted wryly. "He had his arms full of Dolly Douglas, and suddenly it didn't matter what he thought. I did what I did because I wanted to—needed to."

"Honey, I don't want to seem nosy," Ida hesitated, "but . . . you and Colt . . . does he have some hold over you? He didn't tell me a thing when he brought you here. Only that you needed a place to stay. I sense more than that between you."

"You may as well know, Ida—"

"I want to talk to you, Sam—alone, if you don't mind, Ida." While Sam and Ida stood on the porch talking, Colt had finally shaken loose from Dolly and various well-wishers and followed Sam home.

"Colt, what are you doing here?" Sam gasped, startled.

"I oughta tan your hide," Colt bit out from between clenched teeth.

"I'll go inside and make us some coffee," Ida volunteered as she scurried away, leaving the two antagonists alone to hash out their problems.

The moment she disappeared, Colt lit into Sam. "You little idiot! What did you think you proved back there? You could have been killed! You got more gumption than brains."

"I . . . I knew what I was doing," Sam defended stoutly.

"I doubt that. I oughta take you over my knee and beat your enticin' little butt black and blue. If somethin' happened to you I . . ." Sam waited with bated breath for his next words. ". . . would have blamed myself."

"As you can see, Ranger Andrews," Sam sniffed haughtily, "I'm just fine."

Colt bristled for a moment at the girl's defiance, but then his golden eyes softened. "Sam, about this afternoon—"

"No need to explain. It just happened. I'm as much to blame as you are. I know it meant nothing to you and I'm not going to holler rape and demand marriage. Don't worry about it, Colt, you don't owe me a thing. Besides," she added baldly, "I owe you for making my first time—downright memorable.

114

Now if you'll excuse me I've had a full day and would like to retire."

She turned and left him standing alone, more confused than ever. What a contrary little hellion. Things had happened so fast after they had made love this afternoon that he had little time to dwell on what happened between them or to explore the uncertain feelings and emotions she had unleashed in those few brief hours of unsurpassed rapture. Where would this attraction between them end? Colt was just beginning to appreciate the threat Sam presented to the well insulated chambers of his heart.

It was well past midnight and the only light in the entire town of Karlsburg came from the Palace where the revelry continued unabated, albeit without Colt, who had retired early after politely declining Dolly's company. But if one looked closely one could see the barest glimmer of light around the drawn shade of a back room used as an office in the comfortable house belonging to the Logans.

Inside, Calvin Logan sat in brooding silence while his son, Vern, made a substantial dent in the bottle of whiskey sitting between them on the desk. Word had gotten to them about the Crowders' ignominious flight out of town, and they sat pondering that astounding event. In fact, if Vern hadn't been trying to impress his father by remaining home he might have been there to witness it.

"What in the hell is keeping him?" Calvin growled, glancing toward the door. "You don't think he—"

"He'll be here, Daddy," Vern said with more

conviction than he felt. "Crowder may be a lot of things but he's not stupid. If I know him, he's headin' into town for his money right now."

"If you had talked the Howard girl into marrying you, she wouldn't have made such a spectacle of herself in the Palace tonight," accused Calvin relentlessly. "What's that Ranger to her anyway?"

"I talked to her today," Vern rejoined lamely. "I think I'll win her over soon. As for the Ranger, I ain't figured him out yet."

"Bah! You must have inherited your mother's weakness. You're a poor excuse for a man, Vern. If you'd spend less time with that whore down at the Palace and more time tending to business, you might amount to something one day. You're absolutely worthless to me."

Accustomed to being constantly belittled by his father, Vern merely flushed and took another healthy slug of whiskey. One day he'd show him, Vern silently vowed. One day he'd make his father proud of him. And when he did, everything his father had cheated and lied for would be his, including the hot-tempered Samantha Howard. Tonight she proved she had a fire in her that went beyond his wild imaginings. A blaze he longed to quench in a special way she wasn't likely to forget.

A soft rapping interrupted Vern's lewd musings and he leaped to attention. "Let him in," Calvin ordered, jerking his head toward the private door to the office. Vern jumped to obey, and Lyle Crowder sidled into the room, an ugly sneer contorting his features.

"It's about time, Crowder," complained Calvin. "What in the hell kept you?"

"The boys wanted to move on and it took plenty of talkin' to convince them you'd make it worth their time to stick around a while longer," Lyle grumbled. "I hope you don't make no liar outta me, Logan."

"You'll get your money, Crowder, plenty of it. *When* you're finished with this job and not before."

"We wasn't countin' on no Texas Rangers comin' to town," Crowder said sullenly.

"Only one," Vern corrected. Crowder bent him an austere glare.

"Makes no never mind. One Ranger or twenty, they're all bad news. The boys think it's time to move on. There's plenty of towns left in Texas ripe for plunderin'. The Rangers mean trouble—big trouble. Can't do a damn thing with them breathin' down our necks."

"You've still got a job to do for me," Calvin reminded him. "There's a great deal of money involved here."

"That's 'zactly what I told the boys," Crowder concurred. "What about the Ranger?"

"Steer clear of town for a few days. There's nothing further to be gained here. I want you and the boys to concentrate on the Krebs ranch west of town. He's our last holdout. I need his property, and his note doesn't come due until after he sells his cows and then he'll have plenty of cash to meet the note. That can't happen," Calvin said, smiling deviously, "if he doesn't have any cattle to sell, now, can it?"

"You want us to steal his cattle? Just like the other times when we made it look like Injuns done it?"

"Precisely. Any questions?"

"Yeh, I need money. Enough to keep the boys happy till we get the job done."

"You can have half now and half when the job is done. See to it, Vern, I'm going to bed." He rose stiffly and left the room.

Vern's mind had been working furiously while Crowder and Calvin talked. An idea began to form in his mind. If it worked, he could become a hero to Sam and a man his father could respect.

Moving to the steel safe behind the desk, Vern fiddled with the dial before the door swung open on silent hinges. Following his father's instructions, he counted out a wad of bills and wordlessly handed them to Crowder, who grunted and stuffed them in his pocket. Then Crowder watched narrow-eyed as Vern counted out an extra thousand dollars before closing the safe and twirling the dial.

"What's that for?"

"A little private job, if you're willin'. Just between us. Daddy doesn't have to know."

"For another thousand?"

Vern nodded. He could easily replace it before his father noticed it was gone. With Spindler no longer at the bank to keep his eagle eye on things, Vern could juggle the bank ledgers so that the money was never missed. He wasn't his father's son for nothing.

"Who do I have to kill?"

"No one," Vern returned quickly. "In fact, killin' is the last thing on my mind. I want you to kidnap someone for me."

"Kidnap—well, I don't rightly know 'bout that. Do you mean that Ranger fella? If I could get my hands on him I'd kill him."

"What you do with Andrews is your business,"

Vern said with a shrug. "I want you to kidnap a woman and then let me rescue her. I don't want her hurt, mind you, just roughed up enough to make her beholden to me when I save her skin."

"She must be somethin' special," said Crowder, eyeing the money in Vern's hands greedily. "But how will I know if we have the right woman?"

"You'll know her. You already saw her at the Palace tonight."

"You mean that black-haired bitch with the shotgun? Shit! Once I get my hands on her there won't be nothin' left to save."

"Do you want the money or not?"

It took Crowder only a few minutes to make up his mind. "Where do I find her?"

"She's stayin' with Ida Scheuer and works at the grocery. You'll have to keep watch and catch her alone. Oh, yeh, her name is Samantha Howard."

"Howard . . . Howard," mused Crowder, rubbing his stubbled chin. "Ain't her pa the man your daddy paid us to kill? You must want her pretty bad to go to all this trouble."

"Yeh," agreed Vern, "real bad. As soon as it's done, send a man to tell me and I'll ride out to your camp to get her. Be sure and tell the boys she's not to be touched. When I get there we'll pretend to negotiate for her release. We'll reach an agreement, I'll hand you the money and ride off with the woman. Understood?"

"Sure, nothin' to it," boasted Crowder. "Do I get the money now?"

"Half now," offered Vern shrewdly as he peeled off five one hundred dollar bills and pocketed the rest, "and the other half when I ride out to get her."

"Agreed," grinned Crowder. "You'll be hearin' from me soon."

"I'd better," Vern said, "for if you double-cross either me or Daddy you'll find yourself in a heap of trouble. If you think one Texas Ranger is dangerous, wait till there's twenty or thirty on your tail. I understand they shoot first and ask questions later."

"Don't get your dander up, a Crowder keeps his word. You'll be hearin' from me."

"Good enough. And Crowder, this is between you and me. What Daddy doesn't know won't hurt him."

Chapter Seven

An uneasy peace hung over the city. Sam had neither seen nor heard from Colt since the night the Crowder gang rode into town. She assumed he was too busy with Dolly Douglas to spare her a thought. He had taken what he wanted from her and couldn't wait now until he was rid of her for good. If the town was truly free of the Crowders, it couldn't be much longer before Colt would take her to San Antonio to jail.

Sam had no way of knowing that Colt had deliberately kept his distance in order to give her time to cool off—though he wanted her back in his bed so badly his every waking moment was consumed with his need for her. Dolly's silken flesh no longer held any appeal, and ever since he had held, kissed, and made love to Sam he had room for no other woman in his life. He wouldn't be satisfied, he reckoned, until he sated himself with her sweet body and the urge to possess her totally was no longer a demon driving him.

Sam's thoughts took her in another direction—to San Antonio and what awaited her there. If she was to go to jail soon, she wanted to go back to visit the ranch one last time. Besides, the rest of her clothes were there, as well as personal mementos. Mr. Colter may own the land, but that didn't give him the right to her personal belongings. One slow day at the store Sam informed Ida of her intention to retrieve some things at the ranch and asked for the rest of the day off.

Poor Ida was beside herself. Nothing she said could persuade Sam from taking off by herself. Just because the Crowders hadn't returned didn't mean they weren't out there somewhere in the hills waiting to commit mayhem. Why, Ida heard that just last night Herr Krebs had lost half his herd to Indians— another danger to reckon with. Sam was being bullheaded as usual, insisting she had ridden the distance between the ranch and Karlsburg a thousand times in the past and not been molested, so why should today be any different? Sam chose to ignore the volatile situation that existed in the area and scoffed at the danger, daring—no, defying— fate to alter the course of her uncertain future. Changing into tight denim pants and a checkered shirt, Sam picked up her horse at the livery stable and rode off.

Ida sat on the horns of dilemma for all of fifteen minutes before concern for Sam sent her searching for Colt. But to her growing dismay he was nowhere to be found. She returned to the store praying that

Sam's recklessness would not be rewarded by more trouble than she could handle.

Colt reined in Thunder atop a hill overlooking the ranch he now owned. Already he detected an abandoned look about the place and hoped to change all that with the telegrams he had sent shortly after purchasing the Circle H. Not for one minute did he believe the Crowders were finished with Karlsburg, so it looked as if he'd be here for some time. Since his confrontation with the Crowders he had definitely made up his mind about Sam's future, and it didn't include jail. That damn little nuisance had been a thorn in his side from the moment he set eyes on her. The longer it remained, the more it festered into a kind of sickness from which there was no cure.

Colt had spent the entire day searching the hills, valleys, and mesas surrounding Karlsburg for the Crowder gang. He was willing to bet they were camped somewhere nearby and were responsible for the cattle rustling at the Krebs ranch—not Indians as everyone assumed. He had been out there, talked to Krebs, and examined the evidence. The arrow he found was a white man's attempt to copy a technique the Indians had spent centuries perfecting. And he never knew Indians to ride shod horses. He had even discovered a boot print. Too many conflicting signs roused his suspicions, so instead of returning to town he took his search into the hills and eventually ended up gazing down on his own property.

The house, fence, corral, and stock pen looked in worse shape than when he had first set eyes on them weeks ago. A deserted aura had settled over the land and buildings, and if something wasn't done soon, nothing would be left to salvage. Weeks ago he had acted to prevent just such a catastrophe, and now expected that things would look different when his men arrived.

Suddenly Colt noted a movement near the corral and positioned himself for a better view. The horse he saw tethered to a fence post looked vaguely familiar and he moved in for a closer look, his right hand dangling loosely above the holstered gun riding comfortably on his hip. He relaxed somewhat when he recognized the horse as belonging to Sam. But that knowledge served only to release a string of foul oaths tumbling from Colt's lips and bring a ferocious scowl to his face.

What in tarnation was Sam doing out here alone after he forbade her to return? Didn't she realize the dangerous situation that existed since the Crowders had returned? Her father hadn't done her any favors by allowing her to grow up as wild and untamed as a Texas tornado, Colt reflected. Didn't she realize she was a woman whose extraordinary beauty made her more vulnerable than most? Her undisciplined ways had already gotten her into a heap of trouble, but the little firebrand wouldn't listen. He had a mighty urge to turn her over his knee and blister her backside. But he knew exactly where that would lead.

Reining in beside Sam's mount, Colt tethered Thunder nearby and moved noiselessly toward the house. He entered through the front door, but Sam was nowhere in sight, evidently too engrossed with what she was doing to hear his approach. A noise from the back of the house brought a smile to Colt's lips, and he aimed his steps toward the bedroom.

Sam had just finished packing the clothing she had left behind and was tucking into an old carpetbag a few family keepsakes when a shadow loomed above her. With a speed born of panic she reached for the revolver strapped to her waist, the same gun she'd worn when she held up the stagecoach. Colt had put it in a drawer and she had just found it, feeling more at ease with it buckled around her slim hips.

"Don't even think it, darlin'," Colt warned.

"Hellfire and damnation, you scared the living daylight out of me!" Sam scolded, whirling to face the man who had turned her life upside down. "What are you doing here? Have you been following me?"

"Christ! I was about to ask you the same question, you little hellion. What are you doin' here by yourself? Must you be so damn contrary?"

"You told me I couldn't live out here, but you never said I couldn't return for my belongings!" Sam defied.

"I would have brought you here myself if you had said somethin'."

"I haven't seen you since—" she flushed with warm remembrance, "well . . . since the Crowders returned to town," she finished lamely.

"You mean that day we made love?" A lazy grin touched his lips.

"If you want to call it that," Sam returned disdainfully. "Personally I think what we did had little to do with love. We wanted each other and were honest enough to admit it and take what we

125

wanted." Her cynicism was as sharp as a cactus spine. "Besides," she added coolly, "it would have happened with me sooner or later anyway. You were in the right place when . . . the urge struck me to find out what loving was all about. I doubt you'll be the last."

Colt ground his teeth and glared at Sam. Had she used him? Had she known what would happen when she came to his room? Had she *wanted* it to happen? Perhaps he was right in the first place when he accused her of buying her way to freedom with her body. "Well, darlin', 'pears like we're two of a kind. Shall we strike a deal? You're an enticin' little piece, and one taste wasn't near enough to satisfy my cravin'."

Was he testing her? "You lowdown, no-good sidewinder!" Sam spat. "You've no more scruples than a rattlesnake. What makes you think I'd . . ."

Colt's brows arched and he regarded her defiant expression for a long silent moment. "If I created an itch in you, darlin', I'm the one who's goin' to scratch it."

Sam flinched. Damnation, when was she going to learn to keep her mouth shut? "You'd be the last man I'd let touch me."

Impulsively Colt clutched her arm, yanking her to him until their bodies were plastered together tighter than wallpaper on a wall.

"Christ, Sam, you'd try the patience of a saint." This slip of a girl had the uncanny knack of turning his guts inside out. She had him acting like a jealous husband. He had taken his pleasure from dozens of women and knew nothing of jealousy—until now.

The mere thought of another man touching Sam drove him to do and say things he surely would regret later.

Sam was never more aware of Colt as a man. He was so close, so virile, so damn masculine it shattered her self-control. She was positive no other man would never affect her in such a manner, but she dang sure wasn't about to let him know that. Then his words about striking a deal came back to haunt her. "What . . . what kind of a deal?"

"What!"

"You said something about a deal."

Colt's original purpose had been to tell Sam he no longer intended to take her to jail. Never had meant to, actually. But she had angered him so with her open defiance and taunts about taking other men to her bed that he changed his mind. It was obvious he was never going to rest until he satisfied his craving for the little wildcat. Once he appeased this maddening need, he'd be shed of her for good. Colt knew only one way to prove that Sam was merely a woman like all the others who had come and gone from his arms in moments of passion. But, knowing Sam, she was likely to balk unless he continued to maintain control over her life.

"You want your freedom, don't you?"

Wide violet eyes searched Colt's face, wary yet wildly eager. "You know dang well I do."

"Okay, darlin', it's yours."

"Just . . . just like that?" Openly skeptical, Sam waited for his answer with bated breath.

"Well . . . not 'zactly," Colt hedged, smiling wolfishly. "I reckon I did mention a deal."

"Go on."

"I want to continue makin' love to you for as long as I'm around."

"You want me to be your whore?"

Colt frowned, not exactly pleased with her choice of words. "I want to be your lover. I want you to be available when I . . . need you."

"Need me?"

"Christ, Sam, you're not witless. No commitments are necessary for a man and woman to enjoy each other. Bindin' promises only cause resentment. You know what kind of man I am. I live for the moment, knowin' I might not be around tomorrow. I want you, dammit! For as long as I'm in Karlsburg. When I leave, you'll be a free woman."

For some obscure reason Colt was not yet ready to let go of the delightful pleasure her body brought him, totally denying he would ever be ready.

"So I'm to earn my freedom," Sam snarled bitingly.

"However you want to phrase it." Veiled, tawny eyes twinkled at her from the shadows of the broad-brimmed felt hat he wore. "You can't deny we had a wild, reckless sort of passion that first time. Why not explore it more fully?"

The thought was so delicious Colt savored it a moment. He readily admitted Sam had a delightful body that could drive him to the peak of passion, but he damned well didn't intend it to go beyond sensual pleasure.

A ferocious scowl drew Sam's brows together. His outrageous suggestion jolted her with fury as well as with an emotion she'd rather not put a name to. She reacted in a flash of wild and brilliant rage.

"You ornery polecat! Snake! Toad! You despicable—"

"We're definitely goin' to have to do somethin' about your language, darlin'," Colt threatened, his lips twitching suspiciously.

Then he proceeded to shut her up in the only way available to him. Forcefully his mouth seized hers. It was hard and warm and demanding. His questing tongue tugged her lips apart to trace the trembling curves before plunging inside and savoring the sweet moistness within. Sam had every intention of biting down to stop his sensual invasion, but her body turned traitor. Not only her lips but her entire body reacted and responded to his kisses, his closeness, the feel of his hard, lean body pressing against her own soft curves. Though she tried, she could not deny the almost unnatural physical desire she had for him. His kisses left her grappling with the intensity of her conflicting emotions. This ruggedly handsome and wickedly dangerous man was a threat to her very existence.

Reluctantly Colt lifted his head, tawny eyes two smoldering firebrands speaking eloquently of his desire. His hands skimmed lightly over the contours of her body, finding the twin mounds that filled out her trousers so delightfully. Sam felt the strong surge of his desire prodding her thighs, and her pulse quickened in unwelcome response.

Damn his ornery hide, she silently fumed. He knew exactly how he affected her and used her weakness against her. Sam had no idea she was affecting him in the same way. He needed her, craved her; the urge to lose himself in her tempting flesh was so compelling it nearly brought him to his knees—a sad state for a man who prided himself on his nerves of iron.

Against her will, Sam's arms crept around Colt's neck, her body alive and pulsing. Her mouth clung to his with a desperate yearning; seeking, taking, accepting all he had to offer. He chortled, surprised at the ease of her surrender, his kisses deepening, his hands moving upward to cup her breasts, feeling the nipples harden beneath his palms. Tugging the shirttails from her waistband, his fingers caressed the satiny flesh beneath. Each place he touched burned like wildfire. His mouth rolled over hers. It was soft and warm and intoxicating. Then the feel of his hard, seeking hands on bare flesh brought her abruptly to her senses and she made a feeble attempt to resist.

Colt's arms tightened around her, stilling her struggles. Then he was forcing her closer, crushing her, his body hard and demanding against her softness. Sam felt herself melting beneath the intensity of his need, aware of his power, knowing beyond a doubt that he meant to have his way and he *would* have it.

Colt lifted his head, his voice made hoarse with desire. "Once the deal is sealed there's no turnin' back. I'm goin' to make love to you, sweet darlin'."

Despite her misgivings, Sam would have been grievously disappointed if he didn't. She knew she should resist this crazy magnetism that drew her to him like a horse to water, but she wanted him with a passion she couldn't explain.

She also wanted her freedom. Going to jail was the scariest thing she ever faced. If Colt meant what he said, and she had no reason to doubt him, all she had to do was let him make love to her and she would be a free woman. It smacked of blackmail, but he had given her little choice. As long as he was so determined to have her, Sam decided, she may well benefit from the pleasure he gave her. Suddenly a thought came to her, and she voiced it while she still had the breath to do so.

"What about Will? Does our bargain include him?"

Taken aback, Colt paused, his drugged mind reacting slowly. Sending Will to jail was never his intention. He was just a misguided kid who followed his sister's orders because he loved her. What he needed was a strong male to guide him. Someone to mold his character and lead him into manhood. As things stood now, Colt had no idea where Sanchez had taken the boy, and obviously Sam wouldn't say.

"Your brother is safe from me, Sam," Colt said, "as long as you deliver your end of the bargain."

Sam grimaced distastefully as Colt added, "It won't be for long, darlin'. My enlistment is up in less than three months and you'll be rid of me. Sooner if the Crowders have their way."

"Then I agree, Colt. Make love to me."

"Gladly, darlin'." A slow smile tilted his mouth in a crooked grin and tiny lines gathered around his tawny eyes as he swooped her off her feet and carried her to the bed. His gaze softened, riveting on the tempting mounds of her breasts peeping through the gaping shirt he had unbuttoned. Pale gold and perfectly formed, each firm peak was tipped with a pouting cherry bud just begging for his attention.

He dipped his tawny head, nuzzling the delicate

nubs, drawing each one deeply into the flaming heat of his mouth until they swelled and became achingly swollen and deliciously taut against his moist tongue. He sucked vigorously as a moan drifted past Sam's parted lips.

Then, without really knowing how, Sam lay on the bed, Colt's hard body sprawled atop hers, his lips continuing their delicious foray while his hands worked to remove her boots and skin-tight pants. He savored her flesh with sensual enjoyment, moving his mouth slowly, nibbling, tasting—sensing the heat within her—unleashing it in ways she never knew existed. And then she was naked, writhing beneath the intensity of his gaze.

"You're as sleek and beautiful as a newborn filly." His voice was barely recognizable in the heat of passion. "I want to be inside you so bad it hurts."

Highly erotic, his words aroused her as much as his hands and mouth.

Frantically he began stripping off his own clothes until he stood before her in all the glory of proud nudity. His body was a mass of finely tuned muscles; a mountain of steel—hard, unyielding, and intimidating. The fine furring over the flatness of his belly drew her gaze to his lean flanks where his staff stood proud and erect with pulsing anticipation. She stared with unabashed curiosity and awe. The sudden paleness of his lower region highlighted the tawny patch of hair surrounding his maleness, and his tapered hips flared into thighs thick with muscle and hard with strength.

She reached out and touched his skin. It was much coarser than hers, hair-roughened with the feel of softly tanned leather. Her touch was the only invitation Colt needed as he pressed her into the softness of the mattress with the hardness of his body.

Sam ground her hips against him in response and felt his arousal swell to astounding proportions. His hands dropped to her buttocks where he stroked and caressed with maddening results. She lifted her hands to cup his face and, moving her fingers to the back of his neck, pulled him closer still. Her mouth touched his, and when she felt his lips open to her, she slipped her tongue inside. Colt groaned, his arousal approaching physical pain. Need mushroomed into intense craving and fanned the flames of passion into a blazing inferno too hot, too explosive, to deny.

The sinewed column of his thigh gently nudged her legs apart, letting her feel the urgency of his desire. Then he shocked her by snaking his body downward and dropping his head to that aching place between her thighs. She cried out his name in blind and mindless surrender as his mouth touched her heat, his tongue caressed, at first in light, teasing strokes, until she felt she could bear no more. Then he penetrated deeply, seeking to drive her beyond mere pleasure. He succeeded beyond his wildest imaginings as she spasmed and jerked violently beneath his tender torment. Her eyes popped open in surprise and her head strained up off the mattress as Colt continued until there was nothing more to give.

"My wild little darlin'," Colt moaned, trembling with passion. "If I don't put this inside you soon I'm goin' to explode."

Then she felt herself expanding with the hugeness

of him, the core of her body finding new fire, burning hotter and hotter with each relentless thrust. Faster and harder he plunged, driven by a passionate, all-consuming fury. The muscles of her femininity contracted violently against the rigid intruder in her body, squeezing, holding, embracing its hard length as she rode it to blind rapture. Then the explosion began, sending her spinning to the stars. At the same instant Colt found his own release, the breath leaving his chest as he raced to join Sam on her rapturous journey.

Sam dozed in Colt's arms, but Colt was denied the solace of sleep. What he had just experienced with Sam had been devastating. He had taken her only once before and like an arrogant fool thought it would be enough. But it wasn't. Forever would not be enough. Sam had a way of interfering in his life without really trying. If he didn't guard his heart he would never be able to walk away from her, not without leaving a part of himself behind. He had always prided himself on being a free spirit who came and went with the wind. What could it hurt if he appeased his passion while remaining detached? He would tire of Sam long before he left Karlsburg, wouldn't he? At least that had been his thought mere hours ago. If you believe that, Colt old boy, he chided himself, you'll believe the Crowders are as gentle as lambs. A harsh chortle rumbled through his chest and Sam stirred in his arms. Slowly her eyes opened, and Colt floundered helplessly in those compelling violet depths before his gaze faltered and he lowered his lids.

"Colt?"

"What is it, darlin'."

"That first time we made love," she said shyly, "I thought nothing could be more wonderful. But after today—well—it far surpassed anything I imagined. I envy all those other women you've ever made love to."

Her innocent remark startled Colt into acknowledging something he hadn't wanted to face. No other woman had affected him in the same way Sam did, had turned him inside out with a single glance or touch. He had made love to women far more experienced, a few just as beautiful, but none who had captivated him so thoroughly.

"What would you say if I told you it's never been like this with any other woman? That what we shared is unique."

"I'd say you were a liar," Sam replied, the thought intriguing yet somehow ludicrous.

"It's true," Colt insisted, awed by the discovery that he wasn't lying. There was something very special about Samantha Howard. "But if you don't believe me we could try it again," he suggested wickedly.

"If we did I wouldn't have the strength to ride back to town. Unless," she hinted slyly, "you let me remain at the ranch until the new owner arrives. I'm certain he wouldn't mind."

"Oh, but he would."

"How do you know?" Sam challenged. "Are you acquainted with Mr. Colter?"

"I *am* Mr. Colter."

"What! Your name is Colt Andrews."

"My name is Steven Colter. I was given the nickname 'Colt' during the Mexican War and it stuck."

"You bought my ranch? *You?*" The cold reality of what he'd done nearly suffocated her. "You conniving bastard!" She leaped from the bed and began flinging on her clothes.

"Sam, will you let me explain?"

"What's to explain? Where did a worthless, gun-toting cowpoke like you get that kind of money? Did you use the stagecoach money to buy my ranch?" she accused hotly.

"You know I wouldn't do that."

"I don't know what you're capable of. It seems I hardly know you at all. Why do you call yourself Colt Andrews?"

"I was many things before I was a Texas Ranger. One of them was a bounty hunter. There's too many trigger-happy outlaws around gunnin' for Steve Colter so I often use Colt Andrews when on assignment. It's better than findin' my past catchin' up with me when I least expect it. Around Texas Steve Colter is known as a quick draw."

"Why did you steal my ranch?" Sam spat murderously.

"I wasn't plannin' to buy your land when I first met you. Then I learned somethin' that convinced me to do it. I heard Vern Logan tellin' . . . a friend that his father wanted your land. The proposed railroad is goin' through one section of your property. He's been secretly buyin' all the land along the right-of-way with the idea of commandin' his own price. Calvin Logan has the cravin' to become the most powerful man in the state of Texas."

"I . . . I don't believe you. Vern wouldn't allow his father to cheat me like that."

"He would and he did. I wouldn't be surprised if the Logans are behind all the cattle rustlin' in the area. Without cattle to sell, your pa had no way to repay his loan."

"The Indians stole our cows."

"Maybe, maybe not," Colt said cryptically. "Logan is a greedy man. He's a threat to every decent settler tryin' to make an honest livin'."

"We're not talking about the Logans," Sam persisted. "We're talking about you. You still haven't told me where you came by the money to purchase my land."

"I acquired it honestly," Colt volunteered. "Bounty huntin' earned me more than I could spend, and the rest came from the sale of land I owned near San Antonio."

"Do you expect me to believe you? You've lied to me so often I don't know what's the truth. Our deal is off, Colt," Sam glowered. "Go ahead and put me behind bars, I want nothing more to do with you."

Having gotten no farther than slipping into his pants, Colt paused in his dressing to study Sam's flushed features. He could see that explanations would get him nowhere, that she was too riled to listen to reason. There was only one way to capture her attention, he thought as he dropped his shirt and grasped her shoulders, pulling her against the solid wall of his chest.

"We made a bargain, darlin', and you're not goin' to squirm out of it." Resentment and anger melded into a confusing turbulence as Sam grew aware of Colt's intention.

Then hard lips slanted across her mouth, driving the breath from her lungs. Cold fury budded and blossomed into full-blown rage, and with a sharp cry of wrathful indignation she pushed him away. Fire glittered in Colt's tawny-gold eyes but he did not desist. Sam fought valiantly, not only Colt's sensual assault but her own traitorous body. All the while he was dragging her toward the bed, her head was screaming "no" but her heart was whispering "yes."

"Take your hands off my sister." The words were spoken with quiet authority, warning Colt his life hung on his ability to obey.

"Will!" Sam cried, relief washing over her as she welcomed her young brother.

Removing his hands from Sam's slim form with marked reluctance, Colt turned to face his youthful challenger. Will stood in the doorway holding a Sharps rifle, cocked and aimed.

"What's this varmint doin' to you, Sam?" Will asked tightly as he took in Colt's state of undress. "Did he hurt you."

"He . . . no . . . he didn't hurt me," Sam replied, her face poignantly stricken and pale. "What are you doing here?"

"I tried to stop him, Senorita Sam, but he's as stubborn as you are." Sanchez stood behind Will, one shoulder lifting in an apologetic shrug.

"I couldn't stay away, Sam," Will explained. "I'd be a coward to leave you to face the blame by yourself. As soon as we reached Laredo and Sanchez rested up a spell we started back. You're all I have in this world, and I had to return. Don't be angry with me."

"Put the rifle down, Will," Colt said quietly, "before you hurt someone."

"Don't move, Ranger," Will warned when Colt made to step forward. "What are you doin' here with Sam?"

"Please, Will, put the gun down," Sam advised, knowing he was no match for Colt's superior strength and experience.

"I expected to find you in jail, Sam," Will said, confused. "What are you doin' at the ranch? Where is the new owner?"

"One thing at a time, Will." Sam smiled fondly. "Colt . . . didn't turn me in, and I've been living in town with Ida Scheuer. I only returned today to retrieve some of our personal belongings. As for the new owner, he's right here."

"Where? I don't see him."

"I'm the new owner," Colt revealed, his eyes glued to the rifle in Will's hands.

"You? I don't understand."

"I'll explain later, Will, but I think you should lay your gun aside. I . . . I don't think Colt means us any harm."

Will's wide purple eyes shifted to Colt, so like Sam's violet orbs it was uncanny. "Why is his shirt off and what was he tryin' to do to you?" he asked.

"That's between me and your sister," Colt replied.

After several tense moments, Will lowered the rifle. "What happens next?" he asked, slanting Colt a defiant glare. "Now that I'm back you can turn me in and leave Sam alone."

"I'm afraid that's impossible." Colt smiled lazily. "Your sister and I have already come to terms. Neither of you will go to jail unless . . . unless," he repeated, his voice hardening, "she fails to keep her end of the bargain."

Will searched Colt's face, deciding he wasn't a man easily intimidated or swayed. "What kind of bargain? Haven't you hurt us enough?"

"I've hurt no one, Will," Colt insisted, his glance lingering on Sam's flushed face. "Sam has yet to see the inside of the jail, probably never will. If I hadn't bought your ranch, the Logans would own it and Sam would be married to Vern." Will grimaced. "To my way of thinkin' I did you both a favor. I'm not the one who robbed the stagecoach. That was your own doin'."

"Damn your hide, Colt Andrews, or whatever your name is—" Sam exploded, sparks dancing in her eyes like fireflies flitting in the dark.

"Watch your tongue, darlin'."

"Quit badgering my brother. What are you going to do with us? Am I to go back to Ida's?"

"I've been thinkin'. Since Will and Sanchez came back I 'spect it wouldn't hurt to let you both remain at the ranch."

"But you said—"

"That was before Will and Sanchez turned up," Colt said. "I couldn't leave you here by yourself, but the three of you should get along right well until my foreman arrives."

"You're going to work the ranch?" Sam asked, stunned. "I thought you couldn't abide attachments, like a home or . . . wife." What made her say that? Sam silently reproached herself. It made little difference to her what Colt did or didn't do.

"Jake Hobbs recruited ranch hands in San Antonio and they're drivin' several hundred head of cows out with them," Colt explained, ignoring Sam's question. Actually, he had no idea how to reply to her taunt. "There's enough unbranded mavericks roamin' the hills to increase the herd considerably. When Jake arrives, him and the boys will have plenty to do. Will," he addressed the boy, "you must know somethin' about ranchin'. I can always use another cowboy. Sanchez can cook for the men. Both of you will earn the same as the others. Is that agreeable?"

"Si, Senor, that is most generous," Sanchez quickly acknowledged.

"I reckon," allowed Will grudgingly. Actually he enjoyed ranch work and knew a great deal about it, but didn't want to give the Ranger the satisfaction.

"Course that means you'll be livin' and eatin' in the bunkhouse with the cowboys," Colt lectured sternly. The boy needed to be taken in hand, and Jake Hobbs was just the man to see to it. Will still had a heap of growing up to do.

"But—"

"No arguments, Will. I'm callin' the shots, and those are my terms. Believe me, you wouldn't like the alternative. You and Sanchez go and get settled in, I want to talk to Sam."

Will slid Sam an inquiring glance, but when she did not protest he nodded, turned, and left, Sanchez trailing behind. Immediately Sam rounded on Colt. "Just what are my orders, Ranger?"

"You, darlin', will perform housekeepin' chores as well as—"

"—Spread my legs whenever you demand it," Sam finished caustically.

"I wouldn't 'zactly put it that way," Colt said with

141

a laconic smile, "but you know I'll want you again. I aim to gorge myself on your bewitchin' body till I can't take another bite. I'm beginnin' to think you're a witch, darlin', and somehow you keep lurin' me back to your bed. Just as long as I'm the only one to answer your call we'll get along just fine."

"If I was to lure any man it certainly wouldn't be you," Sam returned coolly. "You might have taught my body to respond, but I seriously doubt that you're the only man handy at lovemaking. Perhaps one day soon I may test my theory." The lie burned like acid on her tongue, but Sam couldn't let the randy varmint believe he made her body sing and her heart beat like a triphammer even if it was true. He attracted and repelled her at the same time.

Red dots of rage exploded behind Colt's brain. Her words very nearly strangled him. The thought of Sam responding to another man as wildly and passionately as she did to him tied him in knots. Just because he had introduced her to passion didn't mean she needed to fall into bed with other men to test her reaction to him. Christ! It was almost as if— No, it couldn't be, Colt reasoned, horrified by where his thoughts led him. He could find pleasure with any woman, he comforted himself confidently. This bundle of trouble was no more special than . . . than . . . hell's bells! She had him so confused he couldn't even remember the name of any other woman. Love was such an alien emotion it had no place in Colt's vocabulary, nor in his thoughts. But if love was not involved, why did Sam's words create such a violent inferno in him?

His hands clamped on her shoulders, pulling her

against him. "You're mine, Sam, till I say otherwise. I better not catch any other varmint touchin' you. Once I leave here you can do as you please, but till then there'll be no experimentin', understand?"

His lips came down on hers, putting his brand on her as surely as he intended to do to his cattle. When he lifted his head she tottered on rubbery legs but had no trouble finding her tongue.

"You don't own me, Colt. If it wasn't for Will I'd tell you to go to the devil and take my chances in jail."

"But you won't, will you, darlin'? You'll be here waitin' for me when I want you."

Then he kissed her again, this time moving his hands intimately over her generous curves, molding her to his hips and thighs. All too aware of his arousal and where it was leading, Sam wrenched free.

"You've already put your brand on me, now go."

The corner of Colt's mouth curved up crookedly. It brought crinkles to his eyes and softened his features. "Don't fret, darlin'. Every time we make love I'll give you as much pleasure as I'm capable of. Now be a good girl and stay outta trouble. My men will be arrivin' soon to keep an eye on you."

"What will Dolly say about sharing your favors?" Sam taunted.

Colt frowned, annoyed. "Dolly has nothin' to do with us."

After a long, lingering look filled with poignant promise, he was gone, leaving Sam fuming in outrage.

Not only was her pride wounded by being forced to act as Colt's housekeeper in her own house, but assuming the role of occasional bedwarmer devastated her. She wondered how Dolly Douglas would feel about sharing the honors. Not only was Colt a puzzle but a contradiction as well. He could be the tenderest of lovers while still maintaining strict control over his emotions.

Sam decided she must not delude herself into thinking he had any tender feelings for her; she was merely someone who gave him pleasure. He lusted after her without endangering his status as a free operator. He wanted no involvements, no commitments, no attachments. Why couldn't her heart be as immune to the devastating effect of his brute strength and rugged appeal as he was to her?

It suddenly came to Sam that Colt was a man she loved to hate and hated to love—a man whose touch she craved as desperately as the air she breathed.

Chapter Eight

The next day Colt's partner, Jim Blake, arrived in town. Captain Ford had assigned him to act as backup for Colt at Colt's request. They were ensconced in Colt's room at the Palace discussing the latest developments, a half-empty bottle of whiskey resting on the table between them.

"So what's your theory, Colt?" Jim asked.

Somewhat shorter and stockier than Colt, Jim Blake was no less imposing. Slate black hair curled defiantly against his neck, but it was the thick, ropy muscles of arms and torso that drew one's attention. And the hard, bulging length of thighs and calves. He exuded the same kind of power and authority one immediately recognized in Colt. Together they were a formidable foe to be reckoned with. More than one man had cowered before their brand of ruthless justice.

"I can't escape the feelin' that Calvin Logan and his spineless son are behind the town's troubles," Colt mused thoughtfully. "Since the Crowders obviously made a deal with the Logans not to rob their bank, they've no reason to keep returnin'. Sure, they scared the hell outta people, shot up the saloon and killed a few men. But what did it get them? Why do they keep comin' back instead of movin' on to greener pastures? I can't figure them out unless someone is payin' them to stick around. Someone like the Logans."

"Maybe they like the town?" suggested Jim wryly. "What does the local sheriff think?"

"I have as little to do with that abusive varmint as possible," Colt spat. He went on to explain about Ida Scheuer and the sheriff's attack upon her. "The man's a coward. When the Crowders ride into town he conveniently disappears."

"You mentioned somethin' about Injuns stealin' cattle."

"I suspect the Logans were the ones that did that too. But provin' it won't be easy."

"What are my orders? Cap'n Ford said I was to go along with anythin' you asked."

"So far no one in town knows you're a Ranger," Colt confided. "Keep up the disguise of a drifter lookin' for work. Cozy up to the Logans and if you can, find out what's goin' on. Try to keep our meetin's casual on the surface, but we'll rendezvous in my room late at night to compare notes. Any questions?"

"Yep, where do I stay?"

"Not here, obviously. There's a hotel of sorts

down the street. Check in there and report back to me in a few days. And Jim—take care."

Jake Hobbs arrived in Karlsburg two days later with ten cowboys and several hundred head of cattle. The cattle remained just outside the city limits watched over by the hands while Jake found Colt and received his orders. A friend since the Mexican War, Jake was tall, as lean as Colt, with a shock of light brown hair and intelligent brown eyes permanently etched with laugh lines radiating from their corners. Happy-go-lucky by nature, Jake had yet to find the one woman who could make him want to settle down. But contrary to Colt's theory, Jake believed that such a woman existed, she just hadn't been found yet. Luckily, Colt's telegram had found Jake dissatisfied with his previous job, so it took little coaxing to bring him to the Circle H as foreman.

Jake listened to Colt's instructions about the ranch, asking no questions until Colt finally spoke of Sam. "You took that girl's ranch away from her?" Jake accused, unable to believe that Colt could do so vile a thing.

Colt sighed. "It's a long story, Jake. One you'll learn soon enough. Just watch over the lady for me. It won't be easy, but I have every confidence that you'll keep her out of trouble. Her brother needs a firm hand, he's had little direction since his pa died."

"The filly must be special," Jake remarked cautiously. "The Colt I know would love her and promptly forget her. Is that your intention, Colt? Have you bedded her yet?"

An inscrutable mask settled over Colt's features. "Don't get nosy, Jake. What I do with that little wildcat is my business."

"I can hardly wait to meet the gal. She must be somethin' to set you to itchin' so fiercely."

Colt frowned. "Go on, Jake, I'll ride out in a few days to see how you and the boys are doin'."

Her chin tilted at a stubborn angle, violet eyes glaring defiantly, Sam watched as Colt's newly hired cowboys rode in from the range where they had left the cattle to graze. She hated to admit it, but it was a comforting sight to see the cows spread out grazing in the surrounding hills. All but one man rode directly to the bunkhouse, and he approached Sam with more than a little curiosity.

Sam waited as the tall, laughing man rode toward her. His shirt was half open down his chest, exposing a thatch of curly golden hair. A gunbelt of black leather rode low on his hips. The rider tugged off his sweat-stained stetson to wipe his forehead on the sleeve of his blue chambray shirt, and Sam noted that his hair was a warm brown that glinted with red highlights.

"You must be Samantha Howard," Jake ventured, eyeing Sam appreciatively. He was beginning to understand Colt's preoccupation with the woman. "I'm Jake Hobbs, Colt's foreman." He tipped his hat politely.

"Don't expect a grand welcome," Sam said sourly.

Jake laughed, understanding now why Colt had hinted that the woman was pricklier than a porcupine. "A warm welcome would be right kindly, miss."

"Forget it, mister. I don't need a keeper. You can tell your boss I said so. This land belonged to me and my brother long before Colt stole it."

Jake's eyebrows rose several inches. Looked like Colt had met his match in this little filly. Jake didn't envy Colt the job of taming her, if that's what he had in mind.

"I hoped we might be friends, miss," Jake said, completely disarming Sam. "I had nothin' to do with what's between you and Colt. I'm here to run a ranch, not keep tabs on your comin's and goin's." Not strictly the truth, Jake reasoned, but close enough.

A guilty flush spread across Sam's cheeks. Her anger with Colt had scattered her wits and made her lash out at Jake Hobbs. The foreman was not privy to her private feud with Colt, and she had no right to treat him so shabbily.

"I . . . I'm sorry, Mr. Hobbs," she stammered. "As usual I let my tongue run hog wild."

"The name is Jake." The foreman grinned so engagingly that Sam could not repress an answering smile.

"Everyone calls me Sam," she offered, holding out her hand.

Colt stooped to examine the cold ashes of the abandoned campsite. During the past few days he had found three others—all sites the Crowders had used recently. The Crowder gang were like nomads, Colt reflected contemptuously, moving from place to place to avoid discovery. He wondered why they didn't leave the area, since they hadn't returned to town since their humiliation in the Palace.

Thus far Colt had seen or learned nothing to suggest that the Logans were responsible for the recent cattle rustling. Or that the Crowders were hired by the Logans. But Jim had succeeded in making friends with Vern Logan, and perhaps things would heat up soon. Colt was glad Sam was at the ranch and out of harm's way. She was far too impulsive for her own good and her reckless nature could endanger her life. According to Jim, Vern hadn't given up on making Sam his wife and often spoke of her in a proprietary manner. Colt didn't profess to knowing everything, but he was damn certain Vern Logan would never lay hands on Samantha Howard.

Sam wiped the perspiration from her face with a cloth dipped in cool water. The heat was more oppressive than usual for this time of year, and she spared a twinge of sympathy for Jake, Will, and the cowboys riding the western slopes in search of mavericks. For the first time since she had returned to the ranch Sam found herself alone and at loose ends. Even Sanchez was gone, having taken the chuckwagon to the range to feed the men.

After finishing her chores, Sam thought longingly of the stream behind the house that meandered down from the hills. At this time of year the stream was high from spring rains, running clear and cool, and she longed for a refreshing dip. Later the stream would turn into its normal murky, muddy trickle and provide little comfort. No one was around to stop her or spy on her and she'd be back long before the men returned, so Sam saw no reason not to indulge herself.

Packing her saddlebags with a towel, soap, and clean clothes, Sam saddled her horse and rode out, eagerly anticipating her bath. She did not see the two men following behind.

The stream was high, just as Sam expected, reaching to her shoulders after she threw off her clothes and waded to the middle. It felt delicious and she closed her eyes, enjoying the coolness and solitude. A short distance away hidden eyes watched with avid delight.

"I don't recollect when I've ever seen a purtier sight," sighed Dusty wistfully. "All that soft golden skin makes me itch somethin' powerful. Do you reckon Logan will mind if we—"

"He said we ain't to touch her, Dusty," Lyle warned as he watched Sam cavort in the water. "Not like you mean, anyways. We're just supposed to kidnap her. Once we get shed of this place you'll have money aplenty for whores."

"One that looks like her?" Dusty asked doubtfully. His eyes glittered greedily as he devoured every inch of Sam's exposed flesh. "Reckon we oughta do it now?"

"Naw, let's wait till she comes outta the water," Lyle suggested craftily. "If we show ourselves now, she might swim to the other side and we'd be outta luck. She'll come out soon enough. While you're waitin' you can look your fill."

They settled down behind low scrubs and tall grass a short distance from the stream. Suddenly another rider came into view, and Lyle cursed violently. Dusty tore his eyes from the vision in midstream to watch the horseman enter the clearing.

"Shit!" Dusty spat, incredulous. "I swear that man knows everythin' what's goin' on. He turns up at the dangedest times."

"Hush up. Maybe he'll go away." They flattened themselves against the dusty ground and waited.

Colt had remembered the stream from earlier travels in the area and had aimed Thunder in that direction with the thought of filling his canteen and washing the trail dust from his face and neck. He nearly fell off his horse when he spied Sam this far from the ranch playing naked in the water without a care in the world. He kneed Thunder down to the water's edge intending to give Sam a piece of his mind when the stallion snorted nervously. Colt reined in sharply, his senses alert, his body tense, sniffing the air as if he could smell danger. Smoothing a hand down Thunder's heaving neck, he spoke softly in his ear.

"You sense it, too, don't you, boy? There's somebody else here, isn't there?" Thunder emitted a soft snort in reply.

Colt glanced toward the stream where Sam was gloriously oblivious, her head submerged beneath the surface. Colt's hand inched toward his saddle holster, carefully removing his Winchester and placing it across his knees.

"Let's get the hell outta here," Dusty whispered, frightened. "There's no use hangin' around and lettin' that Ranger feller find us. We can get the girl another time."

Lyle hesitated. He wanted to kill Colt so badly he

could taste it. He raised his gun. Then Colt turned in Lyle's direction, and though he was well hidden, Lyle had the uncanny feeling that Colt could see him through the dense foliage. Lyle's finger fondled the trigger, so close to firing he could smell blood. But at the last second some sixth sense warned Colt and he brought his rifle up, aiming it in Lyle's direction. It was enough to convince Lyle to heed Dusty's advice as he scrambled to his feet and beat a hasty retreat. Colt made to follow the noise, but when a polecat ambled out of the bushes he relaxed, thinking he must be getting trigger happy. Then he turned his attention and well-aimed anger on Sam.

Blissfully unaware that Colt stood on the bank, Sam continued her bath. His voice was harsh when he spoke. "Get the hell outta there!"

"Colt! Where did you come from?" Shock shuddered through her when she saw Colt standing on the bank, fuming with rage.

"Are you nuts, Sam? Don't you realize what a damn fool thing you're doin'? You're askin' for trouble."

"Trouble?" Sam scoffed derisively. "The only trouble here is you."

"What about Indians and outlaws?"

"Indians? Outlaws?" Suddenly she didn't feel quite so confident.

"Yep. You're dang lucky that was only a skunk in the bushes. Who knows what might have happened if it had been the Crowders instead. Now come outta there. Get back to the ranch."

"You go on," Sam hedged, unwilling to bare herself before him. "I'll come along later."

"Don't be bashful, darlin'. I've seen every gorgeous inch of you."

When Sam made no move to obey, Colt began stripping off his shirt, cursing beneath his breath. Wide-eyed, Sam stared as Colt pulled the shirt from his trousers, baring his bronzed chest. Sam knew exactly what he intended, and when their eyes met there was no surprise, just a tingling awareness and anticipation that unnerved yet tantalized her. Colt was the most intriguing, exasperating man she had ever known, and Sam felt herself melting beneath his steady perusal, compelled by something she did not understand. A familiar shiver of arousal set her atremble as Colt's pants slithered over his hips to join his shirt and boots on the ground.

"If you refuse to come out I reckon I'll have to come in after you," he said with casual softness.

Her throat was dry and tight as he waded into the stream. A tangible air of brute strength clung to him as slick muscles rippled beneath taut skin with each step he took. His muscular form had the same vitality and masculinity of the stallion he rode.

Then suddenly their bodies were touching. Sam could feel his big manhood hard and throbbing with life against her leg, knew he was ready to take her, to prove his mastery over her as he had before. But he would not master her, Sam vowed; she would give as good as she got. Taking wasn't just a man's prerogative. She would enjoy him as much as he seemed to enjoy her. She would tease him, taunt him, and bid him good-bye when the time came without tears or recriminations.

When his lips brushed over her nipples she inhaled sharply and moaned her encouragement. His tongue circled one taut peak before taking it into his mouth to suck on it, then he did the same to the other. His hands moved around her softly rounded hips to capture her firm buttocks. Fascinated by his growing desire, she slipped her hand below the water to touch him, hot, throbbing, and growing even larger in her hand as she stroked and fondled him.

"Christ!" he exploded, grasping her hand and holding it in place. "You little tease. Don't stop. Don't—"

Then his mouth was on hers, his tongue discovering its softness as he shifted her upward and his manhood found her sheath. Then she could feel him throbbing deep within her. Impaled on his hard shaft, she felt him move with merciless regularity until she could no longer control the beat of her heart, and she plunged recklessly down into passion's abyss. Once again their fiery lovemaking melted their icy anger and transformed it into a passionate flame.

With Sam held tightly in his arms, Colt carried her out of the water and set her on her feet on the bank, her body sliding down his with provocative slowness.

"Why is it I can think of nothin' but makin' love to you?" It rankled to think that lust for the little wildcat consumed him so completely that his job came in a poor second.

"Because you're randy as a billy goat!" Sam shot back.

The corners of his mouth twitched suspiciously, but Colt would not give Sam the satisfaction of laughing. He had to force the harshness into his voice. "Get dressed, you're goin' back home. I don't have time to stand around listenin' to your insults. Jake's goin' to catch hell for lettin' you wander off by yourself."

"Don't blame Jake. Him and the boys are out rounding up unbranded mavericks. I did this on my own. Go ahead and scold, I can take it." Her stubborn little chin lifted in the air, and Colt suffered a pang of jealousy.

Did Sam admire Jake? Is that why she defended him so staunchly? Colt had to admit Jake was an attractive rascal, but he damn well better keep his hands off Sam.

"Is somethin' goin' on between you and Jake?" His voice was harsh with reproach.

"Do you think all men are like you?" countered Sam angrily. "You've got an active imagination as well as a dirty mind. Jake and I are friends."

"Just remember, darlin', you're mine till I say otherwise. No one has the right to touch you 'cept me."

"You hard-headed jackass! Nobody owns me."

"You're tryin' me somethin' fierce, darlin'. Get dressed and go back to the ranch. I'm goin' to mosey around a spell longer. I'll see you back at the ranch."

That little black-haired bundle of calamity set his teeth on edge more than any woman he had ever known, Colt reflected as he watched Sam ride off. For some dang reason that feisty brat turned his insides to mush. What he should do was kick the dirt off his heels and hightail it out of Karlsburg. He had no earthly business sniffing after a girl like Samantha Howard. Dolly Douglas was his kind of woman, not someone like Sam who threatened his very way of living. What in the hell was the matter with him? Being tied down was worse than a death sentence. Besides, he hadn't entirely given up on finding his sister. Someday, somehow, he'd get her back from those savages who had stolen her. Until then there was room for no other woman in his life. Not even a passionate little hellcat like Samantha Howard.

Sam took her time returning to the ranch. Her heart was racing wildly and her body sang a song composed by Colt. He had only to tempt her and she gave herself willingly, gladly, joyfully. One touch from the handsome devil and her wits scattered like sagebrush in the wind. Originally he might have forced her compliance, but that was no longer true. She wanted him. But was lust all that was involved? Sam asked herself. Sometimes her wanton behavior with Colt downright shocked her. Could it be—? Was it possible—?

Her heart whispered what logic so easily denied. She loved Colt! Yet that same logic spoke of the futility of her love. Colt wanted no commitments— nothing or no one to hold him to one place. In a few weeks he'd move on to another town, another woman—or women. Knowing Colt, she'd be no more than a fleeting memory with the passage of time, while her own heart might never recover.

"She's alone," Dusty crowed. "Best we do it now before the Ranger shows up again and spoils everythin'."

"I knew if we waited around long enough our

luck would change," Lyle said eagerly. "It takes more brains than that Ranger's got to outwit Lyle Crowder. Let's go, Dusty. By tomorrow we'll be a thousand dollars richer."

He spurred his horse cruelly, leaping out from the oak and mesquite lining the trail to confront Sam, Dusty close on his heels. Sam had heard the clatter of hooves but failed to recognize her danger, thinking Colt had changed his mind about letting her ride back to the ranch alone. By the time she collected her wits it was too late. Lyle Crowder was already snatching the reins from her hands and bringing her horse to a skidding halt.

Chapter Nine

Colt reined Thunder in the direction of the ranch, having found little indication that the Crowders were anywhere nearby, although he did find suspicious tracks that left him puzzled. He hadn't talked to Jake since his foreman had taken over at the Circle H, and he was itching to chew him out for allowing Sam to wander off by herself. No doubt the little spitfire had used her feminine wiles on Jake, turning him inside out just like she did him. It took little imagination to picture her astride her mount, a banner of long black hair waving in the breeze, skin tanned golden by the sun, her tight little bottom clad in masculine trousers bouncing enticingly in the saddle and breasts jiggling beneath her shirt. Christ, what a temptress! No man had a chance with her around.

Jake and the hands were engaged in herding two dozen unbranded mavericks into pens when Colt rode up. He watched a few minutes, amused to see Will in the midst of things, obviously in his element and enjoying himself. Perhaps there was hope for the lad yet, Colt thought with a smile. He seemed to be prospering under Jake's able direction despite the sullen glare the boy slanted at Colt when he rode up. Once the cows were penned, Jake detached himself from the cowboys and rode to meet Colt.

"A nice haul," Colt acknowledged, nodding toward the sleek cows.

"About time you showed up, pal." Jake grinned, slapping Colt on the back. "How's things goin' in town?"

"Nothin' new," remarked Colt glumly. "Jim's workin' on a link between the Logans and Crowders, but so far no luck. You seen anythin' suspicious around the ranch lately?"

"Nope. Are you expectin' trouble?"

"Saw signs and hoof prints in the hills but nothin' to suggest the Crowders are still hangin' around. Saw Sam down by the stream."

"Sam was ridin' out alone today? Damnation, I warned her about leavin' the ranch by herself. She's as contrary as a mule and twice as stubborn, but so damn beautiful she'd tempt a monk."

"But you're no monk, are you, Jake?" Colt expelled an exasperated breath. Life would be so much simpler without Sam driving him to distraction. He found himself acting like a jealous fool and didn't like it one damn bit.

"What's that supposed to mean?" bristled Jake.

"I warned you not to sniff around Sam."

"I don't see your brand on her." Jake suppressed an amused smile. He rather enjoyed baiting Colt. Nothing delighted him more than seeing Colt brought low by a woman. Jake always knew that one day a special woman would enter his friend's life. A woman as strong-willed and contrary as he was. It was long past time some of the ice melted from around Colt's heart.

"Sam might not wear my brand but she's mine just the same," Colt announced arrogantly.

"I wonder what Sam would say to that."

A lazy grin lifted the corner of Colt's mouth. "Knowin' her talent for cussin', she'd probably spit out a string of words that would singe your ears."

"You're slippin', Colt," Jake laughed, delighted that he had ruffled Colt's feathers. "Can't you tame the little filly? Want me to lend a hand?"

Colt's smile turned downward into a ferocious scowl. "I meant it, Jake. You're to keep an eye on Sam and your hands off. That goes for the men, too."

"Have either of you seen Sam?"

Both men whirled as Will approached, a frown worrying his young face.

"Probably in the house," Colt said, a frisson of apprehension sizzling down his spine.

"Nope, not there," Will replied tersely, "and her horse is gone from the stable."

"Christ!" thundered Colt. "How can one small woman cause so much trouble? I saw her down by the stream earlier and sent her home. Don't worry, Will, I'll find her, and when I do I aim to blister her britches good. Probably stopped to pick wildflowers or some such foolish female thing." To Jake he said, "Bring a couple of the boys, we'll search the hills. Probably find her sashaying back on her own."

Jake hurried off. "I'm goin' with you," Will insisted.

"I don't—"

"Sam's my sister."

A sigh left Colt's throat. "Okay, Will, c'mon."

Sam had no idea what was happening until she recognized Lyle Crowder. Digging her heels into her mount's flanks and slapping the reins against its heaving sides, she surged ahead, but only briefly. She had responded to danger too late, recognizing her peril when escape was all but impossible. Overtaking her easily, Lyle seized the reins from her fingers and brought her horse to an abrupt halt.

"What do you want, you mangy varmint?" Sam screamed, struggling as Lyle dragged her from her horse and placed her in the saddle in front of him. "Let me go!"

"You ain't goin' nowhere, lady, we got plans for you," Lyle growled gruffly. "Big plans." Wheeling, he took off toward a range of flat-topped hills rising in the distance. Dusty followed, Sam's horse trotting behind on a leading rein.

Sam slumped dejectedly, knowing the exact moment they left the Circle H spread behind. Clinging to the saddlehorn, she attempted to keep her spine rigid so as not to touch the despicable desperado holding her before him in the saddle, but as the afternoon waned so did Sam's strength. She leaned slightly forward but hadn't the energy to resist when Lyle uttered a nasty chuckle and pulled her firmly against his chest. Lyle was aware that Vern Logan didn't want the girl hurt, but nothing had been said against having a little fun with her.

Darkness was approaching when they rode into camp. Sam noted that the camp was located in a natural box canyon which afforded the outlaws maximum protection. From somewhere nearby she heard the lowing and restless movement of cattle. A lot of cattle. Several men milled around a small campfire, some engaged in preparing a meal, others performing mundane tasks. They looked on curiously as Lyle and Dusty dismounted but made no comment. Immediately one of the men detached himself from the group and led the horses to a remuda nearby to join the others.

"What kept you?" greeted a slim man with dirty brown hair and a droopy mustache. "We been waitin' on you for days."

"Ain't our fault," Dusty complained. "This is the first the girl's been out alone. That damn Ranger nearly ruined everythin'."

Lyle pulled Sam roughly from the saddle. Her knees nearly crumbled beneath her, but somehow she managed to remain upright. Someone shoved a plate of food in her hands. "Eat," Lyle ordered brusquely.

Ravenous, Sam hunkered down and wolfed the beans, bacon, and biscuits without asking questions, though she wondered what would happen next and listened closely to the conversation between Lyle and his men.

"What now, Lyle?"

"We follow directions, Blackie."

"You want I should hightail it to town?"

"Naw, mornin' will do."

Blackie slid a lascivious glance in Sam's direction. "She sure is purty. There ain't but ten of us, can we pass her around?"

Lyle would have liked nothing better than to thrust himself between Sam's long golden thighs, but he was a greedy man. He wanted Logan's money. Once he had it, he and the boys could go across the border into Mexico with the cattle now penned up in the canyon and buy themselves a different woman every night of the week.

Remembering that Vern Logan wanted the girl scared enough to be beholden to him for ransoming her, Lyle winked broadly at Blackie. "A good idea, Blackie. Let's draw lots to see who gets her first."

Sam had no idea that Lyle's words were meant mainly to terrify her. "No!" she screeched, her empty plate flying to the ground as she leaped to her feet. "Why are you doing this to me? What good can possibly come of hurting me? Don't you know what will happen when Colt finds you?"

Dusty looked decidedly unhappy and a few of the others shifted nervously from foot to foot. Only Lyle and Blackie seemed unperturbed. "Let the varmint come. Me and him got a score to settle," Lyle replied, scowling. "He ain't no match for the ten of us."

"Colt has all the hands from the Circle H to back him up," shot back Sam, undaunted.

"We ain't afeared of ranch hands," Blackie guffawed. "Give me the girl, Lyle, I'm leavin' in the mornin' and might miss my turn."

Panic-stricken, Sam reacted instinctively, fear lending wings to her feet as she darted off into the darkness. Her tactic so surprised her captors that she was able to make good headway before Blackie, being wiry and lighter on his feet, lurched into motion. She was brought to a shuddering halt when he grabbed the lengthy tail of black hair whipping behind her and yanked viciously. Sam screamed in agony as her body jerked backwards against Blackie's thin chest. Oblivious to her discomfort, he dragged her back to camp protesting violently.

"Nice goin', Blackie," Lyle crowed. "I reckon you deserve first crack at her. She's yours."

Sam blanched. None of this made sense. What did the Crowders want with her? Obviously they had taken her for a purpose. Was she to be cruelly raped by every member of the gang?

Like the rest of the Crowders, Blackie knew his instructions regarding Sam, but he was ready and willing to disregard them if Lyle hadn't winked at him and said, "Enough, Blackie, orders is orders."

"Shit!" Blackie growled, spitting out a dirty stream of tobacco juice at Sam's feet. "Just when I was beginnin' to enjoy myself."

He was so aroused by now that he flung Sam from him in disgust. Like a rag doll she flew through the air and came down with a thud, slamming her head against a rock. She went limp and lay still.

"What in the hell did you do to her?" Lyle roared. "Logan ain't gonna like this." His beady eyes greedily devoured the curve of Sam's breasts beneath the open shirt that had come unbuttoned during the struggle.

"Aw, shit, Lyle, I ain't hurt her none," Blackie said sheepishly. "I was gentle as a lamb. Can't help if she landed on a rock."

"You better pray she's all right when she wakes up," Lyle warned ominously. "If she cries rape, you can kiss your share good-bye."

"Tie her hands and feet and lay her close to the fire," Lyle continued tersely. "Throw a blanket over her so's we can all get some sleep. After Logan gets here with the money, we'll head to Mexico with the cattle. Just hope there ain't no Injuns around. Once those Red savages get wind of the cows, they're likely to lift our scalps as well as our stock."

"We'll find Sam tomorrow, Will," Colt promised as they dismounted in front of the bunkhouse. "Don't give up." He could tell by the boy's drooping shoulders that Will had all but given up hope of finding his sister.

"What could the Crowders want with Sam?" Will asked dejectedly. "Are you positive you read the signs right? Could be Indians."

"Jake and I studied the tracks carefully, son, and it wasn't Indians. I can smell those varmints a mile away."

"I reckon we best all get some shuteye and start out fresh in the mornin'," Jake suggested. "We've done all we can tonight."

On that note they parted, all but Colt entering the bunkhouse to eat the cold meal Sanchez had prepared hours earlier, and bed down. After rubbing down Thunder, feeding and watering him, Colt continued on to the darkened house. He picked listlessly at leftovers Sam had prepared that day, not really hungry, and found himself wandering into her bedroom. He lit a lamp and gazed around the room in numb fascination. It didn't seem possible that he and Sam had made love only hours ago and now she was missing.

Things just didn't make sense. There was a connection here that he was missing. Were the Crowders trying to get at him through Sam? Were the Logans involved? It was all so confusing, Colt reflected as he stretched out on Sam's bed, inhaling deeply of the special aroma that clung to the bedclothes. It was sweet, spicy, and deliciously arousing.

Should he never see Sam again, Colt knew he would remember to the end of his days the images that now burned in his brain as if etched in fire. Sam, her golden body stretched beneath him in wild abandon; Sam, his name bursting from her lips at the peak of her ecstasy. Nothing in his life could equal the pleasure he found in her arms or the strange conflicting emotions she forced him to acknowledge.

It wasn't just the joy of making love to Sam, it was her feisty spirit, her humor, the love packaged in her delectable body, her loyalty when she had come to his defense against the Crowders. She was proud, reckless, and so beautiful it hurt to look at her, and wildly satisfying in bed. Colt had known other women with one or two of those attributes, but not one who possessed them all wrapped in a curvacious little bundle of trouble. She had the face of an angel, the body of a goddess, and a vocabulary that could singe the ears off a brass monkey. And he loved her! Christ! He loved her and didn't want to lose her. The realization exploded brilliantly within him. If need be, he'd search the width and breadth of Texas to find her.

After chewing for a time on the discovery of his feelings, Colt began to wonder what Sam felt for him. Hatred, certainly, for the high-handed manner in which he treated her. He had shot her, taken her home from her, and relieved her of her maidenhead. "Christ!" The oath was ripped from his throat and echoed hollowly in the darkened room.

Yet when they made love he could swear there was something there besides hatred. A spark? No, stronger than a spark. A flame. Yes, a flame that ignited and devoured them with brilliant, consuming fire. Their lovemaking was spontaneous and wild and sweet and—no, don't think about it, he lectured himself sternly. Just find Sam, tell her how you feel and hope she doesn't laugh in your face. On that thought he slid into a fitful slumber.

Sometime during the night Colt awakened to the sound of thunder and a flash of lightning. A short-lived but turbulent thunderstorm passed. In normal conditions it would be a blessing, but tonight the storm produced a feeling of hopelessness. For no one knew better than Colt that there would be no tracks to follow come morning.

Colt's prediction proved correct. If tracks had existed they were obliterated in the storm's fury the night before. It didn't take Colt long to realize there was nothing to be gained by looking for nonexistent signs.

"I'm headin' to town, Jake," he informed his foreman. "You and the boys keep searchin'. The Crowders gotta be camped somewhere in these hills. My gut feelin' tells me the Logans are somehow involved in all this. If you find anythin' send one of the boys after me. Otherwise I'll meet you back at the ranch tonight. I need to talk to Jim and see the sheriff about gettin' up a posse.''

Jake had time for nothing more than a brief nod before Colt rode off hell for leather.

The sensation of muted light against her closed eyelids lured Sam from sleep. Her head throbbed with pain, the blanket covering her was soggy after last night's rainstorm, and she had never felt more miserable in her life. A sudden movement of her limbs brought an agonized groan to her lips. To her horror she found her wrists and ankles bound tightly, the discomfort excruciating. Her bound hands flew to her head, where a Texas-sized lump met her searching fingertips. Then Sam became aware of an urgent need and tried to rise, glancing around frantically to get her bearings.

"Sit down, girl, you ain't goin' noplace." Lyle Crowder stood glowering over her.

"I need some privacy," Sam insisted. Her eyes met his defiantly. "Please untie me." Awkwardly she rose to her knees and the blanket fell away, immediately drawing Lyle's hungry gaze to her breasts. Sam gasped, bringing her bound hands up but unable to do anything about her gaping shirt.

"What did you do to me, you uncivilized jackass?" she accused hotly.

Stunned by her colorful words, Lyle asked, "What kind of lady uses language like that?"

"A lady like me!" Sam responded shortly.

The last thing Sam remembered before awakening this morning was being manhandled by Blackie. Had he raped her? Then she relaxed somewhat, realizing she'd definitely know it if she'd been assaulted. "What did you do to me?" she repeated heatedly.

"No one touched you," Lyle growled. He knew it wouldn't do for Sam to believe she'd been raped, for she'd likely tell Logan and he'd be furious. "Blackie got a mite carried away but he didn't hurt you none."

"I didn't get this lump on my head by myself," Sam accused. "Nor did my shirt unbutton itself."

"I told you Blackie was being a mite playful and you bumped your head when you fell. As to your shirt—" He shrugged, leaving his sentence dangling and Sam's temper soaring.

"Release me at once, you bushy-tailed skunk! You dirty, stinking—"

"Shut up, girl!" roared Lyle, losing what little patience he possessed. "Ladies ain't supposed to act like you. You're more trouble than a horde of hungry grasshoppers at harvest."

"You don't know what trouble is until Colt catches up with you," Sam taunted relentlessly.

Slanting her a quelling look, Lyle turned on his heel.

"Wait! I . . . need to go—I need a few minutes privacy. Untie me . . . please," she added, the word nearly choking her.

"I reckon you ain't goin' nowhere with all of us nearby," Lyle allowed grudgingly as he stooped to untie her ankles and then her hands. While she hastily fastened her shirt, Lyle led her to several large boulders to the left of their campsite. "Make it snappy. If you ain't out in five minutes I'm comin' after you." Nodding grimly, Sam scurried behind the rocks.

Finishing quickly, Sam surveyed her surroundings, noting the thick brush and stand of cedar trees stretching out behind her. Without giving the matter a second thought, she turned and darted into the thicket. Behind her she heard Lyle's rough voice calling. "Time's up, girl. Come out now or I'm comin' in." A moment of silence was followed by a vile curse and the sound of footsteps crashing through the bushes.

The sounds of pursuit grew louder, but Sam refused to surrender despite the fact that her head pounded painfully and her breath shuddered in her chest. But in the end all her effort was wasted and she was brought down by Lyle's heavy body. Pinned to the ground, she glared murderously at the outlaw, eyes spitting violet flames. Hauling her roughly to her feet, a thoroughly disgruntled Lyle dragged her none too gently back to camp.

What did these desperadoes have planned for her? she wondered glumly. It was obvious by now they wanted her for a purpose other than rape. Yesterday Lyle had said something about following orders. Whose orders? What kind of orders? No doubt she'd find out shortly, she reflected as Lyle shoved her to the ground and retied her feet while leaving her hands free long enough to eat the unappetizing meal set before her. Then, after a short interval, her hands too were bound as tightly as before.

Colt dismounted in front of the sheriff's office, wrapped Thunder's reins around the hitching post, and walked inside. Sheriff Bauer looked up, grimaced in annoyance, and asked nastily, "What brings you here, Ranger? You sure as hell didn't need me when you chased the Crowders out of town."

"Samantha Howard is missin'," Colt said without preamble. "I believe the Crowders are responsible."

"If she was stupid enough to ride out by herself, she probably got what she deserves," Bauer grunted. "That was a foolish thing she did at the Palace Saloon. What lady would burst into a dangerous situation brandishing a gun and spouting threats?"

"That's more than you did," Colt returned bitingly. "That little lady has more gumption in her little finger than you do in your whole damn body." Bauer had the grace to flush. "But I didn't come here to trade insults, I came to ask you to head up a posse. A woman has been abducted and it's your duty to help find her. The Crowders have gone too far this time."

"Are you so sure it's the Crowders? Indians have been raidin' in the area. Just recently Herr Krebs lost nearly all his herd."

"I'm not askin', Bauer, I'm tellin'," Colt delivered with cool authority. "Get up a posse and start searchin' the hills outside town."

"Gott in himmel!" Bauer blustered. "This is my town. You got no right to—"

"*Now*, Bauer!" Colt's words left no room for argument as he turned and stalked out the door.

Colt paced impatiently in his room above the Palace while Sheriff Bauer rounded up a posse. As the townspeople gathered to watch the men ride out of town, a lone figure detached itself from the crowd, slipped into the saloon and up the stairs where he tapped out a prearranged signal on Colt's door. The door swung open almost immediately.

"Where in the hell you been, Colt?" Jim Blake questioned, stepping into the room and closing the door behind him. "Vern Logan is up to somethin'."

Bells went off in Colt's head. "Spell it out, Jim."

"This mornin' I moseyed over to Logan's office to ask about a job he promised me and saw a man sneakin' out the back door."

"Did you recognize him?" Colt asked eagerly. "This could be the break we been waitin' for."

"Nope, didn't get that good a look, but I'm certain I never saw him before." Colt's hopes plummeted. "But that's not all."

"Go on," Colt urged.

"When Vern let me in, the safe was open and he was in a damn hurry to leave. Said we'd talk later and lit outta there like a skunk was on his tail. He had a wad of money in his hand."

"Did you follow?"

"Only until he joined up with the other fella west of town. Then I hightailed it back to tell you. Where've you been?"

"Did you hear about Samantha Howard?"

"Yep. Almost joined the posse till I spied you goin' into the Palace. What's goin' on, Colt?"

"Does old man Logan know about Vern's visitor?"

"Nope. Old Calvin is in San Antonio conferrin' with officials from the railroad, accordin' to Vern. Reckon there's a link between the Logans and the girl's abduction? Or do you suspect Indians?"

"Definitely not Indians. You know my gut instincts are usually right, Jim, and this time they tell me the Crowders are workin' for Vern in this. I wish you had followed Vern. I think he might lead us to Sam."

"Damn, Colt, I wish I'da known."

"You couldn't have, Jim. Don't worry, I'll find Sam if it's the last thing I do."

"Do I detect somethin' other than duty where Miss Howard is concerned?" Jim asked bluntly. "From what little you've told me about the lady, 'pears she's rather . . . er . . . unique. Has the invincible Ranger Colter finally met his match? I thought Dolly had an inside track."

"That's neither here nor there, Jim, but I will admit Sam is special," Colt admitted. "How long ago did Vern light outta here?"

"Two, three hours ago," Jim calculated.

"If I leave now, there's a good chance I can pick up his trail."

"Want me to come along?"

"Nope. Stay here and keep an eye on things. I'll be in touch."

Sam hated the way the Crowders kept looking at her—with hungry, sidelong glances. She knew what they were thinking and tried to make herself as small as possible. She still remained in the dark as to the gang's intentions for her but knew they couldn't be good. By now Colt must know she was missing and would be out combing the countryside. But would he? Did he care enough about her to endanger his life? Even if Colt wasn't actively searching for her, Jake, Will, and the ranch hands surely must be. Her mind worked furiously, clutching at any straw, clinging to the slightest hope.

The restless shuffle of livestock caught Sam's attention and she turned to where several hundred head of cattle were milling about in the natural box canyon which provided a perfect stockade when fenced across the open end. Sam reckoned if she was to look closely the cows would bear brands of nearly every rancher in the area, including the Circle H. She heard snippets of talk indicating that the gang intended to drive the cattle across the border into Mexico and sell them.

The hours dragged by slowly, and Sam was surprised when her bonds were released and she was allowed to move about a bit before being bound loosely around the middle to a tree, her arms and legs left free. This arrangement was still far from comfortable but much better than the previous one. She was grateful for that much, for the pains in her limbs had become unbearable.

Suddenly a commotion brought the desperadoes to their feet and their hands groping for their weapons. Two horsemen approached camp and Sam blanched, immediately recognizing the man with Blackie. Vern Logan! What was he doing here?

Vern glanced surreptitiously around the crude camp, spotted Sam, and leaped to the ground. "Samantha! Are you hurt?" He raced to her side, hunkering down beside her. Sam was beyond speech, but Vern could see at a glance that other than a few bruises she appeared unhurt. "Thank God I've come in time."

"I . . . I don't understand," Sam stammered, finally finding her tongue. "How did you find me? What is this all about?"

"I found one of the Crowders at my door this mornin' demandin' ransom," Vern said, using the story he had decided upon.

"Ransom! Is that why I'm here? Why did they come to you?"

"It's no secret you're my intended wife. I've said as much often enough, to anyone who would listen. The Crowders need money and thought to use you as a means of gettin' it. They know Daddy is rich and I'd pay anythin' to get you back."

"They stole all the cattle, Vern. They're thieves. You can see the many different brands from here if you look closely. How can you expect these no-good varmints to keep their word? They'll kill us both."

"I had no choice but to trust them, Samantha," Vern temporized. "The cattle are no concern of ours. We gotta get outta here as quickly as possible."

"How much is that skunk demanding for ransom?" Sam bit out, glowering murderously at Lyle.

"Ten thousand dollars," Vern lied, slanting a warning glance at the outlaw. He wanted Sam to think he was parting with a fortune for her release.

"Ten thousand! Why . . . why, that's robbery!" Sam blasted, paling. It shocked her that Vern was willing to part with so much money in her behalf. Perhaps she had misjudged him. Maybe he did care for her. Colt could be wrong about him and his father. If Calvin *was* guilty of fleecing the ranchers, perhaps Vern wasn't aware of it.

"You're worth every penny, Samantha," Vern said, gloating. He had the little vixen right where he wanted her. To Lyle he said, "Leave us alone for a few minutes, I want to talk to Samantha privately."

A frown drew Lyle's shaggy brows together, but he ambled off to converse with Dusty. "Thank you, Vern," Sam said sincerely. "I'll not forget this. Somehow I'll find a way to repay you."

"There's only one way you can repay me, Samantha," Vern said, impaling her with his piercing gaze. "I've arranged for us to be married the moment we return to Karlsburg. Daddy's badgerin' me to marry, and you're the only woman I'll settle for."

"No, Vern, it won't work," Sam said with conviction. "Please untie me. I won't breathe easy until we put distance between us and these dirty renegades."

Vern's voice was low and strident. "You mistake what I'm tellin' you, Samantha. I'm willin' to part with a fortune only if you cooperate. I risked my neck for you, and if you value yours you'll agree to my terms." His meaning couldn't be any plainer, putting a whole different light on his selflessness.

"Sounds like blackmail, Vern. What happens if I refuse to do what you want?"

"I'll be blunt, Samantha. I thought you'd be grateful enough to marry me. But I can be stubborn, too. If you don't agree to my terms you'll find yourself on the way to Mexico, where Crowder will make a small fortune sellin' you to a brothel, after they finish with you. I'd advise you to think carefully before you refuse. As my wife you'll lack for nothin'. If you please me I might even purchase the Circle H from the new owner and give it back to you."

Sam laughed harshly. Buy the ranch from Colt? She seriously doubted that Colt would give the time of day to Vern, let alone sell him the ranch. Yet she had to say something to appease Vern or he might leave her to the Crowders as he threatened. She could always agree to marry him and worry about it later. Surely Colt wouldn't stand idly by and allow her to marry a polecat like Vern. When Vern had arrived at the Crowder camp she'd looked on him as a savior, but now she saw him for the vile varmint he was.

"Release me, Vern, we'll talk about marriage later," Sam pleaded. She wanted to lash him with all the stinging oaths she knew, which were considerable, but instead she concealed her anger and attempted to placate him.

"Enough chit-chat, Logan. Where's the money?" Growing impatient, Lyle butted into the conversation that was beginning to bore him.

Vern reached into his inside pocket and extracted a thick envelope, slapping it into Lyle's hands. Lyle sneered at Vern with something akin to loathing, then turned his back to count it.

"Are we gettin' married, Samantha?" Vern persisted doggedly.

Sam searched her mind for words that would convince Vern to untie her without offering ridiculous promises. The man was completely ruthless in his demands, and Sam very nearly gave up trying to reason with him. What happened next would live forever in Sam's memory.

A raiding party of a dozen or more Indians came whooping and hollering from the surrounding hills waving bows and arrows and outdated single-shot rifles. If Sam thought it odd that these savages carried firearms, she had only to remember that unscrupulous men often traded whiskey and guns for prime pelts.

The surprise attack brought Vern abruptly to his feet. The blood froze in his veins when he saw the raiders split up, half riding toward the cattle, which was what had drawn them in the first place, half racing toward the outlaw camp.

"Shit!" Lyle spat, nearly swallowing the wad of tobacco in his cheek. "Those red bastards want our cattle."

"Who cares?" Dusty called as he sprinted past. "I'm outta here."

Gun in hand, he vaulted into the saddle and dug his spurs sharply into his horse's flanks. Kidnapping women and killing a few hapless men were one thing, but fighting Injuns was another. He was willing to cut his losses and hightail it to Mexico with his skin intact. One by one, Lyle's men joined Dusty, fleeing for their lives.

Deserted by his men, the cattle all but lost, it took Lyle only seconds to realize that retreat was the better part of valor. He had Logan's money, and Mexico began to look increasingly attractive, coward that he was. Before Vern could catch his breath, those Crowders that weren't killed by Indians had already scattered to the wind.

"Vern, help me!" Sam screamed, struggling against the bonds that defied her meager strength. "Hurry, damn you, untie me."

Faced with the terrifying prospect of being killed or captured by Comanches should he linger a moment longer, Vern panicked, showing his true mettle. Nothing or no one was worth dying over, he decided, sliding Sam an apologetic look. Keeping a wary eye on the Indian thundering down on him, he darted away. Sam knew what Vern intended long before he leaped into the saddle and galloped off, an Indian brave hard on his heels.

"Don't leave me, Vern!" Sam wailed, cursing him for a lily-livered polecat. "Come back, you cowardly varmint!"

Sam's voice all but lost in the thunder of hooves, Vern hardly gave her a second glance as he rode hell for leather. The brave soon became bored with the chase and turned back to where Sam struggled with the ropes Vern had neglected to cut. In the canyon the raiding party had already scattered the cattle, cutting out and herding together enough to satisfy their needs. The rest were left to roam at will. Comanches raided regularly to replenish their supply of meat and acquire horses, usually stealing only what they needed to survive. Beeves promised by the government rarely arrived in their villages, and buffalo were increasingly scarce with the spread of civilization onto Indian lands.

Sam watched with dread as the tall, powerfully built Indian stared down at her, a curious expression on his proud, handsome features. His dark eyes widened in recognition though Sam knew she had never seen the warrior before. His magnificent torso, slick and shiny with sweat, was thickly roped with corded muscles.

He carried himself with arrogant grace, and Sam felt a morbid curiosity about the noble savage. Naked to the waist, he wore only a breechclout. Buckskin leggings hugged long sturdy legs and thighs, and moccasins encased his feet. He wore his shiny ebony hair long and flowing to his shoulders except for one thin plait adorned with a single eagle feather. His body was decorated with bright yellow, white, and black splotches of paint, and a colorful band held his hair in place. Sam could not help but admire his sternly handsome face and the wild nobility of his features.

One lithe motion brought the Indian off his horse to his feet. Drawing a knife from the sheath strapped around his narrow waist, he approached Sam with the rolling gait of a stalking panther. Hunkering down beside her, he stared pointedly into her wide violet eyes. Sam cringed as one bronzed arm rose high in the air and assumed a downward path. She closed her eyes, conjuring up a picture of Colt, certain she was about to breathe her last and wanting her final thoughts to be of the man she loved.

Expecting to die, Sam was shocked when her bonds fell away. Her lids flew up just as the imposing Indian brave grasped her around the waist and literally tossed her on the back of his pony, leaping behind her with agile grace. Whooping triumphantly, he galloped off.

Hanging on for dear life, Sam's violet eyes widened when she saw the braves splinter into two groups, each driving half the cattle before them. Vaguely, she wondered which path her captor would choose, and was more than a little confused when he chose neither, riding instead in a straight westerly direction toward a mesa just visible in the distance. Sam had no way of knowing the purloined cows were being driven north into Kiowa Territory, a tribe friendly with the Comanches, while she was being taken to the Comanche village of Chief Black

Bear near the Oklahoma border. Sam had the dubious distinction of being captured by Brave Eagle, the chief's son.

They rode all day and far into the night. The fearless brave appeared tireless, while Sam slumped exhausted against the hard wall of his chest. When they finally stopped beneath the protection of a narrow cliff, he lifted her off his pony and indicated she was to sit on the ground. Then he shoved a stick of pemmican and a handful of parched corn in her hands. Cowering, Sam waited for his attack, and when it did not come, began to gnaw hungrily on the pemmican. After a few bites she curled into a ball on the hard ground and fell asleep, too exhausted to care what the Indian intended. Brave Eagle sought only sleep as he settled down beside Sam and closed his eyes.

Before the sun rose in the cloudless sky, Sam was shaken rudely awake, allowed a few minutes of privacy, then hoisted unceremoniously atop Brave Eagle's pony. Attempts at conversation proved fruitless, for the stoic brave offered nothing but the shake of his majestic head and what surely must pass as a smile in answer to her questions.

As on the previous day, they journeyed with only one or two short breaks. At mealtimes Sam gnawed at the tough but surprisingly tasty pemmican and chewed the parched corn the Indian provided. When exhaustion claimed her she slept against his bronzed chest. When they stopped for the second night, Sam stiffened when the Indian dropped down beside her, so close she could feel the hard contour of his virile body beneath the breechclout.

Sam steeled herself for his assault, prepared to

defend herself as best she could, but the brave merely rolled over and went to sleep. His behavior contradicted everything she'd ever heard about Comanches, whose killings, rapes, and scalpings were legend among Texans. This same pattern continued for one torturous week. When at length they entered the village of Black Bear, Sam had no idea she was so close to Kiowa Territory.

Chapter Ten

Brave Eagle's arm tightened proprietarily about Sam. Though the warrior had all but named his bride, he would have pressed this golden woman to his mat long before now if not for Spirit Dancer, the wise shaman well known among the People. It was Spirit Dancer who had foretold the coming to their tribe of a woman with eyes the color of spring violets. According to the shaman, she would walk among them but a short time but she would have great import for the People. Prosperity would soon follow. If finding the large herd of cattle was any indication, Violet Eyes had already wrought a miracle, Brave Eagle thought solemnly. The beeves would keep their people from hunger for a long time to come, without depending on the meager offering from government agencies.

Spirit Dancer had also told of a man with golden

eyes and hair who would ride fearlessly into their midst to challenge them for the right to take Violet Eyes away. Brave Eagle didn't always believe Spirit Dancer's visions, treating many of the old man's tales with open skepticism. But in this instance it seemed to have happened just as Spirit Dancer dreamed. Violet Eyes was their link with prosperity, and she wasn't to be violated like other women captives, Spirit Dancer had warned, promising ominous results if she were harmed.

When Brave Eagle first spied Violet Eyes bound to a tree he could scarcely believe his eyes. It was just as Spirit Dancer had seen in his vision, though the shaman didn't know when or where her spirit would call to theirs. From all indications, her own people had abused her, leaving it to the Comanche to set her free. Now her spirit belonged to them.

Stretched across the length of a narrow meadow, the Comanche village was a beehive of activity in the late afternoon sun. A frisson of fear raced down Sam's spine as all work came to a halt and everyone turned to watch Brave Eagle's slow progress through the village. Even the children stopped their play to stare curiously at the white captive who entered their camp on horseback instead of being dragged at the end of a rope.

Brave Eagle reined in his spotted pony before a tipi brightly painted with designs and mystical signs. He waited politely for the occupant to appear. At length an old man, still proud and erect despite his great age, appeared through the tent flap. Besides breechclout and leggings, he wore a pure white buffalo robe and a curious headdress using horns from the same animal. He was most impressive, and Sam assumed him to be the chief, though she was wrong. His sharp black eyes, quick with knowledge not entirely of this world, slid over Sam with a thoroughness that embarrassed her. They widened perceptively when curious violet orbs met his own dark, probing gaze.

Brave Eagle slipped from his pony's back, pulling Sam with him. When her feet hit the ground, her knees threatened to buckle, but she stiffened her spine, pride and the knowledge that she hadn't been hurt thus far lending her courage. Sam understood none of the conversation passing between the two Indians, for they spoke in the dialect of the Comanches. Spirit Dancer's probing eyes never left Sam's face all the time he and Brave Eagle conversed.

"Look closely, Spirit Dancer, is this the maiden of your visions?" Brave Eagle asked eagerly. "Gaze deeply into her eyes and see the violets growing there. I found her tied to a tree and much abused by her own kind. I did not touch her and await your decision, Spirit Dancer."

Spirit Dancer circled Sam slowly, carefully noting her tight-fitting male attire and torn shirt. He studied her bruises, including the rope burns on her slender wrists. He lifted her chin with a long gnarled finger and stared deeply into the violet pools of her eyes. Sam did not flinch despite her pounding heart.

For more moons than he cared to count, Spirit Dancer's visions had taken him on strange journeys and told many bewildering stories, some that defied explanation. With increasing regularity they involved a maiden. Most confusing was the fact that despite her midnight black hair and golden skin she appeared as a warrior woman in his visions, exhibiting a courage and pride that few White Eyes possessed. Somehow this violet-eyed woman's spirit was linked with that of the Comanches, and Spirit Dancer had been expecting her for many moons. The Great Spirit had yet to unravel the mystery surrounding the maiden, but he was confident that all would be revealed when the time was right.

Spirit Dancer studied the smooth golden-hued face of the girl in contemplative silence. Taut flesh stretched tightly across high, prominent cheekbones, and full red lips pursed in a sensual pout beneath a slim, straight nose. The face was hauntingly familiar yet oddly strange. For a brief space of a heartbeat Spirit Dancer felt a flicker of recognition, then just as swiftly it was lost. He knew that all would become clear with the passage of time, but first his judgement must be relayed to his people. Except for Chief Black Bear, who was visiting a neighboring tribe, the entire village had gathered around to hear his sage words.

"My visions indicated a maiden would come to us. One with skin the soft gold of a newborn fawn and eyes the color of spring violets. She would be possessed with the heart and soul worthy of the People. I believe the maiden who stands before us has been sent to us by the Great Spirit for a purpose yet to be revealed." His wise words brought nods from the People as well as shy, sidelong glances in Sam's direction.

"Will you speak to the woman, Spirit Dancer?" Brave Eagle asked, "or shall I summon Fawn?"

"The white man's tongue does not come easily to my lips."

Brave Eagle nodded, turned to scan the crowd gathered behind him, and motioned a young woman forward. He spoke to her at length.

"What is it? What's happening?" Unable to stand idly by while her fate was being decided by a bunch of savages, Sam's fragile control snapped. Her outburst earned her nothing but a stern glance from her handsome captor.

Two could play this waiting game, Sam decided as her chin tilted at a defiant angle. It was almost as if the Comanches had a specific purpose in mind for her. Yet it was comforting that she had not been molested or abused and seemed to be looked upon most kindly. Though the old man was formidable, he appeared to wish her no harm, and she saw nothing to suggest she was viewed as a hated enemy.

Sam's thoughts skidded to a halt when a pretty girl about her own age approached, her eyes properly downcast as befitting a modest Indian maiden. Though her skin had turned golden from living in the open, it did not have the reddish tint or underlying duskiness of her people. In fact, Sam's own skin seemed much darker. The girl wore her inky hair in two braids. Upon closer inspection Sam noted that those ebony locks looked as if they had been touched by a paint brush, clashing oddly with the unusual tone of her skin. It wasn't until the girl looked up through a thick fringe of golden lashes that Sam learned the girl was no more Indian than she herself was. A pair of inquisitive tawny eyes eagerly devoured every detail of Sam's appearance.

A jolt shot through Sam. No wonder something

about the maiden seemed strange to her. Now the golden roots of her hair nearest the scalp became glaringly apparent. Some concoction had been smeared on that shiny head to turn it dark. The girl was white! The words that came from her lips were strangely halting, as if English were unfamiliar to her and she had to search her memory for the right pronunciation and meaning.

"I am called Fawn," she said in a soft, lilting voice. "Spirit Dancer, our holy man, bids me welcome you to our village, Violet Eyes."

"You're white!" Sam cried excitedly. "I knew it!"

"You are mistaken, Violet Eyes, I am Comanche," Fawn corrected gently. "My father is Chief Black Bear. Brave Eagle, who stands beside you, is my brother. I will soon marry Long Bow and eagerly look forward to giving him many strong sons."

Astutely Sam decided not to question Fawn's rather terse explanation of herself, preferring to learn what these savages wanted with her. "My friends call me Sam. Can you tell me what your people intend for me?"

Once again Sam was struck with poignant memory when Fawn's tawny eyes searched her face. In all her life Sam had known only one other person with eyes that color. She shook her head to rid herself of the picture of Colt, those distinctive golden eyes demanding her soul but offering nothing of himself in return. Certainly there could be no connection between that uncivilized varmint and this fragile, shy creature who wasn't what she appeared.

"Spirit Dancer wishes me to convey our greetings and tell you that you are to be our guest," Fawn said, a shy smile hovering about her lips.

"Your guest?" Sam repeated, thoroughly bewildered. "But I don't want to be your guest. I want to go home."

Fawn translated her words and waited for the shaman's reply. "That is not possible," Fawn repeated Spirit Dancer's answer. "We have awaited your coming for many moons. You cannot leave until the Great Spirit's wishes have been revealed. Perhaps you will never leave."

"You . . . your people have been waiting for me?" Sam stuttered, astounded. "You've never seen me before."

"Spirit Dancer has seen you in his visions. Until we learn why your coming is important to us, you will remain as a guest in our village."

"Am I a prisoner?" Sam asked bitingly. "Will I be punished if I try to escape?"

"You are not a prisoner," Fawn replied, her eyes dimming beneath Sam's verbal attack, "and I hope you will not want to leave. I want to be your friend, Violet Eyes, if you will allow it. My people wish you no harm."

Fawn's wounded expression made Sam realize how unfair she was being when Fawn was obviously following orders. Besides, the girl was white despite her staunch denial.

"I would like to be your friend, Fawn."

"It is done. I will introduce you to my father, Chief Black Bear, when he returns. Meanwhile, I will find something fitting for you to wear. Tonight a great feast with dancing and much food will be held in your honor."

* * *

Colt reined in Thunder sharply, his body tense, ears attuned to familiar sounds echoing across the hills. Gunshots! he realized, instantly alert. His keen senses served him well as he turned Thunder and pounded in the direction of the shots.

Not once did Colt consider that he might ride into a situation he couldn't handle. Neither the Crowders nor Indians could keep him from riding to Sam's defense, the odds be damned. She was infuriating, headstrong, argumentative, contrary, and proud to a fault, but he'd have her no other way. The love he had just discovered was a fragile thing, perhaps not even strong enough to last, but he wanted the opportunity to put it to the test.

Colt had given little thought to where their volatile relationship might lead. His first inclination had been to blurt out his feelings the moment he saw Sam. But on second thought he decided it was pure folly to bare his soul when he had no idea how Sam felt about him. They made love wonderfully yet seemed unable to say a civil word to each other. Cautious by nature, he had no reason to change now, Colt ruminated, deciding to carefully guard the fragile love he felt for Sam and nurture it only if it was returned. But first he had to find her.

Suddenly a lone rider appeared, racing across the plains. Bent low over the saddle, whipping his horse to a froth, the man seemed immune to all but his need to escape some unseen danger. Acting instinctively, Colt gave chase, urging his noble mount to even greater speed. Colt was nearly abreast of the man before recognition dawned. Vern Logan! What in the hell was that slimy varmint doing out here?

He bet his ass it had something to do with Sam. Colt decided there was only one way to gain Vern's attention as he drew his gun and fired over his head.

More fear than he had ever known accompanied Vern on his headlong flight across the grassy plain. The shot only increased his terror, and he reacted by digging his spurs into his mount's heaving flanks, caring little that the poor animal had already been driven beyond its endurance. Intuitively Colt knew the valiant beast must be stopped before his heart gave out. Drawing alongside, he snaked out his arm, snatching the reins from Vern's hands. Both horses shuddered to a halt, Vern protesting vigorously until his panic-stricken mind accepted the fact that it was not Indians pursuing him. At the same time he recognized Colt.

"What's your hurry, Logan?" Colt drawled with deceptive calm.

His breath still ragged in his chest, Vern gulped and replied, "Injuns! A whole damn raidin' party. Let me go, they're on my tail."

"You're loco," Colt returned, looking pointedly in all directions. "What are you doin' out here?"

Glancing fearfully behind him, Vern saw nothing but rocks, hills, and trees. Maybe the Indians had given up on him. "They . . . they were right behind me," he stuttered, his heart slowing to a steady bounce. "They must have decided the cattle were more important than me."

"Cattle?" repeated Colt sharply. "What cattle? Might as well start from the beginnin', you're goin' nowhere till I hear everythin'. Includin' what happened to Sam."

"Later, Andrews," Vern pleaded, growing desperate. "The Injuns—"

"Talk, Logan. The faster I learn the truth, the sooner you'll be on your way."

Licking his parched lips, Vern explained reluctantly, "The Indians were after the cattle the Crowders stole from ranchers. They were penned up in a canyon back yonder in the hills."

"I don't give a hoot in hell about those red devils, or the cattle. I want to know about Sam. Do the Crowders have her?"

Vern nodded slowly. "They were holdin' her for ransom."

"Why didn't I hear about it?"

"I'm the only one with money enough to ransom her. They knew how I felt about Samantha and demanded ten . . . ten thousand dollars for her safe return," he stumbled over the lie. "One of their members led me to their camp where the money was exchanged."

Colt eyed Vern narrowly, slowly and pointedly looking all around him. "That's odd, either Sam has made herself invisible or you lost her somewhere along the way."

"That . . . that's what I been tryin' to explain," Vern muttered nervously. What would the Ranger do when he learned the Injuns had Samantha?

"I'm waitin'," Colt ground out, his patience swiftly deserting him. "Where's Sam?"

"The . . . the Injuns took her. The Crowders tied her to a tree and the camp was overrun before . . . before I could free her."

"What! You left her!" roared Colt, shaking with

fury. "You yellow-bellied sonofabitch! I'da fought till the Injuns hacked me to pieces. Nothin' would have made me leave Sam, or any woman, to Comanches. I oughta kill you and rid the world of your slimy presence."

Beads of sweat gathered on Vern's forehead, and after looking into the golden inferno of Colt's condemning eyes he knew icy fear. In the brief span of a moment his entire life passed before his eyes, certain he was on his way to meet his maker. But the instant Colt might have made him a corpse passed with the approach of riders. Vern tried desperately to escape, but Colt held tightly to the reins of his horse, preventing his flight. Keeping a firm grip on his emotions, Colt watched as Jake, Will, and riders from the Circle H wheeled to a halt.

"We heard shots, boss," Jake said anxiously. "Are you okay?"

"I'm fine, Jake," Colt replied tightly, still grappling with his profound anger.

"Colt, what about Sam?" Will injected.

Colt swung his gaze to Will, his expression conveying such pity that Will immediately assumed the worst.

"She's dead, isn't she?"

"No, not dead, Will, don't even think it. It's a long story, but the short of it is that the Crowders had Sam."

"Let's go after them!" Will exclaimed recklessly.

"It's not that simple. The Crowders were attacked by Indians and they took Sam, or so Logan says."

"What's Logan got to do with it?" Jake asked.

"Logan was with the Crowders when it happened.

Claims he was there for the purpose of payin' ransom for Sam's safe return."

"And he stood by and let the Indians take her?" Will cried, his face mottled with rage. "Let me at the yellow polecat, I'll kill him!"

Before Colt could react, Will drew his gun and got off two rounds. He was blinded by anger and both shots whizzed harmlessly by Logan's head, missing by mere inches. "Someone stop that crazy kid!" Vern yelped, ducking.

Jake sprang into action, wresting the weapon from the enraged youth when he would have squeezed off another round.

"Let me at him, Jake, the sonofabitch deserves to die!"

Colt had other plans for Vern Logan and they didn't include being killed by a green kid. One day Vern and his shifty father would get what was coming to them. Leaving Sam to the Indians would not put Vern in jail, but cattle rustling and illegal manipulation would. Soon he would have enough proof to hang them both. "Let him go!"

"What! Are you loco?" Will protested violently.

"Nope, just older and wiser," Colt said evenly. "Don't worry, son, I'll get your sister back." Vaguely Colt wondered how he would keep his word when he had failed to find his own sister after years of searching.

"What're you gonna do, boss?" Jake questioned worriedly.

"Ride to the Crowder camp and look around. Then decide what to do next."

Vern didn't linger for further discussion. Puzzled

by Colt's decision to let him go and fearing he might change his mind, he spurred his horse, quickly putting distance between him and Colt.

"Colt!" Will cried in warning.

"It's okay, Will, I have other plans for the Logans. Findin' Sam comes first."

The Crowder camp yielded little in the way of clues as to Sam's whereabouts. Colt found tracks indicating that Indians had raided the camp and driven off the cattle. He saw where they had split up into two groups, each traveling a different route toward Kiowa Territory. The tracks wouldn't be difficult to follow, Colt surmised, but Sam could be with either group, complicating things.

"What do you make of it, boss?" Jake asked.

Suddenly Colt's eyes found the tree and severed ropes indicating Vern hadn't lied about Sam being tied up by the Crowders. A string of curses singed Jake's ears. "This is where Sam was bound to a tree," he pointed, his eyes two flaming pools of rage. "If they harmed her, I swear I'll personally gun down every last man ridin' with the Crowders."

Jake examined the ropes carefully, as well as the ground surrounding the tree. He found a scrap of plaid material that matched Sam's shirt and held it up for Colt's inspection. If either had a lingering doubt that those ropes had once held Sam, none remained. "It 'pears like Logan was tellin' the truth. The Crowders might have had Sam at one time, but the Comanches have her now," Jake said, a pained expression on his face.

While Jake and Colt conferred, Will came up to join them. A sob wrenched past his throat when he heard Jake's sober words. "No! They can't have her! Colt, do somethin'!"

Will's plea struck a responsive chord in Colt's heart. He had felt exactly the same when his own sister had been taken by Comanches and his parents killed. He hated Indians with a deep abiding emotion.

"I promised I'd find Sam, son, and I will," Colt said tightly. "If we split up we'll more than likely find them before nightfall. Take half the men, Jake, and follow one set of tracks. My group will trail the others. If Sam isn't with the Comanches you followed, don't bother with them. We'll need our strength and numbers to take on the party that does have Sam. Meet back here at dark to compare notes and plan our attack. Surprise is on our side. Cattle travel slow, and the Injuns don't know we're trackin' them."

Breaking into two groups, they took off in clouds of dust and jangling spurs. No one noticed the single set of tracks separating from the two main parties of Indians and cattle, heading alone into the hills.

"Sam's not with them," Will hissed hoarsely. "I don't see her anywhere."

"Just our damn luck," spat Colt disgustedly.

Perched in the rocks high above the narrow gorge into which the cattle had been herded, Colt and his men scrutinized the valley below. Several Indians dressed only in breechclouts and leggings, their bronzed torsos glistening in the setting sun, faces streaked with paint, crouched in the dirt talking in low voices.

"That's them all right," one of the cowboys said

beneath his breath. "Comanche. I'd recognize them red bastards anywhere. Where do you reckon they're takin' the cattle?"

"My guess is Kiowa Territory," Colt replied. "They make their summer camp with their Kiowa brothers."

"How do you know so much about Indians?" Will questioned.

"I've spent years trackin' them and lookin' for my sister," Colt revealed, a pained expression darkening his features. "I traveled from village to village as far north as Colorado and even learned their language in an effort to find Laura. But it was like she disappeared into thin air."

"I . . . I didn't know," Will stammered, embarrassed. He was stunned to learn that they both had lost a beloved sister to the Indians. "Did you ever find her?"

"Nope. Someday I'll tell you all about it, Will," Colt promised, "when Sam is with us to hear the tale."

"Let's get the murderin' thieves," Will urged, his gun slipping easily into his hand.

"I have reason to hate the Comanche more than any man alive," Colt said through clenched teeth, "but we can't spare the time. If Sam is not with this group she's bound to be with the other. We have to find Jake and figure out how to get Sam back before they reach Kiowa Territory."

Suddenly a commotion at the entrance of the gorge captured their attention. From out of a cloud of dust rode several Indians driving a dozen or so head of cattle to join the others. Evidently this was the meeting place agreed upon ahead of time by the raiding party. Anxiously Colt studied each rider, hoping to recognize Sam's beloved face.

"Sam's not with them, boss." Colt started violently, turning to find Jake crouching beside him. "I reckoned I'd find you somewhere up here when I saw this was some kind of meetin' place."

"Sam has to be with the Indians you followed," thundered Colt.

"Look closely, boss, there's nothin' but Comanches down there. I figured Sam was with those you followed till I got here and found out different. I told the boys to spread out, that you'd be holed up here someplace."

Darkness was only a breath away but Jake could see clearly the agony and desperation on Colt's expressive face. No longer could he doubt Colt's feelings where Sam was concerned. Somehow the feisty filly had penetrated Colt's thick skin and found a home in his heart whether he realized it or not.

"Christ, they tricked us!" Colt spat, tight-lipped with disgust.

"What now?" Will asked worriedly.

"'Pears Sam was taken directly to their village," Colt said thoughtfully. "Won't do no good trailin' these cattle thieves. Take the boys and go on home, Jake."

"Home!" croaked Will, aghast. "You can't mean that! What about Sam?"

"I'm goin' after Sam, son, alone," Colt explained as patiently as time allowed.

"I'm goin' with you."

"Not this time. I'll be travelin' through Indian territory. The Kiowa are as fierce as Comanches and

I'll likely meet up with both of them. I know their language and how these savages think. Alone I have a chance of bringin' Sam home. Besides, you're needed on the ranch. Jake tells me you've more than earned your keep these past weeks."

Refusing to be mollified, Will protested vigorously, but it did him no good. Colt had melted into the darkness, and within minutes the sound of hoofbeats vanished too.

Chapter Eleven

Sam knelt in the dirt outside Black Bear's tipi helping Singing Wind, the chief's wife, grind corn into flour. She didn't mind this chore. It was rendering deer hides smooth and pliable that she couldn't abide. First they were scraped clean with a sharp knife, then spread with a mixture of animal brains and left to soften and cure. Later the mess had to be scraped off. Thankfully, after the first time she had been spared that task and assigned simpler duties by the chief's kindhearted wife. Her treatment by the Comanches had been a contradiction to everything she'd ever heard about these fierce warriors. Yet she fully believed that the stories about the atrocities they committed were true. What made her different from those hapless victims? she wondered, her apprehension growing with each passing hour.

Sam was convinced she'd awaken one morning to learn the Indians had mistaken her for someone else and would kill her. Or worse, torture her. A shudder of fear rippled down her deerskin-clad back.

That first day in Black Bear's camp Fawn had provided her with a beautiful beaded doeskin dress and leggings. The workmanship was exquisite, and Sam was stunned to learn that Fawn had made it herself as part of her trousseau. At first Sam had refused such a lavish gift, but Fawn was adamant.

Sam wondered if she would ever escape to return to Will—and to Colt. Did Colt miss her? Probably not, she decided. It stung to think that someone else would promptly take her place should she never return.

In the meantime there was Brave Eagle to contend with. In the nearly four weeks since her arrival in the Comanche village, the handsome brave had made his amorous intentions known. Sam had quickly picked up a smattering of the Comanche language, and with Brave Eagle's limited knowledge of English, plus sign language, they had been able to communicate. It soon became apparent that the proud brave was courting her. The bold, assessing glances he slanted in her direction were the same the world over and could not be mistaken. His looks spoke of desire and need and an emotion she'd rather not define.

Sam couldn't begin to explain the Comanches' reasons for keeping her with them and treating her with respect. Perhaps when Spirit Dancer returned from his vision quest, all would become clear. The holy man had left over a week ago, and when he returned Sam felt in her bones that she would know things that might be better left hidden. She never set much store in superstition, but somehow this defied everything she'd been taught. Sam wasn't certain she was prepared to face what Spirit Dancer's vision unveiled, but at least she would escape the uncertain existence in which she found herself.

Sam paused in her task to wipe the sweat from her brow with a tanned forearm. A pair of moccasined feet appeared at the edge of her vision, and she raised her eyes past muscular calves, corded thighs, and massive bronzed chest to gaze into Brave Eagle's impassive face.

"Greetings, Violet Eyes."

"Greetings, Brave Eagle." Sam curbed her annoyance as Brave Eagle devoured every detail of her face and form. From past experience she knew it would do little good to lose patience. In good time she would learn the reason for his visit.

"Spirit Dancer has returned from his vision quest. He is speaking now with Chief Black Bear. Though he is weak and exhausted from his long fast, he is much enlightened and anxious to see you. I think you will be surprised at what he has learned, Violet Eyes. Come, I am to bring you to Black Bear's tipi." It was the longest speech the taciturn Comanche had ever made in Sam's presence.

Rising swiftly, Sam ventured a glance at Fawn before following Brave Eagle. The girl's tawny eyes were wide and encouraging, bolstering Sam's courage as she trudged off after Brave Eagle. There was no question of refusing, for Sam was anxious to find out the mystery surrounding her, if indeed there was a mystery. Perhaps when the Comanches learned that she was not what they thought she'd be allowed to return home.

Soon Sam stood before Chief Black Bear and Spirit Dancer, who looked drawn and wasted after his week-long ordeal of fasting and prayer. "Sit down, Violet Eyes," Black Bear invited. The chief spoke passable English which Sam followed easily. Sam saw that Brave Eagle was to be a part of this powwow as he hunkered down on his haunches beside her. Spirit Dancer was already sitting, his face a wrinkled mask carved in stone.

"Spirit Dancer has returned from his vision quest much enlightened," Black Bear intoned. "The Great Spirit has blessed him with knowledge and revealed things long forgotten about Violet Eyes and the Comanches."

Sam sucked in her breath, waiting, anticipating, speculating. Did Black Bear look at her with more fondness than usual? There was a spark of some profound emotion in the dark depths of his eyes. More confusing was Brave Eagle's uncharacteristic behavior. Why did he keep looking at her in such a proprietary manner?

Black Bear cleared his throat, fixed Sam with a piercing stare, and asked in a commanding voice, "Tell me about your mother."

Confusion numbed Sam's senses. Her mother? What did that gentle creature have to do with all this? "My mother was Elizabeth Ashley from Virginia. She died birthing my brother Will."

Suddenly Spirit Dancer came out of his trancelike state as he pointed a bony finger at her. "Not so, Violet Eyes. Your brother's mother was Elizabeth

Ashley. Your mother was a beautiful Comanche maiden named Shy Deer. The spirits do not lie. My vision pointed the way, and my memory of the past provided the answers."

"That's not true!" Sam refuted hotly, probing her brain to recall the beautiful blond angel who had been her mother. But all her searching provided were vague memories of gentle hands, a sweet voice, and sad blue eyes. Sam had been only six when Elizabeth died giving birth to Will.

"Your mother was Shy Deer," Spirit Dancer repeated with a conviction that stunned Sam. "Once, she was the chosen bride of Chief Black Bear."

Sam's eyes swung to Black Bear. "Then I can't be Shy Deer's daughter. William Howard is my father."

"True, Violet Eyes, William Howard is your father," Spirit Dancer acknowledged, his voice dry and raspy. "Clear your mind of all you believe to be true and listen to Black Bear's tale. Afterwards, no doubt will remain in your heart or mind about your heritage."

Black Bear began speaking in a singsong voice heavy with sadness, his eyes closed, his body moving to a silent rhythm. "Shy Deer was a virtuous young Comanche maiden. Her gentleness and beauty appealed to me and I desired her. She was a chieftain's daughter, dutiful and obedient to her father and compliant to his wishes. It was time I took a wife, and when I expressed a desire to join with Shy Deer her father was agreeable and arrangements were quickly made. We were to be joined on the next full moon. Her bride's price was ten ponies, and I considered her worthy of the high price. I fell deeply in love and assumed Shy Deer shared my feelings."

Sam searched the proud chief's lined face and thought he must have resembled Brave Eagle in his youth. He still cut a handsome figure despite his years.

"One day Shy Deer and another maiden wandered far from camp gathering wood. It was winter and we were camped far south of here. Catastrophe struck when Shy Deer was bitten by a rattlesnake. The maiden with her ran for help, but they had roamed a long way from the village. In the meantime Shy Deer was found by a man rounding up stray cattle. He knew he must help her or she would die. He carried her to his home.

"When I learned Shy Deer had been stricken, I immediately set out with braves from the village to the place described by her companion. When we arrived it was as if she had disappeared into thin air. I was devastated when no amount of searching led us to my love. For many moons I refused to consider another woman until I learned Shy Deer's fate." His voice broke, and Spirit Dancer took up the tale.

"William Howard took Shy Deer to his ranch and saved her life. During her long convalescence the two fell deeply in love. But being the dutiful daughter that she was, Shy Deer eventually convinced your father to take her back to her village so she might fulfill her destiny as Black Bear's wife. It must have been painful for your father, but he could not keep her against her will.

"Shortly before the wedding ceremony joining Shy Deer to Black Bear, she found herself with child. She was too honorable to enter into a marriage with Black Bear under those circumstances and confided in her father."

Black Bear struggled for composure as he continued the story. "I still would have taken Shy Deer to wife and accepted her child, but she refused, saying it would bring dishonor to me. Her father, Walks Tall, was a proud man and cast her from the tribe. She lived on the fringes of the village, eating scraps and surviving on her own. In due time her child was born. A healthy girl with violet eyes. I felt great compassion for Shy Deer and her daughter, but the laws of the Comanche are strict."

"I was that baby," breathed Sam, her voice trembling with emotion. "But what happened to Shy Deer, and how did I end up with my father?"

"One day the village was attacked by soldiers. No one but women, children, and old men were in camp, the others were hunting buffalo," Spirit Dancer said, looking twenty years into the past. "From her tipi at the edge of the village Shy Deer saw her mother struck down. She hid you in the forest and rushed to her mother's aid, only to be struck down herself and left for dead. But she wasn't dead. Somehow she found the strength after the soldiers left to collect her child and bring her to her father."

"Shy Deer knew she was dying," Black Bear added sadly, "and could expect no help for her motherless child. We knew none of this until much later. Somehow Shy Deer survived the trek to your father's ranch, dying in her lover's arms after presenting him with his daughter."

"How . . . how do you know all this?" Sam asked, astounded as well as deeply skeptical.

"From your father's own lips. After Shy Deer's death he went in search of her father but found the village annihilated and the People scattered," Black Bear revealed. "Eventually he found our new campsite and told me what had happened when he learned Shy Deer's parents had both died in the raid. He said Shy Deer was buried on his property and announced his intention to keep his child. Because Shy Deer had once meant so much to me, I allowed your father to go in peace to raise their daughter as Shy Deer would wish. In the ensuing years we heard nothing more of the Howard family until Spirit Dancer's vision foretold your coming. Shy Deer and her child were all but forgotten. It took a vision quest before answers were given and truths made clear. You are the granddaughter of Walks Tall and daughter of my beloved Shy Deer. It is right that you should return to your own people."

"But . . . but what of Elizabeth Ashley?" Sam asked, by now beyond mere shock.

"The spirits revealed that when your father found himself with a small infant to care for he traveled to Virginia to propose to a woman he had known before he settled in Texas," Spirit Dancer answered. "She must have been a remarkable woman to take on the added burden of another woman's child. A half-Comanche child would not have been easy to accept. Yet you say you have nothing but fond memories of Elizabeth Ashley."

Sam was silent a long time, absorbing all the astounding revelations concerning her heritage. As long as she could remember she had hated Indians, especially Comanches, whose cruelty was legendary among Texans. To find herself the daughter of a Comanche mother was devastating.

She searched her brain for some hint, something her father might have said or done in the past to suggest that Elizabeth was not her mother, but nothing came to mind. And in her heart Sam knew that Elizabeth had been a kind, gentle woman who had always loved her, even though she was her husband's half-breed daughter.

Because of the hatred that Texans bore Indians, Sam knew that her father had kept mum all those years to protect her. But what if . . . what if Spirit Dancer were lying?

As if reading her mind, Spirit Dancer said, "Accept the truth, Violet Eyes. Once the vision was revealed to me, I recalled everything as it happened long ago. You are Shy Deer's daughter. Learn to live with your new life."

"But I'm happy the way I am," Sam objected. "I like what I was. I have a family. My brother needs me. I want to go home."

"This is your home, Violet Eyes." This came from Brave Eagle, who until now had done nothing more than listen to the amazing story.

When Sam expressed a desire for her old way of life, Black Bear injected words that left her reeling. "Walks Tall has been gone these many moons, but I gladly and willingly open my heart and home to you, Violet Eyes. We are your people, and I will become your guardian. My son has expressed a desire to mate with you, and I have given my permission. The ceremony will take place on the night of the next full moon. You have three weeks in which to prepare yourself. Until then you will learn the customs of our tribe and develop skills needed to make Brave Eagle a proper mate."

Sam leaped to her feet. "No! I won't do it! You can't make me marry against my will. I don't love Brave Eagle."

Black Bear's eyes went cold and his face settled into harsh lines. "Brave Eagle is a fearless warrior, strong, proud, and capable of leading the People when the time comes. He will provide well for you and the daughters and sons you give him. Love will surely come of such a strong union."

"But I can't!" Sam cried.

"Do you already have a mate?" Brave Eagle asked, frowning.

If only she could say yes, Sam thought bleakly. The only man who had asked for her hand was a lily-livered coward who thought only of saving his own skin. The man she wanted didn't want her, not on a permanent basis anyway. Why did she have to love a gun-toting womanizer with no room in his cold heart for love? In the final analysis there was but one answer to Brave Eagle's question.

"No, I have no mate. There is no one."

Suddenly Spirit Dancer stirred uneasily, impaling Sam with his piercing black eyes. But it was to Brave Eagle and Black Bear that he spoke. "The lion, not the eagle, will mate with Violet Eyes."

His cryptic words were all but ignored by Brave Eagle, whose love for Violet Eyes transcended all else. "The eagle is cunning and can defeat the lion. It is the eagle who will banish the lion and mate with Violet Eyes. Your eyes have dimmed, old man.

Look at me and tell me I am not a fit mate for Shy Deer's daughter."

Spirit Dancer's eyes slid away, unwilling or unable to refute the proud warrior's claim. "Time will tell," he said through bloodless lips. His meager strength was all but depleted and nothing more could be gained by arguing with Brave Eagle, who was ruled by his heart, not his head, where Violet Eyes was concerned.

Turning to Sam, Brave Eagle said, "You will be mine on the next full moon, Violet Eyes." Then he turned and strode away with the arrogant gait of a man who knows what he wants and is willing to fight for it.

Sam tried to make sense of the conversation but decided that too much had been lost in translation. What was all the talk about eagles and lions? Her vigorous protests did little good as she was summarily dismissed by Black Bear. Fuming in impotent rage, she returned to her tipi, waiting until she would be alone with Fawn to spit out her objections.

Meanwhile, Spirit Dancer and Black Bear resumed the conversation. The shaman leveled an inscrutable look at Black Bear, predicting ominously, "Even as we speak the lion is stalking his prey."

"Will the lion find what he is seeking?"

"He will come," nodded the shaman, looking inward.

"You heard Violet Eyes deny she has a mate."

"My visions do not lie. A man with hair and eyes of tawny gold possessed with the heart of a lion will come to claim his soulmate."

"Brave Eagle will fight for her," Black Bear remarked sagely.

Spirit Dancer nodded as if a confrontation were unavoidable. "They will fight."

"Will my son emerge victorious?" Black Bear asked anxiously. It wasn't that he doubted his son's courage or stamina, for he had proven himself many times over in battle. Brave Eagle had counted many coups on the enemy. Rather it was fear of the unknown lion that caused Black Bear to question Spirit Dancer. Besides, he had just found Shy Deer's daughter and didn't want to lose her as he had lost her mother.

"The outcome is in the hands of the Great Spirit above," Spirit Dancer chanted, looking heavenward. "You must be prepared to accept whatever happens. If Violet Eyes is meant to remain with the People and become Comanche, Brave Eagle will defeat Lion Heart and win her love. If not, she will leave with Lion Heart, but with her will go a valued possession of the People."

"Can you not consult the spirits again to learn the outcome?" Black Bear suggested.

"I am weary, my chief, and have exhausted all my resources on this vision quest. I fear there is nothing more to learn. Patience and time will bring all the answers you seek."

Colt crouched behind a large boulder at the edge of the Comanche village, his eyes avidly following the comings and goings of the inhabitants. He had come upon the village late yesterday. It was the fourth such encampment he had investigated in his weeks of traveling through Indian territory. Each time, he left Thunder tethered a good distance away and approached the village on foot, concealing himself in such a way that he could watch the camp undetected. Each time, he had experienced profound disappointment when several days of observation produced no sign of Sam. Colt prayed she was still alive as he continued his search with renewed desperation.

Now he watched as two Indian maidens left one of the tipis hand in hand and headed in his direction. Before he ducked down he had seen that each woman carried a basket over one arm as they walked toward a berry patch some distance beyond the boulder he crouched behind. A powerful, fierce-looking brave, handsome in a primitive way, watched their progress, his expression inscrutable. As the two women left the perimeter of the camp, the brave turned to follow, his long, lithe steps reminding Colt of a stalking panther. The brave caught up with the women as they disappeared into the trees. Colt could see them clearly, but very little of their conversation reached his ears. He wished they would conclude their business so he could get on with his surveillance.

Fawn and Sam did not hear Brave Eagle's silent steps behind them—not even a snap of a twig gave him away. Besides, Sam could think of nothing but her impending marriage to the chief's son. He was handsome and brave, and seemed quite fond of her, but she didn't love him and had no intention of living the rest of her life with the Comanches. It annoyed Sam the way Brave Eagle's black eyes flamed with desire whenever they lit on her.

Suddenly Sam's ruminations were interrupted

when a steel band encircled her waist, slamming her against a solid wall of rock encased in smooth, bronze flesh. Swiveling her head, she saw Brave Eagle's noble face looming above her.

"Why do you and my sister stray so far from camp, Violet Eyes?" he asked, his voice low and strident.

"We go to pick berries, brother," Fawn quickly pointed out.

He graced his sister with a brief but brilliant smile, his fondness evident. "Leave us, Fawn, I wish a moment alone with my intended bride." Fawn started to protest until Brave Eagle added, "I would do nothing to harm Violet Eyes. She will join you shortly."

"What do you want, Brave Eagle?" Sam asked in halting Comanche. Thanks to Fawn's perseverance, she grew more proficient in the language with each passing day.

"Only to speak with you, Violet Eyes. To ask if you have resigned yourself to our joining. The day cannot arrive too soon for me. You fill my heart with joy and my loins with longing."

Sam flushed, choosing her words carefully. "I admire you, Brave Eagle, truly I do. You are all an Indian maiden could wish for. But I am the wrong mate for you. Through an accident of birth I may be Comanche, but in my heart I belong to the white world."

Brave Eagle ignored her words. "You learn quickly, Violet Eyes. Soon you will possess all the knowledge that is natural to a Comanche maiden. When I take you to my mat, my first thrust between your thighs will end your fears and make you mine forever. I will cherish you and take no other wife as long as you give me strong children."

Sam knew that Brave Eagle made quite a concession by promising to take only one wife, but she could offer him no hope for their future.

"You honor me, Brave Eagle, but it changes nothing. I've noticed that Pretty Dove looks at you with adoring eyes. Why not look to your own kind for a mate?"

Brave Eagle stiffened. "You *are* my own kind."

What did this exasperating woman want from him? Brave Eagle wondered glumly. She was as beautiful as she was infuriating. He yearned to press her down into the spongy earth and thrust into her yielding flesh until she was breathless and pliant beneath him. If his father hadn't taken her under his protection, he would have done so long ago. But soon—soon he would know her tempting flesh, experience her succulent warmth, sire strong sons on her body, and she would love him. But until that day he would satisfy his longing with the taste and smell and feel of her.

Pulling her slight form into the curve of his muscular body, Brave Eagle's hard lips slanted across Sam's, his burgeoning desire a living thing between them. It did little good to struggle, for Sam realized his strength was tremendous and he would not be deterred. Resting limply in his arms, Sam quietly endured. Intuitively she knew that Brave Eagle would not hurt her, that for the time being she was safe even though his desire for her was enormous. With that in mind she neither struggled nor protested, just patiently waited for him to finish so she might join Fawn. What his kisses did was convince Sam she couldn't marry this stalwart Indian brave when another man equally imposing already possessed her heart.

From his concealment Colt watched the tall Comanche embrace the slim maiden dressed in a beautiful beaded doeskin dress. Her shiny black hair hung down her back in two long braids held in place by a headband with a lone eagle's feather protruding from the back. Though her back was to Colt, the golden flesh of her arms reflected the dappled sunlight stabbing through the tall trees towering above them. A feeling of recognition jolted through him.

Curiously Colt wondered if the couple were lovers, then laughed at his own stupidity. Of course they were lovers, their very actions indicated they were more than just friends. The maiden did not protest when the brave's kiss deepened or his hands roamed freely over lush curves. He felt like an intruder and hoped the brave didn't intend to mate with the woman here in the woods with him looking on. Then suddenly the couple parted and the maiden whirled, for the first time presenting Colt with an unobstructed view of her face.

What struck Colt initially was the look of absolute hopelessness on her lovely features. His next thought was that if he didn't know better he'd have thought Sam really was a Indian. Christ! How could she let that filthy savage maul her? He fully expected to find her either dead or a much abused prisoner. Instead, she appeared healthy and obviously well

216

treated, though her defeated expression proclaimed her far from happy. If the Comanche brave meant nothing to Sam, then Colt reckoned she was being forced into a situation beyond her control. Had the Indian already taken Sam to his mat? The thought brought an urge to kill, cold sweat running down his spine.

Abruptly the Indian released Sam and she ran off to join her companion. The brave watched as she fled down the path, obviously loath to let her go. The possessive smile on his face and an air of expectancy about him spoke volumes, and Colt was consumed with a terrible fear. If the Comanche had taken Sam into his tipi, as Indians sometimes did white women captives, how in the hell would he get her out of the village? As Brave Eagle returned to the village, Colt allowed himself to relax, his mind working furiously.

From his previous dealings with the Comanches, Colt knew he had little hope of spiriting Sam out from under their noses. His years of searching for his sister had taken him deep into Indian territory, into countless Indian villages, and if the experience had taught him anything, it was that savages valued courage above all else. As he had done many times before, Colt planned to bluster his way into the village, present his demands, and bluff his way out, hopefully with Sam. While Colt went back for Thunder, he mentally prepared himself for the ordeal facing him, realizing that both he and Sam could very well end up dead. Their deliverance depended solely on his wits and cunning. He dare not think about failure, or dwell on the relationship between Sam and the handsome warrior who handled her with such familiarity. He could only pray that Sam wanted to leave as badly as he wanted her out of there.

His hat pulled low over his eyes, shoulders set at a determined angle, Colt rode Thunder boldly into the Indian village. Barking dogs announced his arrival and all activity ceased as countless pairs of black eyes followed his slow progress through the camp. Appearing relaxed though actually alert and watchful, Colt rested his right hand on his thigh mere inches from the butt of his six-shooter; his left hand held the reins in a loose grip, belying the tension that sent adrenaline pumping at a furious pace through his veins. It was late afternoon and the women were preparing food over open fires before their tipis.

Colt's tawny gaze searched for the face he knew as well as his own, but Sam was nowhere in sight. Nor was the maiden who had been with her earlier. Christ, how he hated these stinking savages! No matter how lovely some of their women appeared, never could he bring himself to feel desire for one of them. His hatred for Indians, Comanches in particular, went deep, leaving him with a profound aversion for anything having to do with heathenish savages. Colt could barely stand the stench of the village. Poor Sam, he commiserated, thinking of her terrible ordeal as a captive of the Comanches. As long as a breath remained in his body, Colt vowed, he would not abandon her as Vern Logan had done.

A shiver danced along Colt's spine. The dark eyes

that bore into his back were like hundreds of tiny pinpricks, yet no one challenged him. If he didn't know better he would have sworn there was a hint of expectancy in the air, as if his coming were the climax of some long-heralded event. Whatever it was, Colt didn't like it—not one damn bit. From the corner of his eye he saw a figure dressed in chief's regalia step from a tipi brightly painted with signs and symbols. Assuming the man to be the leader of the tribe, Colt directed Thunder toward the imposing figure. From another tipi nearby an old man emerged, joining the chief as Colt reined in several feet short of the two. With easy grace he slid from the saddle.

Colt aimed his tawny gaze at Black Bear, then slid an equally probing look toward Spirit Dancer.

"Behold the lion," Spirit Dancer said quietly, unaware that Colt understood his every word.

Black Bear merely nodded, and once again Colt was stunned with the knowledge that his appearance was no surprise. He didn't hold much with heathenish superstitions practiced by Indians, but he had the eerie feeling these red devils knew who he was and why he was here. If it would help his cause any, Colt reckoned he could play along with them by answering to any name they chose for him.

Biding his time, Colt held his tongue, aware from previous experience that Indians employed strict protocol when dealing with their chief. He chafed restlessly while waiting for Black Bear to speak, knowing the chief was deliberately baiting him. It wasn't until a younger man appeared to stand beside the chief that Black Bear spoke. Colt easily identified him as the same young brave he had seen earlier embracing Sam so intimately. Apparently this proud Comanche was the chief's son.

"I am Chief Black Bear. Why do you come to our village, Lion Heart?" He surprised Colt by speaking in halting English.

Lion Heart! Why had they given him a name, when he'd never encountered this particular tribe before? Colt puzzled. Truth to tell, the name did not displease him.

"If you know my name then you also know why I'm here," Colt proclaimed arrogantly. He'd be danged if he'd show fear to his lifelong enemy.

Black Bear nodded, his face a mask carved in rock. "Spirit Dancer's vision spoke of you."

Colt frowned, assuming Spirit Dancer to be the old man at the chief's side and the shaman of the tribe. "What did Spirit Dancer's vision tell him?" Colt probed.

"That Lion Heart wants Violet Eyes." Colt's wits sharpened.

"Violet Eyes? If you mean Samantha Howard, then your shaman speaks the truth. I have come to take her back to her people."

Bristling, Black Bear refuted, "Violet Eyes *is* among her people. In three suns she will join with my son, Brave Eagle."

"The woman you call Violet Eyes has a brother who needs her and people who love her," Colt revealed, thinking of his newly discovered feelings for Sam. "When I leave here she goes with me."

"The lion roars, but can he fight?" sneered Brave Eagle. "Does he have the courage to challenge Brave Eagle for the right to possess Violet Eyes?" He spoke in Comanche, then waited for his father to translate. But Colt answered in fluent Comanche before Black Bear could form the words.

"You wish to fight me for the woman, Brave Eagle?"

Stunned by Colt's command of his language, Brave Eagle eyed Colt sourly. "You might speak our language, White Eyes, but you know nothing of our customs. If you want Violet Eyes you must fight me, for I have already claimed her."

Colt wanted to fling himself at Brave Eagle's throat when he heard the Comanche lay claim to Sam, but wisely held himself under tight control. "Sam doesn't belong to you and never will."

"She belongs to the Comanches." Colt did not take Brave Eagle's words literally when he referred to Sam as belonging to the Comanches, thinking he meant she was their prisoner.

"Then we fight," Colt asserted boldly, taking careful measure of the warrior's superb physique. Colt thought them evenly matched and reckoned it would be a fierce battle.

At this point Black Bear stepped forward. "Heed my words, Lion Heart. According to our customs the fight will be to the death. You will be armed only with knives." He waited for this information to sink in, then advised, "There is still time to withdraw with no shame to you. If you do so now you will be allowed to leave in peace, a concession rarely granted. But you leave alone."

"Then I must refuse, Black Bear," Colt drawled. "When I leave—if I leave—the woman goes with me."

"You are named well, Lion Heart," Black Bear

allowed, a spark of admiration lighting his eyes. He hated to see so brave a man die an ignominious death.

"If I win, will I be allowed to leave with Samantha Howard?" Colt persisted.

A tense silence ensued. A nudge from Spirit Dancer brought Black Bear's reluctant answer. "I have said so. A Comanche is as good as his word."

"You will not win, Lion Heart," offered Brave Eagle. "Violet Eyes is mine. She is Comanche, and one day our son will be chief. Prepare yourself to meet your white God."

Brave Eagle's taunts pierced Colt sharply. Was he implying that Sam was already carrying his child?

"You will rest and prepare yourselves tonight," Black Bear decreed with an air of finality. "The fight will take place when the sun is at its peak tomorrow."

"No!"

Ignoring Black Bear's stern warning to remain inside the lodge, Sam charged from the tipi, protesting wildly. She loved Colt too much to permit that supreme sacrifice of him. If she could persuade Colt to leave, she would somehow survive, even if it meant marrying Brave Eagle. Since Spirit Dancer had established that she was half Comanche, Sam knew she wouldn't be harmed. Indeed, she was treated like any other Indian maiden belonging to the People.

The first that Sam knew anything unusual was taking place had been when Black Bear told her and Fawn to remain inside the lodge. She had made nothing of it until she recognized a voice she thought she'd never hear again. Motioning to Fawn, they had peeked through the tent flap, listening, until Sam heard Colt agree to a fight that could result in his death. And if Colt won, Brave Eagle would die. Chief Black Bear would be devastated by the loss of his only son, and Sam had grown fond of the aging warrior and his shy wife. Even Brave Eagle had many good qualities to commend him. She just didn't want to marry him. Colt's words brought her leaping from the tipi with Fawn close on her heels. Colt's face lit up the moment he saw her.

"Sam! Are you all right? They haven't harmed you, have they?"

A ferocious scowl darkened Black Bear's features, and Brave Eagle stepped forward to prevent Sam from rushing into Colt's arms. He managed to snare her around the waist and hold her in place beside him while Colt looked on helplessly.

"I'm fine, Colt," Sam said. "But you must leave here. If you go now Chief Black Bear will keep his word. No harm will come to you."

Colt looked perplexed. "I don't understand. Do you want to marry that . . . that savage?" he supplied for lack of a better word.

"No, of course not," Sam refuted, "but there's nothing either of us can do."

"I can fight Brave Eagle."

"I don't want you dead, Colt," Sam said softly.

His tawny eyes drank in the sight of her. She was so damn beautiful it hurt to look at her. The doeskin dress she wore was soft and supple, molding her lush curves perfectly. Intricate beading interspersed with fringe decorated the neck, sleeves, and hem. A beaded band sporting an eagle's feather held back her jet black braids. The golden skin of her arms and face had turned a deep tan beneath the relentless Texas sun, and Colt thought she looked as much an Indian as those surrounding her.

"The choice has already been made, darlin'," Colt said softly, tenderly. "Whatever happens tomorrow, I want you to know—"

"Enough!" Brave Eagle grunted, jealous of the display of warmth between Violet Eyes and Lion Heart. "Save your words for your God when you meet him tomorrow." Then he shoved Sam back inside the tipi while Spirit Dancer led Colt off to prepare for the morrow's confrontation between him and Brave Eagle.

Inside Black Bear's lodge Sam fretted and fumed, cursing the fates that had brought this mess. Learning that she was part Comanche had nearly devastated her, but knowing that Colt might die in her defense was an even greater blow. She was so consumed with her own misery that she failed to notice Fawn's strange preoccupation.

From the first moment Fawn laid eyes on Colt she had been struck speechless, her tawny eyes wide with shock. Long-forgotten memories, painful recollections, and shadowy figures from her past played cruel games with her mind. It was some time before Sam noted Fawn's quiet introspection and pale features. When she did, she searched her brain for a hint of what could have upset the girl.

"Fawn, what is it? Are you ill?"

Fawn raised stricken eyes to Sam; her narrow shoulders trembled and her hands clenched into tight fists. "It . . . it is nothing, Violet Eyes," she disclaimed, her voice quavering.

"You're upset. Something happened. Something to do with Colt."

"C . . . Colt?"

"His real name is Steven Colter but he was given the name 'Colt' during the Mexican War."

"What is this man to you, Violet Eyes?"

A becoming flush crept up Sam's neck. "He . . . I . . . love him," she admitted shyly. "He's a man like no other I've ever known."

"He must love you very much to be willing to fight Brave Eagle."

Sam shook her head sadly. "I wish it were so. Colt loves his freedom. He wants no wife or romantic attachments to complicate his life."

Fawn looked so troubled that Sam would not let the subject drop. "Does something about Colt upset you?"

Fawn's eyes swept downward, her lashes like golden butterfly wings against the paleness of her cheeks.

"I'm your friend, Fawn. Please tell me what's troubling you."

Up came the fringe of gold, Fawn's tawny eyes so hauntingly familiar the breath caught painfully in Sam's chest. She had noticed the similarity before but had been too consumed with her own problems to recognize the truth when it stared her in the face. "I know you're no Indian, Fawn, you're white. You're no half-breed like I am, either. Do you want to tell me about it? Does it have something to do with Colt?"

A frown worried Fawn's smooth brow, fearful of digging up painful memories of a past she had tried to forget. Remembering brought heartache and sorrow. Why dredge up things better left buried or dwell on mental images that produced only tears? Yet the urge within her to speak of things she had held within herself for years was strong.

Fawn trembled so badly that Sam silently berated herself for badgering the girl. If Fawn wished to confide in her she would do so of her own accord. Yet Sam couldn't help her curiosity—there were too many unanswered questions and intriguing possibilities.

Suddenly Fawn seemed to come to a decision and the words tumbled from her lips in a long-suppressed torrent. "Steve is my brother. I haven't seen him for years, not since I was ten. I idolized him. Besides my parents he was all I had in the world until that terrible day when life dealt me a bitter blow."

She paused to lick dry lips, and Sam jumped into the void to ask, "What happened?"

"Steve was very young when he went off to fight in the Mexican War. He hadn't been gone a month when Indians raided our ranch south of San Antonio and made off with the livestock and killed both my parents."

"Dear God!" Sam gasped. "Your parents were killed by Black Bear and his people?"

"No, it was another tribe of Comanches. They burned the house and took me with them. It . . . it was terrible." A haunted look turned her eyes bleak. "I was beaten every day, starved, shackled at night, and made to work until I dropped from exhaustion."

"But now you are daughter to a chief," Sam said, amazed. "What happened?" She had known that Colt's parents had been killed by Comanches, but this was the first she heard about a sister. No wonder Colt hated Indians so much.

"Somehow I survived six months of unspeakable brutality before I was bartered to Black Bear for six ponies. Singing Wind had just lost a daughter to illness, and Black Bear hoped to assuage her grief by giving her another. From that time on I never knew another unkind word or suffered abuse. I was adopted into the tribe, and consider myself as much Comanche as my brother, Brave Eagle."

"But you have a brother, Fawn, a true brother. I must tell Colt, he'll be overjoyed to find his little sister after all these years."

"No." The girl shook her head emphatically. "It will serve no earthly purpose. By now Steve, or Colt as you call him, has all but forgotten his sister Laura. She ceased to exist years ago. He always hated Indians. He will despise what I have become. Besides, if he values his freedom as highly as you say, I will only complicate his life.

"You misjudge Colt, Fawn . . . Laura," Sam corrected, preferring to use her American name. "From the beginning I sensed a restlessness in Colt, as if he had been searching for something to make his life complete. I think finding you is just what he needs."

Laura shook her head, objecting vigorously. "No! I owe my life to my adopted father. I will marry

Long Bow as Black Bear wishes and become a proper Comanche wife. I know nothing of the white man's world. My life is with the Comanche. Please, Violet Eyes, promise you won't tell my brother."

"Don't ask that of me, Laura."

Laura shrugged. "You will have no chance to speak with my brother before his confrontation with Brave Eagle. If he still lives after tomorrow, I will simply express my desire to remain with my adopted family. My father will respect my wishes."

When Sam tried to persuade her to reconsider, Laura turned a deaf ear, leaving the lodge and the subject behind.

Overwhelmed, Sam slid to her knees, wondering how it would affect Colt when he learned his sister was alive but wanted nothing to do with him or her former life. Sadly, Laura had become thoroughly Indian. Suddenly a devastating thought assailed her. How would Colt react when he learned that she, Sam, was half Comanche? Knowing his hatred for the Indian race, it took little imagination for Sam to realize he would despise her for something she had no control over.

From that terrifying thought her mind skipped to the confrontation tomorrow between Colt and Brave Eagle. Equally matched, both men possessed bravery and cunning, both were superbly conditioned and mentally and physically fit. Sam found it impossible to predict the outcome, nor did she wish to contemplate what would happen to Colt if Brave Eagle became the victor. Life without Colt seemed bleak and dismal. The thought of another man touching her intimately was repugnant to her. If she couldn't have Colt, opinionated and arrogant though he might be, she wanted no one.

Chapter Twelve

Ensconced in Spirit Dancer's lodge, Colt was provided with a substantial meal and told to eat hearty, for no food would be forthcoming the next day until the winner partook of the feast prepared in his honor. Then he bedded down while the old shaman sat cross-legged beside him, seemingly in a trance. Sleep skittered around Colt but did not claim him, though he desperately needed to restore his strength and stamina.

Colt did not fear the fierce warrior, but he did respect his formidable strength. Defeating Brave Eagle would not be easy, and it was a battle he could not afford to lose. He already had lost one loved one to the savages and wouldn't give up another. The thought of losing Sam to that redskin made him break out in cold sweat. And his own survival rested on his ability to outwit the proud Comanche.

In Colt's rather tarnished estimation, Indians

were the world's worst abomination. Nothing could persuade him to take an Indian woman to his bed. He hated to think of Sam being forced to share that savage's mat. On that note he fell into a fitful sleep, his dreams fraught with visions of Sam. Making love beside the stream, in her bed, in his room above the Palace. In her arms he had found something that had been missing from his life. A love to compensate for the pain of losing Laura. Was his life to end before those tender feelings could be thoroughly explored?

Dressed simply in breechclout and moccasins, Colt stepped outside Spirit Dancer's lodge. The old man pointed him toward an open area in the center of the camp where the entire population of the village had gathered in avid anticipation of the fight. The sun was directly overhead, its white-hot glare heating the trodden earth beneath Colt's feet. By the time he reached the designated area, beads of sweat dampened the ropy muscles of arms and torso, turning his bronzed skin slick and shiny. He might have been mistaken for Comanche were it not for his shock of wheat-colored hair and tawny eyes.

Brave Eagle awaited him in the center of a large circle formed by excited spectators acting like children about to be given their favorite treat. He was similarly clad in breechclout and moccasins. Impressive, powerful, lean, Brave Eagle's impassive features wore an inscrutable mask. Both men resembled well-oiled fighting machines; both determined to win, neither willing to abandon Sam to the other.

Black Bear approached. From the corner of his

eye Colt saw Sam standing with an Indian maiden at the edge of the crowd. Then the chief began to speak, and Colt had to satisfy himself with a brief glimpse of Sam's worried face.

"The rules are simple," Black Bear intoned. "You will each be armed with a knife. You may also use any part of the body to defend yourselves. If one is disarmed by the other, the weapon cannot be replaced by a spectator though it may be retrieved by a combatant. Upon the death of one, the other will be declared winner and claim the reward. Are you ready, my son?"

Colt did not miss the pride in the chief's voice or the look of confidence bestowed upon the young warrior. When Brave Eagle nodded eagerly, Black Bear turned to Colt, his dark eyes hooded. "Are you prepared, Lion Heart?"

"Ready," Colt said, his voice taut.

Each man was handed a Bowie knife, a weapon thoroughly familiar to Colt, who gripped it firmly with one hand and saluted cockily with the other, a mocking grin on his mouth. The circle around them widened, allowing ample space for the combatants though little leeway for intricate maneuvering. It took skill and concentration to fight in such a manner, and no one was more aware of it than Colt.

Colt circled Brave Eagle warily, feeling, testing, taking full measure of the Comanche's strengths and weaknesses. Both men moved cautiously, each deliberately postponing the initial moment of contact yet knowing it was unavoidable. Brave Eagle looked awesome and dangerous stripped down to breechclout, his muscles rippling under a fine sheen of sweat. His stoic features revealed nothing of his thoughts or the turmoil churning his guts. Colt was equally imposing, his face harsh with the need to win.

Of the two, Colt was taller by an inch or two, but their bodies were similar in size and strength. When Brave Eagle launched the attack with a sudden slashing motion, Colt anticipated the move, easily deflecting the blow. Since the sun was directly overhead, neither had the advantage over the other when it came to avoiding the blinding glare, and Colt began to appreciate Black Bear's sense of fairness by arranging the match at high noon. Then Brave Eagle crouched low, but once again Colt was ready, warding off the attack with a counterthrust of his own.

Deflecting Brave Eagle's attempt to emasculate him, Colt danced around the brave, confusing him, then lashed out with a speed born of desperation. Colt drew first blood with the tip of his Bowie, a superficial cut that caused Brave Eagle little concern. The Comanche retaliated by viciously kicking out at Colt with a moccasined foot, catching him in the groin. Though Colt turned aside at the last minute, avoiding the brunt of the blow, it nevertheless brought a grunt of pain from his lips. He recovered before Brave Eagle could move in for the kill, but not fast enough to entirely avoid the flashing knife. A jagged line of red appeared across Colt's chest—not deep but bleeding freely. From somewhere behind him Colt heard a stifled scream. Sam?

Eyeing Colt's wound with a measure of satisfaction, Brave Eagle made the mistake of pressing closer, wielding his knife in a wide arc aimed directly at Colt's heart. Naturally ambidextrous,

Colt slapped his blade into his left hand and blocked with the right, at the same time nicking Brave Eagle's right thigh. By now both men were covered in sweat mixed with blood, and Colt swiped at his eyes with a forearm in order to clear his vision.

Suddenly Colt found himself on the ground, pinioned by the Comanche's considerable weight, a brawny arm pressing against his throat. For long suspenseful minutes they grappled in the dirt as Colt grasped Brave Eagle's wrist, suspending the knife just inches from his face. Exerting all the strength he could muster, Colt slowly turned the advantage in his favor as he reversed their position, straddling the Comanche's hips while his legs thrashed wildly in an attempt to dislodge Colt's bulk. Not really knowing how it all came about, both men were on their feet again, circling, feinting, retreating. Colt's face wore a grim smile—more like a snarl with teeth bared and lips a taut slash across his face. Brave Eagle's expression was equally intense, his features carved in stone, eyes cold as death.

Brave Eagle attempted another well-aimed kick, but this time failed to connect. Once again the knife slid into Colt's left hand as he delivered a hook to the Comanche's chin that left him shaken. Though he was trained in wrestling and adept at fighting with his feet, fisticuffs were relatively unknown to Brave Eagle. Sensing his confusion, Colt carried through with another righthanded blow, quickly followed by a third. A low murmur rippled through the crowd, which was clearly displeased by Colt's unorthodox tactics.

Colt could feel the strain, his muscles screaming in protest at each violent jolt, each precise movement. His body was on fire, his heart pumping at a furious pace, every motion an agony of pain. Despite their herculean efforts, neither of them appeared to be gaining an advantage over the other. Suddenly it occurred to Colt that the only way to defeat this apparently indefatigable savage was by cunning and a whole lot of luck.

Though it tore Sam apart to watch the terrible punishment the men inflicted upon one another, she was unable to turn away. Each time Colt sustained an injury, no matter how minor, she flinched and clung tightly to Fawn's hand. It seemed impossible that one man could win when they were obviously so evenly matched. She inhaled sharply when Colt and Brave Eagle grappled in the dirt, pummeling each other furiously, neither willing to give an inch. Brave Eagle used his feet to advantage, but Colt's fists proved just as lethal.

Drained by the relentless sun and battered by Brave Eagle, Colt grew desperate, and out of that desperation an idea was born. If it worked, it could mean the difference between death and walking out alive with Sam. If it failed, in all likelihood he and Brave Eagle would kill each other, or else still be fighting when the moon came up.

Warily the men circled, Colt carefully observant as he maneuvered Brave Eagle into a position favorable for his purpose. A little good luck wouldn't hurt either. Brave Eagle thought nothing of Colt flashing the blade over his head and from hand to hand. He assumed that the White Eyes was

merely trying to impress him with his prowess—
until he discovered that the blade was catching and
reflecting the glare of the sun directly into his eyes.
He cursed himself for failing to recognize the man's
cunning and fought to overcome the disadvantage.
But no matter how hard he tried he couldn't escape
the debilitating blindness that stalked him at every
turn.

When Brave Eagle ducked, the sun followed. His
eyes burned, not only from sun blindness but from
sweat and blood. Instinctively, he blinked, and in
that brief instant Colt reacted. He leaped at Brave
Eagle, sending the knife flying from the Indian's
hand. It lay at the fringe of the circle and according
to rules must remain there until Brave Eagle retrieved it. The chief's orders had been explicit.
Before strength returned to the Comanche's limbs
and breath to his lungs, he was forced to the ground
by the sheer weight of Colt's surprise attack. So
quickly that no one actually saw the movement,
Colt's knife pressed against Brave Eagle's throat,
only one swift stroke away from death.

There was no fear in Brave Eagle's eyes, for fear
was unknown to a Comanche warrior. He could
laugh in the face of pain and scorn death, for it was
but an adventure into another world. The pressure
increased, and Brave Eagle sought his father's eyes.
He saw fierce pride in their black depths—a hint of
regret and overwhelming sadness. Colt followed the
direction of Brave Eagle's gaze and realized that
father and son were silently communicating their
love and bidding one another good-bye.

"Colt, please, don't kill him!" Over the stunned

silence of the crowd, Sam's voice soared out to stay Colt's hand.

It was fully within Colt's right to end Brave Eagle's life—expected, actually. The warrior wouldn't have hesitated to deliver the fatal blow were the circumstances reversed. Yet Sam's plea stopped him, even though he hated the Comanches enough to kill each one single-handedly.

Why did Sam plead for Brave Eagle's life? Colt wondered angrily. Did she harbor tender feelings for the savage? Jealousy jolted through him as the knife bit deeper into Brave Eagle's throat. The Comanche's black eyes did not waver from Colt's face. But for some unexplained reason Colt postponed the fatal slash. Maybe it was Sam's plea that stopped him, but he didn't think so. Some sixth sense told him that one day Black Bear might prove useful to him, that sparing his son's life would cost him little and gain him much.

Undaunted, Brave Eagle watched the play of emotion across Colt's face. His lip curled derisively. "Kill me, Lion Heart. Were I in your place I would not hesitate. My intuition tells me you have killed many times in the past."

"Many times," Colt concurred, his own breath harsh with fatigue. "And I'll kill again, but not today."

Suddenly the pressure on Brave Eagle eased as Colt leaped to his feet and faced the chief, who appeared stunned by the turn of events.

"Is the victory mine?" Colt asked loudly enough for all to hear.

Black Bear nodded, his face giving away nothing

Connie Mason

of his great sadness. "It is your right to take my son's life."

"Am I free to leave with Samantha Howard?"

"You are free to go where you please. Both of you," Black Bear advised harshly.

"Then I choose to spare your son's life."

Picking himself up off the ground, Brave Eagle scowled, certain he hadn't mistaken the hatred for his people inherent in Colt's attitude. Such a man would not balk at killing an enemy. In his own defense, Brave Eagle felt no loss of face for Colt's strange behavior. He was prepared to die, would have done so bravely, and his people knew it. He had fought with courage, but the white man's cunning had defeated him. It stung to think he would never taste the sweetness of Violet Eyes, for he loved her well and truly.

Black Bear didn't trust himself to speak. Losing his only son would have been a terrible blow, but Lion Heart had won the right to take his son's life, and should have. His refusal to do so bewildered Black Bear. Never would he understand the White Eyes. Lion Heart had fought as courageously as Brave Eagle and won Violet Eyes fairly. Lion Heart didn't strike him as being particularly tender-hearted or squeamish, and Brave Eagle surely would have killed Lion Heart had he the opportunity. What was Lion Heart's reason for sparing his son's life? Was it because of Violet Eyes' plea?

Spirit Dancer sensed his chief's confusion. "The Great Spirit has seen fit to spare your son. Give thanks by offering Lion Heart something in return. Brave Eagle acquitted himself bravely. There is no shame in defeat at the hands of another of equal strength and courage."

Black Bear considered Spirit Dancer's words carefully, deciding to follow the astute shaman's advice. Turning to Colt, he said, "I did not ask for my son's life but I willingly accept your gift. But in return you must accept mine. It is the way of our people."

Colt mulled over the chief's words, his eyes searching out Sam, who appeared stunned and unbelieving. He wanted to grab her and run as far away from the Comanches as he could get. With that in mind it was not difficult to agree to whatever Black Bear suggested.

"I agree," Colt replied warily. "I will accept your offerin'." Christ! He hoped it wasn't an Indian maiden to warm his bed because he'd sure as hell have to refuse.

"Come to me, Violet Eyes," Black Bear motioned. Sam approached cautiously, her eyes shimmering with all the pent-up love and longing for Colt she had locked away in her heart.

Christ, she's beautiful, Colt thought as he watched Sam approach. Her black hair glistened like polished ebony in the brilliant sun, and her skin appeared to be molten gold. But it was her violet eyes that drew his attention. He didn't want to put a name to what he read in those dark, mysterious depths, but he hoped he hadn't been mistaken. Once they left this savage environment, he meant to explore all that they promised.

Sam had no opportunity to unburden her heart to Colt, for Black Bear was speaking again. "The Great

Spirit above has shown us your future is not with the People, Violet Eyes. But because of the love I bore your mother and the fact that you have no father to see to your welfare, I will assume his authority."

Sam looked puzzled, while Colt could not think past Black Bear's statement that he had loved Sam's mother. His attention sharpened as Black Bear continued. "My gift to you, Lion Heart, is a joining ceremony. When you leave here, Violet Eyes will be your mate. At the feast tonight Spirit Dancer will join you to Violet Eyes."

"What! A marriage ceremony?" exclaimed Colt, stunned. Though he might eventually come to offer Sam marriage, he didn't want to be pushed into that decision before it was time.

"Did you think your bravery would go unrewarded? The outcome of the fight with my son made Violet Eyes yours. Are your intentions less honorable than Brave Eagle's who wanted Violet Eyes for his mate?"

Colt flushed. He was almost certain he loved Sam, but marriage would take some getting used to. Still, an Indian marriage ceremony was hardly binding in the white man's world. He looked to Sam for guidance and saw only her willingness to comply with the chief's wishes. Had she planned it this way? Had she conspired with the chief to trap him into marriage? Ridiculous, he told himself—they had had no idea he would win.

Colt realized that the chief had asked him a question and was waiting for an answer.

"Like Brave Eagle I am an honorable man, but I came here to return Sam to her own people, not lookin' for a mate."

"Violet Eyes is with her mother's people. We do not harm one of our own."

"One of your own? Her mother's people? I . . . I don't understand."

Suddenly Colt's eyes widened as his gaze slid to Sam, seeing her in an entirely different light. Hair as black as a raven's wing, skin golden bronze, eyes slightly aslant in a face that could very well belong to a half-breed—all combined to convince Colt that Black Bear spoke the truth. Why had Sam lied to him? She knew that he despised Indians. Had he known her secret, he probably would never have touched her. And if you believe that you're a lying varmint, he told himself with a snort of disgust. Suddenly the look on his face changed from one of disbelief to one of utter contempt, causing Sam to catch her breath painfully.

"Colt, I didn't know," she attempted to explain. "Please believe me . . ."

Black Bear motioned her to silence, then turned to Colt, scowling darkly. "Violet Eyes is the daughter of Shy Deer, a Comanche maiden who fell in love with William Howard. She bore him a daughter, but they did not marry. I do not wish the same fate for Violet Eyes, who has become like a daughter to me. You risked your life for her, it is only right that you should take her as your mate. Giving Violet Eyes to you according to our custom is my gift to both of you. You cannot refuse, for you have given your word just as I gave mine. Unless," the chief said shrewdly, "you are like most White Eyes who speak with two tongues. Should I find your words false I will give Violet Eyes to my son, who greatly desires her."

Black Bear had spoken the right words. With brutal clarity Colt knew he was trapped. If Sam thought this sham wedding would be binding, she was dead wrong. In fact, everything had changed the moment he learned she was part savage. He was seeing her as if for the first time. Christ! She was a damn redskin! He had made love to a woman with Indian blood flowing through her veins, something he'd sworn he'd never do. Her nasty temper and vile tongue should have given him a clue to her heritage. Colt fumed in impotent rage at the way he had been manipulated, yet he knew there was only one answer.

"Brave Eagle will have to look elsewhere for a mate, Black Bear," Colt acquiesced none too gallantly. "I'll join with . . . Violet eyes." Now that he knew what she was, her Indian name came easily to his lips.

"No, that's not necessary," Sam protested. Colt's reluctance hurt dreadfully, but she tried not to show it. "It is not our way, Black Bear."

"Trust me to know what is best for you, Violet Eyes," Black Bear said shortly. "Go with Fawn and prepare yourself for the ceremony."

"But . . ." She got no further as Fawn approached and tugged gently on her hand. Fawn did not look at Colt but kept her eyes properly downcast.

Colt's face settled into harsh lines as he watched Sam being led off. Had he known how this would end or the secrets that would be revealed, he might have left Sam to her own devices, he reflected, knowing in his heart he lied.

"Go with Spirit Dancer, Lion Heart," Black Bear said, interrupting Colt's dark thoughts. "He will

tend your wounds and prepare you for the ceremony."

Sam's heart plummeted to her feet. Forcing Colt
to participate in something he obviously found so
distasteful was the last thing she'd intended. If only
she could talk to Colt, tell him that this was none of
her doing and remind him he need not honor
Indian vows once they returned to civilization. The
look he had given her when he learned she was part
Comanche was so filled with loathing and contempt
that it tore her apart. It hurt, hurt terribly, to think
he would never again touch her with love and
tenderness. Her entire world had turned upside
down since learning the truth about herself. What
would Will think? Would it change his brotherly
feelings, or would she still be his beloved sister?

While Fawn helped Sam bathe and dress in a
sleeveless pure white doeskin dress elaborately
fringed and beaded, she thought about all that Fawn
had revealed to her yesterday, and longed to tell Colt
she had found his sister. The way things were
progressing, Sam seriously doubted she'd find the
time before the ceremony. What would he do when
he learned Fawn was his sister Laura? Naturally
he'd want to take her away, and no doubt Black
Bear would protest since Fawn herself was unwilling to leave her adopted family. She eyed the girl
speculatively. Fawn had become so thoroughly Indian that Sam came to the sad conclusion that a
miracle was needed to pry her from the bosom of
the Comanches. Perhaps she shouldn't tell Colt
about Laura, Sam debated, knowing in her heart
she must.

Sensing the direction of Sam's thoughts, Fawn said, "It would serve no purpose to tell him, Violet Eyes. I will not go with him."

"Would returning to your people be so bad, Laura?"

"I . . . I wouldn't know how to act in a white world. The White Eyes have been my enemy for too many years."

"Colt is your brother," Sam reminded gently.

"I . . . hardly know him. He has changed."

"So have you, but you have the same blood flowing through your veins," Sam persisted. "Besides, I couldn't keep the truth from Colt. He hates me enough already."

"He wouldn't be here if he hated you," Fawn said astutely. "It will not matter to him if I refuse to leave my people."

Sam snorted derisively. "Colt doesn't want a half-breed wife. He hates Comanches for killing his parents."

"Then he will hate me, for I am Comanche," Fawn insisted stubbornly.

Sam sighed despairingly. Was there nothing she could say to change Laura's mind? If the girl refused to leave with them, it would add more fuel to Colt's already burning hatred of Indians. And naturally his anger and disappointment would be directed at her, Sam.

The sun was just setting when Sam was led to the center of the village, where Colt waited with Spirit Dancer. Like her, he was dressed in soft white buckskin elaborately beaded and fringed. Instead of boots he wore moccasins, and his loose-limbed stance belied his raging anger. He looked so handsome it literally stole Sam's breath away. The breadth of his shoulders, the rippling muscles, slim waist and narrow hips—dear God, no man had a right to look so magnificently male! Why couldn't he return a tiny part of the love she felt for him? Sam sighed despondently. Then she made the mistake of looking in his face. If Black Bear hadn't been directly behind her, she would have turned and fled, so fierce and austere was Colt's expression.

In a surprisingly short time the Indian men circling them began whooping and dancing while the women clapped their hands in time to the drums, which had taken up their beat the moment Spirit Dancer signaled the end of the ceremony. According to Comanche custom, Sam was now Colt's mate.

By now darkness had dropped like a curtain about them and the women began passing around food to the men seated around the huge campfire watching the dancers. The Indians loved a celebration and participated fully, dancing, eating, and drinking their own particular brew of strong drink. It was an awesome spectacle, one Sam wouldn't soon forget.

Throughout the ceremony Colt maintained a stoic expression, gaining perverse pleasure from glancing at Sam from time to time from beneath shuttered lids. She looked more beautiful and provocative than he had ever seen her. His loins ached at the sight of her supple curves moving sinuously inside the clinging doeskin dress. He recalled distinctly how soft her skin had felt beneath the roughness of his fingertips, how her breasts had swelled to the touch of his hands. She tasted delicious; so sweet, so responsive to his need.

Then he remembered the Comanche blood flowing through her veins. It stung to think he had made love to a damn half-breed and enjoyed it. Had he known— His train of thought skidded to a halt. If he wanted to be brutally honest, had he known Sam was part Indian, he still would have made love to her. He couldn't deny he'd wanted her from the first moment he set eyes on her. He glanced at Sam where she sat sedately beside him and was startled to find himself being regarded somewhat warily by eyes the color of the sky at midnight.

"Violet Eyes," Colt muttered with something akin to contempt. He made her Comanche name sound dirty and vile. "Whether you like it or not, you're my squaw now."

Sam winced, his words as cutting as the Bowie he had used to defeat Brave Eagle. The term he used was derogatory. No self-respecting Indian would call his wife a squaw. Only white men called their Indian whores squaws. Was that how Colt thought of her? As his whore? His Indian whore? Did he despise that half of her so much?

"Colt, don't look at me like that," Sam choked on a sob. "I haven't changed. I'm still the same person you—"

"No!" Colt injected rudely. "Everythin' is changed, Violet Eyes."

"Why did you come here?"

"Because I thought I . . . because I told Will I'd find you," Colt amended before he revealed too much.

"You know this ceremony means nothing," Sam said softly. She didn't want Black Bear to think she was finding fault with her husband so soon, but neither could she let Colt believe she had planned things this way. "When we return to civilization we can forget this."

"You're wrong, Violet Eyes," Colt refuted sarcastically. "Nothin' will ever be the same. Black Bear gave you to me. You're my squaw for as long as I want you. Though Lord only knows if I'll be able to touch you knowin' you're a—"

"Violet Eyes, come, it is time to prepare yourself for your husband." A bevy of giggling maidens descended on Sam, dragging her away from Colt and his cutting words. It was just as well. One more snide remark about her heritage and she would have exploded. The mule-stubborn varmint needed to be taught a lesson.

It did little good to protest as Sam was led off toward a tipi that had been hastily erected in honor of her joining. She was bathed, anointed, stripped naked, and settled on a mat that was to be her nuptial bed.

Chapter Thirteen

Colt partook freely of the bitter concoction brewed by the Indians for special occasions and ceremonies. It was as potent as whiskey but not nearly so good, he reflected as he watched Sam being led off to their nupital tent. How could he still want her so fiercely when he now knew what she was? With brutal clarity Colt realized this could easily be the same tribe that had killed his parents and carried off poor Laura, perhaps even killed her. That thought was instantly sobering, though it did nothing to diminish the intense throbbing in his loins.

With frequent regularity Colt's gaze went to the tipi where his bride awaited. A knowing grin curved Black Bear's lips as he noted the direction of Colt's eyes with a certain amount of satisfaction. "Do you grow impatient, Lion Heart? Your woman is beautiful, possessing much courage and strength. She will give you strong sons. May your seed be swift and true tonight."

Children! Colt thought grimly. He had no desire to sire children with the blood of savages running in their veins. It rankled to think he could not lift his mind past the ache in his loins. Raising his cup, he drank deeply of the intoxicating brew. He had lost count long ago of the amount he had consumed, hoping it would take the edge off his longing.

Black Bear rose unsteadily to his feet. "It is time, Lion Heart. Your bride awaits. I will escort you to your lodge."

All Colt's senses came alive as he staggered beside Black Bear, potently aware of Brave Eagle's black eyes boring into him. Colt had tried to drink himself senseless and failed. Though far from sober, he still had faculties enough to feel, to think—to make love. When it came right down to it, he wasn't convinced he could make love to a half-breed Comanche. Did he want to? The answer thrummed through his body like a Comanche arrow. Christ, yes!

The chanting and dancing continued as Black Bear left Colt standing uncertainly at the entrance to the tipi. Vividly Colt recalled the last time he had made glorious love to Sam. But since then everything had changed. Everything but the desperate need riding him.

Inside the tipi Sam stirred restlessly. It had grown so late she seriously doubted Colt would come to her. Did he despise her so much? Squirming on the pallet of soft skins, Sam felt a draft and intuitively knew that Colt stood beside her long before she saw him.

"Waitin' for me like a good squaw, darlin'?" Colt slurred.

"Why did you bother coming at all if you can't tolerate me?" Sam shot back.

"It was expected of me," Colt rejoined lamely. "What kind of man could neglect a beautiful bride on her wedding night?"

"The kind that never wanted a bride in the first place."

"Just so you understand that I don't intend to honor your heathenish rites," Colt reminded her sternly. "You're my squaw, nothin' more."

"It's no more than I expected from a blackhearted skunk."

Above the blanket Sam had pulled up to shield her nude form, her shoulders gleamed like antique gold in the dim glow from the fire burning in the center of the tipi. Colt's eyes glinted wickedly as he dropped to his knees and stripped away the thin covering with one fluid motion, tossing it aside.

"Damnation, you're beautiful!" he muttered. "Maybe a saint could resist such outlandish temptation, darlin', but as you well know, I'm no saint. I swore I'd never touch an Indian squaw, but when I look at you nothin' matters 'cept puttin' myself deep inside you where it's warm and wet and so enticin' a man could go crazy wantin' it. I want you, Violet Eyes. I'd be lyin' if I said I didn't."

"Won't taking a half-breed Comanche to bed offend your sensibilities?" Sam taunted chillingly.

"Why should I deny myself? I'm only doin' what's expected of me. Besides, I need a woman and you're my squaw to use in any way I see fit. Indian or not, I'm gonna do what we both want."

"You loathsome—"

Abruptly her words stopped as he took her lips in an eager, demanding kiss, and for long minutes his mouth worked its magic on her. Just when Sam thought she'd expire from lack of breath, his mouth began a tantalizing foray to her ear, sliding down to the base of her throat, his tongue sending flashes of flame to her body as he nipped and licked at the tiny pulse beating in her throat. She inhaled sharply when Colt's lips burned a path to her breasts, nibbling hungrily at the dusky pink tips puckering delightfully beneath his touch. Every nerve came alive as he licked a path down her stomach, stopping briefly at her navel, then continuing downward. Her legs were nudged apart and she nearly exploded when the tip of his tongue probed and prodded. One exquisite thrill after another sang through her as he raised her hips to meet his mouth. With a will of their own her hands found his hair, her fingers tangling in the tawny mass to pull him closer.

Keen disappointment produced a groan from Sam's lips as Colt brought her to the brink of ecstasy, then deliberately let her dangle on the edge, denying her the ultimate victory. Cruel! Cruel! How could he make her suffer when it was within his power to grant her release?

"Colt, please!"

Abruptly Colt rose to his knees and tore off his clothes, releasing that part of him she yearned for most. Mindlessly she reached out, enclosing his throbbing strength in her hand, and Colt jerked violently. It felt smooth and hard and hot in her palm and Colt cried out as if in pain when she stroked the pulsing length back and forth. Sam delighted in the satiny feel of him in her hand and drove him beyond physical endurance by rubbing him against her belly, smiling with devious delight at his response.

"Christ!" Colt exploded, bolting upright. "What in the hell are you tryin' to do?"

"Exactly what you did to me," she taunted, pleased with herself. "How does it feel to be teased unmercifully?"

"Indian witch! Is this what you want?" Slapping her hand aside, he mounted her and entered swiftly.

She rose up to meet his thrust, feeling herself filling with the incredible length of him, stretching further than she thought humanly possible. Colt pressed himself into the depths of her and felt her enclose him, hold him, caress him. Then suddenly it no longer mattered that Sam was part Comanche and he hated Comanches. Or that he was forced to participate in a heathen marriage. He knew only that the woman in his arms, responding to him, loving him, was sweet and warm and made his body thrum with joy.

Driven by a thousand demons, Colt seized Sam's lips, plunging his tongue inside in rhythm to his thrusting below. Her body was a savage blending of ecstasy and torment as wild and wonderful sensations attacked her senses. But it became too much for her when his hand slid between their driving bodies to find the tiny hidden button in the secret folds of her flesh, intensifying her pleasure by gently massaging the swollen nub with thumb and forefinger. Sensation after sensation erupted within her, her mind whirling, pleasure mounting until she was consumed in delicious agony. Her world spun dizzily and rapture flung them into endless space.

They descended slowly, drifting contentedly until Colt broke the spell. "I could easily grow accustomed to this if you weren't . . ."

It was as if Colt had dashed cold water in Sam's face. "Go ahead, say it."

His face hardened, his eyes turned a murky brown. "You know my feelin's about Indians. I almost imagined myself in love with you until I learned . . ."

". . . That I'm a savage?" Sam contended, completing Colt's sentence. "Have I changed so much? Do I feel different, taste different? You had no problem making love to me just now."

Colt had the grace to flush. In that respect Sam was right. Making love to her was as enjoyable as ever—more so, in fact. Surprisingly, his skin didn't crawl when he touched her, nor had his manhood reacted differently in the tightness of her sheath. They were as fully attuned to each other's needs as if they were truly man and wife. Christ! What was he thinking? He wanted no wife, especially no Indian squaw. Yet, to his chagrin, Colt found himself impatient to taste Sam's sweetness again, savor her unique response. And most of all Colt wanted no other man to sample what was his.

Suddenly Sam moved in such a way as to bring Colt's thoughts to her nude body rubbing against him. He tried to banish his renewed desire by concentrating on answering her questions.

"I should hate you, yet I want you so fiercely it hurts," he admitted. "I'm probably drunker than

I've ever been in my life but I've never felt stronger. My hunger for you is mind-bogglin'. I feel I could make love to you ten, no, twenty times tonight and not tire. You inspire me with a stamina few men will ever know. You taste and feel the same and, yes, dammit, I still want you."

"Even though I'm part Comanche?" Sam asked quietly.

"Yep," he acknowledged tersely. "I must be crazy but it makes no difference, though deep down it hurts to think you share the same blood as the savages that took my sister."

Sam tensed. Laura! She had to tell Colt about his sister. "Colt, about Laura . . ."

"How do you know my sister's name? Has Jake been talkin'?"

"No, not Jake. It's . . ."

"I don't want to talk about Laura, Sam. If I think about what those heathens did to her, I wouldn't be able to make love to you again, and I want to more than anythin'."

"But Colt, I need to tell you . . ."

He brushed his lips over her forehead, then trailed them ever so slowly and enticingly over her brows, temples, nose, and cheeks before capturing her mouth to stop her words. He fondled her breasts lightly, leisurely, his thumbs and forefingers trapping the two buds between them and gently kneading until they hardened and grew erect. Then his lips and tongue moistened the peaks, tantalized them, his hands roaming downward to more fertile ground. He explored her thoroughly, lush hills, a tiny peak, enchanting valleys, secret crevices, and a dark and damp cave.

Beneath his probing fingers, tongue, and mouth, Sam squirmed uncomfortably, her chest rising and falling with excruciating slowness. Suddenly his hands grew rough as his passion spiraled into a burning need so intense it threatened to turn him to cinder. Sam cried out as his fingers dug painfully into tender flesh, but Colt was beyond tenderness. He could wait no longer. He grasped her hips, his fully extended organ pressed against her softness, firm and powerful. Flexing his hips, he pushed inside and Sam prepared herself for a brutal assault. But to her surprise, Colt's roughness turned gentle and she gave herself up to his loving. Later, he loved her again, and yet again. His stamina was amazing. Dawn was tinging the eastern sky when exhaustion finally claimed them.

Colt was pulling on his buckskin trousers when Sam opened her eyes. She stretched languidly, feeling glowingly content despite twinges of discomfort in certain places. Then with amazing clarity she recalled everything that had transpired during the long night. She flushed and slid a shy glance at Colt, startled to find that he was watching her. The urge to say something—anything—seized her.

"Where are you going?"

"To prepare for our trip home. It's a long way and we'll need supplies. Go back to sleep, you need the rest."

Though he didn't say so, his words hinted of the wildness of her response to his loving last night. She had acted like a wanton in his arms, and she was ashamed of the way he seemed to command her body to do as he wanted. During those magic hours he had completely controlled every aspect of her mind and body. She hated Colt for using her to assuage his lust when he felt nothing but contempt for her. But at the same time she loved him. It seemed she didn't know her own mind where Colt Colter was concerned. A throbbing anger seized her when she thought of all the ways he manipulated her.

"Damn you for a pig-headed jackass! I won't be your whore," she blasted hotly. "After the way you made love to me last night I thought . . ." Her sentence trailed off.

"I needed a woman," Colt said in a feeble attempt to explain his overwhelming ardor and surprising tenderness. "Chief Black Bear gave you to me, and I merely took what he so kindly offered. Besides, you're a beautiful woman, Violet Eyes, with the body and face of an enchantress. I told you I wanted you, that you're hard to resist no matter what or who you are. I'm not made of stone."

"Once we return to civilization you won't have to worry about being tempted," Sam contended. "I'm leaving the ranch and taking Will with me. There's no reason for us to remain."

"Have you forgotten somethin'?"

"I think not."

"You can't leave until I say so. Unless you and Will want to rot in jail. Have you forgotten that stage-coach robbery so soon?"

"You conniving rattlesnake!" Sam snarled. "If it weren't for Will I'd take my chances with Sheriff Bauer and confess. Do you intend to hold that over my head for the rest of my life? You despise me, so why should you care if I leave?"

Deliberately ignoring her taunts, Colt said, "I don't hate you, Violet Eyes, it's what you represent. You'll stay at the ranch till I say otherwise. I still aim to put the Logans and Crowders behind bars, but Jake is capable of handlin' you in my absence. One way or another," he hinted slyly, "you'll earn your bride-price."

"Bride-price?"

"Chief Black Bear demanded ten beeves delivered each fall to feed his people durin' the long winter months."

"And you agreed?" Sam asked incredulously.

"I had no choice." He turned to leave.

Suddenly Sam remembered that she had had no opportunity to tell Colt about Laura. "Colt, don't leave."

A slow smile altered the harsh lines of his face. "I would have thought after last night your—cravin' had been satisfied. But I'll gladly oblige if you're still hankerin'." Deliberately he unfastened his pants.

"Hellfire and damnation! You randy billy goat! I ought to let you go on thinking Laura is either dead or beyond your reach."

Colt froze, all his senses alive as he fell to his knees and grasped Sam's shoulders, pulling her to a sitting position. "What do you know about Laura? Speak, damn you!"

"Colt, you're hurting me! I tried to tell you last night, even though she begged me not to."

"Who?" His hold eased somewhat but not enough to stop the bruises that were sure to show up tomorrow.

"Laura. Black Bear adopted her. She's his daughter. She is called Fawn."

"Christ! Why didn't you tell me sooner?" Colt exploded, releasing her so quickly she fell back with a thump. "Where is she?"

"She lives with Black Bear and his family."

"You mean she sleeps in the same tipi with Brave Eagle?" His face was a mask of rage.

"He's her brother," Sam said, exasperated.

A string of curses fell from Colt's lips. "I'll find her."

"She insists she won't leave the Comanches."

"Like hell!"

"Colt, they're her family now. She's reluctant to leave them. She was a child when she ame to them, and they've treated her with kindness. She loves them."

"They killed our parents! I can't believe she'd live with savages and enjoy it."

"No," Sam refuted, rising and shrugging into her dress. "It was another tribe who killed your parents and took Laura captive. They traded her to Black Bear later. Singing Wind, the chief's wife, lost a daughter and wanted Laura to replace her. According to Laura she's had a good life with them. She's to marry soon. A . . . a brave Black Bear considers worthy of a chief's daughter."

"Over my dead body!" erupted Colt. "I have to talk to her."

"I'll get her, Colt," Sam offered. "She's not the Laura you once knew. She's a woman now. You've already seen her and failed to recognize her. She said she doesn't want to return to the white world, so be gentle with her."

Colt's jaw clenched tightly and he merely nodded, unwilling to trust his voice.

The Indian maiden who entered the tipi couldn't be Laura, Colt decided. The Laura he remembered had golden hair and creamy white skin. This dusky maiden had coal-black braids. Surely Sam had been mistaken. Or was she using unfair means to repay him for forcing her response last night? He was on the verge of dismissing the Comanche girl and lighting into Sam when she raised her head to stare unblinkingly into his eyes. Abruptly his world spun dizzily when a pair of tawny eyes locked with his. Colt searched the sun-bronzed face, and what he saw jolted through him like a bolt of lightning. The features were white. The delicately tanned skin, slightly upturned nose, distinctive Colter eyes. It *was* Laura. Christ! After all these years.

"Laura," he whispered, his breath catching on a sob. "Little sister, thank God I've found you." He felt her stiffen when he enveloped her in a crushing hug. "I'd nearly given up hope."

"Steve." Laura rolled the name around experimentally on her tongue. "Violet Eyes told you, didn't she? I asked her not to." She bent an accusing glare at Sam, who had retreated mutely to the rear of the tent in order to allow brother and sister privacy.

"Have you forgotten your brother, little sister? Have you abandoned your white heritage? Our parents didn't raise you to become Comanche."

"Black Bear and Singing Wind are my parents," Laura insisted, tilting her small chin at a stubborn angle.

Colt winced, wounded deeply by Laura's denial. For years he had searched for her, thinking her lost to him forever, and now that he'd finally found her, she wanted nothing to do with him. "You don't mean that, Laura."

"My name is Fawn."

"Your name is Laura. It was our grandmother's name."

"I'm not the girl you remember."

"You're not a savage," Colt snarled harshly.

"How could you be so hateful?" Laura accused, glowering darkly. "Your own wife is part Comanche."

"My wife!" spat Colt disparagingly. "Are you referrin' to my Indian whore!"

A gasp of horror escaped Sam's lips, echoed by Laura, who stared at Colt in stunned silence. Was this brutish, opinionated man the brother she remembered with love? How could he treat Violet Eyes so cruelly? She retreated a step, her tawny eyes dark with condemnation. Immediately Colt realized his mistake and sought to remedy it.

"I'm sorry, Laura, I didn't mean that. I've searched years for you. I've traveled the length and breadth of Texas and far into Kansas Territory. Christ, Laura, you're all I have left in the world!"

Laura's expression softened. "I'm Comanche, Steve. I've long forgotten my white beginnings. I . . . I wouldn't be happy with whites. They're my enemy. They killed my friends as well as members of my Indian family. I'm to marry soon."

"Once you're back with your own kind, all that will change," Colt promised. "You'll see, things will be the same as when Mother and Father were alive. I own a ranch, you can stay there with Sam. Life will be good again, I promise. Just give yourself a chance to adjust."

"Life is good now," Laura insisted. "Besides, my father would not allow me to leave."

"We'll see," Colt said with grim determination. "Prepare yourself. When Sam and I leave here, you'll go with us." Turning on his heel, he stormed from the tipi.

"My brother is a stranger to me, Violet Eyes," Laura sobbed. "Why was he so hateful to you? Doesn't he know you love him?"

"Colt can't see beyond his own prejudice," Sam replied astutely. "He's spent half his life fighting Mexicans and Indians. He can't stand the thought that I'm part Comanche. You have to admit he has good reason to feel as he does."

"I'm Comanche," Laura contended.

"No, Laura, you're Colt's sister, his own flesh and blood. He hates what the Indians did to you but loves you regardless. It's me he wants nothing to do with."

Colt sat cross-legged on the hard ground beside Black Bear. As usual, Spirit Dancer was present. Thankfully Colt had calmed down enough to speak coherently as he presented his demands to the chief. Spirit Dancer was the only one who appeared unmoved when Colt revealed that Fawn was Laura, his long-lost sister. His wise old eyes held certain knowledge that was denied the others.

"Fawn is my daughter," Black Bear stated with unrelenting firmness. "I will not give her up."

"Laura is my sister," Colt refuted tightly. "I won't give her up, either."

"Have you spoken with my daughter?"

"We . . . talked," Colt admitted tightly.

Spirit Dancer grunted, recognizing the impasse. Turning to Black Bear, he intoned, "My vision foretold such a happening, but until now I did not fully understand it. You love Fawn, but for the good of your people you must give her to Lion Heart. What Lion Heart offers in return will benefit the entire tribe. And in the end you will not lose your daughter."

"You speak in riddles, old man," Black Bear said irritably.

But Colt understood the wily shaman better, perhaps, than Black Bear. He wanted something. Something only Colt could provide. Silently he mulled over Spirit Dancer's words, until it dawned on him what the shaman was hinting at.

He cleared his throat loudly. "You know, of course, that I own a ranch and many hundreds of acres in the hill country where you rest and hunt during the winter months. It is the same land that once belonged to William Howard."

Black Bear nodded slowly. "That is so."

"Release my sister and in return your people are welcome to camp in the hills surroundin' my land to hunt and fish as you see fit to supplement the beeves I promised as bride-price for Violet Eyes. Laura can ride out frequently to visit. It won't be as if you're losin' her forever."

It was a concession Colt had never expected to make, but an unavoidable one. Though he hated the

Comanches, he was prepared to promise anything for Laura's sake. Even if it meant consorting with the enemy. "You'll have beeves to replace the buffalo that no longer roam the prairie as freely as they once did. What I offer will be good for your people."

Black Bear mulled over Colt's offer, knowing in his heart it was a good one. "What about Long Bow? Fawn is promised to him."

"Long Bow will have to find another wife," Colt threw out tightly. "Eventually Laura will marry one of her own kind. I've spent years searchin' for my sister. I just can't leave her behind now that I've found her."

"I will give you my answer after I've spoken to Fawn," Black Bear said dismissively.

"Chief—"

"Go now, Lion Heart," Spirit Dancer advised. "Our chief's heart is heavy, but he is wise and will come to the right decision."

Fuming impotently, Colt left. He had plans to make. If Black Bear refused him, how in the hell would he get Laura out of here? And he didn't dare leave Sam behind or that damn Brave Eagle would be all over her like honey over biscuits.

"What are your feelings for Lion Heart, daughter?"

Laura knelt beside Black Bear, her luminous eyes bright with unshed tears. "I hardly know him, Father," she whispered tremulously. "My life is with you and my Comanche family."

"Your brother wishes you to return with him to the white man's world. Do you want to go?"

Laura's eyes widened with an unnamed fear. With the Comanches she felt safe, she knew what to expect. Life with her own kind offered unknown challenges, uncharted territory. She'd been still an untried girl when taken from the bosom of her family and had grown to womanhood during the intervening years. A woman who knew only the simple life of the Comanche. How could she hope to make a future with the whites she had been taught to hate? And yet, some nearly forgotten memory inspired her with a warm feeling she could not explain.

"Why do you hesitate, daughter? Are you uncertain of your feelings?" Black Bear asked astutely.

"I was thinking of my marriage to Long Bow," Laura hedged.

"Do you love Long Bow so much? I do not possess the wisdom of Spirit Dancer, but my feelings tell me you agreed to the joining only to please me and Brave Eagle."

Laura squirmed beneath Black Bear's scrutiny. Impaled by his dark, inscrutable gaze, she could not lie. "I . . . do not love Long Bow, Father, but he is brave and strong and will make me a good husband, just as I will be a dutiful wife to him. I am grateful for the love you have given me all these years and want only to obey you."

Black Bear searched Laura's face carefully, looking into her soul through the window of her tawny eyes. What he saw there neither pleased nor displeased him. He merely accepted what he saw as the design of things. Spirit Dancer had said the People would prosper with the coming of Violet Eyes, and it would be so if Lion Heart kept his word. Spirit Dancer had also predicted that they would forfeit something of value in order to gain prosperity, and it had come about. Fawn was dear to him, and losing her would leave a definite void in his heart, but the Great Spirit had spoken and the People would obey.

Black Bear read indecision in Fawn's eyes. Panic, confusion, and fear of the unknown all warred within her slim body. Buried deep within her heart Black Bear sensed a yearning, recognizing it immediately as a feeling of kinship with Lion Heart she could not deny. It was enough to provoke a decision.

"You have been a good and loving daughter, Fawn, and it would pain me to lose you."

"Then I may stay?" Laura asked hopefully.

"You will leave with Lion Heart."

"Father, no! You and Singing Wind are the only family I know. I can't bear the thought of not seeing either of you again."

"We will meet again, daughter. Lion Heart has invited us to make our winter camp on his land, to hunt and fish to supplement the beeves he will provide us as bride-price for Violet Eyes."

"I don't believe it!" Laura gasped, stunned. "My brother hates Indians, especially Comanches. He holds his own wife in contempt because of her mixed blood. My brother has changed. He's a hard, cruel man."

"He's a warrior," Black Bear chided gently. "He might appear hard and inflexible, but he loves you. His eyes do not lie."

"What about Violet Eyes? She loves Lion Heart and he treats her like . . . like his whore," she whispered, lowering her voice. "It isn't right, Father. I don't think he will honor their marriage once they leave here."

"I have done all in my power to provide for Violet Eyes' future," Black Bear replied. "Lion Heart defeated Brave Eagle fairly and joined with Violet Eyes of his own free will. Now it is up to Violet Eyes to capture her husband's love and banish his prejudice. Proud blood flows through her veins; she will persevere. With your help, daughter, Lion Heart will one day recognize the love in his heart."

Laura seriously doubted her brother's heart would melt so easily.

Colt was ecstatic when told that Laura would be allowed to leave with him and Violet Eyes. Damn, there he went again, referring to Sam by her Indian name. If only things could return to the way they were before he had learned that Sam belonged to the despised Comanches. At least one good thing had come of it. Laura. He couldn't get her out of here soon enough to suit him.

Colt chafed impatiently while he waited in the center of the village for Sam and Laura to appear. His wits sharpened when the two women emerged from the tipi and were met by Black Bear, who escorted them to where Colt stood. Once again Colt was struck by Sam's beauty, vividly recalling how she had been in his arms last night, all response and feeling, fire and ice, and how he enjoyed making love to her. Christ, she was wild in bed. A touch was all it took to set her on fire. Vaguely he wondered if she would have acted the same with Brave Eagle had the Comanche won the right to wed and bed her. The thought set his teeth on edge.

Soon they were mounted and ready to ride. Colt still found it difficult to believe he was riding out of the Comanche camp with his skin intact and both Sam and Laura in tow. He had fully expected to fight Long Bow for Laura, but Black Bear had convinced the warrior to look elsewhere for a wife, freeing Laura to leave with him despite her vigorous objections. To compensate for his loss, Long Bow was appointed a chieftain and promised another bride equally as beautiful.

In the years Laura lived with the Comanches she had become thoroughly Indian, even down to the walnut stain used to dye the golden hair he remembered so well. That practice would stop immediately, Colt decided with firm resolve. Already he could see hints of lustrous gold mingling with inky strands and wondered how long it would take to bring it back to its natural color.

Though he yearned to dig his spurs into Thunder's sleek flanks, Colt deliberately refrained. Sweat poured down the inside of his collar, his body tense, waiting for the cry indicating the savages had changed their minds. Only when they were out of sight of the village did his breathing return to normal and he hastened their pace.

They rode in silence for hours. Both women were grateful when Colt finally called a halt by a stream so they might rest and water their horses. Taut silence reigned as they refreshed themselves and ate a meal of pemmican and parched corn. After Colt drank his fill he sat on the ground resting against a tree, regarding Laura with tenderness as well as a good bit of frustration.

"I know you're unhappy now, Laura, but in time you'll come to appreciate Black Bear's decision. Black Bear is wise," Colt allowed grudgingly. "He did the right thing. Do you seriously believe you could be happy married to a savage?"

Laura bristled, taking exception to Colt's choice of words. "Long Bow is no savage. He is a brave and courageous man and has proven his prowess many times over. I doubt there is a white man to compare with him."

"Christ, Laura, you sicken me with your continual praise of the same savages who killed our parents," Colt exploded angrily. "You should hate them as much as I do."

"Black Bear wasn't responsible for our parents' death," refuted Laura tearfully. "It was a raiding party of renegade Comanches."

"Comanches are all alike," glowered Colt, deliberately avoiding the more colorful language he normally employed when speaking of Comanches.

Laura glared at him with stricken eyes, leaped to her feet, and stalked off toward the woods.

"Don't wander too far," Colt called after her departing back. "We'll be leavin' soon."

"Damn your ornery hide, Colt!" Sam hissed furiously. "Leave the girl alone. Can't you see she needs time to adjust to the change in her life? She's still as much an Indian as . . ."

". . . You are," Colt finished disparagingly.

"You can treat me as vilely as you please if you feel the need to strike out at someone, I can take it,"

Sam retorted tartly. "Laura is too vulnerable and open to hurt to take your needling. Let her grow accustomed to you slowly."

"Maybe you're right," Colt allowed, eyeing her sourly. "Laura is white, she'll come around soon enough."

"Colt," Sam ventured, hesitant to broach the subject yet anxious to settle things between them. "What happens now?" Her words brought a puzzled frown to Colt's face. "With us, I mean. Are you going to hold that ridiculous robbery charge over my head or am I free to leave with Will?"

"You call robbery a ridiculous charge?" Colt demanded. "Men have hung for less. Have you forgotten our 'marriage'?"

"Marriage!" snapped Sam, dismayed. "Surely you don't mean to hold me to those vows. They were Indian rites, hardly binding, and you know it."

"But you're Indian, Violet Eyes, or so I've been told. Don't you consider them bindin'?"

"Me?" Sam squeaked. "Of . . . course not." Colt noted the slight hesitation in her voice, and a slow smile settled over his harsh features.

Sam wasn't certain what she believed. Spirit Dancer's words at the joining ceremony had as much meaning to her as if a preacher had married her and Colt. "I know you hate Indians, Colt, and I couldn't live with a man who considered me less than human because of my mixed blood."

Colt's tawny eyes darkened with an emotion Sam found difficult to decipher. "I never thought the day would come when I'd desire an Indian squaw like I do you," he admitted. His anger was directed not only at her but at himself. "Christ! I can't remember when I've loved a woman so thoroughly, or received so much satisfaction in return. I didn't think it possible to—I've hated Indians for so long—What I'm tryin' to say is that makin' love to a half-breed isn't as repulsive as I reckoned."

"Damn you, Colt! You're a cold-blooded polecat with no heart and even less scruples. A braying ass has more brains than you do. Nothing could convince me to stay with you. If you need a whore, go see Dolly Douglas."

She turned away, sickened. Colt leaped to his feet, his hurting grasp on her arm stopping her in her tracks. "You're goin' nowhere till I say so, Violet Eyes. You're stayin' at the ranch with Will and Laura. Your brother needs some stability in his life right now, and so does my sister. I doubt if I could keep Laura with me if you weren't around. She's grown to depend on you in the short time she's known you. Besides," he added, a slow grin curving his lips, "I still want you despite—everythin'." His tawny eyes turned a dark, smoldering gold, and Sam fought the surge of hot desire his look evoked.

Colt did not miss the expression that passed over Sam's face. It spoke eloquently of the passion they shared, of the response she could not deny. He pressed forward, his intention all too apparent, when Laura stepped into view.

"Hell's bells," Colt muttered beneath his breath. "Mount up. We've wasted too much time already."

That night Sam was careful to make her bed next to Laura's. Though Colt offered no objection, he bent her an austere look before placing his own bedroll a short ways apart from theirs. As long as he kept his distance, Sam reasoned, she could resist him. But if he decided he wanted her and used his considerable power over her, she was lost.

Several days later Sam recognized landmarks indicating they were on Howard property. No—not Howard property, she thought bitterly, Colter property. During their long days and night of travel, she and Laura maintained their close friendship while Colt became more sullen and withdrawn. Sam assumed it was due partly to Laura's lack of acceptance of her brother and the white world. She failed to recognize the primary reason for Colt's moodiness—her own remoteness and lack of response while he still desired her desperately.

Jake saw them first. He was working near the corral when he spotted three riders approaching the house. His hand poised above his six-shooter, he waited until they were close enough to recognize before relaxing his guard. Then he took off running, waving and shouting to alert the others. Hearing the commotion, Will came rushing from the bunkhouse, his face wreathed in smiles when he saw Sam.

Sam slid from her horse, holding her arms wide as Will ran into them, hugging her tightly. "I knew Colt would find you, Sam, I just knew it!"

Sam realized that after today Colt would be a hero in her brother's eyes and didn't know if she liked that or not.

Colt and Jake exchanged meaningful glances and a hearty round of back slapping. Then Jake hugged

Sam fiercely. At length he noticed Laura standing quietly at Colt's side. "What's with the squaw? Is she some kind of hostage?"

Colt bent Jake a warning look that the foreman found confusing. Grasping Laura's hand tightly, Colt pulled her forward. "Jake, this is my sister Laura."

Dismay marched across Jake's face, quickly followed by delight. "Sweet lovin' Jesus, you found her! Only you could go after one woman stolen by Indians and bring back two. Amazin', simply amazin'. Welcome back, Laura. Your brother's been lookin' for you as long as I've known him."

Will approached Laura hesitantly, smiling shyly. He offered a hand in welcome. "I . . . I hope you'll be happy here. Colt owns the ranch now, but it was ours, mine and Sam's, once."

Laura looked confused. "Violet Eyes didn't tell me that."

"Violet Eyes!" The words exploded from Jake and Will at the same time.

"It's the name the Comanches gave me," Sam remarked apprehensively. She looked helplessly at Colt, hoping he wouldn't mention her Indian ancestry until she had time to prepare Will.

Colt correctly interpreted the plea in Sam's eyes and decided it would serve no purpose to tell Will his sister was born of a different mother, an Indian one at that. It was best left to Sam to choose an appropriate time to tell him. Laura sensed Sam's reluctance to reveal her Indian heritage at this time and also remained silent.

"Those dirty savages didn't hurt you, did they, Sam?" Will asked anxiously.

Sam saw Laura stiffen and decided to have a talk with her brother as soon as possible. It wouldn't do to have him offend Laura with his disparaging remarks.

"Do I look harmed? Thanks to Laura, I was well treated. She was adopted by Chief Black Bear and lived all these years as his daughter."

"Knowin' Injuns, it's hard to believe they let you go without a fight," Jake said thoughtfully. "Comanches aren't usually so obligin'."

"Colt did fight," Sam revealed. "He fought with Brave Eagle and won."

"Brave Eagle?" Jake questioned.

"My brother," Laura returned.

Jake quirked an eyebrow in Colt's direction, noting the pained expression distorting his features.

"Laura's *adopted* brother," Colt corrected, holding his temper under rigid control. "The man Sam would have married if I hadn't turned up when I did."

"That must of been one helluva fight," Jake remarked, whistling. For the first time he took a long, hard look at Laura. At first glance she gave the appearance of being thoroughly Indian, but closer observation revealed that she hadn't one Indian feature. He could see traces of gold amidst dark strands of braided hair and realized it must have been dyed black with walnut stain. Though her skin was darkly tanned, it lacked the red tint distinctive to the race. In fact, with her dark hair arranged in braids, Sam looked more Indian than Laura.

Beneath the doeskin dress Laura's petite figure appeared distractingly feminine. Somewhere around twenty years old, Jake reckoned. He thought

Colt's sister lovely and wondered how she would look in a becoming dress with her hair combed out and restored to its own natural blond. He was astute enough to realize it wasn't going to be easy for the girl to adjust to a world she had forgotten long ago. He sensed her confusion, her fear, her unwillingness to leave her Indian family, and his heart went out to her.

Reluctantly pulling his eyes away from Laura's bowed head, Jake turned his attention to Sam. "It's good to have you back, Sam. You gave us all a good scare."

"I missed all of you," Sam said, swallowing the lump forming in her throat.

"Is it true that Brave Eagle wanted you for his wife?"

"I . . . yes," Sam admitted, flushing. "But as you can see, everything turned out just fine."

"Take Laura inside, Sam," Colt ordered, scowling. The look Jake bestowed on Sam was so filled with concern and caring that Colt felt a slow anger building inside him.

Slanting Colt a venomous glance, Sam took Laura by the hand. "Come on, Laura. I'll show you the house. You can have Will's room. He seems happy enough bunking with the ranch hands."

Will readily agreed, and the three men watched silently as the women disappeared into the house. Then Jake dispatched Will on an errand and turned to Colt, his brows raised in question. "What really happened in that Indian village, boss? You were gone so long we talked about sendin' out a search party."

"My search took me north into Kiowa Territory.

It seems the tribe that killed my parents and took Laura traded her to Black Bear, who then adopted her. Findin' Sam and Laura together was somethin' I never expected."

"What about Sam and this Brave Eagle she was supposed to marry? Was she mistreated? She looks well enough."

"Brave Eagle wanted Sam," Colt said succinctly.

"Why do I get the feelin' there's more to it than that?"

"Because there is." Colt's face revealed an emotion Jake had never before seen in his friend. Then Colt proceeded to tell Jake everything that happened in Black Bear's village. Jake's eyes grew wide as secrets he would never have guessed at were revealed to him.

"Jesus! It's hard to believe Sam is part Comanche. I . . . I don't know what to say." Then he turned thoughtful, sliding Colt a sly look. "So you two are married."

"Married, hell!" Colt thundered. "I don't hold with heathenish rites. Besides, you know how I feel about red savages."

"Dammit, Colt, Sam is no savage! She's a beautiful, intelligent woman. Her father is a white man. You have no cause to treat her so disrespectfully."

"Are you sayin' I should honor this forced Indian marriage? You and I know it's not legal. So does Sam."

"I'm not tryin' to run your life, but we've been friends a long time. Somehow I got the idea you were fond of Sam."

"I . . . was, Jake," Colt admitted, wishing Jake would stop badgering him. How he treated Sam and what he intended to do about their stormy relationship was his business. For the time being he needed her for Laura's sake—or so he tried to tell himself. Later, once his enlistment expired and he returned to the ranch, he'd decide what to do about Sam.

"I don't mean to interfere, boss," Jake admitted wryly, "but I won't allow you to hurt Sam. Her mixed blood makes no difference to me. I don't reckon it will to Will, either, when he finds out."

"Sam is my concern, Jake," Colt returned possessively. "Keep away from her and let me deal with her in my own way."

Jake shot Colt a reproving glance before turning abruptly on his heel and stomping away.

Chapter Fourteen

It's . . . very nice," Laura stammered, her eyes wide as she surveyed her surroundings.

"It's been my home for as long as I can remember," Sam said wistfully. "I hope you'll be happy here."

"You're not leaving?" Laura exclaimed, suddenly frightened. "Please, Violet Eyes, this is your home. You're Steve's wife. You belong here more than I do."

"Colt has no intention of honoring a marriage legal only to Comanches. He hates what I am. He never wanted a wife. He wants me here only for your sake. But one day, Laura, Will and I have to leave. It's inevitable. We no longer belong on the ranch."

"I don't understand my brother. Can't he see how much you care for him? If you leave, so will I," she declared staunchly.

Sam mulled over Laura's words for several tense minutes. Laura was white and belonged with her brother, not the Comanches. All she needed was time to adjust to her surroundings and circumstances. Intuitively Sam realized that Laura depended on her for support and friendship, and she couldn't leave her, not yet. One day she'd depart, but not until Laura was better able to cope with her new life. She owed Colt a great deal for rescuing her. One way of repaying him was to remain at the ranch until Laura grew accustomed to the changes in her life.

"I'll stick around a while," Sam allowed grudgingly. "Until you no longer need me."

"I'll always need you, Violet Eyes. You're my friend."

Tears moistened Sam's eyes. "And you're my friend, Laura. But I reckon you should call me Sam. Now come along, I'll show you your room."

It was already dark when Colt entered the house. He was surprised to find Laura standing by the window staring forlornly into the blackness. She looked lonely, bereft, and completely lost.

"Where's Sam?"

"In bed," Laura replied. "It's been a long day and these past weeks have been difficult for her."

"Why aren't you in bed?"

"I . . . I want to talk to you. We really haven't had much of a chance, you know."

Immediately Colt's face softened, the lines around his mouth curving into a tender smile. His little sister was all the family he had left in the world and the one person worthy of his unqualified love. If she was finally willing to open up to him, he was ready to listen. He settled an arm around her shoulders and led her to a chair, hunkering down beside her.

"What is it, honey? What do you want to tell me?"

"Is it all right to call you Colt? Somehow Steve no longer seems appropriate. You aren't the Steve I knew long ago."

Colt nodded. He would have agreed to anything to preserve their tentative new beginning. "Sure, honey, call me whatever you're comfortable with. I'm here to listen."

Still somewhat in awe of the tall, powerful man Colt had become, Laura said, "I want to talk about Violet—I mean, Sam."

Colt stiffened. "What about Sam?" Sam was the last person in the world he wanted to discuss. Especially with Laura.

"She's your wife, why do you treat her so badly? Brave Eagle loved her. My brother would have—"

"*I'm* your brother!" Colt barked, trying to control his temper. "You're smart enough to know that Indian customs mean nothin' to white men."

"What will become of Sam? You've already taken her land."

"Did she tell you that?"

"She told me some things but not everything. I don't want her to leave, Colt. She will if you continue to act in such a disgraceful manner toward her. Must your hatred for Indians blind you to your own feelings?"

"I know my own mind, honey. The same blood flows through Sam's veins as the savages that killed our parents. One day, after Black Bear's influence is gone and your life is back to normal, you'll come to understand how I feel."

Laura shook her head in vigorous denial. "No, Colt, you're wrong, about many things. Sam and her brother will leave once you're gone. You can't keep her here against her will."

"Did Sam tell you she meant to leave?" Colt demanded.

"She said she'd leave when I no longer needed her. She's your wife, Colt, can't you stop her?"

Intuitively Colt realized his threat to turn Sam and Will over to the law no longer served as a valid reason to keep her under his thumb. He had procrastinated, threatened, and cajoled too many times in the past for Sam to take him seriously now. Obviously, if he meant to put her in jail he would have done so long ago. And Sam was smart enough to realize it.

"Sam's not goin' anywhere," he said with a determination that secretly pleased Laura. "She belongs here. This is her home."

He'd do anything within reason to keep Sam, Colt realized, startled by the intensity of his feelings. If Sam left he'd lose Laura, and he couldn't bear that. Not when he'd just found her. Ten years! Ten long, frustrating years he'd searched for his sister and he'd be damned if he'd have her rushing back to her adopted family at the first opportunity. Colt fully intended to make his home on the Circle H once his enlistment expired, and if Sam was the key to keeping his sister happy, then it was imperative Sam remain. He tried and failed to make himself believe that was the only reason he needed Sam.

Laura smiled an amused smile. "Do you realize what you just said?"

Colt nodded slowly, suddenly realizing he had just admitted he wanted to keep Sam with him forever. "Go to bed, honey, it's late. I'll see you tomorrow."

"I . . . could I ask a favor?"

"Anythin'." Colt grinned, elated at the strides they'd made tonight. At least they were talking like kin instead of strangers.

"I want to sleep outside tonight. Under the stars. This is all so strange—the house, the bed. Give me time, brother. With Sam here to guide me I'm sure I'll adjust in time."

Brother! Laura called him brother. Did she know how badly it had hurt to have her constantly refer to Brave Eagle as brother? Perhaps things weren't as hopeless as he previously thought. But one thing became increasingly evident. Laura's willingness to adjust as well as her happiness depended on Sam. He let that thought roll around in his head before replying.

"Okay, honey, sleep outside if you reckon it will help," he said, lacking the heart to deny her anything. He'd warn the hands before he retired and have Jake make damn certain she wasn't bothered.

Sam struggled with sleep, so elusive and disturbed by dreams and images it was difficult to judge where fantasies ended and reality began. From somewhere out of her deepest longing Colt appeared beside her, a lamp held aloft in one hand. Her eyes ran over the incredible, sensual length of him, from his chin with its day's growth of beard, over the rich outline of chest and shoulders straining against the fabric of his buckskin shirt, down long lean hips and thighs, pausing a breathless moment on the bold proof of his masculinity. Her eyes lifted from their avid contemplation of him to find him studying her with wry amusement. Warmth penetrated her body, winding its way around her heart, consuming her soul.

Carefully placing the lamp on the night table, Colt's gaze went over her hungrily. He knew a gut-wrenching longing to claim her tremulous lips and devour their sweetness. He wanted to probe the honeyed depths of her mouth and feel her return his kiss full measure. With a will of their own his hands reached out to touch her soft, full breasts and he longed to weigh their softness in his palms. He wanted to—The profoundness of his need jarred him.

Sam knew she was dreaming, had no doubt she had conjured Colt up from her erotic fantasies. Although the hands that explored her body intimately felt like flesh and blood, she knew that Colt wouldn't dare come to her room with Laura in the house. Then her drugged thoughts scattered as her fantasy lover captured her lips, his kiss firing her passion as his tongue slipped between her teeth into the moist cavern of her mouth. His kiss was forceful, demanding a response as one of his big hands stole under her nightgown to fondle her between her legs, moving slowly, insidiously higher and higher.

Surrounded in a misty haze, Sam encouraged the shadowy form crouched above her, reaching out to stroke broad shoulders that somehow had lost their buckskin covering. The flesh beneath her fingertips was warm, vital, pulsing with life. The muscles flexed and jerked as her lips tasted the slight saltiness of his skin.

She breathed in the special scent of him, a clean woodsy aroma blended with the pungent fragrance of soap. Though Sam knew he was but a figment of her imagination, the proud arrogance of his dark features loomed bigger than life before her. She loved the confident way he carried himself, the bronze perfection of his rugged form, the way his tawny eyes glowed when he made love to her. She sighed happily, imagining for a moment that this incredible man was hers.

"I love you," she whispered to the phantom who could neither hear or speak.

In dreams anything was possible. She could delude herself into thinking Colt had tender feelings for her instead of considering her merely a possession. If Colt were truly in the room with her she would never admit to loving him, knowing the contempt he felt for her.

His voice was deep and rich, and it went over her like a velvet caress, stoking the already fiery desire she was experiencing. "Do you mean that, Violet Eyes, or are you dreamin'?"

Colt was shocked but immensely pleased by the way Sam welcomed him to her bed. He had expected fierce resistance but found her soft and accepting in his arms. He hadn't planned things this way, but when he returned to the house for the night an unexplained force drove him to Sam's room. And once he saw her there was no turning back.

The single lamp cast its golden glow on Sam's sleeping form. Tiny gasps escaped her lips, and her movements were so erotic that all thoughts of leaving fled. Flinging off his shirt and stretching out beside her, Colt assumed she was awake when her hands discovered his chest and her lips tasted his flesh. For some reason those three words she uttered sent his senses reeling.

As she tottered on the fringes of awareness, Sam's eyes widened, suddenly aware that the warm weight pressing her down into the softness of the mattress was no fantasy. Confused, groggy, her senses drugged, Sam wrongly assumed she was back in Black Bear's village where she was known as Violet Eyes. Her next grave mistake was thinking it was Brave Eagle who had just spoken her name—her Indian name.

"Brave Eagle?"

"Christ! Do you think I'm that damn Comanche?" Colt spat disgustedly. "Is he the man you love?"

"Colt? I . . . you called me Violet Eyes. I . . . thought . . ."

"You thought it was that savage makin' love to you. Sorry to disappoint you."

She looked up at him, arrested. "What are you doing in my room?"

"It's obvious, isn't it? I want you."

"I don't want you! Leave me alone."

"Your body wants me." Colt smiled with slow relish. "It's been so long, Sam, you need me as much as I need you."

"I don't need you at all."

"Who do you love, Violet Eyes?" he taunted, reminding her of her careless words. "Did you fall in love with Brave Eagle? Did he bed you?"

"Please, Colt, don't torment me."

"I wouldn't do that, Violet Eyes. I want to love you. Chief Black Bear would be the first to remind you of your wifely duty." His tone was light and teasing.

She formed a scathing retort, but it died in her throat as his mouth slanted across hers in a fiery kiss that left her breathless. Just when she thought she would suffocate, his lips drifted down her cheek to the hollow at the base of her neck, then back to her mouth. He cursed when her nightgown prevented him access to her breasts. His breath warm in her mouth, he tore at her single garment, baring her in seconds, then stripped off his boots and pants, as frantic for her as she was for him. She felt the heat of his skin, the abrasion of his body hair as he settled on top of her, thrusting one knee between her thighs.

Sam gasped when Colt's open mouth found the peak of one breast. His tongue teased the nipple, then sucked greedily upon the tender flesh. His hands slid down her belly, molding her hips, her buttocks, then sought a deeper warmth.

Sam thought she would never be able to bear the swirling torrent of fiery need that stirred deep within her the moment he began his loving torment. She knew she should resist, willed herself to hold back her response, but Colt was an unstoppable force, driven by incredible passion. He was a mass of sinewed strength—a powerful, imposing creature, half-man, half-beast. He was a cunning, calculating male who had learned to survive by his wits, and she was powerless against his imposing will.

There was no logic in the kind of passion Colt evoked in her. It was raw emotion, so fierce and potent that nothing could contain it. She made a half-hearted attempt to resist but gave up when one earth-shattering sensation of rapture piled atop another.

"Do you want me to stop, Violet Eyes?" Colt rasped, his tawny eyes dark with desire.

"Hellfire and damnation! No!" Sam flung back, clutching desperately at his broad shoulders and moaning in sweet torment. "Love me, Colt. Love me for all the empty tomorrows when I'm nothing to you but a vague memory."

Colt would have challenged her words if he hadn't been too caught up in the moment for coherent speech.

The aching between Sam's legs built to a crescendo of need. She arched her hips against him and was impaled by his hard strength. A trembling sigh left her lips; her body a mass of tremors as Colt's sensuous mouth whispered over hers, coaxing her lips apart to taste deeply of his offering. He moved with easy grace, plunging, thrusting, withdrawing, setting her afire as sensation after sensation turned her into a living flame. She cried, she cursed, she begged Colt to release her, but he continued to toy with her senses until her own urgency drove him toward completion. His silken strokes created an inferno in her and Sam felt herself ready to explode.

Then she did, soaring to the heavens, lifting out of space and time into the star-studded universe. Colt's climax began almost simultaneously, his body trembling, his hoarse cry resounding loudly in the stillness of the night.

A profound contentment came over Sam as she floated back to earth, and she snuggled against the curve of Colt's body. If only—but the thought barely registered before she felt Colt stiffen beside her and turn away. "Colt? What is it?"

"Why do I forget everythin' 'cept the need to possess you when I'm with you? This terrible urge to fill my senses with the taste and smell of you is a weakness in my character I'm unfamiliar with."

"Can't you just accept our attraction for one another without rationalizing?"

Colt turned to face Sam, his tawny eyes glowing hotly. "I can accept the fact that I want to make love to you, Violet Eyes, and keep you close, but it's the reason for that need I question."

Colt's bald statement stunned Sam. What did it mean? Did he actually feel something for her besides sexual attraction? Something stronger than the contempt for that part of her that was Indian?

"I want you to stay here, Sam," he coaxed. "Stay and share the ranch with Laura."

"As your wife?" she challenged boldly.

"No . . . no, of course not," he quickly denied. "You know that's impossible, the way I feel about Indians."

"Will you expect to share my bed?"

Colt hesitated, eyeing her shrewdly. "I don't see why not. As long as it's what we both want. And if our couplin' tonight was any indication, I'd say you enjoyed it as much as I did."

"I won't be your whore, Colt. If that's what you think of me, there's no hope for any kind of relationship between us. No matter how badly Laura needs me, I won't remain here a moment longer than necessary. There will be no repeats of tonight."

Christ! Colt cursed beneath his breath. He didn't really think of Sam as a whore. He had been the first with her and was certain there had been no one else unless Brave Eagle had seduced her. Perversely, he wanted to keep her for himself where no other man could touch her. Did that make her his whore? Was there no cure for the terrible ache of wanting her with a passion bordering on desperation? What he needed was to sate himself with her golden flesh until he tired of her. Only then, Colt reasoned, would he be free of her.

"You don't mean that, darlin'," Colt murmured huskily, teasing her lips as he pinned her to the mattress. His mouth drifted downwards to capture a pouting nipple, and the magic began anew.

"Damn you, Colt!" Sam gasped, arching into his mouth. "So blasted sure of yourself, aren't you?"

"You're mine, darlin', for as long as I want you. Nothin' can deny this—" Her body jerked convulsively as his hands sought a deeper warmth, his fingers separating the petals of her womanhood to stroke the fires of her passion. "Or this—" Unerringly he found the velvet sheath, carefully inserting one finger, then another, thrusting, withdrawing, until Sam's ragged breathing and muffled cries sent his own passion rocketing. Then Sam felt the bold proof of his desire replace his fingers and she knew nothing but the spiraling shards of pleasure turning her body to ash and cinder.

Hazy wisps of mist hung lopsided in a sky streaked with mauve and scarlet when Laura returned to the house the next morning. Accustomed to rising at dawn to begin her numerous chores for the day, she had found it difficult to change habits overnight. Folding her bedroll neatly and placing it on the bed she had yet to sleep in, Laura wandered into the kitchen to begin preparations for breakfast. Selecting wood from the woodbin next to the cookstove Sam's father had purchased shortly before his death, Laura lit a fire and searched the cupboards for food. She was delighted with the staples on hand and set coffee to boil while she fried bacon and made biscuits.

When the coffee was done, Laura filled a cup with the fragrant brew and crossed to Sam's room, wanting to surprise her with her skill. Noiselessly she opened the door, so startled by the sight of Sam and Colt intimately entwined on the rumpled bed that the cup flew from her hand, nearly scalding her. Sam and Colt were nude, their bodies stirringly beautiful in the early morning light. A glowing smile curved the corners of Laura's mouth. Her brother might deny his feelings for Sam to himself but to no one else. It was obvious he cared deeply for his wife, and Laura hoped he would realize it before he lost her. Returning to the kitchen, she placed the food on the back of the stove to keep warm and went outside to wash up in the stream that rambled through the woods behind the house.

Colt jerked awake with a start, suddenly aware of

the sun stabbing his eyelids. Hell's bells! How could he sleep so late? Had Laura returned to the house yet? If so, he hoped she hadn't discovered him in Sam's bed. It would be difficult to explain to his sister why he found it necessary to sleep with Sam when he repeatedly denounced their Comanche marriage vows as heathen rites he had no intention of honoring.

There was no denying that his need for Sam overruled his scruples. It was a need so potent that he could take her again despite the fact he had made love to her repeatedly until the sky turned from black to dirty gray and exhaustion claimed them. Was there no way to break the spell she wove around his senses?"

Rising, Colt struggled into his pants with a haste born of guilt, grabbed up the rest of his discarded clothing, and spared a last glance at Sam's sleeping form before leaving the room. Seeing no one about, he finished dressing on his way out the front door and hastened to the bunkhouse to wash up and breakfast with the ranch hands.

Sam stretched lazily, a contented smile tilting the edges of her lips. Her body ached—but pleasantly so. She felt vaguely tired—yet glowingly refreshed. Then memory eroded the corners of her brain, intruding upon her feeling of happiness. She reached out to where the indentation and warmth of Colt's body still lingered, and breathed a sigh of relief to find he had already gone. After her wanton behavior last night she didn't want to face him yet.

A timid knock sounded on the door and Laura poked her head inside. Hastily Sam pulled a cover

over her nudeness. Laura appeared not to notice—
all Indian women slept nude.

Laura felt no qualms about intruding on Sam, for
she knew that Colt was gone. She had spied him
walking to the bunkhouse on her way back from the
stream. "I thought you'd like some coffee, Sam."

Sam flushed guiltily, thinking Laura's words a
mild rebuke for sleeping so late. "I didn't realize it
was so late," she replied sheepishly, reaching for
the coffee.

"You deserve to sleep after all you've been
through." Laura smiled.

"What!" Sam replied, startled. Was Laura referring to the sleepless night she had spent in Colt's
arms? Had she heard their rather vocal lovemaking?

Laura soon put Sam's worst fears to rest. "I slept
outside last night. It will take me some time to
adjust to sleeping in a bed."

"Oh," Sam said in a small voice, lowering her
gaze to hide her relief.

"Breakfast is cooked. When you're ready we'll eat
together."

"Is . . . is Colt . . . sleeping?"

"I saw him walking to the bunkhouse when I
returned from bathing."

"Oh," Sam said again. "I think I'll bathe first."

"Hurry, then, I'll wait."

Some time later, shaved, bathed, and dressed in
clean buckskins, Colt returned to the house. He
found the women in the kitchen.

"I'm leavin' for Karlsburg," he said, shifting his
gaze from Laura to Sam. "Can't say when I'll return.
I reckon Cap'n Ford has been in touch with Jim by

now with new orders. I'll get word to you if my orders take me out of town."

"Do you have to leave?" Laura asked.

"I've a job to do, honey. I'm a Texas Ranger. I go where I'm needed."

"Who is Jim?"

"Jim Blake, my partner. He's been in Karlsburg posin' as a hired gun hopin' to learn more about the Logans. I'm convinced they're behind most of the cattle rustlin' in the area."

"What do they hope to gain by it?" Sam asked, puzzled. "I know Vern Logan is a vile worm whose only thought is for his own skin, but why do he and his father want to ruin the ranchers?"

"Power and money," Colt explained. "They stand to make a fortune from the railroad. They want to be the most important men in Texas."

Sam chewed on that for a while before asking, "When will you return?" She could have bit her tongue for asking, but it was too late to take it back.

Colt's considering gaze flicked over Sam and a slow smile lit his dark features. "Why, will you miss me?"

"Hardly," Sam lied. "I just wanted you to know that I won't be here when you return."

A cry of dismay slipped past Laura's lips. Sam flung her a pitying look but stubbornly maintained her position, undaunted by Colt's fierce scowl.

"Laura, I'd like to speak with Sam privately before I leave." Though the words were addressed to his sister, his intimidating gaze never left Sam.

"Of course," Laura agreed with alacrity as she left through the back door.

"If you know what's good for you, you'll be here when I return," Colt warned ominously.

"What difference does it make to you? You don't care about me, so why try to keep me against my will?"

"I care about Laura and she needs you."

"What makes you so damn contrary?" Sam fumed angrily. "You admitted last night you needed me. Can't you care a little?"

Shoving his hat to the back of his head, Colt raked her slim figure suggestively. "You're a damn allurin' woman, darlin', despite your Comanche blood. Only a fool or a blind man would deny it, and I'm neither. I'm also no saint. A man takes his pleasure where he finds it. When I want someone or somethin', I take it. Last night I *did* need you."

"And now you don't," Sam stated flatly.

"Don't put words in my mouth. Just be here when I return."

"If I'm not? What then?" Sam challenged.

A sly smile quirked Colt's lips. "What if you're breedin', darlin'? Have you thought of that? How will you support a child?"

A baby! The thought had never occurred to her.

"After last night I reckon it's possible," he drawled.

His calm words sent Sam's temper soaring. "Damn your black heart to hell and back! I want nothing of yours. Including your baby. If I am breeding I'll find a way to get rid of it."

Colt's face paled and his hands balled into tight fists, making Sam sorry she had said such a terrible thing. Especially since she didn't mean it. She would love Colt's baby as dearly as she loved its father. But she dare not admit she cared for Colt and risk being laughed at.

"You'll do no such thing!" Colt thundered, his face mottled with rage.

"Let's say I am pregnant," allowed Sam quietly. "What then?"

If it was possible, Colt grew even paler. Was he prepared to accept a half-breed bastard? *Could* he accept one? Christ! How had his life become so damned complicated? A month ago he was concerned only with killing Indians and bringing outlaws to justice. Now he was saddled with a half-breed squaw who might be carrying his child. To complicate matters, he was bombarded with feelings for the little wildcat that might be construed as love had circumstances been different. Her being half Comanche had changed everything except his confounded need for her, and it would take more than Indian blood in her veins to quench the inferno of desire she inspired in him.

"I asked you a question, Colt," Sam repeated.

"I won't let you starve, if that's what you're hintin' at," he said evasively. Sam bent him an oblique look, prompting him to add, "If you're askin' for a commitment, forget it. I don't want a half-breed wife or . . ." His words faltered.

". . . half-breed bastard," Sam completed, flushing angrily. "Don't worry, this entire conversation is pointless anyway."

"How so?" Colt asked.

"You'll never know whether or not I'll have your child. I won't be here long enough for you to find out." Then she whirled on her heel and flounced out the door, leaving Colt fuming in impotent rage.

Colt fervently wished he could forget his duties for once and stay in one place long enough to tame the little hellion. Violet Eyes, bah! The Indians should have named her Wildcat or something in keeping with her fiery temperament. He had already told her what he expected of her, now all he could do was trust that Laura and Jake would keep her here until he returned. Colt knew Will loved the ranch and would resist any attempt to drag him away as long as he could.

Why couldn't he come to grips with his feelings for Sam? Colt asked himself glumly. Why couldn't he admit he never wanted her to leave him and tell her he'd love any children she gave him? He knew exactly why. In his mind's eye he could picture those same savages Sam claimed as relatives murdering his parents and carrying off his little sister, eventually turning her into one of them. Who could blame him for despising all Sam stood for and using her for his pleasure instead of offering her marriage as he might have done had things been different?

Chapter Fifteen

It was midnight when Colt admitted Jim Blake to his room above the Palace Saloon. The slim Ranger slipped inside, then turned to grasp Colt's shoulders.

"I saw you ride in today. Thank God you're safe. You were gone so long I was afraid somethin' happened to you. Did you get your woman back from the Indians? Is she all right?"

"If you're talkin' about Sam, she's back at the ranch," Colt replied crisply. "The Comanches took her into Kiowa Territory. We returned just yesterday. To make a long story short, Sam wasn't harmed."

"Sweet Jesus, you're a lucky bastard! Goin' alone into Injun country would have intimidated a lesser man. You're either very foolish or very brave."

"It's not the first time I traveled alone deep into

Indian territory. Have you forgotten all those years I spent searchin' for my sister? Not only did I live to tell of it, but my diligence finally paid off. I found both Sam and Laura in Black Bear's village."

"Sweet lovin' Jesus! You found your sister after all these years? I'm as pleased as a cowpoke on a Saturday night."

Colt grinned, Jim's enthusiasm heartwarming. "Enough of me, Jim, what's happened in my absence? Have the Logans tipped their hand yet? Have you managed to gain their confidence?"

Jim snorted derisively. "I'm in their employ but have yet to earn their trust. Their kind trusts no one, least of all a gun-totin' drifter. They purchased the Krebs ranch shortly after his cattle were run off by the Crowders and stolen by Comanches. The poor man couldn't raise enough cash to pay the note due at the bank. So far my duties have consisted merely of ridin' guard on the gold shipments between here and San Antonio."

"Have you talked to Cap'n Ford lately?"

"I saw him in San Antonio two days ago."

"What are his orders?"

"Mine are to remain in Karlsburg till I gather enough evidence to hang the Logans. Several ranchers swindled out of their land learned about the railroad and turned up at Ranger headquarters to register a complaint against the Logans. The ranchers accused them of employing illegal methods to cheat them out of their property but they've nothing on which to base their charges."

"What are my orders?"

"Still the Crowders," Jim revealed. "They've been

givin' ranchers down around Laredo a hard time. Cap'n Ford wants you to go down and investigate. 'Pears like they're rustlin' cattle and hightailin' it into Mexico to sell their stolen livestock. He suggests you leave immediately."

"Christ," muttered Colt crossly. He had hoped to remain in the area long enough to see Laura settled and happy. Now it looked as if everything would have to remain on hold until he was released from his Ranger duties. "Will you go out to the ranch and tell Jake what you've just told me? He'll know what to do in my absence. We've already discussed it. Tell Laura I'll try to keep in touch."

"Does everyone in Karlsburg still think your name is Colt Andrews?" Jim asked curiously.

"Yep, except for Sam, Jake, and Dolly Douglas, and I'd like to keep it that way for a spell."

"What about Sam?"

"What about her?" Colt asked sharply.

"Is there a . . . special message you'd like me to deliver?"

"What makes you think there should be?"

"C'mon, Colt, I've been with you a long time. When you go chasin' after a woman like you did Sam Howard, I know she's someone special to you."

Colt felt his body tense. Was he so transparent?

"The whole town is talkin' about Vern Logan and how he abandoned the girl to Injuns. They say you're a brave man to take off after her alone. The bastard never will live that down. Even his old man is furious with him."

"I'd do the same for any woman," Colt contended. "Sam is—merely a woman who—attracted me. You know me well enough to know I'm not ready to settle down."

Jim's eyes narrowed shrewdly. "What did you do, bed the girl and then tire of her? I'd be willin' to bet she was a virgin before you got hold of her." The slight stiffening he noted in Colt's spine told him he had struck pay dirt.

"Since when has it been your business to keep track of the women I bed?"

"Forget it, Colt, I didn't mean anythin' by it. Hell, we've been friends too long to let a woman come between us. I'll go out to the ranch and deliver your message. How soon you leavin'?"

"I'm headin' out at daybreak."

"Then I'll let you get some shuteye. Take care, you know where to reach me."

"Jim, much obliged."

Easing his big body down on the bed, Colt sighed wearily, aware that too few hours remained before the arrival of dawn. Stripped to the waist, his six-shooters positioned nearby, he punched a comfortable place in his pillow, then groaned in annoyance when a knock at his door disrupted his plans. Thinking it was Jim returning to tell him something he had forgotten, Colt bade him enter.

To Colt's dismay, Dolly Douglas stood poised in the doorway. He could hear evidence of late-night revelry wafting through the hallway behind her before she closed the door.

"I've missed you, Colt," she purred huskily. Without waiting for an invitation, Dolly glided toward the bed where Colt lay, undulating her hips seductively.

"I've got a demandin' job," Colt replied evasively.

"Is chasing little fillies over the countryside one of them?"

"If that little filly was stolen by Indians, it is. Did you want somethin', Dolly? I'm leavin' at daybreak and have had blessedly little sleep these past weeks."

"Was your mission successful? Did you find the Howard girl?"

"Yep," Colt said tersely. His succinct reply seemed to nettle Dolly.

"Damn, but you're a close-mouthed bastard," she muttered, disgruntled. "Sheriff Bauer told me more than you just did. The whole town knows how that cowardly Vern Logan ran off and left the girl to Injuns. I hope she wasn't harmed none."

Colt's expression softened. Dolly wasn't a bad sort. He'd trust her more than most women he knew. She was just too damn nosy. "Sam is fine, Dolly. I'm sure she'll appreciate your concern."

"I thought you might like some . . . company," Dolly suggested boldly, moistening her lips with the pink tip of her tongue.

"Some shuteye is what I need, Dolly," Colt replied.

Undaunted, Dolly leaned over to lightly stroke Colt's bronzed chest, her breasts all but spilling over the low-cut, vivid green satin dress she wore to perfection. Colt felt a familiar tightening in his loins, recalling the expertise with which Dolly plied her trade. He reached up to fondle the outer curve of a soft white mound and unconsciously compared it to Sam's golden-tinged flesh. For no apparent reason his hand dropped limply to his side, his body completely devoid of desire.

"Christ! That little hellion's turned me into a steer with no balls," he muttered beneath his breath.

"What did you say?"

"Nothin', nothin' at all."

Dolly's brow wrinkled as comprehension dawned. "It's the Howard girl, isn't it? You're hung up on her. I never thought I'd see the day Colt Colter would be tied in knots over a woman. Does she know you love her?"

"Damnation, Dolly, you're too perceptive for your own good," Colt grumbled irritably. "And nosy. I never said I loved anyone. You know I'm not hankerin' to settle down. Vamoose, woman, tomorrow's gonna be a long day."

Dolly eyed Colt curiously. "What's eating at you, Colt? We've known one another quite a spell now. Long enough for me to know when something is bothering you. Do you want to tell me about it? I assume it concerns Samantha Howard."

Colt remained silent for a long time, favoring Dolly with a speculative glance. At length he said, "I don't know how long I'll be gone, Dolly. If you really want to help you'll keep your ears and eyes open. I don't trust the Logans. If you see or hear anythin' of value tell Jim Blake."

"That gunslinger! He works for old man Logan."

"He's my partner, workin' undercover."

"Well I'll be hanged."

"I'm tellin' you 'cause I trust you. And 'cause I want you to do somethin' for me should I . . . fail to return." He drew an envelope from his shirt and lay at the foot of the bed. "A Ranger's life is precarious at best. Should somethin' unforeseen happen to me, give this to Sam." He had meant to give it to Jim but had forgotten.

"What is it?"

"The deed to the Circle H. It's rightfully hers anyway. There's also a will leavin' the balance of my estate to Laura."

"Your sister? But I thought . . ."

"I found her, Dolly, with Sam in the Indian village. She's stayin' out at the ranch with Sam."

"Sure, Colt, I'll see to it," Dolly said, accepting the envelope with a certain reluctance. "Anything else?"

"Nope. You're quite a woman, Dolly Douglas and I'm . . . sorry about . . ."

"Forget it, Colt." Dolly shrugged. "I hope things work out for you and Sam."

"Not likely," he muttered. But Dolly was already out the door and did not hear him.

Two days passed before Jim Blake found the opportunity to visit the ranch according to Colt's wishes. As it happened he had a legitimate reason to do so—one that satisfied his employers as well as served his own purpose. The same day that Colt left Karlsburg, Calvin Logan summoned Jim to his office. Vern sat across the room, puffing on a stogie.

"I've got a job for you, Blake," Calvin said. Immediately Jim's wits sharpened.

"Sure, boss, whatever you say," Jim agreed, trying not to sound too eager.

Vern smiled thinly. "As long as the price is right."

Calvin leveled a quelling look at his son before turning back to Blake. "I want you to get out to the Circle H and hire on as a ranch hand."

"What if they ain't hirin'?"

"Use your brains, man. Surely there's some skill you can impress them with," Vern snorted, earning himself another sharp rebuke from his father.

"Say I do get hired, what then?" Jim asked.

"Find out all you can about Steven Colter, the new owner," Calvin directed. "I want to know why he's never showed up after he bought the place and just how interested he is in keeping the ranch. If the foreman knows how to get in touch with Colter, I'd like to know. I want that ranch."

"Any particular reason?" Jim asked with deceptive innocence.

Calvin eyed him with a measure of distrust. "Just do as I say, you're being well paid to follow orders without asking questions."

"Sure thing, boss, you'll be hearin' from me soon." Jim rose to leave, only to be stopped when Vern jumped to his feet, placing a restraining hand on the Ranger's arm.

"One more thing, Blake. I want to know what's goin' on out there with Samantha Howard. I understand Ranger Andrews brought her back from Injun territory. Find out what shape she's in. Knowin' the Comanches, I reckon they made good use of her durin' the time she was their prisoner, if you get my meanin'. Serves her right, the little bitch," Vern spat. "She made me look like a coward. The whole damn town is laughin' at me. She could have been my wife and well fixed for life if she hadn't turned down my offer of marriage. She made a damn whore outta herself by beddin' that Ranger."

"That's enough, Vern," Calvin admonished sternly. "Blake isn't interested in your private life. Go on, Blake, keep in touch."

Shielding her eyes against the sun, Sam watched the lanky cowboy ride up toward the house. His hat was pulled low over his forehead, shading his face, and the six-shooters strapped to his slim waist and tied down around his thighs sent Sam's heart racing. Colt! Had he come back to tell her that he . . . he what? Certainly not that he loved her. Her pulse beat like a triphammer until she realized with keen disappointment that the man approaching was a stranger. She fidgeted nervously while he reined in before her and dismounted. Something about him made her rest her hand on the gun strapped to her own slim waist.

"Howdy, ma'am," Jim said, doffing his hat politely.

Eyeing his guns warily, Sam nodded, waiting for him to state his business. Suddenly Laura appeared at Sam's side, lending her support.

Jim's dark eyes slid from Sam to Laura, having no difficulty identifying Colt's sister. The dark one had to be Samantha Howard, the woman who had his friend going around in circles, and Jim could easily see why. Though Laura was a beautiful woman, Sam was stunning. Never had he seen eyes that particular shade of violet. He felt himself drawn into their mysterious depths, lost to an emotion totally foreign to him. Could it be he was experiencing some of the same magic she wove around Colt?

"What do you want?" Sam asked rudely when the stranger continued to stare at her with unabashed interest.

"Sorry, ma'am," Jim apologized, removing his hat. Rich brown hair gleamed darkly in the sunlight, momentarily distracting Sam. "I don't mean to be rude but it ain't often I see two beautiful women at one time."

Sam suppressed a smile but said nothing. "Are you the owner of this ranch?" Jim asked, feigning ignorance.

"No," Sam said tightly, refusing to elaborate.

"Then you're the lady of the house," Jim grinned cheekily.

"N . . . no, not exactly," Sam stuttered, flushing.

Laura came to her rescue. "What exactly is your business, Mr. . . ."

"Jim, Jim Blake, ma'am. I'm lookin' for work. I reckon a ranch this size can always use another hand."

"Are you from these parts, Mr. Blake?"

"Nope," Jim admitted. "Been travelin' some and decided to settle for a spell. This looks to be as good a place as any."

"You'll have to speak to the foreman, Mr. Blake," Sam advised. "He does the hiring around here in the owner's absence. And if I'm not mistaken, that's Jake riding in now."

Jake recognized Jim Blake instantly. Though Jake had never been a Ranger, they had met while fighting in the Mexican War. The three men had formed a lasting friendship. Jake knew Jim was in town, so he was not unduly surprised to see him.

"Jim!" he greeted, slapping him on the back, "you old cuss. Been wonderin' when you'd pay us a call."

"You two know each other? I . . . I thought you were a drifter," Sam said.

Laura echoed her sentiments.

Chuckling, Jake revealed, "Far from it. Jim is a Texas Ranger workin' with Colt. I know Colt trusts both of you, so I don't mind tellin' you all this."

"You're the partner Colt mentioned," Sam said, comprehension dawning. "Is Colt all right?"

Jim did not miss the note of anxiety in Sam's voice and was shocked at the twinge of jealousy he felt. "Colt's fine. He's on his way to Laredo."

"Laredo!" Sam repeated stupidly. "Colt's in Laredo?"

"He's been ordered to Laredo to investigate rumors that the Crowders are raidin' down by the border. He left before he could get back here and tell you about it."

"He went alone?" Laura asked, scandalized. "What are you doing here if Colt is in danger?"

"Colt can take care of himself." Jim smiled indulgently. "Besides, I'm still on assignment here in Karlsburg."

"What are you doing at the Circle H?" Sam demanded to know. She had a profound premonition that Colt was heading straight for trouble and wanted to know why his partner was safely tucked away in Karlsburg.

"Orders," Jim answered cryptically. "To all appearances I'm workin' for the Logans."

"Do they know you're here?" Jake asked anxiously.

"They sent me."

For some reason his eyes sought out Sam, finding himself enthralled with her dark, sultry looks. If he thought Colt truly had no interest in her he'd waste little time staking his own claim.

"The Logans seem determined to get their hands on this piece of land. They're payin' me to hire on as a ranch hand in order to learn all I can about the owner."

"Why?" Laura asked, bewildered. All this was still new to her.

"They're wantin' to buy the ranch so they can make a bundle off the railroad when it comes through. But they have no idea where to find the present owner," Jake revealed, his eyes softening as they lingered on Colt's sister. It was obvious to both Jim and Sam that the foreman held tender feelings for the petite blond.

"Exactly," concurred Jim. "I'm supposed to learn all I can and report my findin's to the Logans."

"Do you have evidence to connect the Logans with the Crowders?" Jake wondered.

"Nothin' but a gut feelin'. And a jury needs more evidence than that. I'm hopin' it will all bust wide open soon. Calvin Logan is a slick operator, but one day he'll slip up and the game will be over. He's ruined too many good men to get away scot free."

"Then I reckon I oughta find you a job to keep up appearances," Jake concluded. "C'mon, Jim, you can jaw at the ladies later."

"Join us for supper," Laura invited impulsively, surprising Sam. Immediately Laura regretted her rash invitation and looked to Sam for support.

Sam hesitated but a moment before adding her own approval. Why not? she reasoned. It's been dull around here these past days without Colt. "Yes, please do join us for supper tonight. It will give us a chance to put our cooking skills into practice. Jake and Will can come too. They're probably tired of Sanchez's cooking by now."

After that Jim and Jake ate their evening meal with Sam and Laura whenever possible. Will joined them when duties permitted, but mostly it was just the four of them. Recently Laura had admitted to Sam that she thought Jake a fine man, and obviously Jake felt more than mere friendship for Laura. More often than not Sam found herself alone with Jim while Laura and Jake wandered off by themselves. At first Sam felt uncomfortable, but after a while she began to relax in Jim's company, discovering an extraordinary man beneath the rough exterior. He reminded her a lot of Colt.

Soft-spoken, sensitive, kind, and gentle with the opposite sex, Jim was nothing like what she'd expect of a gunslinger. Not that he didn't look the part with his dark, brooding looks, tall, lithe form, and aura of danger about him. When fixed with his steely gaze, Sam could understand one's fear of the man. But to his friends he revealed none of the harshness of his nature that simmered just below the surface.

During their times together Sam learned that Jim and Colt had met during the Mexican War. Older than Colt by a few years, Jim was born in a covered wagon somewhere on the prairie between Illinois and Texas. His family eventually found their way to Fort Worth and settled on land north of the city. Unlike Colt's family who were slaughtered by Indians, Jim's folks prospered and now owned one of the largest spreads in Texas.

After the war Jim found it difficult to settle in one

place, and when Colt announced his intention of joining the Rangers, Jim quickly followed his friend into their ranks despite his father's protests. The elder Blake had high hopes of Jim taking over the Triple Bar Ranch. Jim's two sisters had married men with no inclination for ranching, and his parents waited, albeit impatiently, for Jim to give up his wild ways and shoulder his responsibilities. But Jim had no intention of settling down, until he met Samantha Howard. Barely two weeks had slipped past before Jim realized he was falling in love for the first time in his life.

"It's so nice out tonight, Laura, we oughta take advantage of it," Jake suggested hopefully. They had just finished supper and since the men had been out running down strays for the past week, it was the first meal they had shared since their return.

"I should help Sam with the dishes first," Laura replied with a shy smile.

"No need," Jim said with alacrity. "You two go on and enjoy the night. I'll help Sam with dishes."

"Yes, go on, you two," Sam urged, thinking how happy she'd be if Colt expressed the desire for her company. Needing no further urging, Laura gave Sam's hand a squeeze and left with Jake.

"There's no need for you to help, Jim, it will take me but a few minutes to do these dishes."

"I want to help, Sam. I like to be with you," Jim admitted somewhat sheepishly. "Haven't you caught on yet? I want you."

Jim's passionate confession nearly caused Sam to drop a plate. She stopped in mid-stride and turned to gape somewhat stupidly at the attractive man she had come to like and trust.

"No, Jim, you mustn't," she whispered as he stepped forward and grasped her arms just above the elbows. "Surely you know that Colt and I are—that we're—" The pained, constrictive words were jerked out of her.

"I know what happened between you and Colt, and it doesn't matter," Jim said tightly. "He took advantage of you. I've known Colt a long time and he always was a bastard where women were concerned."

"No!" Sam's eyes flew up, meeting Jim's probing gaze squarely. "It . . . wasn't like that."

Her words came to him on a breathless sigh, and suddenly Jim knew a moment of intense pain. "You love him." It was more of an accusation than a question.

Her silence provided the answer far better than any words she might have uttered. Jim's eyes narrowed and his mouth hardened.

"Jesus, Sam, don't you know how futile, how utterly misplaced your love is? I don't think Colt is capable of returnin' your love. He might be my best friend, but I hold no illusions about him and his dealin's with women. He attracts them in droves but allows no lastin' attachments. At first I thought you might be the woman to change all that but . . ." Not wishing to hurt Sam, he fell silent.

"But what?" Sam prodded, pain thudding through her body.

"Dammit, Sam, do you really want to know?"

Jim's obvious reluctance spurred her curiosity, but words weren't necessary to describe Colt's feelings for her. Sam knew he wanted her; that he enjoyed making love to her. She even conceded the fact that he might feel a certain possessiveness towards her, but not love. No, never love. He would never forget she was part Comanche or forgive her for the blood that ran through her veins—the same blood claimed by those savages who killed his parents. Colt was a man who harbored too much hate in his heart for love to take root and grow.

"There's nothing you can tell me that I don't already know," Sam said slowly, relieving Jim of the need to say things about his friend better left unsaid. "At one time there might have been a chance for me and Colt. But I recently learned something that killed whatever feeling Colt felt for me."

"I can't imagine what that could be." Jim frowned thoughtfully.

"Didn't he tell you?"

"Should he have?"

"I don't know—I thought— You may as well know the reason I've earned Colt's contempt. He discovered I was part Comanche."

"Jesus!" Jim rasped, stunned. But once her astounding disclosure sunk in, he noted all the subtle hints that pointed to her heritage. Golden skin, hair as black as a raven's wing, high cheekbones, and eyes tilting subtly upwards. She was so vital, so alive and beautiful it hurt to look at her. If the savage part of her offended Colt, that was his problem. As for himself, Jim reckoned there was not a part of Sam that didn't please him—including her Indian blood. Colt's loss was his gain, if he could persuade Sam to consider him seriously.

"I'm sorry, Sam, if bein' Comanche bothers you," Jim allowed. "Knowin' Colt's aversion for Indians, I can understand his . . . er . . . reluctance to continue your relationship. Perhaps now that you know how much I care for you you'll consider my proposal."

"At the moment it's impossible to think beyond the fact that I love Colt," Sam said dryly. "I've tried to forget him. Now that Laura no longer needs me, I'll be leaving."

"I need you, Sam," Jim insisted, drawing her into the circle of his arms. "My enlistment is up soon and I've been seriously thinkin' of settlin' down."

"Jim, please, I . . ."

"I'm offerin' marriage, Sam."

"But you hardly know me."

"I know that I love you."

"I have to think of Will."

"There's plenty of room on the Triple Bar Ranch for Will."

Unable to contain himself another minute with the object of his affection so close and attainable, Jim slipped his arms around Sam's supple waist, pressing her into the hard wall of his chest. Then abruptly his lips slanted over hers, sampling the sweet nectar she sought to withhold—but failed in the face of his perseverance. Before she succeeded in freeing herself, she felt the bold proof of his desire rising like a hot brand between them.

The kiss was pleasant but not earth-shattering like Colt's, prompting Sam to struggle free before Jim's ardor got out of hand. "I'm sorry, Jim, it just won't work," Sam persisted, backing away. "Whether Colt realizes it or not, I belong to him. Did he tell you we were married in an Indian ceremony?"

"Sweet Jesus!" Jim mouthed with suitable shock.

"We had little time for talk, but he mentioned no such thing to me. You must realize, of course, that the marriage is hardly legal."

"I'm not stupid, Jim. I know Colt was more or less forced to participate in the joining ritual. I have no false expectations where Colt is concerned. I took care of myself before and will do so again."

"If I have the story straight," Jim said with a lazy smile, "you were in trouble when you and Colt met."

Annoyed, Sam nodded. Of course Jim would know about that fiasco. "The money was returned," she snapped.

"I wasn't accusin' you, Sam," Jim returned. "I was tryin' to prove a point. It's difficult for a woman on her own."

"I have Will," Sam said stubbornly.

"A half-grown boy."

"Nevertheless, we'll manage."

"Marry me."

"I . . . can't. You'd better leave, Jim."

Disappointed but hardly defeated, Jim acquiesced. "The last thing I want to do is anger you. But don't think I've given up. If I thought Colt wanted you I'd back off gladly. But I've known him too long, been privy to the workin's of his mind too many years not to know that he neither wants nor deserves your love."

He left then, leaving Sam with an empty feeling in the pit of her stomach. Everything Jim said was true. And it hurt—hurt dreadfully. It stung to think that her Indian blood made her good enough to bed but not to wed. Perhaps she should consider Jim's proposal, Sam thought despondently. Soon everyone would know she was expecting Colt's child. Then what?

It had been nearly two months since their joining ceremony in Black Bear's camp, and there was still no sign of her monthly flow. Since the onset of brief bouts of morning sickness, Sam was convinced that Colt's seed had taken root in her womb on their wedding night. That's why it was imperative she leave the ranch before anyone found out. Though Colt didn't want her he'd feel obligated to support her and their child. But Sam didn't fancy being kept for that reason. She'd starve before accepting charity from a man who felt nothing for her but lust.

As the days sped by, Calvin Logan fumed over Jim Blake's lack of communication. Vern was the recipient of the lion's share of his anger.

"Dammit, Vern, what could that man be doing out there all this time?" Calvin raged as he paced his office. "Surely he's found out something by now."

"We shouldn't have hired the man without askin' more questions about his past," Vern acknowledged irritably. "I'da sworn he was a drifter on the run from the law, but looks are often deceivin'."

"We had no choice," Calvin growled crossly. "Once the Crowders left the area, we needed someone. Blake happened to be handy. But I certainly expected to hear from him before now."

"What are we gonna do, Daddy?"

"Nothing, for a day or two. If we still haven't heard from him by then, you ride out to the Circle H and arrange a meeting. Let him know we're not too happy with him. Time is running out. The railroad men will be here soon and I hate to lose the profit I could make on the Howard place. If things go my way I'll be rich beyond my wildest dreams."

Vern's brows drew together in a scowl. "What about me?"

"You're a disappointment to me, Vern," Calvin remarked hurtfully. "I want grandchildren and I won't get any as long as you keep fooling around with that whore over at the Palace. You lost Samantha Howard by playing coward. The whole town knows you for what you are."

"Would you prefer I lost my life because of that woman?"

"It might have been a blessing," Calvin muttered beneath his breath.

"Daddy!"

"Oh, hell, Vern, you're all I've got so it looks as if I'm stuck with you. Just don't disappoint me this time. Find out what's going on with Blake."

"Have you changed your mind about the will?" Vern asked hopefully.

Calvin eyed Vern with distaste. How could this spineless creature have sprung from his loins? "Bring home a suitable wife and give me a grandchild, then we'll talk about it."

"Do you still consider Samantha suitable after that Ranger bedded her?"

"I like the girl. She's got guts, something you lack. Besides, her indiscretion is no worse than your penchant for whores. Marry the chit and I'll not find fault with your choice."

Several days later Vern rode out to the Circle H, arriving some time after dark. His orders were to contact Blake under the cover of darkness and find out if the gunslinger had learned anything about the new owner.

Vern approached the bunkhouse cautiously, peering through one of the windows. The hands were seated around a long table making inroads in the piles of food Sanchez placed before them. Blake was not among their ranks. Disappointed, Vern slunk away, his gaze turning toward the house where soft light glowed invitingly through the windows.

His steps took him to the rear of the house. Suddenly the back door opened and Vern melted into the shadows when a couple stepped out into the soft, star-studded night. At first he thought it was Samantha, but moonbeams reflecting off long blond tresses revealed his mistake. He knew then it was the sister Andrews had recently rescued from the Comanches. Vaguely, he wondered what the woman was doing out here. The Ranger had left Karlsburg some weeks before, and Vern had naturally assumed his sister had accompanied him.

Hand in hand, the couple disappeared in the direction of the creek and Vern emerged from his concealment. The sound of voices drew him toward a window that looked into the parlor. Dismay settled over Vern's bland features when he saw Jim Blake seated next to Sam on the divan. Swallowing his shock, Vern concentrated on the words flowing between them.

Ever since Jim had declared his feelings for her, Sam had felt uncomfortable being alone with him. Luckily Jim had been too busy of late with ranch work to pursue her as he might have liked. But tonight everything conspired against her. One thing led to another and she soon found herself seated next to Jim in the parlor while Laura and Jake escaped out the back door, holding hands and giggling like children. Sam wanted to disappear in a wisp of smoke when Jim broached the very subject she wished to avoid.

"Have you thought any more about what we discussed the other day?" Jim asked, impaling her with eyes as black as midnight.

"Jim, I appreciate your asking but—"

"I want you for my wife, Sam."

Crouched outside the window Vern's gasp drew little attention.

"It's impossible."

"Because you love Colt?"

"That's part of it."

"Look, Sam, I'm Colt's best friend. We've been together for years. Through the Mexican War and now the Rangers. If I thought he wanted you for his wife, I'd bow out."

"A goddamned Texas Ranger," Vern muttered beneath his breath. Daddy's going to explode when he learns he hired a lawman, Vern thought as he withdrew from his uncomfortable position beneath the window. Blake's undercover activities told Vern things that neither he nor his father had been aware of. It told him that they were under suspicion and the Rangers were on to their illegal dealings. Perhaps even linked with the Crowders. Suddenly a devious smile lit Vern's features. He saw a way to redeem himself in his father's eyes and rid them of a traitor at the same time.

"You don't have to remind me that I'm nothing more to Colt than a convenience," Sam choked, the notion that Colt's feelings were widespread knowledge a knife-thrust in her heart.

"No!" Jim contradicted. "I'm sure it wasn't like that. I know Colt felt somethin' for you, he wouldn't use you for—well, he just wouldn't. What I meant is that he's not a marryin' man. Especially when—" His words skidded to a halt, afraid of immersing himself more deeply in hot water than he already was.

". . . especially when the woman in question is half Comanche," Sam saved him from saying. "It's getting late, Jim, you'd better leave."

They soon parted after one last plea from Jim exhorting Sam to seriously consider his proposal.

Thoughtfully leaving a lamp burning for Laura, Sam wandered into her bedroom, undressing almost immediately after the door closed behind her. She had gotten no further than her shirt when the stillness of the night was shattered by gunfire.

"Good God!" cried Sam, jerking her arms into her shirtsleeves and rushing from the room.

A terrible premonition turned her legs to rubber as she staggered outside. Heading toward the bunkhouse, she nearly tripped over a prone form sprawled in the dirt. Realizing at once what it was, Sam screamed. Suddenly she was surrounded by light and faces.

"Jesus, it's Blake!" someone shouted, holding a lamp high in the air. "Some bastard ambushed him."

"What is it?" This came from Jake who had just arrived with Laura in tow.

"Someone gunned down Blake, boss."

"Who saw it?"

All eyes swung to Sam. Shock suspended her senses, rendering her unable to move or speak. Jake had to shake her gently before reason returned.

"Sam, did you see who did this?"

"N . . . no," Sam stuttered, mesmerized by the pool of blood congealing beneath Jim's body. "Is he dead?"

"He's alive—barely." This came from a cowboy kneeling at Jim's side.

"Get him inside," Jake barked. "Easy does it. Someone get Sanchez, he has some experience with things like this."

"I'm here, Senor." Sanchez stepped forward, following on the heels of the men carrying Jim into the house. With stricken eyes Sam watched the lifeblood flow from Jim's body, somehow feeling responsible.

"What happened, Sam?" Will appeared beside Sam, lending her a supporting arm.

"I . . . I don't know," Sam quavered, still in shock. "Jim had just left the house when I heard the shot. Who would shoot him?"

"The man is a Ranger, Sam," Will said with keen perception. "He must have dozens of enemies." Of the ranch hands, only Will knew Jim's true identity.

Jim hovered on the brink of death, the bullet having lodged just inches below his heart. Crippled by age, Sanchez's hands shook too badly to attempt delicate surgery, so one of the men rode hell for leather into town for the doctor. In the meantime all Sam could do was stop the bleeding. When the doctor finally arrived, the bullet was removed successfully, but Jim was in grave danger of losing his life. It was now up to God whether Jim lived or died.

The doctor held out little hope that Jim would survive the fever that would surely strike, and before he left provided a vial of laudanum to keep him sedated and immobile. When the fever raged through Jim's body, Sam sat helplessly by, wringing her hands and praying. It was Laura who took things out of God's hands and into her own. Scouring the woods the next morning, Laura found the ingredients to brew an infusion of herbs according to her knowledge of Indian remedies, which she spooned with great patience into Jim's mouth. In a matter of hours the fever broke and a glimmer of hope rose in Sam's breast.

Chapter Sixteen

Much to everyone's surprise, Jim survived the odds and slowly but surely began to mend. He remained comatose for a week, then suddenly opened his eyes one day, managing a weak smile at Sam who, along with Laura, had been taking turns tending him. That day marked his steady but slow progress toward full recovery. Then something happened to send Sam's world plummeting.

Shortly after Jim regained his senses, a stranger arrived at the ranch. Covered with road dust, trail weary and clearly distressed, the man asked for Jim Blake. When informed Jim was gravely ill, the stranger became distraught.

"I gotta speak with Blake, ma'am," the man insisted grimly. "I'm carryin' a message . . . from a friend."

"I told you," Sam replied, equally determined,

"Jim is still very ill. Whoever you are you'll have to deal with me."

A flash of anger hardened the man's weathered features. "Beggin' your pardon, ma'am, but you're a woman. I need to speak with a man." Sam's implacable expression brought a curse to the man's lips. "Dammit, a man's life is at stake!"

Suddenly all Sam's senses came alive, each nerve ending tingling in warning. "A man's life?" she whispered, clutching at her throat. "What man? Please, tell me his name."

"As I mentioned before, you're—"

"It's Colt! Something has happened to Colt! Oh, God, he's dead."

"No, no, he ain't dead, but he will be if you don't let me talk to Blake. My name is Phil Smith, I'm a friend of Colt's. He's hurt, hurt bad. I figured Blake would know what to do. I'm afeared if Colt ain't seen to soon he'll die."

"What happened?" Sam choked out, dazed.

"The Crowders. Colt was ambushed near the Mexican border, shot and left for dead. It's a miracle he survived this long—if he's still alive."

"Has Colt been treated by a doctor in Laredo?" Sam asked with rising panic.

"There ain't no doctor in Laredo, ma'am. Not since old Doc Foley drank himself to death. I dug out the bullet but it looks bad. Colt told me all about his partner workin' in Karlsburg and I figured he'd know what to do. When I didn't find Blake in town I asked at the Palace Saloon, and the owner told me I might find him out here. Are you certain I can't talk to Blake?" Sam nodded, bereft of speech.

"After Colt was shot he kept callin' out for someone named Sam. Is he around? Mayhap I can talk to him. Seems like I recall Colt askin' for his wife. Do you know where I might find her? 'Pears to me a man oughta not die without kith or kin to give him comfort in his final hours."

A strangled cry escaped Sam's lips; lips that were suddenly bloodless. Colt die? No! He was too vital, too alive to die an ignominious death in some godforsaken town. "I'm Sam," she said at length. "I'm Colt's . . . wife. And I'm afraid if you tell your story to Jim Blake it will do more harm than good. He was shot several days ago and still isn't out of the woods. This kind of news will surely cause a relapse. Besides, he can help no one in his condition."

Lines of weariness etched Phil's face, making him appear much older than his forty-five years. "Then that's it," he said flatly, sagging in defeat. "I come all this way for nothin'."

"I won't let Colt die!" Sam raged determinedly. "Jim can't help, but I can. If you'll guide me, Mr. Smith, we can leave immediately." She was afraid to wait until Jake and the boys returned from the range, for Jake surely would go by himself and insist she remain home.

Phil Smith stared at Sam a full minute before reaching a decision. He had met Colt in Laredo under less than favorable circumstances, but against all odds they had become friends. A drifter and loner, Smith was about to have his neck stretched for cattle rustling when Colt stepped in to stop the hanging. Smith was guilty of many things, but this time it was a clear case of mistaken identity, which thankfully Colt had been able to prove. Smith had been mistakenly identified as one of the Crowders.

Eternally grateful, Smith had taken it upon himself to become Colt's guardian angel. When Colt failed to return to Laredo one day after a trip across the border to check on the Crowders, it was Smith who rode out in search of him. And Smith who found him near death on a lonely stretch of desert. When the ride back failed to do Colt in, and Smith's crude probing for the bullet did not kill him, Smith left him with Lola, a whore from the cantina. Then he set out for help, leaving enough money for Colt's care to last until his return. If Sam was indeed Colt's wife, then Phil reckoned she deserved to be with her husband at the end.

"I'll take you to your man, Miz Andrews," Smith said somewhat reluctantly.

"The bunkhouse is behind you, Mr. Smith, tell Sanchez to feed you. The ranch hands are branding strays today and won't be in till dark. I'll be ready in an hour if you feel up to traveling so soon."

"I'm game if you are," Phil returned, "but it ain't gonna be easy for a woman. I'll sleep in the saddle if need be. It's a far piece to Laredo, and Colt could be . . . well," he shrugged, "we won't know till we get there."

"I'll manage, Mr. Smith," Sam said tightly. And she would, no matter what it took.

"You can't mean to go alone with a complete stranger," Laura cried, distraught. It was bad enough learning about Colt, but discovering that Sam intended to leave without informing Jake, and with a man she knew nothing about, was too much. "The man could be lying. It could be a trap. Please, at least wait for Jake."

"There's no time, Laura. Colt needs me."

"Then I'm going with you," Laura insisted stubbornly.

"No, someone has to stay here to care for Jim," Sam contended. "I'll be all right, truly. I believe Mr. Smith is telling the truth. Colt's life might depend on my ability to reach him as quickly as possible. Please don't worry, Laura."

Sam was glad neither Laura nor Jim knew about the baby, for there would be the devil to pay.

Seeing that her words were having little effect on Sam and that she meant to go anyway, Laura produced several packets of medicinal herbs, which Sam carefully packed along with a few necessities in a saddlebag. Then Sam joined Smith at the remuda, where they selected horses for the trip. Smith's mount was so worn out he could not have lasted the return journey. Without telling Jim what she intended, and extracting a promise from Laura to keep him in bed at all costs, Sam rode out with Smith, heading directly south toward the border town of Laredo.

The journey took four days of hard riding; riding until Sam's backside was a mass of bruises and every bone in her body ached; riding until the insides of her thighs felt like raw meat. Through it all Smith remained a perfect gentleman, given his calling. He spoke in glowing terms of Colt, carefully omitting any mention of his own colorful past. Mostly, though, they rode in silence, each to their thoughts.

What would she do if she arrived too late? Sam worried despondently. No, she mustn't think about that. Wouldn't she feel it in her heart if Colt were already dead? Those times spent in his arms had been pure rapture. Whether Colt meant it to be that way or not, she found him to be a tender and considerate lover, careful to give her as much pleasure as she gave him. She often thought God meant for them to be together—until the truth about her mixed blood earned her Colt's contempt. Even then he still desired her, still seemed incapable of letting her go. It surprised Sam that Colt had told Smith he had a wife. Surely that meant he cared a little, didn't it?

But even if Colt hated her, Sam reflected, it made little difference, she would still rush to his aid. Her own love was strong enough for both of them.

During the long, exhausting days Sam thought often of the baby growing beneath her heart. Colt's baby. She loved it already though it was still a tiny being within her. It mattered little to Sam that Colt didn't want a child with her, for he would never know. Once she nursed him back to health she fully intended to disappear from his life. She had also come to a decision about Will. He was happy on the ranch, and Sam decided to allow him to remain. Eventually she'd communicate with Will but not tell him her whereabouts until he had grown up and could accept her as an unwed woman with a child. Marrying Jim would solve that problem but in so doing create others, and Sam rejected that solution immediately.

It was dusk when Sam and Smith rode into

Laredo. The dusty border town offered few amenities and Sam's thoughts of a hot bath to soothe her sore backside fled as Smith led her toward a small, dingy cantina located on the main thoroughfare.

"You left Colt in *this* place?" Sam asked, horrified.

"I had no choice, Miz Andrews," Smith apologized. "Colt took a room at the cantina when he arrived and there was nowhere else to take him. I was lucky to find Lola to look after him. Nearly all the women in Laredo are whores—beggin' your pardon, ma'am—and Lola is a mite cleaner than most. She promised to see to Colt's needs till I returned with help."

"Let's hurry, then, Mr. Smith," Sam urged, despairing of what she'd find. It was worse than she expected.

Colt lay on a tangled heap of dirty bed linen, the heat and stench nearly gagging Sam. He was naked and a blood-soaked bandage badly in need of changing covered his stomach. Flies buzzed around his head and angry red mosquito bites dotted his flesh. He lay so still that at first Sam feared he was dead, until the steady rise and fall of his chest instilled her with hope. He looked sadly neglected, and a foul curse left Smith's lips as Sam pushed through the door to kneel at Colt's side.

Sam's small cry of distress brought the first response from Colt she had noted since entering the tiny, airless room.

Colt's eyes cranked open, their normal golden depths muddy brown and glazed with fever. A parody of a smile curved one corner of his mouth into a grimace of pain as recognition lit his eyes. His cracked lips moved and Sam had to lower his head in order to hear his words.

"Violet Eyes."

A sob tore at Sam's throat when his lids slid shut again and a sigh slipped past his parched lips.

"Water, Mr. Smith, hurry!" Sam ordered crisply, immediately taking charge. "Plenty of hot water first and clean cloths, if there is such a thing in this den of filth. Then cold water, lots of it. I won't let Colt die. I won't!"

Six hours later Colt rested more comfortably on clean sheets, though he had stirred little during Sam's ministrations. She had washed Colt's sweat-soaked body with hot water, soaked off the blood-encrusted bandage, and thoroughly examined the ugly wound on the upper left side of his stomach. It appeared that no vital organs had been damaged, but the loss of blood had been considerable. The wound was a raw, gaping hole that needed tending immediately if Colt were to survive. His entire body burned with fever, and white pus oozed freely from his wound. It was obvious Lola had done little to earn the money Smith had left for Colt's care. Sam fully intended to give Lola a verbal lashing, but caring for Colt consumed all her time and energy.

With Smith holding down Colt's emaciated form, Sam replaced the filthy bandage, spread a healing salve provided by Laura, and wound a clean cloth around his torso, fastening it snugly in place. From somewhere Smith had produced clean sheets and together they changed the soiled linen. Then Sam painstakingly spooned an infusion of herbs, also provided by Laura to reduce the fever and combat infection. Afterwards Smith went to his own rest while Sam spent the night sponging Colt with cold water when his temperature rose dangerously and shooing away flies and mosquitos.

From the cantina came sounds of revelry, men's rauctous laughter and women's shrill voices raised in flirtatious invitation. A continual procession of footsteps echoed in the hallway as well as soft titters and gruff replies.

During the long night Sam had more than sufficient time to study Colt and fret over his deplorable condition. Had he been properly cared for from the beginning it might have made a world of difference in his recovery. His strong constitution and superb physical condition were probably what saved his life. He was so thin it was obvious little effort had been made to feed him. Serious loss of blood and infection had combined to lay waste his once magnificent body. His face was gaunt and white beneath the two-week growth of beard, contrasting sharply with the deep tan of his chest. His tawny mane of hair lay flat against his scalp, and the sharp angles of his cheeks stretched the skin taut across his face. He was still the handsomest man Sam had ever seen.

Sam prayed fervently that night for Colt's recovery, knowing it was still touch and go. Only a strong will to live could pull him through, she thought as she knelt at his bedside. Perhaps if she could get through to him . . . The thought was riveting and she acted on it immediately.

"Colt, don't die!" she begged, her voice ragged with emotion. "Please don't die. I need you. Our child needs you. Please live for our baby."

Did Colt hear her? Did he understand? Wanting to

believe, Sam thought he did for his thrashing ceased and his breathing became less ragged. Though Sam wasn't entirely certain Colt knew she was here, she hoped her words had helped.

From somewhere in the cantina Smith produced a plate of beans and tortillas for Sam's breakfast the next morning, along with a cup of strong steaming coffee. Though it didn't set too well on her delicate stomach, the food was nevertheless nourishing and somehow she managed to keep it down. It took more ingenuity to provide something suitable for Colt to eat. About noon Smith returned bearing a bowl of chicken broth, a not inconsiderable feat given the circumstances, and Sam patiently fed Colt nearly the whole bowlful before his throat refused to swallow the last drop. When he was once more resting comfortably, Sam finally succumbed to Smith's urging and accepted the offer of his room to sleep and refresh herself. Whatever Colt had done for the man, Sam reflected, he was being amply repaid by the man's loyalty.

After a bath and a change of clothes, Sam felt almost human again. Knowing that Smith would inform her of any change in Colt's condition, she collapsed on the bed and slid instantly into a deep, dreamless sleep.

The next day Lola made an appearance in Colt's room. Hips swaying seductively, shiny ebony hair tossed carelessly over bare shoulders the shade of deep gold, black eyes alert and snapping, she boldly entered the room to stare rudely at Sam.

"He told me he had a wife but I did not believe him," Lola stated, her pouting red lips accusing.

"Who are you?" Sam really didn't need to be told that the girl was Lola.

"I am Lola," the girl replied, moving to stand beside Colt. She appeared to be about Sam's age or younger.

Lola was outrageously beautiful with smooth tan skin the texture of velvet, slanting brows over almond-shaped eyes surrounded by thick black lashes, and provocative mouth. Her flirting eyes gave mute testimony to her calling. A knowing hardness reflected in those ebony orbs, and a cynical awareness lingered at the corners of her wide lips.

Sam's eyes narrowed dangerously. This was the woman who had allowed Colt to wallow in filth and neglect despite the fact she'd been amply paid to care for him. "Hellfire and damnation! How could you allow my husband to suffer under your careless tending?" she rounded on the beautiful Mexican. "I found him lying in his own filth. You deserve a beating and I just might give it to you."

Lola sniffed, one well-rounded bare shoulder lifting haughtily. "He's alive, isn't he? I did what I was paid to do. I could not neglect my . . . duties to care for your man."

Sam's look was vemonous, speaking eloquently of her contempt. "You wouldn't fare so well had I found Colt dead," she hissed.

"It *would* be a shame for such a virile animal to have his life ended in his prime. Such a macho man," Lola sighed lustily, casting greedy eyes on Colt.

A bolt of riveting pain shot through Sam. "Did you and Colt . . . did you . . ."

"He is a man," Lola's answer was short, her implication clear, "and I am a woman." She did not tell Sam that Colt had refused her, for no man had ever refused Lola.

"Yes, he is a man," Sam agreed, closing her eyes and insulating her heart against the hurt Lola's words evoked. "My man. Please leave, Lola, my husband needs rest."

"Of course, Senora," Lola agreed sweetly, too sweetly. "I am needed in the cantina anyway." Casting a long, lingering look at Colt's sheet-clad body, she quietly left the room, her breasts bouncing beneath her thin white camisa and generous hips setting her short red skirt awhirl about bare tan legs.

Three days later full awareness returned to Colt. He'd experienced brief intervals of lucidity before, but since that first day when he h d called Sam Violet Eyes he seemed not to recognize her. So it came as somewhat of a shock when she looked up from her inspection of his wound to find him regarding her with interest.

"What are you doin' here?" he croaked, moistening dry lips with the tip of his tongue. "Where am I?"

Sam's hand immediately went to Colt's forehead, noting with heartfelt relief that it was only moderately warm. "What's the last thing you remember?"

Colt's brow knitted in contemplation. At length he said, "I was trailin' the Crowders across the border, hopin' to find their hideout. They must have ambushed me. Came out of hidin' with guns blazin'. I remember bein' hit, then nothin' else. Am I back at the ranch?"

"You're in Laredo, in your room at the cantina."

Colt frowned. "How in the hell did you get here? For that matter, how did I get back to Laredo?"

"You can thank Phil Smith for that. He found you badly wounded and brought you back to town. He paid Lola to look after you and then took off to find Jim Blake. Dolly Douglas directed Phil to the ranch, where he told me his story. We left almost immediately."

"Thank God Jim is with you," Colt said, vastly relieved. "Where is he?"

Sam hesitated. "Jim isn't here. He was shot by an unknown assailant several days before Mr. Smith arrived. I . . . came alone."

"Christ! Is Jim dead?"

"He was well on his way to recovery when I left."

"I'll have his hide for allowin' you to come out here alone."

"Don't get your dander up, Colt, Mr. Smith was all the escort I needed."

"What about Jake?" persisted Colt. "I can't believe he'd let you ride through Indian territory with no one but Smith to protect you. What in the hell was he thinkin' of?"

Sam studied her fingernails with great interest. "No one but Laura knew I left with Mr. Smith. Jake and the ranch hands were branding mavericks, and I couldn't tell Jim because he was too ill to be disturbed."

Though still too weak to bestir himself, Colt found the strength to let loose a string of well-aimed oaths.

"Why are you so angry?" Sam wondered. "If I hadn't come you'd be dead. Lola's skills hardly lend themselves to nursing, and you weren't up to enjoying what she does best. Though she hinted you made good use of her while you were still able."

"Dammit, Sam, the whore is lying'. She—"

Just then the door opened and Smith stepped inside, bringing the conversation to an abrupt halt. A wide smile split his weathered face from ear to ear.

"Damn if your voice ain't music to my ears," Smith remarked. "You were more dead than alive when me and your missus arrived in Laredo. You can thank the little woman for pullin' you through. Truth to tell, I gave up all hope the minute I laid eyes on you. Yes sir, Colt, you're one lucky hombre."

"My . . . wife is extraordinarily talented," Colt said wryly, his voice beginning to fade after the exertion of talking with Sam.

"You ain't just flapping your jaws," Smith said, grinning cheekily. "And powerful beautiful."

Colt's eyebrows shot up a notch, but further conversation was delayed as weakness and exhaustion combined to plunge him once more into the healing world of slumber. He awoke later to find Sam still seated beside him, sponging him with cool water as darkness brought on a resurgence of the fever ravaging his body.

Each day brought Colt much closer to recovery. Finally Sam felt secure enough to leave him a few hours at a time, returning only to find him petulant and complaining of her neglect. Once she entered Colt's room to find Lola leaning over him, her camisa gaping open and her full breasts all but falling into his face.

"I was inquiring if there was anything I could do for Colt," Lola explained in a seductive whisper. "Anything," she stressed.

"Colt is hardly up to doing what you're suggesting," Sam bit out. "Vamoose. If my husband feels in need of a whore I'll certainly let you know, but I seriously doubt it will be anytime soon."

Indignant, Lola drew herself up, hissing a string of Spanish the meaning of which Sam could only guess at. She flounced out the door, leaving Sam immensely satisfied with herself.

"She was just tryin' to help," Colt remarked blandly. "She took care of me till you arrived."

"I'm well aware of *how* she took care of you," Sam snapped with ill-concealed rancor. "I reckon a randy goat like you made good use of her while you were able."

Sam's barb earned her a reproachful look. It rankled to admit he couldn't bring himself to bed Lola despite her blatant invitation. She had come to him on a night when thoughts of Sam's soft, yielding body and lush curves, responding to him, loving him, had driven him nearly crazy. At first he considered taking what she so brazenly offered, but in the end he sent her packing and it didn't sit well with the little puta. Now she was trying to make trouble between him and Sam.

Colt couldn't forget Sam; could only remember the sweet taste of her flesh, the smell of wildflowers he associated with her. And their explosive coming together. Like nothing he'd ever experienced before. Not in a million years could he forget those incredible violet eyes—or her Comanche blood.

He couldn't purge Sam from his mind no matter how hard he tried, no matter how many exciting women flaunted themselves before him. His biggest worry had been that Sam might leave the ranch before he returned. Then Lola had approached him, his mood dark and perverse. Surely, he thought, a woman as gorgeous, provocative, and experienced as Lola had the power to cure him of his all-consuming need for Sam—a woman whose Comanche blood made her an enemy. What transpired next proved to Colt beyond a reasonable doubt that only Sam was possessed with the power to move him. Using all her considerable skill, Lola tried desperately to coax Colt to her bed, but failed miserably.

Strangely, Colt felt as if he were cheating on someone he loved, though he thought himself crazy for refusing Lola, for whores as young and fresh as she were an exception. But Colt had spurned her generous offer. Did that mean he loved Sam? Did it really matter that Sam was a half-breed? Suddenly Colt became aware that Sam's remark still hung in the air between them, heavy and encompassing.

He wanted badly to dispense with the pretense they had erected between them, to toss aside the cloak of bitterness, but he had no idea how Sam felt about him after the deplorable way he had treated her and the terrible things he'd said to her. He wanted to tell her the truth about Lola. Yet some perverse demon within him made him say, "I'm no monk. We made no vows to one another."

Sam paled. Had Colt forgotten already the joining ceremony in Black Bear's village? Of course he had, Sam answered her own question. Because it meant nothing to him. She meant nothing to him, and neither would their child. "I have no right to question your actions. You're free to bed whoever you please as long as it isn't me." Then, noticing his trembling, which she attributed to weakness, Sam quietly left the room.

Later that day Sam had a violent row with Lola, and it shook her up more than she cared to admit. She stopped the woman from entering Colt's room and Lola loudly voiced her displeasure.

"Are you afraid I will take your man?" Lola challenged contemptuously. "Is that why you guard him so jealously?"

A slow anger built up inside Sam. "Colt is still too ill for visitors. Jealousy has nothing to do with it. If my husband," she stressed the word, "asks for you, I'll see that you're notified. Until then, I suggest you tend to your customers."

"Puta! I've already had your man," Lola lied. "He is too much man for a puny woman like you. When he is well enough to speak for himself he will ask for me."

Lola knew full well Colt would not ask for her. He had repeatedly resisted her best efforts and stubbornly opposed all attempts to get him into her bed. It surprised her to learn Colt had a wife—he didn't look the type to be faithful to one woman. The more she thought about the way Colt had spurned her advances, the angrier she became. Her beauty was legend, and men came from far and wide to buy her body. She was probably the best-paid whore in Texas. She had no need to throw herself at one man when dozens of others begged for her favors. Someday she'd make that Texas Ranger sorry he'd ever turned her down, Lola thought vengefully. His wife would rue the day she looked down her nose at Lola Cortez. Little did Lola realize that her revenge was close at hand.

For some reason Colt was restless tonight. Being confined to bed was definitely not to his liking. But weakness and pain prevented him from rising. He hated to think of the long days of convalescence ahead of him. He still wasn't entirely free of fever— it rose and fell with alarming frequency. But tonight something else nagged at him. His glance fell on Sam as she lay sleeping on a cot nearby.

He recalled the surge of elation he had felt on seeing her when he awakened from his stupor for the first time. Smith had told him how she insisted on coming to Laredo despite the arduous journey. Smith's words gave him a warm feeling he was hard pressed to explain.

"You're a lucky man, Colt, to have such a faithful missus. If I hadn't brung her here she would have taken off on her own. I reckon she loves you somethin' fierce."

Did Sam love him? Colt pondered. If she didn't, would she have faced the rigors of travel across Indian territory to come to his aid? In the deep recesses of his brain he could still hear her calling him back from the edge of death. Her words came back to haunt him—urging him to live, telling him she needed him, that their child— Sweet Christ! It couldn't be. Did Sam really tell him she was breeding, or was he hallucinating? A groan of anguish left his lips, and Sam stirred, alerted by his cry.

"Colt? What's wrong? Are you ill?" Clad only in a thin shift, Sam approached the bed. A lamp left burning in the corner cast its dim glow on the man tangled in the covers on the narrow bed. His eyes were wide and staring, alarming Sam. She raised her arm to test his forehead, but Colt's hand shot out to capture her wrist.

He had to know. Was she carrying his child or had he imagined those words? "Sam, lie with me," he urged, pulling her down beside him. "I want to talk to you."

"Can't it wait till morning? You need your rest."

Colt was adamant, and rather than agitate him further, Sam acquiesced, lying full length beside him. Hips and thighs touched, a bolt of fire jolted his loins, and suddenly all thought of talk fled. He wanted this special woman in his bed, in his arms, loving her, forever.

"We'll talk in the mornin' if you prefer, darlin', but lie with me for what's left of the night."

His request startled her. "I . . . I might hurt you."

"It would be worth it. I need you beside me, Sam. Please stay, you don't belong on that cot."

"All right, Colt," she consented with reservation.

Fitted snugly in the curve of Colt's body, Sam began to relax, her breathing slowing as she slipped naturally into a light doze. She was aware of nothing but the comfortable warmth against her, the tingling sensation in her breasts and the slow acceleration of her heart. The tingling grew. The heat spread to her loins, and Sam could not still the erotic movement of her hips in response to the mysterious stimulation that caused her breath to leave her chest in ragged gulps.

Hands. Warm hands, teasing hands. Hands sure and gentle were stroking her breasts, fondling her nipples, exploring the softness between her thighs.

"Sam, turn around."

Fully awake now, Sam lacked the will to resist the low seductive pull of his voice coaxing her into the web of sexual yearning. It had been so long . . . so very long.

"Kiss me, darlin'."

His lips, soft as down, touched her eyes, caressed the high ridges of her cheekbones, slid down the lengthy curve of her throat as she arched her neck to give him unlimited access. After pressing tantalizing kisses in the fragrant hollow at the base of her throat and across her shoulders, his mouth slid upwards. Desire was a bright flame within her when Colt finally found her lips. A sigh parted them and his tongue found the opening.

Colt groaned, savoring her taste as his tongue sipped greedily. She was sweet—oh, so sweet, and he deepened the kiss, continuing his gentle plunder until she lay breathless and quiescent in his arms.

"Colt, you can't," Sam gasped, fully aware where this kind of play would lead.

"It's okay, darlin', I won't hurt myself. Not if you help me. I need you so damn bad I'll go up in smoke if you don't let me love you."

The protest died on her lips as Colt raised her

shift and she felt his persuasive mouth on her nipple, the sucking sound he made highly erotic. While he diligently sucked one breast, long supple fingers toyed with the other. Sam worried about the effect that lovemaking would have on his wound and made protesting noises deep in her throat.

"Don't stop me, Violet Eyes, just help me."

Why did Colt insist on using her Indian name when lost in the throes of sexual excitement? Sam wondered distractedly. Yet this time she sensed no derision, no contempt in his words. Then he was urging her to her knees, whipping her shift over her head and lifting her to straddle him. Her train of thought was completely lost when Colt settled her on his chest and nuzzled her stomach. He hadn't let her shave him and his beard felt rough against her tender flesh.

"I want to give you pleasure first, darlin'," Colt murmured against the satin nest of her belly.

Exerting a strength that belied his condition, he lifted her upward, placing her knees on either side of his shoulders. She wasn't certain of his intentions until he buried his face in the warm fragrance at the juncture of her thighs. His tongue parted the black curling hair and unerringly his lips found the core of her femininity. He drank greedily, his tongue slipping into the moist opening, sucking, licking, lapping. Sam's mouth worked in a soundless plea, aching for that which only Colt could give her.

Desperately she clutched at his shoulders, taking pleasure in the tautness beneath her fingertips, in his exertion in her behalf. A muted scream left her throat as his tongue delved deep—deeper, while his hands cupped her buttocks, skimmed her hips, the tiny indentation of her waist, before fitting her breasts in his palms. Sam's legs shook like jelly as the pressure built, Colt's face all but invisible as he continued his erotic torture.

"Colt! Oh my God!"

Her hips undulating wildly against his mouth, the tension unbearable, Sam felt the powerful contractions beginning in the region of her loins and surging upward until her entire body was vibrating. Still Colt did not let up his marvelous loving until the telltale shriek, the last sigh, the final shudder left her body.

Then, urging her downward until she straddled his hips, he seized her lips, his tongue moving in and out with sensual torment that began anew the upward spiral. Afraid to put her weight on him, Sam balanced on her knees above him. He reached for her hand and placed it on his erection, her fingers curling naturally around the hard pillar of smooth velvet.

"Help me, Sam," Colt whispered, his need never greater as his towering strength jerked forcefully against her palm.

Raising her hips she took his hardness inside her, closing snugly around him. It amazed her that she fit him so well. Colt moaned in response to the moist heat surrounding him, and Sam thought she was hurting him until he groaned mindlessly, "Good— so damn good."

Grasping her buttocks, he set the pace, holding her weight away from his wounded side. Sam sensed his purpose and tried to ease away but his hands held her tight. "I don't want to hurt you, Colt."

"The only way you can hurt me is by stoppin'. No pain, no matter how severe, could make me leave your warmth. You feel so damn good inside I feel like I've died and gone to heaven," Colt drawled slowly. "Come with me, darlin'. Show me what I do for you. Tell me how you feel."

Mesmerized by his soft, seductive lovetalk, Sam's response was immediate. "No one could make me respond as you do, Colt. I feel all wet and melting inside. When you thrust inside me I want to scream in pleasure. Only you, my love, only you can make me feel like this."

Lifting his head to the breast that dangled so temptingly above him, Colt drew the erect nipple deep into his mouth, sending her senses reeling and her desire soaring. Tunneling her fingers into his crisp hair, Sam allowed him to work his magic once again on her willing body. He released her sweet flesh to whisper urgently in her ear, "Hurry, darlin', I'm nearly there and I want you with me in heaven."

His words were all it took to push her over the edge. Feeling her first tremors, Colt unleashed his tightly controlled ardor and stroked them furiously toward explosive, mind-numbing release. "Violet Eyes!"

Afterwards, Colt eased Sam to his side, the strain of their strenuous loving already taking a toll on his depleted strength and weakened body. But he did not let her go far as he curled an arm possessively around her slim form and pulled her into the curve of his body. Colt's last thought before he slid into

Chapter Seventeen

Heat. Flames seared her along one side. Sam sought to escape from the scorching warmth, but it followed her. Suddenly her eyes flew open as a terrible sinking knowledge jerked her awake. Colt lay beside her still as death, his breathing shallow and labored. His skin was damp and flushed, and Sam instinctively knew that the recurring fever was ravaging his body.

Leaping from bed, Sam flew into her clothes, noticing that the sun steamed brightly through the window. They had overslept. Their vigorous love-making had been exhausting and sleep had come instantly. But when had Colt's temperature risen so dramatically? Had it been the result of their loving? Sam cursed herself for ten fools. She should have realized that Colt was still too weak for the kind of activity they had engaged in last night, but his touch and his erotic words had rendered her completely mindless.

Fully dressed now, Sam headed for the door, intending to brew the herbs Laura had given her to combat fever. An insistent knocking startled her.

"Colt, Miz Andrews, wake up! We got trouble, a heap of trouble." Sam recognized Smith's rough voice and flung open the door.

"Mr. Smith, what is it?" The grave expression on his face set Sam's heart to pounding.

"It's the Crowders, ma'am," Smith said. "They're back in town and bound and determined to finish Colt." He directed his gaze to Colt and was stunned to see him flushed with fever and barely conscious.

"It's the fever again, Mr. Smith," Sam said worriedly. "Tell me what you know about the Crowders."

"Lyle Crowder paid for Lola's favors last night. I was passin' her door just now when I heard Colt's name mentioned. The door was ajar and I stopped to listen. Lola was tellin' Crowder that Colt wasn't dead, that you were here nursin' him back to health."

"Hellfire and damnation! That spiteful bitch! To think they were in the same building last night." A shudder passed through her.

"That ain't all, ma'am," Smith continued, blanching at her colorful language. "As soon as his men sober up they're gonna kill Colt and take you prisoner. I don't need to tell you what that means."

It took little imagination for Sam to realize what the Crowders intended to do with her. "Damn that jealous bitch to hell and back," Sam muttered. "What can we do?"

"I don't reckon the Crowders will be sober enough to ride for a couple of hours yet," Smith calculated. "Enough time to find a wagon for Colt and hightail it outta here before the gang comes gunnin' for him."

"No! The ride will kill Colt in his condition," protested Sam.

"Miz Andrews," Smith said earnestly. "If we stay here, the Crowders will kill him. There's a good chance Colt will survive a wagon ride, but waitin' for the Crowders means sure death for Colt and worse for you."

Sam bit her lower lip. "You're right, of course, Mr. Smith. Get the wagon and bring it around to the back door. I'll gather up our things and get Colt into his clothes. Hurry!"

"Was that Smith?" Sam whirled to find Colt's overbright eyes regarding her curiously. "Somethin's wrong. What is it?"

There was no reason to lie. "It's the Crowders. They're in town and been told you're still alive."

"I was afraid somethin' like this would happen." Colt grimaced. "They'll finish me off this time. How long do we have?"

"An hour at the most."

"You gotta leave, darlin'," Colt said urgently. "Your life's too precious to me to waste."

Precious? Her life was precious to Colt? Was he delirious? Regretfully, there was no time to pursue that intriguing thought. "I won't leave you, Colt. Don't ask that of me. Smith has gone after a wagon. We'll leave here together."

"I'll only slow you down. Don't be so dang mule-stubborn, Sam. I'm burnin' with fever, my wound is hurtin' somethin' fierce, and I'm too weak to hold a gun. When Smith gets here you're to go with him, no argument, no tears—just get."

"You know I've never taken orders well," Sam returned stubbornly. "And if you don't help me with your clothes, we'll drag you out of here bare-ass naked."

Colt smothered a smile with a groan of pain. Someday he was going to have to do something about her mouth. But he knew defeat when it stared him in the face. The feisty wildcat he had come to love—he was finally willing to admit to it—had him cornered. If he didn't leave with her and Smith, she would remain and surely be taken by the Crowders.

Grudgingly, Colt lifted his legs so Sam could slide his pants over his hips and shove on his boots. Helping him to a sitting position, Sam struggled with his buckskin shirt until finally he was dressed. He lay back exhausted and perspiring, watching while Sam swiftly gathered up their meager belongings.

The door opened and Sam whipped around, the six-shooter strapped around her waist already in her hand. She relaxed when Smith slipped inside the room. "All set?" he asked, glancing with obvious relief at Colt's fully clothed form.

Sam nodded. "Did you get the wagon?"

"Yep. It's in the alley."

"Did anyone see you?"

"Nope, but the Crowders are movin' around in the cantina. Ain't certain how much time we got. All depends on how drunk they got last night."

"We're ready. Help me get Colt on his feet."

"Christ, I feel like a mewling infant!" Colt complained, wincing as he tried unsuccessfully to rise by himself. Instantly Smith came to his aid, but Colt resisted.

"Take Sam and go without me, Phil," Colt urged desperately. "I'd only slow you down, and I don't want those bastards gettin' their hands on my wife."

Smith looked uncertainly at Sam, leaving it in her hands.

"Ignore him, Mr. Smith," Sam said briskly. "Obviously my husband is delirious. I'm not going anywhere without him."

Colt gave Sam an obstinate look but was too weak to back it up in view of her palpable determination, with her trim legs in tight trousers planted wide apart, hands on hips, an implacable expression furrowing her brow, and those incredible violet eyes daring defiance. Colt acquiesced with ill grace, allowing himself to be hoisted up between Smith and Sam and half-dragged, half-carried from the room. His legs were like rubber beneath him and he eyed the long hallway with misgivings. But somehow they made it through the hall and out the door without being stopped.

Smith had thoughtfully lined the wagon waiting at the back door with straw. Both Sam's and Smith's horses were attached to the leads, with Colt's stallion tied behind. Smith had thought of everything, Sam reflected as they settled Colt in the wagon bed. He was perspiring heavily from the exertion, and the grimace on his face mirrored his pain. The moment his head hit the straw he was out. Sam climbed in beside him, took his head in her lap, and motioned Smith forward.

Deliberately avoiding the center of town, Smith

skillfully drove the wagon through back streets and alleys until they arrived at the trail leading north.

"We made it!" Sam exulted, leaning over Colt. "Don't give up, my love. Hang on, I need you."

Steeped in misery, Colt gave in reply only a tormented groan.

Had Sam known their stealthy leaving had been closely observed, she wouldn't have been so optimistic. From the window of her room facing the back of the cantina, Lola watched long enough to see the wagon carrying Colt and Sam turn north. Then she hurried off to find Lyle Crowder.

However, it was hours later before the gang rode out after their prey, fuming because they had let the trio escape while they were engaged in drinking and whoring. But Lyle wasn't worried. Sooner or later they'd catch up with that damned Texas Ranger. He had more lives than a cat, but his time on earth was running out. Lyle decided the black-haired wench would be kept alive to serve as their own private whore.

"How's Colt holdin' up?" Smith threw over his shoulder.

"He'd do better if you slowed down," Sam advised, worried over the blood staining Colt's shirt. "Colt's bleeding again."

"Can't do it, not yet, Miz Andrews," Smith apologized. "We gotta put more miles between us and Laredo."

It was night before Smith pulled off the trail and stopped beside a dried-up stream with a thin trickle of water running down its center. Daring a small fire, Sam brewed herbs for Colt's fever while Smith filled the canteens and then went in search of small game for their supper. He returned later with a brace of rabbits, one of which Sam used to make a nourishing broth for Colt. Afterwards she settled down beside Colt in the wagon bed while Smith made do with stretching out on the hard ground and resting his head on his saddle.

Colt stirred restlessly. "I'm sorry, Violet Eyes," he murmured huskily, finding comfort in her nearness. "If it wasn't for me you'd be safe at home now."

"And you'd be dead," Sam returned irritably. "What's done is done. I'd have it no other way. Are you sorry I came, Colt?"

No answer was forthcoming, and his even breathing told her that he had fallen asleep. Thanks to Laura's medicine, he felt blessedly cooler. With any luck they'd be back at the ranch in five or six days, considering Colt's condition and their slow method of travel. Once they reached home, Sam reflected, she could decide whether or not to remain. These past days Colt had seemed a different man. He had truly needed her and freely admitted it. She desperately wanted to tell him about the baby but decided the time was not right.

They were on the road early the following morning. Colt's body had been refreshed by a cool sponge bath and his wound rebound, and he felt nearly human again. But when the wagon bounced along the rutted road, he realized he still had a ways to go toward full recovery, if the Crowders didn't catch up with them first. Colt knew those desparadoes better than anyone, and though he said nothing to Sam, he was well aware they would not give up on him so easily. They were as tenacious as they were lawless. Once they set their minds to something they weren't likely to back off.

Colt's small improvement allowed them to quicken their pace; and the third day found them more than halfway from Laredo to Karlsburg. Sam was jubilant, certain they no longer had anything to fear from the Crowders. Unwilling to cast a pall upon her happiness, Colt said nothing, remaining watchful and alert.

It was mid-afternoon, the white-hot sun high in the sky, when the first inkling of trouble came. Propped against the side of the wagon, Colt was the first to note the trail of dust rising behind them in a billowing cloud. With pounding heart he watched it until its ominous tidings could not be ignored.

"Riders!" Colt pointed, alerting Sam who dozed in the straw beside him.

Panic-stricken, she rose to her knees and squinted into the sun at the cloud of dust. "The Crowders?"

Grimly, Colt nodded. "Reckon so. Hand me my guns, darlin'. I can't ride, but I sure as hell can still shoot straight." To Smith he said, "Stop the wagon."

"What? Are you crazy?" Sam gasped, stunned.

"I'm bein' practical," he said cryptically as the wagon rolled to a halt. "Get out, unhitch the horses, and ride like hell. Smith will see that you get to the ranch safely." A meaningful look heavy with dire predictions passed between the two men.

"Hellfire and damnation! I'm not leaving, Colt."

Smith was already unhitching the horses.

"I'm countin' on you, Phil," Colt said, ignoring Sam's protests. "Get Sam outta here."

"You can trust me, Colt," Smith said solemnly.

His lined face was etched with sadness as he dug the saddles from beneath the straw in the wagon and readied the horses.

"No! You can't make me leave," Sam spouted belligerently. Desperately she clung to Colt, ready to die with him if need be. "There's three of us, it won't be so bad. We've plenty of ammunition."

"Darlin', look at me." Sam turned her head and it was the last thing she remembered. Mustering all his meager strength, Colt doubled his fist and aimed at her jaw. Sam went out like a light. "I love you, Violet Eyes," he said, handing her limp form up to Smith. "Be sure and tell her that, Phil, when she comes to." Smith nodded, too choked to reply.

"I'll keep them occupied while you get Sam safely away. They're still a long ways off and that's in our favor."

"I'll send back help, Colt."

Colt smiled ruefully. "Yeh, you do that. Now get!"

Pulling Sam's limp form up before him in the saddle and tying the leading reins of her horse to the pummel, Smith gave a blood-curdling yell and took off in a flurry of dust and gravel, leaving Colt to face the combined fury of the Crowders.

Heaving a regretful sigh, Colt turned his attention to the matters at hand. Now th t Sam was safe he could concentrate on giving her and Smith as much time as possible. First he untied the leading reins of his stallion and slapped his rump. No sense losing a good animal to stray bullets, he reasoned. Perhaps someone who needed a good mount would find him. Next he piled straw around the sides of the wagon to act as a cushion. Then he loaded his guns, arranged the ammunition nearby, and sat back to wait, breathing heavily from the exertion and cursing his limited strength. Colt had no idea how long he could hold out against ten determined men, but for Sam's sake he prayed it would be sufficient.

Sam was unconscious nearly an hour. She emerged slowly from thick layers of black gauze, fighting through the encompassing shroud into the light of day. Confusion stole her wits until she felt strong arms holding her upright in the saddle. With a jolt she remembered everything. How had they escaped the Crowders? Why had she blacked out? She turned in the saddle to question the man holding her so protectively.

"Colt, what happened?"

It wasn't Colt.

"Mr. Smith! Where's Colt?" Suddenly comprehension dawned. "Noooo! You bastard! You left him! You left Colt to die. Stop! I want to go back."

"I'm only doin' what Colt wanted, ma'am," Smith managed to convey over the hammering of hooves. "He didn't want you hurt."

"He hasn't a prayer against the Crowders and you know it!" Sam sobbed, struggling against the band of steel holding her firmly in place.

"It won't do you no good to carry on, Miz Andrews. It's for your own good."

"How . . . how long have I been out?"

"An hour, I reckon. Colt only tapped you, but it did the trick."

"Colt hit me?"

"He knew you wouldn't go on your own."

"It's not too late to turn back," Sam said hopefully. Smith's jaw tightened but he said nothing. It hurt him almost as much as it did Sam to leave Colt alone to face the Crowders. Colt hadn't a chance in hell of living through it. If he hadn't promised Colt he would take care of his wife, Smith would be fighting at his side right now.

Sam sensed Smith's determination and abruptly changed tactics. "I can ride by myself, Mr. Smith. Your mount will tire quickly if we continue this way."

Suspecting a ruse, yet recognizing the truth of Sam's words, Smith reined in sharply and carefully transferred Sam onto the back of her own horse. Sam smiled a secret smile, preparing to spur her mount and bolt in the opposite direction —back to Colt. But when she reached for the reins she saw them tied to the pummel of Smith's saddle.

"The reins, please," she said tightly.

"Sorry," Smith replied sheepishly. "It's for your own good, ma'am." Then they were hurtling forward, Sam clinging to the horn in order to keep from falling off.

Tears stung her eyes and a low wail of despair left her lips. She'd never even told Colt about the baby. Never said she loved him. All those days and nights spent fighting for his life were all for nothing— nothing! How could she live knowing Colt no longer walked the earth?

In the midst of her terrible agony, Sam became aware that both horses were being pulled to an abrupt halt. Smith was sawing violently on the reins, and a curse exploded from his lips. "Ho-ly shit! Injuns! From the fryin' pan into the fire."

Sam's head jerked upwards, her eyes widening. A

dozen or so Indians rode out of the brown hills. Comanche; probably a raiding party, judging from their vividly painted faces, Sam thought, and riding straight for them.

Smith reached for his rifle, and Sam unholstered her own gun as she drew abreast of Smith. The Indians approached at incredible speed, and Smith raised the rifle to his shoulder, taking careful aim. His target was a garishly painted brave who appeared to be the leader.

"No time to ride for cover," Smith barked. "Aim true and shoot to kill."

Nodding grimly, Sam raised her six-shooter, but something kept her from firing. A yellow flag caught her eye. Only it wasn't a flag. It was a banner of long blond hair flowing behind a small woman riding with the Comanches.

Laura! Both Jim and Jake rode beside her, flanked by Brave Eagle and his friends. Panic seized Sam when she suddenly realized that Smith didn't know Brave Eagle and was already squeezing the trigger of his rifle. "Noooo!" Her hand flung out and the barrel of Smith's rifle flew skyward, discharging harmlessly into the air.

"What the hell!"

"Don't shoot, Mr. Smith, they're friends."

"Friends? Them redskins ain't friends."

"I'll explain later. They've come to help. Look closely, you can see Colt's sister, his foreman, and his partner riding with Brave Eagle."

"Well, I'll be a pea-brained jackass," Smith said, his heart slowing as he lowered his rifle.

Sam chafed impatiently as she waited for the riders to approach. Each moment's delay lessened

Colt's chances for survival. Finally the group reined in sharply before the waiting pair.

"Sam, thank God you're safe!" Jim shouted gleefully. "I was furious when Laura told me you left without a word to anyone. Jake was madder'n a wet hen and wanted to take off after you immediately, but I convinced him to wait until I was able to join him. We came as soon as I could sit a horse. Where's Colt?"

"He's in big trouble, Jim," Sam said. "You've got to help him!" She looked pleadingly from Jim to Jake to Brave Eagle. "He's wounded and ill. I don't even know if he's still alive."

"Where is he?" Laura repeated Jim's question, looking frightened.

"About ten miles back," Smith revealed. "Holdin' off the Crowders so's me and his missus could get away."

"You must be Smith," Jake said. "I'm Jake Hobbs and this is Jim Blake. You already know Colt's sister. The braves ridin' with us are Brave Eagle and his friends. Comanche relatives of Laura's."

Smith nodded warily, obviously confused by Jake's last statement.

"Black Bear is camped nearby. It's a miracle that we ran into them," Laura explained. "They were following the buffalo further south than usual when we encountered them. I explained our mission to Brave Eagle, and he insisted on escorting us to Laredo. My adopted brother expressed his wish to help Violet Eyes and her husband."

"Can't all this wait?" Sam exploded, clearly distraught. "Colt needs us." Abruptly she kneed her mount in the opposite direction and galloped off.

Laura offered a brief explanation to Brave Eagle, and the party thundered after Sam.

Crouching down in the high-sided wagon, Colt reloaded his rifle with the last of his ammunition. This is it, he thought, his heart sinking. His bullets were nearly gone and all that remained were the rounds already in the chamber. But he had acquitted himself well, he reflected proudly, allowing Sam and Smith a considerable head start. He could think of no better way to lose his life than in defense of the woman he loved. His one regret was failing to tell Sam how much he loved her before rendering her senseless.

Two of the Crowders lay dead on the dusty ground surrounding the wagon, and the others had sought shelter behind various rocks. The shooting had all but ceased, but Colt wasn't fooled. He knew that Lyle Crowder was no fool and would realize by now that Colt was short of ammunition. Colt sat back to wait. The pain in his side robbed him of precious breath and the sun-baked earth wavered before his eyes. His hands trembled and he could feel blood seeping through his bandage. Resting the rifle on the wagon rail, Colt watched warily as the Crowders crept out from their hiding places, mounted, and prepared to attack en masse.

Colt grimaced, realizing his time was running out and he hadn't accomplished half of what he wanted to during his all too few years on earth. Thank God he'd had the foresight to leave a will. At least Sam and their child, if there was a child, would be well provided for.

Suddenly Colt's control snapped. He was hurting, angry, and driven to the point where nothing mattered any more but bringing down as many Crowders as time allowed. Rising to his knees, he aimed the rifle at the outlaws, who were now fanned out and riding toward him with deadly intent.

"C'mon, you worthless bastards!" he shouted, carefully picking out a target and smiling grimly when the rider lurched from the saddle into the dirt. "Come and get me if you got the guts! I'm takin' as many of you with me as I can."

His bravado had little effect on the Crowders as they rode in for the kill. Lyle Crowder's ugly face was split in half by an evil grin as he urged his men forward. Colt's return fire became sporadic as he conserved his ammunition, making every shot count. But he knew he was only prolonging the inevitable.

Not much longer now, Colt reflected, suddenly numb at the thought of dying. He was surprised at how calm he was when the last round left his rifle. Death wasn't so bad if one set one's mind to it, he reasoned, slumping down in a corner.

What happened next would remain forever etched in his brain. The thunder of hooves grew loud, then abruptly stopped. Colt prepared to meet his maker, only to be thrown into utter confusion when one of the Crowders cried, "Injuns!"

Peering over the side of the wagon, Colt saw that the outlaws had reined in a few yards away and were staring at something behind him. Whatever it was threw them into a panic, terror rendering them nearly immobile.

Then Colt became aware of a commotion behind him. Savage hoots and blood-curdling yells raised goosebumps on his flesh, and he jerked around. From behind him rode a Comanche raiding party, looking fierce enough to strike fear in the bravest hearts. Colt thought it ironic that they were all—the Crowders and him—likely to lose their lives violently and swiftly—if they were lucky.

Suddenly Colt blinked, then blinked again. Riding with the Indians were three white men and two white women. Even more astounding, he recognized them all, including the Indians. Brave Eagle. Somewhere Sam and Smith had run into Laura, Jim, Jake, and Brave Eagle's party. And miracle of all miracles, they had arrived in time. His strength depleted, Colt could do little more than cling to the side of the wagon and watch the ensuing battle.

Sam and Laura made straight for Colt and the wagon while the men attacked the Crowders, who, realizing they were outnumbered, turned tail and rode hell for leather. They were quickly cut off, and the ensuing fight was fierce but short. The Crowders were felled by either arrows or bullets and one by one bit the dust.

"Don't kill Lyle Crowder!" Jim shouted to Brave Eagle, who was aiming an arrow at the outlaw leader. "I want him alive!"

Lyle whirled his horse and urged it forward, but Brave Eagle charged after him, leaped off his horse, and threw Lyle to the ground. Two other Comanches joined him to wrestle Lyle into submission.

"You're a welcome sight," Colt said to Jim. "I was gettin' a mite worried." A gross understatement.

Turning to Brave Eagle, Colt said in Comanche, "Thank you, my friend. I owe Brave Eagle my life."

Eyes black as the darkest night regarded Colt solemnly. "A life for a life. A Comanche never forgets a debt. Lion Heart is husband to Violet Eyes who is dear to my heart."

Colt held out his arm. Brave Eagle hesitated only a moment before grasping it.

"Colt, are you hurt?" Sam asked anxiously, closely examining Colt's beloved features. Her eyes widened as they settled on the blood-soaked bandage circling his middle. "You're bleeding again."

"I'm okay, Sam, just tell me where you met up with Brave Eagle and the others."

"Let me explain," Jim interjected. "We were all furious when Sam left without tellin' anyone but Laura. It was a few days before I felt strong enough to ride after her. Of course Jake and Laura insisted on comin' along. We didn't know what we'd find when we got to Laredo."

"We met Brave Eagle and his hunting party late yesterday," revealed Laura, taking up the tale. "Black Bear is camped in the area and the braves were out hunting buffalo when we came upon them. After hearing our story, Brave Eagle insisted on escorting us to Laredo. We passed the night with my adopted father and started out early this morning. We met Sam and Mr. Smith on the trail, and you know the rest."

During the time it took for the telling, Colt had grown increasingly pale; his hands shook and sweat popped out on his forehead.

"Colt!" Sam cried, distressed. "He needs help!"

"Black Bear is camped nearby," Jim said. "Brave Eagle can escort you there."

"Spirit Dancer will heal Colt," Laura said with conviction before turning and speaking rapidly to Brave Eagle.

"What about Crowder?" Colt asked, his eyes sliding to the outlaw crouched in the dirt.

"I'm takin' him to San Antonio," Jim replied. "To testify against the Logans."

"I ain't squealin' on no one," Crowder refuted, clamping his lips tightly together.

"I think you will." Jim smiled ominously. "Course I could give you to Brave Eagle. The Comanches have devised methods of torture guaranteed to make a man talk. They can peel the skin from a man's body piece by piece and still leave him alive to suffer further indignities."

Crowder gulped, looking with terror-stricken eyes at Brave Eagle, who had caught the gist of the conversation and moved threateningly in his direction. Crowder cringed, the menace in the brave's obsidian eyes making up his mind.

"I'll talk. I'll do anythin' you say, Ranger," Crowder offered, blanching. "Just keep that savage away from me."

"C'mon, Crowder, on your feet, it's a long way to San Antonio."

Colt watched dispassionately as Crowder struggled to his feet. Then he turned to Smith. "What about you, Phil? Are you goin' back to Laredo?"

"I reckon I done wore out my welcome in Laredo," Smith drawled. "I've a mind to go to San Antonio. Maybe Jim can use some help with Crowder."

"Much obliged, Smith," Jim said. "I'd appreciate the help."

"Phil, if you need a job, there's one available at the Circle H," Colt offered. "We can always use another good hand."

"I might just take you up on it, Colt," Phil replied, grinning.

"You've been a good friend, Phil. I always take care of my friends."

"You got a deal. See you at the Circle H right after Crowder is delivered to the sheriff in San Antonio."

"What are you goin' to do, Jake?" Colt asked. "You comin' with us to Black Bear's camp?"

"I'd best be gettin' back to the ranch, boss," Jake replied. "We're smack in the middle of roundup and I reckon the men need me."

"I'm going with Jake," Laura announced, ready to argue should Colt refuse.

"You don't want to see Black Bear?" Sam asked, surprised.

"I will see my adopted father soon," Laura replied. "When he leaves this place he will settle his people nearby for the winter. I wish to return with Jake."

A smile hovered at the corner of Colt's lips, soon replaced by a grimace of pain. He had nothing against a match between Jake and Laura, and would not stand in the way if they truly loved one another. Besides, he was too ill to protest.

Soon afterwards Jim and Smith left with Lyle Crowder. A search of the surrounding area yielded nothing but dead bodies. All the Crowders save for Lyle were dead. Three of Brave Eagle's men were wounded, but they were still able to ride. Then Jake and Laura departed for the ranch with several Comanches accompanying them for protection. Two horses were caught and hitched to the wagon, and the party continued on to the Comanche village. By now Colt was writhing in pain, and the intervening miles were a nightmare.

Chapter Eighteen

Do not despair, Violet Eyes, Spirit Dancer will cure your mate."

"He's so weak, Black Bear," Sam lamented, casting anxious glances toward the tipi where Spirit Dancer worked over Colt.

"Lion Heart is strong and of brave heart. He has much to live for. Spirit Dancer tells me you will give him a son."

Sam blushed. "Spirit Dancer says the child I carry is a boy."

"Your husband must be pleased."

"He . . . I haven't told him yet."

"Then you must do so at the first opportunity," Black Bear advised sternly. "A man has a right to know he is to become a father."

Later, Sam mulled over Black Bear's words, realizing it was cowardly not to tell Colt about the baby. He deserved the opportunity either to accept or reject her and their child. If he did not want them she would leave and make a new life for herself and her babe.

That night, after Spirit Dancer left Colt, Sam slowly made her way toward the tipi.

"Is Lion Heart good to you, Violet Eyes?" Brave Eagle asked with grave concern. "I sense a sadness in your heart."

"I love Colt very much, Brave Eagle."

"That is not what I asked." He waited, his body taut, his noble features inscrutable. "If you are not happy, Black Bear will gladly welcome you into our tribe. It would be simple for Spirit Dancer to dissolve the union between you and Lion Heart, leaving you free to join with another. I still want you, Violet Eyes."

His eyes were dark and probing, his words impassioned.

"Much obliged for bringin' my woman to our tipi."

"Colt!"

Colt stood in the doorway of the tipi, holding his side and tilting dangerously. His face wore a ferocious scowl; his eyes were an inferno of molten gold.

"What are you doing out of bed?" Sam scolded.

"I was waitin' for you." His eyes never left Brave Eagle's face.

"I will leave you," Brave Eagle said. "Remember my words, Violet Eyes." With obvious reluctance the Comanche whirled and disappeared into the shadows.

"Let me help you back to bed," Sam offered,

slipping an arm about Colt's waist. "You're in no condition to be wandering about."

"What did he say?" Colt asked sharply.

"Nothing important," Sam hedged. "Did you want anything special?"

"You belong here with me. I'll rest easier with you beside me," he replied lamely. "Take off your clothes, darlin', and lie beside me."

"Colt," Sam protested, "you're too weak."

Colt smiled wanly. "I know. I don't aim to do nothin' but fall asleep with you in my arms."

Taking into consideration his weakened condition, Sam sighed in resignation and began to undress. The tipi was dimly lit by a small fire burning in its center, but enough light remained for Colt to observe the slender curves of Sam's body.

She wore a thin chemise beneath her shirt, but it enhanced rather than hid the full contours of her breasts. Tight pants slid effortlessly over rounded hips, her taut buttocks inviting his attention. Colt protested when Sam would have slipped beneath the blanket still wearing the short chemise.

"Take it off, darlin'."

Hesitating but a moment, Sam slowly pulled the garment over her head. Colt caught his breath. The pale gold of her shimmering flesh inspired him with a tenderness he never knew he possessed. She was lovely, more alluring than any woman had a right to be. He had wanted her from the first moment he saw her and would always want her. Without removing his eyes from Sam's enticing form, Colt lifted a corner of the blanket and she slid in beside him, being careful not to disturb his wound.

"Ummm, you feel good," Colt murmured, stroking her breasts with one hand while the other found the warm place between her thighs. "You smell good, too."

"I just had a bath in the stream," Sam said, already beginning to tingle and burn in the places where his hands caressed. Suddenly Sam came to her senses. "Colt, you musn't! You're much too weak."

Colt sighed regretfully. "I know. I reckon I'll have to recuperate real fast, won't I?" Several long moments passed while Colt rehearsed his next words. "Darlin', there's somethin' I want to tell you. Somethin' long overdue."

"Can't it wait 'til morning? I'm really too exhausted for conversation. And Spirit Dancer says you need rest."

"This has waited too long already," Colt argued. "I don't want another minute to pass without tellin' you how much I love you. I love the way you look, the way you talk. I love your courage and spirit, and I don't think I'll ever get enough of watching the way those tight pants you like to wear hug your sweet little bottom."

Sam simply stared at Colt, a stunned expression on her face. She wanted to pinch herself to make certain she wasn't dreaming. She had longed to hear those words for so long, she had imagined them many times. "You love me?" she repeated stupidly.

"More than my own life, more than I ever thought it possible to love a woman."

"I'm a half-breed Comanche," Sam reminded him. She hadn't forgotten how quickly Colt had rejected her when he'd learned about her Indian mother.

"I was a fool," Colt admitted wryly. "I've hated Indians for so long it robbed me of the sense God gave me. I'm not much at speechifyin', darlin', but I promise if you forgive me I'll never hurt you again. I want your love, Violet Eyes. I want you with me forever."

Tears stung Sam's eyes. She longed to believe Colt, needed to trust him. She loved him with her whole heart and would forgive him anything—anything. But he had hurt her so many times, she was more than a little reluctant to bare her soul.

"I'm afraid, Colt. I have no pride where you are concerned. I allowed you to make love to me when you hated that part of me that was Indian. I was worthy of your lust but not your regard. Now you ask me to love and trust you. In the past, loving you caused me nothing but pain."

"Forget all that, darlin'. I've banished the devils that drove me. I know your love is too precious to lose. I admit I was a bastard and I want to make amends. Please give me another chance. Without you my life is nothin'. I need you."

Colt's impassioned words were all Sam needed to unleash her pent-up emotions. "Oh, Colt, I love you, I do! It's just damned difficult to believe you love me after . . . after everything."

"I know I've been a jackass, but that's all in the past. My enlistment is up soon and I want to settle down and raise cattle and children. I want you for my wife, Sam. Though in truth I won't feel any more married than I have since Spirit Dancer joined us."

A joyous smile illuminated Sam's features. She

believed Colt. He sounded so sincere, so contrite, she could not doubt him. And now that she knew he loved her she could finally tell him about the baby.

"I feel the same way, my love. In my heart we've been married since that night long ago in Black Bear's village. And . . . well . . . there's something I should tell you."

"You mean about the baby?" Colt prompted. A devilish smile split his handsome features.

"You know? How? I've told no one but Spirit Dancer and Black Bear and they promised to say nothing."

"Don't you remember? You told me yourself. Only I didn't recall your words until a day or two ago."

Sam frowned, puzzled. "You must have been delirious."

"You have no recollection of beggin' me to live the first day you arrived in Laredo? Tellin' me you and our child needed me? Your words pulled me through, darlin'. Just knowin' you were there with me gave me the will to live. Do you think we'll have a son?" His face assumed a thoughtful look.

"Spirit Dancer thinks so."

The thoughtful look on Colt's face changed to one of incredible joy.

"You're pleased?"

"Need you ask? 'Course I'm pleased."

"But . . . he'll be a half-breed, Colt. You told me once you wanted no half-breed children."

"I must have been loco. I'll cherish our child just as I will you. I said those things because I was fallin' in love with you but didn't want to admit it even to myself. I know I've a lot to answer for, darlin', but you've got to believe me when I say I want our child. You . . . you want him, don't you?"

His expression was so woebegone, so filled with remorse, that Sam eased his mind immediately. "I can't think of anything I'd rather do than have your baby. I wanted him when I thought you hated me, and I want him now. Nothing has changed except the fact that you'll be with me to raise our child."

"Then you'll marry me?" Colt asked anxiously.

"Whenever you want," Sam assured him, snuggling against his warmth. "Now go to sleep, we both need rest."

"If I wasn't so damn weak I'd show you how much I love you," Colt murmured, his hands discovering the smooth heat of her flesh.

"If you weren't so damn weak I'd insist you back up your words with action. But since you're in no condition for that kind of activity, I suggest you go to sleep."

The time spent with Black Bear and his people was a happy one for Sam. Not only was she able to renew her friendship with the chief and learn more about her mother, but she had Colt's undivided attention while he regained his strength. Sam's nursing skills proved more than adequate as did Spirit Dancer's herbal remedies.

Within a week after his arrival in Black Bear's camp, Colt was on his feet again. Though Colt and Brave Eagle never became close friends, they grew to tolerate each other. Actually, the brave's tender consideration of Sam had much to do with Colt's swift recovery. Colt knew Brave Eagle still wanted Sam and was reluctant to remain longer than necessary in Black Bear's village.

A fortnight in camp found Colt ready to ride. Sam learned of his full recovery in a way that left her in little doubt of his strength and agility. When Sam cuddled beside him on the mat that night, Colt did not settle down to sleep as he'd been wont to do during the course of his illness.

Instead, Colt's hands roamed provocatively over Sam's warm flesh, settling on the rise of her hips as he pulled her close. The bold thrust of his manhood against her softness brought a gasp of surprise to Sam's lips.

"Colt, it's too soon!"

"It's long past time, darlin," he murmured in a voice made low and husky by desire.

"You're still weak," Sam offered lamely. Her body flushed with heat, a familiar warmth that only Colt could assuage.

"Weak?" Colt challenged, nuzzling the soft skin of her neck. "Does this feel weak?" Sam exhaled sharply as he slid atop her, his thick manhood probing her softness. "Or this?" In one fluid motion he easily penetrated the moist nest between her thighs.

Sam gasped, her eyes flying open as Colt buried his steely length full and deep inside her.

"Weak, am I?" Colt repeated, grinning with devilish delight.

Then he proceeded to disprove her words as he began rocking forcefully inside her, back and forth, thrusting, withdrawing, demonstrating his strength over and over as he drove her to the brink of madness. And beyond.

Later, when Sam was drifting off to sleep, completely sated and incredibly content, Colt once again demonstrated his returned vigor by launching another assault on her senses.

"Colt," she protested drowsily, "there's no need to overdo. I agree that you're fully recovered."

"Overdo? Hogwash," Colt chuckled, highly amused. "These past weeks have been pure torture. I've wanted to make love to you so badly it nearly killed me. Now hush up and let me love you again. If my son growin' inside you doesn't object, why should you?" She didn't.

Afterwards, Colt expressed his desire to leave the following day. "I'm anxious to know if the Logans have been brought to trial yet and if Lyle Crowder testified against them."

That wasn't precisely the truth. Colt hated the way Brave Eagle looked at Sam. The Indian was too virile and handsome for Colt's liking. The sooner he removed Sam from Brave Eagle's company the better he'd like it.

"Will we go directly to the ranch?" Sam asked. Though the Circle H was no longer hers, it was the only home she knew.

"Nope. I aim to take us first to San Antonio. It's important I speak to Cap'n Ford and Jim. When we return to the ranch it will be as husband and wife. I'll find a padre to marry us in San Antonio."

"Are you going to accept another assignment?" Sam asked fearfully. She never wanted to be separated from Colt again.

"Not if I can help it, darlin'. There's only a few weeks left on my enlistment and once Cap'n Ford learns I've married, I'm hopin' he'll release me early. I want to be around to watch my son grow up. And perhaps a daughter or two," he added, leering wolfishly.

"You mean you're through with the Rangers?" Sam asked hopefully. "For good?"

"For good, darlin'," Colt promised. "I'm no longer that hard-as-nails, gun-totin' drifter you once knew. You and Laura changed all that."

"I love you so much," Sam sighed happily, covering his face and neck with teasing kisses. "Even though you're ornery and tough as a two-bit steak. We're going to be so happy, I just know it."

"Forever," Colt vowed, warming to her kisses. "Now go to sleep before I'm forced to demonstrate my strength again."

Smiling contentedly, Sam promptly squirmed into a comfortable position against Colt and went to sleep.

San Antonio was just ahead, but Sam felt strangely reluctant to enter the city. She hung back, spurring her horse forward only when Colt halted and turned back to her with a questioning look. Forcing a smile, Sam joined him, trying desperately to shake the sense of impending doom as they rode into town. The feeling was so palpable she suppressed a shudder. Dismissing her misgivings, Sam squared her shoulders and tried to remember that she'd soon be Colt's lawful wife, not just his Indian squaw. Not only would her son carry his father's name, but she wouldn't be forced to leave her beloved ranch.

Before Sam knew it, Colt had reined in before the hotel, dismounted and was lifting her to the ground. After tethering the horses to a hitching post, Colt led her inside. Her unfeminine attire attracted stares and Sam was glad when Colt quickly signed the register and ushered her up the stairs. He had only one key in his hand and Sam belatedly realized he had engaged only one room. A slow flush crept up her neck when she imagined the knowing smirk on the clerk's face. Colt seemed oblivious as they entered the room, firmly closing the door behind him.

"You deserve a rest in a real bed, darlin'," Colt said, surveying the room with satisfaction. He wanted only the best for Sam. "Take a nap, then order a bath."

"What about you?"

"I'll be at Ranger headquarters for a spell. I hope to have good news about the Logans when I return."

Sam looked longingly toward the bed. It would feel good to lie down on its soft surface, she reflected. Her bottom felt like it was still a part of the horse.

"A bath first," she decided, "then rest."

"Sounds invitin'," Colt drawled. "As much as I'd like to stay and wash your back, I reckon I'd be delayed longer than I'd like. When I return you can shop for somethin' fancy to be married in while I bathe and change. First business, then pleasure," he said, his voice low and husky with promise. Then he grabbed her for an exuberant kiss.

Sam melted into his embrace, and when he began to pull away, she clung to him, reluctant to let him leave the room. Ridiculous, she scolded herself, Colt would only be gone a short while.

Colt sensed her fear and was puzzled by it. "What's wrong, darlin'? You seem upset. I'll be back before you know it."

"I know, Colt, it's just . . . I don't know, I can't explain it. Maybe the baby is making me sentimental."

Colt let out a relieved sigh. Of course it was the baby. Being a father was so new to him at times he forgot Sam was breeding. Didn't all women experience strange feelings during pregnancy? After reassuring her again, Colt left, somewhat reluctant but anxious to conclude his business and return to Sam.

"You mean there was no trial?" Colt exploded. "Damn! What happened?"

Colt stood facing Captain Rip Ford in his office at Ranger headquarters. As luck would have it Jim Blake had been there when he arrived. Now he sprawled in a chair listening to Colt's angry tirade.

"Did Lyle Crowder refuse to testify?" Colt raged.

"Not exactly," Captain Ford hedged. "Actually, both Logans were arrested and brought to San Antonio. A swift trial date was set. We were afraid Crowder would turn nasty and refuse to talk. And then—"

"Then—" Colt prompted, growing impatient.

"Calvin Logan suffered a heart attack in his cell and died."

"Christ!" cursed Colt, long fingers tunneling through his hair as he began to pace. "What about Vern? Surely Crowder's testimony indicated Vern was privy to all his father's fraudulent deals."

"Crowder never testified."

"What!"

"He was hung before Vern's trial," Jim explained in disgust.

"A lynch mob stormed the jail and dragged Crowder outside, despite the sheriff's best efforts to protect him," Captain Ford explained. "By the time I got there it was too late."

"Damn! Why couldn't the citizens of this town wait for the due process of the law?" Colt spat.

"The Crowders had terrorized the area far too long for rational thinking," Captain Ford replied. "Tempers were hot. People feared that Lyle Crowder might escape the fate he richly deserved. Most knew nothing about the Logans' dealings in Karlsburg. Some drunks starting talk of a lynching and the idea was promptly taken up by the mob.

"Vern Logan got off scot free," Ford continued. "When Crowder was lynched we lost our star witness. We had no choice but to release Vern due to lack of evidence."

"Jim worked for the Logans. What about his testimony?" Colt wanted to know.

"I didn't have enough evidence to convict Vern," Jim replied. "My orders came mostly from Calvin. He was a wily old man who kept his dealin's to himself. I reckon he had little use for his son."

"Why do you say that?" Colt asked sharply.

"It's common knowledge that Vern was disinherited by the old man. Vern was a big disappointment to his father. The bank was left in the hands of trustees until a nephew from Chicago shows up to claim it. Vern got the house and little else."

"What about the land Calvin cheated the settlers out of?" Colt wondered.

"It all goes to the nephew, his brother's son and by all accounts an accomplished businessman. I imagine he'll make a killin' by sellin' it to the railroad. Calvin despised Vern's weakness and penchant for gambling and whores. Vern squandered the fortune his mother left him on those activities as well as unwise investments."

"At least Vern didn't escape entirely unscathed," grumbled Colt. "Is the case closed, Cap'n?"

"It is as far as I'm concerned. Vern Logan may not be behind bars, but he's been made to pay in other ways. If you're wondering about your next assignment, Colt, there's a renegade Indian on the rampage up around Fort Worth and I thought—"

"Forget it, Cap'n," Colt interrupted. "No more assignments for me. I'm gettin' married today and my enlistment's nearly up an way."

Jim leaped to his feet, his face revealing his surprise. "You're gettin' married! It damn well better be to Sam. She loves you, you know."

"I know, and I love her." Colt grinned foolishly. "It took awhile but I finally came to my senses when I realized how close I'd come to losin' her."

Jim's expression brought Colt to an abrupt halt, and he suddenly realized that Jim cared deeply about Sam. He recalled that Jim had been at the ranch during his absence and had had time aplenty to fall in love with Sam. A pang of jealousy churned his gut until he remembered that Sam loved him, Colt, and not Jim. Compassion guided his words. "I'm sorry, Jim."

Jim merely nodded, his lips tight, eyes bereft.

"What are your plans, Colt?" Captain Ford asked. "Are you certain you're ready to settle down?"

"Damn right, Cap'n! I recently bought a ranch near Karlsburg and intend to settle down with my wife and child."

"Child?" quizzed Captain Ford, his eyebrows raising several inches. Colt had the grace to flush and the captain understood perfectly. Being a gentleman, he discreetly dropped the subject. Instead, he said, "Jim tells me you've found your sister."

Colt beamed. "It's a dang miracle. I'd nearly given up. I think Laura's finally settlin' down to the life she was meant to live."

"Good luck in all your endeavors, Colt," Captain Ford said. "You're a damn good Ranger, the best, and I'll miss you." He held out his hand.

"Same here," Jim added. "I couldn't ask for a better partner. I'll be goin' home myself soon."

"To Fort Worth?"

"Yep. I reckon I've had my fill of excitement for a spell. Pa is gettin' on in years and needs my help." They shook hands. "If there's ever anythin' I can do for you, just holler."

"The same goes for me," Captain Ford offered.

"Well, there is somethin'," Colt drawled. "I was hopin' you'd both act as witnesses at my weddin'."

Jim grinned. "Just name the time and place."

"I'd be honored," Captain Ford said.

"Meet us at seven o'clock this evenin' at the mission church," Colt responded happily.

"We'll be there."

"Stop at the paymaster and collect your pay,"

Chapter Nineteen

Sam savored every delicious minute of her bath. Afterwards she felt so invigorated a nap no longer seemed as inviting as it had. Dressing quickly in clean pants and shirt, Sam decided to buy a simple frock to surprise Colt when he returned. By now he must be tired of seeing her in nothing but masculine attire.

Counting the meager coins in her pocket, Sam decided she had sufficient funds to buy something attractive. The wedding dress could wait until Colt returned. Debating on whether or not to leave a message with the desk clerk for Colt, Sam decided against it, certain she'd be back long before he was.

Excitement seized Sam as she left the hotel. She paid little attention to her surroundings, never even noticing the man stepping into the lobby behind her. Vern Logan had fully intended to check out of the hotel today, but seeing Sam altered those plans. During the long days in jail Vern had laid all the blame for his troubles on Samantha for refusing his marriage proposal and on that blasted Texas Ranger for ruining everything his father had worked for. It was Samantha's fault that Vern had been disinherited and left with nothing but a house he didn't want. All the money and land amassed by his father was to go to a cousin he barely knew. It had shocked Vern to learn that his father had actually carried out his threat and left him penniless.

As for the Ranger, his snooping into things that didn't concern him had led directly to Vern's downfall. Damn Lyle Crowder for not finishing the Ranger off when he'd had the chance.

Finding Samantha in San Antonio stoked the fires of revenge burning in Vern's heart. Rage seized him and he wanted to hurt Samantha and that blasted Ranger in the same way they had hurt him. He was a broken man, Vern ruminated darkly, and someone must be made to pay.

The minute Sam walked out the front door, Vern rushed to the desk and inquired of the clerk, "Is that Miss Samantha Howard I just saw leavin'?"

"The lady's name is Colter. Mrs. Steven Colter. Just checked in today."

"Hmmm, I could have sworn she was a friend of mine from Karlsburg. Can you describe her husband to me?"

Obligingly the clerk described Colt perfectly. Vern blanched as comprehension dawned. The Ranger! Now he understood everything. Colt Andrews and Steven Colter were the same man! For some reason the Ranger used an alias. More importantly, he had purchased the Circle H using devious methods. Did Samantha know? Was she a part of the plot to keep the land from becoming part of the Logan empire? That thought inspired Vern with a burning desire for vengeance. No one made a fool of a Logan and lived to tell of it. If Vern had learned only one thing from his father it was that the Logans were a vengeful lot.

Vern Logan knew exactly what he had to do. Abruptly he turned and sped out the door, leaving the clerk with his mouth hanging open. Vern reached the street in time to see Sam ambling unhurriedly along the boardwalk. He followed discreetly until she entered the mercantile two blocks down the street from the hotel. His lips curving in a malevolent smile, Vern slipped into the alley between the mercantile and the feed store to wait and plan his next move.

It took no more than a few minutes for Vern to map a course of evil with Sam and Colt as the victims. Aware that Sam, like most women, would spend some time in the mercantile, Vern hurried off toward the livery stable where he boarded his horse. It was but a brief distance away at the end of the street. A short time later he was tethering his saddled mount behind the mercantile near the rear exit of the alley. Then he proceeded to the opposite end, where he slouched in the shadows, hat pulled low, waiting for Sam to emerge from the store.

Eagerly Sam sifted through the wealth of dresses offered by the mercantile. She was pleasantly surprised at the rather large selection and took her time choosing an attractive dress within her means. She finally settled on a pale violet linen with scooped neckline, puffed sleeves, and fitted bodice. The full skirt fell softly around her slim hips to the tip of her toes. Sam had no use for the hoops fashionable in more civilized places where clothing played an important role. Truth to tell, she loved wearing denim trousers, but realized that pants had no place in the wardrobe of an expectant mother. Already they were becoming too snug in the waist. And Sam wanted to look her best when Colt returned to their hotel room. She also bought a pair of soft slippers to match her dress.

Then she carefully studied the fancier offerings until she found what she considered the perfect wedding gown. It was a long dress fashioned of fine lawn in a pale shade of pink and lavished generously with lace. The color and style suited her well. The store clerk promised to hold the gown until closing, and Sam left the store with her dress and slippers done up in a neat package beneath her arm. Her afternoon had ended exceptionally well and she couldn't wait to greet Colt in her new finery. He had rarely seen her in a dress, and she smiled when she pictured his surprise.

Concealed in the shadows of the alley, Vern Logan watched Sam emerge from the mercantile and walk in his direction. His eyes glittered unnaturally as she drew abreast. Quickly glancing about, Vern satisfied himself that no one was in the vicinity before acting.

Sam never knew what happened as a long arm snaked out and she was dragged into the alley, one hand clapped against her mouth, the other around her waist. There was no time for struggle or even to call for help as her mouth was suddenly released, for the hand that had previously stifled her cries now clenched into a fist and slammed into her jaw. She dropped her package as she crumpled into Vern's outstretched arms.

Holding his breath, Vern listened for an outcry of alarm. When none was forthcoming, he scooped up Sam's limp form and quickly made his way along the narrow alley to the opposite end, emerging behind the mercantile where his horse was waiting. Mounting with some difficulty, Vern settled Sam in front of him, supporting her sagging body against his own. Taking a circuitous route out of town, he headed directly into the rugged country south of the city. Once out of sight, he stopped long enough to reach for his rope, tie Sam's hands together, and secure them to the pummel.

Struggling upward through layer upon layer of thick, suffocating cotton, Sam groaned, wondering why her arms and legs were numb. Gingerly she attempted to move, but found herself paralyzed. One eye popped open, then another, and the terrible nightmare she found herself in became reality. The last thing Sam remembered was leaving the mercantile in a happy mood. What happened after that, and where was she?

Excruciating pain penetrated the numbness in Sam's limbs, and she struggled to free herself, abruptly realizing that she had been bound hand and foot and left lying on a hard, uncomfortable bed. Slowly adjusting to the dim light, Sam surveyed her surroundings. From all appearances she was inside a damp, dark hole. A cave? Perhaps, though it was small and shallow with a hard, rocky surface, attested to by the sharp stones digging painfully into her back. Dragging herself into a sitting position, Sam felt a cold roughness behind her. She shuddered with the knowledge that solid stone hemmed her in and enclosed her. The opening to her dank prison was tall and narrow, and in it stood the figure of a man.

"Who . . . who are you? Why was I brought here?" Sam demanded to know. Her raging anger left no room for fear.

"So you're finally awake, Samantha."

Samantha! Only one man called her Samantha. "Vern? What is the meaning of this? I demand you untie me."

"You're in no position to demand anythin'," Vern observed, sneering.

"Release me now, before my husband discovers I'm missing and comes looking for me. Why are you doing this to me?"

"Are you referrin' to Ranger Andrews? Or do you mean Steven Colter? Are you really married to that meddlin' fool?"

Disconcerted by Vern's knowledge as well as his frank question, Sam stumbled over her words. "I . . . I . . . damn you, Colt and I have been married for weeks." She failed to add that her marriage was legal only among the Comanches.

Vern smirked. "Are you surprised I know about Colter? He's the man who bought your ranch and you knew it all along."

"N . . . no! I didn't know it until later," Sam refuted. "But that still doesn't explain why you are holding me prisoner. Or how you got out of jail."

"Did you know Daddy disinherited me?" Vern

asked, moving farther into the cramped, cavelike enclosure.

"I . . . didn't know. I'm sorry. What happened?"

"It's all your fault, Samantha." He paused to let his words sink in. "If you had married me, none of this would have happened. I'd be wealthy now and you'd be leadin' a life of luxury and raisin' my children."

Sam grimaced distastefully. "I didn't love you."

"I suppose you love Colter."

"Yes. Yes I do. Very much. You can't blame me for something that was entirely your own doing. It wasn't me who hired the Crowders to frighten and kill unsuspecting ranchers in order to cheat them out of their land," Sam spat, warming to the subject. "You and your father were probably responsible for Pop's death," she added in a sudden burst of insight. Until this moment she hadn't considered the possibility that either Vern or his father had ordered Pop's death in order to seize the Circle H.

"You can't prove that," Vern denied sourly. "The court hadn't a shred of evidence to link me with Daddy's dealin's or even suggest I knew what Daddy was up to. Daddy is dead. He died of a heart attack before the trial, and Lyle Crowder was hanged by a lynch mob. I was released from jail shortly afterwards due to lack of evidence."

"You know damn good and well what your father was doing," Sam said shrewdly. "Someday, somehow, you'll be justly punished, even if I have to see to it myself."

Vern laughed raucously, dropping to his knees before Sam. Grasping her chin between thumb and forefinger, he tilted her face upwards. "When I'm finished with you and your lover, neither of you will be in a position to do anythin'."

"What will you do?"

"First I get Colter out here, then I kill him."

"What makes you think he'll come? Colt's not stupid."

"You're my bait. When he learns I have you he'll hightail it out here so fast it'll make your head spin. Once I have him in my sights he's a dead man."

"Where are we?" Sam asked.

"In a cave formed by rocks above a shallow valley. It's called Twin Butte because of the double spires rising from the valley floor. Colter don't stand a chance. The minute he rides into view I'll put a bullet through his heart."

Sam froze, terror-stricken. Her own desperate situation was nothing compared to what Colt faced. Of course he'd ride out after her if he thought she was in danger. But how will he know? She posed the question to Vern.

"We're but a short distance from San Antonio," he informed her. "I selected this spot very carefully for its accessibility as well as its ruggedness. It'll be simple to slip back into town and leave a note for your lover with the desk clerk at your hotel."

"Vern, please, don't do this," Sam tried to reason. "You're not a vindictive man. I've always known you to be kind and thoughtful." She nearly choked on the lie, hoping to placate him despite the indisputable fact that Vern was a despicable varmint.

"Someone has to pay for everythin' I lost. Because of you and that Ranger, I'm penniless." Vern's eyes grew cold and empty, his lips tightened, and suddenly Sam realized he was quite mad.

Driven, no doubt, by his father and by circumstances that left him bereft of friends, family, and wealth. Or had he always been like that?

Vern turned to leave. "I'll be on my way now, Samantha. Hopefully I'll be back before dark."

"Vern, wait!" Sam wailed. "Don't leave me like this."

"Nothin' will happen to you. You'll be safe enough till I return."

"What happen then? What are you going to do with me? I won't marry you. I'm already married."

"Marry you?" laughed Vern nastily. "You're plumb loco. I wouldn't touch you after that Ranger and all those Comanches had you. True, I might have considered it once, to appease Daddy, but after I learned how you and Colter plotted against me, I wanted nothin' more to do with you. I've somethin' far more subtle planned for you."

"You're going to kill me?"

"Too messy."

"You'll let me go?"

"Not likely. I reckon you're a born whore. Once I kill Colter I'm sellin' you to Injuns. I reckon you've whored for them before and won't mind doin' it again. Only this time there'll be no Texas Ranger ridin' out to rescue you. You'll quietly disappear."

"You cowardly swine! Despicable jackass! Why not let me go?" Sam appealed. "I won't tell a soul what happened. I . . . I'm expecting a child. Colt's child."

It was the wrong thing to say. "Whore! If you really married the varmint you'll soon be a widow. And I reckon the savages will rid you of your bastard soon enough."

Tossing her a venomous glance, Vern turned on his heel and stormed away.

Colt hurried back to the hotel, anxious to tell Sam all that had transpired. Particularly the arrangements he'd made for their wedding. No one was going to call his son a bastard, so the ceremony had to take place as soon as possible. Besides, Sam belonged to him. He loved her. Christ, how he loved her! Though it was later than he had anticipated, Colt reckoned there was still plenty of time left to shop for their wedding clothes.

To Colt's consternation Sam was not in the room. All that remained was a tubful of cold water. Why hadn't she rested as he suggested? he wondered. Where had she gone off to?

Colt spent an anxious hour stomping about the room waiting for Sam to appear, still not overly worried, assuming she had become bored and gone out for a walk. But when another hour passed, Colt became convinced that something had happened to Sam, and cold fear motivated him into action. He rushed from the room to question the desk clerk and learned that Sam had left earlier in the afternoon and had not returned. He snorted in disgust, for he knew that much without asking. What the clerk failed to mention, for at the time it seemed unnoteworthy, was the fact that Mr. Vern Logan, a guest of the hotel, had inquired about Sam.

Starting at one end of the street, Colt made inquiries at each store until he reached the mercantile, where the store clerk recalled waiting on Sam earlier in the day. Encouraged yet strangely disheartened, Colt continued down the street, taking only a few steps before something in the alley next to the mercantile caught his eye. It was a bundle neatly wrapped and tied, and Colt snatched it up from where it lay on the dirty ground. Breaking the string, he carefully inspected the contents. The dress and slippers looked like things Sam would buy.

Unwilling to trust his own intuition, Colt retraced his steps to the mercantile, where the clerk identified the items as those purchased by Sam. In a daze Colt left the store, a terrible dread gnawing at his innards. He returned to the alley and carefully read the signs. What he found only added to his distress.

There were strong indications of a struggle, and tracks that suggested someone had been dragged through the alley. Following the prints, Colt found where a horse had been tethered, and surmised that whoever had been in the alley rode the animal away. The signs were all there. Someone had taken Sam away—but who? And why?

Colt was of a mind to get his horse and follow the tracks until he realized it was growing dark. As much as he hated to admit it, nothing could be accomplished until daylight. Clutching the package containing Sam's new clothes to his chest, Colt stumbled back to the hotel, numb and in more pain than he had ever experienced in his life, and he'd experienced plenty.

"Oh, Mr. Colter," the desk clerk greeted as Colt walked past the desk. "I've a message for you." He waved an envelope in the air. Colt froze.

"Yes, sir, a boy delivered it just minutes ago."

Snatching it from the clerk's hands, Colt merely nodded his thanks, then continued to his room, staring at the missive as if it were the snake in the garden of Eden.

The room was just as Colt left it, except the tub of water had been removed. He tore open the envelope, drawing out the single sheet of paper with shaking hands. His heart pounded, his body grew taut as a bow string as he read the brief note. At the end, he read it again, then cursed violently.

"I'll kill him!" Colt thundered. "If he's hurt Sam I'll kill the bastard."

Several long minutes passed before Colt realized someone was banging on the door. Jim's insistent voice brought him to his senses, and reluctantly he answered the summons. To Colt's chagrin both Jim and Captain Ford stood before him.

"What in the hell happened to you, Colt?" Jim asked worriedly. "Where's Sam? When you failed to show up at the church, we hightailed it over here. You were so eager about your weddin' we grew concerned when seven o'clock came and went with no sign of the bride and groom. Where's Sam?" he repeated.

"Gone," Colt said, his voice thin and reedy, his emotions drawn taut.

"Gone?" Jim echoed, stunned. "What happened?"

Abruptly Colt recalled the words in the note left by Vern Logan. He warned Colt to tell no one if he wanted to see Sam alive, and that included his fellow Rangers. Sam would live only if Colt followed directions. He was to go to Twin Butte, a local landmark south of San Antonio named for its tall spires, alone, at noon, unarmed and prepared to exchange himself for Sam.

Colt agonized over the terse words. It had been hand delivered by a messenger boy, and Colt neither doubted its authenticity nor discounted its threat. He was given no choice but to follow directions. He would gladly lay down his own life to save Sam's. He had only his cunning to rely upon, and his friends must not know the torment he was going through. At the moment Logan was calling the shots, and it was vital that neither Jim nor Captain Ford guess at what was going on.

"The weddin' is off," Colt growled, hoping to convince Jim. "Sam left."

"Hogwash!" Jim said, dismissing the notion. "That doesn't sound like Sam. Somethin' is wrong. What is it?"

"If you or your lady are in trouble, Colt," Captain Ford injected, "the Rangers will rally behind you. You can speak freely. You have my word it will go no further than this room."

"Much obliged, Cap'n, but I can handle it," Colt replied stubbornly.

"What is this all about, Colt?" Jim's brow puckered in concern. "Is Sam in some kind of danger?"

"Jim, we've been friends a long time, please trust me. Don't ask questions I'm not at liberty to answer. When the time is right, you'll both know everythin'."

"I'm convinced, Colt," Captain Ford said. "Be careful." He turned to leave. "Are you coming, Jim?"

"Give me a minute, Cap'n. I'll meet you in the lobby." Captain Ford left, quietly closing the door behind him.

"I want to help, Colt," Jim beseeched, undaunted

by Colt's obstinance. "I think you know how I feel about Sam. If she's in danger, I want to know."

"I appreciate your concern, Jim, but there's nothin' I can tell you. You'll have to trust me in this."

Jim's lips thinned as he studied Colt from beneath narrowed lids. He knew that something was terribly wrong but was powerless to help unless Colt confided in him. Then suddenly an alarm went off in Jim's brain. "It's Vern Logan, isn't it? Jesus, Colt, Logan has Sam!"

"No, Jim," Colt said tightly. Jim was too astute for his own good. "You're way off track."

Jim found himself being rudely edged toward the door, and before he knew it stood in the hallway staring at the closed panel. Momentarily stumped by Colt's stubbornness, he left, determined to find some way to help two people he cared about.

Sleep was impossible. Colt spent the endless night pacing and planning. Vern Logan had to be insane, he reasoned. A sentence in his note made it abundantly clear that Vern blamed Sam for the loss of his inheritance, and him, Colt, for bringing about his downfall. Logan wanted revenge, and Colt seriously doubted that Logan meant to let Sam go despite his offer for an exchange. There wasn't an ounce of honor in the man's black soul.

The longer he thought about it, the more convinced Colt became that Logan meant to kill both him and Sam. With this in mind he formulated a plan that had a slim chance of working. Colt hoped to beat Logan at his own game.

* * *

Sam writhed in pain, wondering if Vern meant to leave her alone in this godforsaken hole all night trussed up like a Christmas goose. Just when she gave up all hope of leaving this place alive, Vern returned. He spared her little more than a contemptuous glance.

"Vern, please untie me, I'm in agony."

"I don't trust you, Samantha."

"I promise I won't try to escape."

Vern seemed to consider her words, then made up his mind and untied the ropes binding her wrists and ankles. If Sam thought she'd been in pain before, it was nothing compared to the excruciating agony she suffered now as the blood rushed to her limbs. Tears streamed from her eyes and the power of speech left her as incoherent sounds gurgled in her throat. With a notable lack of compassion, Vern turned away to prepare a makeshift meal for them. Evidently he had shopped for supplies. As he set about opening various tins of food, he chattered on as if he and Sam were the best of friends. His lively mood sent Sam's spirits plummeting.

"Everythin' went quite well, Samantha," he confided. "I paid an urchin to deliver my message to the hotel, and by now your lover knows you are in my hands. By noon tomorrow he'll be dead. Wild animals will carry off his body and no one will ever know what happened to him. Or to you."

"This . . . this will solve nothing, Vern," Sam croaked, finding her voice with difficulty.

"Maybe not," Vern admitted, "but I'll feel a helluva lot better for it." He noted her wary look and laughed. "You think I'm crazy, don't you?"

"I . . . no, no, of course not!" Sam refuted, not wishing to rile him.

"Don't lie, Samantha. Nothin' will stop me from gunnin' down that blasted Texas Ranger."

"What did your note say?"

"I told him to be at Twin Butte at precisely noon tomorrow if he wants to see you alive. His life in exchange for yours."

"You're nothing but a stinking polecat with a yellow stripe running down your back," Sam blasted. "You're too cowardly to meet Colt like a man."

"You always did have a smart mouth, Samantha. Too bad you never saw fit to accept my proposal. I would have enjoyed taming you into a proper wife. We could have ruled Daddy's empire together."

Sam bit back a scathing retort. Obviously she was getting nowhere with Vern. He was beyond reasoning with, utterly ruthless in his desire to kill Colt and punish her for both imagined and real offenses. Instead, she said, "I . . . need some privacy." Her bladder was near to bursting and her discomfort acute.

Vern eyed her sharply, then waved vaguely toward the rear of the cave.

"I . . . I can't. I want to go outside."

"No! It's here or not at all." Calmly he returned to his preparations. "Don't worry, I told you before I no longer have the slightest interest in you as a woman. You sicken me. I'm surprised Colter wanted you after the Indians finished with you. No doubt he's not as fastidious as I."

Sam saw no reason to explain about Black Bear and her Indian ancestry. Instead she rose unsteadily to her feet and stumbled to the far reaches of the cave. Her legs felt like rubber, but the circulation was returning. Vern paid her little heed as she found a private niche in the solid stone walls. Evidently Vern had inspected this place thoroughly and knew there was no possibility of escape. Disheartened, she returned to her place near the entrance.

Silently Vern handed Sam a plate and cup of water. She ignored the food but drank thirstily, draining the cup and asking for more. Setting her plate aside, she asked, "What now?"

"We sleep. Then we wait for Colter to show up. I don't trust him. I'm willin' to bet he'll try somethin', and I'll be waitin'."

Colt reached Twin Butte an hour after leaving San Antonio. The rugged area was well known to him and he immediately recognized the twin spires rising in the air like a sentinel against a clear blue sky. There was a nip in the air, and Colt hoped that Logan had provided Sam with a blanket to ward off the chill. He hadn't.

Colt reined in some distance from the butte, tethered his horse to a tree, and traveled the rest of the way on foot. He reached the appointed place well before noon, selected a concealed boulder, and crouched down to wait—and watch.

Carefully Colt scanned the surrounding hills, looking for anything out of the ordinary. Somewhere up there Sam was the prisoner of a madman. But not for long, Colt reflected—not if he could help it.

Nothing moved. It was as if Colt were the only

person left on earth in the pristine stillness. The dun-colored hills looked newly created by God, so fresh, so silent, so peaceful in the early hours of morning.

An hour elapsed, then two, and still Colt waited. He estimated the time at about nine a.m. He grew anxious. What if Logan lied to him and Sam was already dead? Then he saw it. Halfway up a craggy mesa Colt spied a lone figure emerge from what looked to be a tall, narrow opening between two rocks. It was Vern Logan. He walked to the edge of a narrow ledge and carefully scanned the ground below. Colt remained well hidden behind the boulder, his sights fixed on the place from which Logan had emerged, committing it to memory. Then Logan turned and disappeared back into the slim opening.

Just thinking about Sam being held prisoner in that dark hole nearly cost Colt his sanity. But he knew Sam's life depended on his remaining calm. He took his time making a slow survey of the area, noting that the place where he had seen Logan was easily accessible. It sat above a narrow ledge or lip about halfway up the north face of a rocky butte. His mind worked furiously, finally deciding that the only way he could possibly reach Sam without being seen was by climbing up from the opposite direction and working his way around.

While Logan remained out of sight, Colt dropped to his stomach and inched his way into the open, praying Logan wouldn't suddenly appear on the ledge anytime soon. It was slow work but luck was with him, and once he reached a point where Logan could no longer see him, he rose to his feet and made his way around to the south side of the butte. He quickly found a place to scale it, hoping to surprise Logan when and where he least expected it.

It was rough going, and Colt stopped often to wipe the perspiration from his brow. By now the sun had effectively banished the morning chill. Colt's steps were sure and nearly soundless due to long practice stalking outlaws and Indians. Halfway up the butte he encountered the ledge that appeared to be part of the same one Logan had stood on earlier. Evidently it girdled the entire butte. Grasping the edge, Colt carefully pulled himself over the lip.

It proved an easy task, and soon Colt was crouching on the ledge, pausing to catch his breath and get his bearings. He decided to follow the ledge around to the north side and surprise Logan long before the hour of noon when he was expected to appear. Only he failed to consider Vern Logan's cunning.

Colt's first inkling that he wasn't alone came when a twig snapped just off to his right. Whirling, he reached for his gun but was stopped dead when Vern Logan calmly ordered, "Don't move, Ranger."

Colt looked up to see Logan's gun trained on him, his finger caressing the trigger. He had materialized like magic from behind a scrub pine. "Did you reckon I was fool enough to trust you not to pull some dumb stunt like this?" Logan smiled nastily. "I'm way ahead of you, Ranger."

Colt cursed violently. He should have known Logan would expect a trick and be prepared for it. Though Colt wouldn't give a wooden nickel for his own life, his thoughts were only of Sam.

"Where is Sam? Is she all right?"

"I've not harmed Samantha," Logan sneered.

"Then let her go. Now that you have me, Sam isn't important to you."

"You're right, Colter, Samantha isn't important enough to kill. I have somethin' altogether different planned for her. Somethin' she's not gonna like."

"I want to see her."

"Take your guns out very carefully and drop them over the ledge. One false move and you're dead."

Colt did exactly as he was told, tossing his guns over the ledge to the valley below. Then he felt Logan's six-shooter poking his ribs.

"Walk," Logan prodded. "Slow and easy."

They followed the ledge around to the north side of the butte until Logan suddenly called a halt. Colt looked around, his eyes widening when he saw the narrow opening in the rocks to his left. Rudely Logan shoved Colt inside. It took several minutes for his eyes to adjust to the dim light, but when they did he bellowed in outrage.

"You cowardly bastard! What have you done to her?"

Sam lay on her side, hands and feet tightly bound, eyes closed. Logan had tied her up again so he could grab a few hours sleep during the night. She had been released briefly in the morning to relieve herself and eat, then rebound. Logan strongly suspected that Colt would try to pull off something unexpected, so at dawn he had begun patrolling the entire area. He had just reached the south side of the butte when he saw Colt pull himself over the ledge. It wasn't yet noon, but Logan wasn't foolish enough to think Colt would meekly allow himself to be killed without a fight.

"I haven't touched Samantha," Logan said peevishly.

Colt dropped to his knees, turning Sam to face him. Only when he saw the steady rise and fall of Sam's chest did he draw in a ragged breath. "Thank God."

Voices reached out and beckoned at Sam. She imagined Colt was here, touching her, offering comfort. She had begged Vern not to tie her up again but he ignored her. The past night had been pure hell. Numb with pain and chilled to the bone, Sam wondered how much abuse she could endure without it affecting her baby. When morning came she was untied for a spell. Then, despite her fierce pride she had broken down and cried when Vern bound her again and left her alone. She prayed that Colt wouldn't appear, for she wanted him to live— even if she did not.

Slowly Sam opened her eyes, the dim contours of Colt's beloved features floating directly above her. "Colt? Oh my God, why did you come?" she sobbed. "He'll kill you."

"Has that swine hurt you, darlin'?"

"N . . . no, not like you think."

"Our baby, is he all right?"

"I . . . I think so."

"How touchin'," Logan said, his voice dripping with sarcasm. "Are you two really married? Or is Samantha your whore?"

Colt whirled, crouching low and coiled to strike, until he heard the metallic click of a pistol hammer.

Of what good would he be to Sam dead? Breathing deeply, he forced himself to relax.

"You're smart, Colter. One more move and I would have blown you away. Answer my question. Are you really married?"

"We've been married for months," Colt snarled, baring his teeth. "Sam's expectin' my child. What do you want from me, Logan?"

"Your life. Because of you and Sam I'm a ruined man. She had the gall to refuse my marriage proposal and made me look like an inept fool in front of my father. Then you came to town and brought ruination to the empire Daddy was buildin'. Everythin' would have been mine. It *should* have been mine. You'll both pay for what you did to me."

"Sam can't hurt you, let her go."

Logan laughed. "Get up." Colt complied, his mind working furiously. Was there no way to stop this lunatic? "Walk." Logan motioned toward the narrow entrance.

"Colt!" Sam's voice quivered in terror. It was a sound Colt would never forget.

"Don't fret, Sam, I'll take care of you." It was a rash promise and Colt knew it, but nothing comforting came to mind.

Logan laughed again, prodding Colt out into the bright sunlight toward the ledge. "What do you hope to gain from this?" Colt asked, playing for time.

"Satisfaction," Logan ground out.

Behind them, Sam mustered what little strength she had left and began moving toward the opening, dragging herself forward on her bottom using her bound limbs as levers. She emerged into the sunshine at the same moment Colt was forced out onto the ledge. He turned to face Logan just as Logan pointed his weapon at Colt's head and pulled the trigger.

"C-o-o-lt!" Sam's warning came a fraction of a second before the shot, and instinctively Colt ducked. But it was too late. Colt plunged headlong over the ledge, tumbling down, down, to the valley below. Sam's scream followed him to the bottom, where he lay in a broken heap.

Chapter Twenty

Jim Blake was not one to give up easily. His night had been every bit as sleepless as Colt's. He and Colt had been close friends for many years; they had saved each other's skin, shared meals, confidences, women. Jim had no intention of abandoning his friend now, despite Colt's obvious reluctance to confide in him. For Colt's good and his own peace of mind, Jim was prepared to meddle in affairs where his help was actively discouraged.

It was noon the following day when Jim decided to disregard Colt's plea not to interfere and resolutely headed for Colt's hotel room. His knock brought no response. Undaunted, Jim tried the knob, and was surprised to find it turned easily. Evidently Colt had left in so great a hurry he failed to lock the door behind him. Stepping inside, Jim gave the room a cursory glance, finding nothing amiss or even suspicious. But his Ranger training dictated that he investigate more thoroughly, for things were not always as they appeared.

His perseverance paid off. Within minutes Jim found Logan's note where Colt had carelessly kicked it, under the bed. It was wadded up in a ball and badly wrinkled but still legible. The message therein brought a groan of anguish from Jim's lips. He held little hope that Colt still lived. Nor could he be certain that Sam had survived Logan's cold-blooded vengeance. Logan had made it abundantly clear that he held both Sam and Colt responsible for all his troubles. A foul oath burst from Jim's taut lips. Why in the hell hadn't Colt trusted him enough to confide in him? Had Logan's threats on Sam's life robbed Colt of his senses? It was the only reason Jim could think of to explain Colt's behavior.

Realizing he had wasted enough time with conjectures, Jim swallowed his worst fears and rode immediately for Twin Butte. It was a landmark he knew well, and suspected that Logan had concealed Sam somewhere amid the buttes and mesas in the rugged area. He prayed he would find Colt still alive, that Logan hadn't already disposed of him. It heartened Jim somewhat when he considered Colt's cunning as well as his vast experience in dealing with desparadoes of all kinds. He had always known Colt to keep a cool head in tight situations. But the woman Colt loved had never been involved before, and that could make all the difference in the world.

Shock and disbelief froze Sam's face into a mask of abject horror. A silent scream formed in her throat as she watched Colt topple over the ledge. Lowering his weapon, Logan walked to the edge and looked down for what seemed to Sam like an eternity, frowning in annoyance.

"It was too damn easy," he muttered sourly. "I had hoped the bastard's death would give me more pleasure."

Suddenly Sam found her voice as hysteria seized her and refused to let loose. She screamed, and screamed, and screamed, the sound bouncing from hill to hill and echoing through the valley below. Spitting out a curse, Logan sped to Sam's side, grasped her shoulders and struck her face several times, the blows sharp and violent.

"Shut up, damn you, shut up! He's dead, and all your caterwaulin' won't bring him back."

The blows had the desired effect, for Sam's screams disintegrated abruptly into sobs, moans, and hiccups. Once she had quieted, Logan untied her ankles, and a new agony assailed her. Only this one was short-lived, not like the pain she would have to live with the rest of her life—if she had a life after Vern finished with her.

"Get up," Logan prodded, nudging Sam with his toe. "We're leavin'."

Leaving? Leaving Colt? "No, Colt needs me." Struggling to her feet, Sam tried out her legs, fully intending to stumble down the butte to Colt's side.

"Samantha, your lover is dead," goaded Logan cruelly. "He hasn't moved a muscle since he fell, and the sooner I get rid of you the happier I'll be. Soon as I get me enough money I'm gonna hire a lawyer to break Daddy's will."

Sam heard nothing beyond Logan's words confirming Colt's death. "Colt's not dead! Let me go, I have to go to him."

"You're comin' with me, Samantha. Didn't you hear? Colter is dead. I killed him."

"How do you know he's dead? He could be badly wounded."

"Look for yourself, damn you." He dragged Sam over to the ledge, forcing her to look down where Colt's body lay sprawled against a stubby pine. Her eyes easily picked out the path his body had taken down the butte, noting the trail of broken brush left in his wake, and a wail of despair left her bloodless lips.

Though logic told Sam that Colt was dead, her heart said otherwise.

"C'mon, Samantha, it's time to leave."

Reluctantly Sam allowed herself to be dragged by her bound wrists away from the ledge, though her eyes remained on Colt until she could no longer see him. And in that split second before he was torn from her sight, she saw something that filled her heart with joy. Colt wobbled to his knees, then flopped back down into nearly the same position in which he had fallen.

Fear lancing through her veins, Sam swiveled to look at Vern. Thank God he was too intent upon settling her on his horse to notice. And Sam was determined that he didn't. If he had the slightest inkling Colt lived, he would surely finish the job. Don't move, Colt, she silently implored. Please don't move. As they began the slow descent down the trail, Sam wracked her brain for a way to keep the knowledge that Colt still lived from Vern.

Dear God, she wanted to go to Colt. Was he badly

hurt? Or bleeding to death? Or had he broken bones? Deliberately stilling her rampaging emotions, Sam decided to distract Vern somehow in order to keep him from examining Colt more closely. She began to struggle against his imprisoning arms, making certain his attention was on nothing but preventing her flailing arms and legs from unseating them. It took all Vern's strength just to keep Sam in the saddle and left little time to watch Colt.

A short time later and after much travail, they reached the valley floor. Sam was seated in front of Vern, her hands tied to the pummel. They rode within ten feet of where Colt lay, but thankfully he hadn't moved again and Logan was so intent upon subduing Sam he barely spared a glance in Colt's direction.

From the corner of her eye Sam saw buzzards circling overhead and stifled the scream rising in her throat. Vern pulled out his pocket watch, noting that it was exactly noon. He smiled, pleased that everything was going so well. He rode northwest into the hill country.

Jim Blake found Colt's horse grazing contentedly some distance from Twin Butte. After a few minutes of indecision, Jim decided to ride on instead of traveling the rest of the distance on foot as Colt had done. It proved a prudent decision, for it saved him precious time when he needed it most.

Nearing the butte, Jim reined to a halt, cautious and watchful. His Ranger training had lent him a courage and icy calm few men possessed. With cool deliberation he divorced his emotions from everything but the need to save his friends. Then he saw the buzzards circling overhead and his heart sank into his shoes.

Tethering his mount to a branch of a nearby mesquite, Jim continued on foot, knowing without being told what he would find. The silence was profound. Jim's intuition screamed that he was too late, that Colt was dead, and maybe Sam, too.

He found Colt at the foot of the butte, sprawled against a stunted pine, arms and legs akimbo. "Jesus!" The word exploded from Jim's mouth, meant more as a prayer than a curse. "Sweet, blessed Jesus!" Jim broke into a run, sliding to his knees when he reached Colt's still form. Employing extreme care, he turned Colt onto his back.

He spotted the blood immediately, and a cursory inspection revealed a bloody crease in Colt's tawny head. Someone—Logan?—had shot Colt at close range. Jim sucked in his breath, amazed that Colt was still alive. Resuming his examination, Jim halted abruptly when his hand on Colt's ribs produced a long, pained groan and an upward sweep of his eyelids.

"Wha—where am I?" moaned Colt, gingerly testing his limbs with slow, deliberate movements.

"Don't move," Jim warned, sighing in relief at hearing Colt's voice. He never expected to find his friend alive. "Did Logan shoot you?"

"Logan!" Suddenly Colt's head began to clear and he attempted to rise. Pain exploded in the vicinity of his ribs and he fell backwards. Then his head began to pound in unbearable waves of agony. "Christ!"

"I reckon you've broken some ribs, Colt," Jim

said. "And there's a new part in your hair. Lie back while I perform some first aid. You can tell me what happened while I work."

Retrieving his canteen, Jim first offered Colt a drink, then cleansed his head and face of blood. "It's not as bad as it looks."

While Jim tore a spare shirt into strips to bind Colt's ribs, Colt spoke haltingly, trying to recall everything over the pounding in his head.

"Where's Sam?" Colt asked.

"I . . . don't know. There doesn't seem to be anyone about. Did Logan shoot you?"

"Yeh, and I don't understand why I'm not dead." He paused, deep in thought. "I probably owe my life to Sam. Somehow she crawled out of that cave and screamed a warnin' just as Logan pulled the trigger. I jerked my head and the bullet must have grazed me. The last thing I remember is tumblin' over the ledge." He pointed to the place he meant.

"You're the luckiest varmint I know," Jim said in wonder. "There, you're bound up nice and tight." He tied the last strip. "Can you ride?"

"Damn right I can. I've got to go after Sam and Logan. I don't know what he's got planned for her, but it can't be pleasant."

"Colt, you gotta be loco," Jim admonished. "You're in no condition to chase after anyone. You need a doctor. You've probably got a concussion and Lord knows what else. I'll take you back to San Antonio and go after Sam myself."

"Like hell!" Colt exploded, stumbling painfully to his feet. But the effort proved too much. He crumbled in a boneless heap at Jim's feet.

Jim made Colt as comfortable as possible, placing

his jacket beneath his head and covering him with the blanket strapped to his saddle. Then he scoured the area for clues. First he rode up the butte to the ledge Colt had pointed out, where he found the narrow cave and signs that showed it had recently been occupied. He peered over the ledge, finding the path Colt had left on his downward plunge, once again marveling at Colt's stamina as well as his rare good luck for having survived such a perilous descent. Then he found horse tracks and followed them to the valley floor, noting that they veered northwest. He returned to Colt, who by now was moaning incoherently and thrashing about.

Comforting him as best he could, Jim went to retrieve Colt's horse. This time Colt remained upright when he was helped to his feet, though his pain was considerable. How he managed to sit on a horse was a mystery to Jim, but he clung to the saddle horn while Jim led Thunder in a slow and easy gait to San Antonio.

Though Colt hated the thought of returning to the city without Sam, he did not protest, for he knew he was in no condition to pursue Logan. But once his ribs were properly bound and his head cleared, nothing or no one would keep him from following Logan and Sam. A miracle had saved him, and a miracle would restore Sam to him.

Something Logan had said earlier led Colt to believe that he wouldn't kill Sam outright, that he had devised some vile method of punishment. What was it? If the lowdown skunk harmed any part of Sam or their child, Colt swore vehemently, the bastard would die a slow and painful death.

* * *

Vern Logan rode with a purpose. An almost demonic desire to set into motion the final phase of revenge drove him north to Kiowa territory. Though he greatly feared those fierce savages of the Kiowa tribe, he believed they wouldn't harm him. Several years ago he had gambled excessively, losing vast sums. When his money was gone he signed IOUs, hoping his father would bail him out. Only it hadn't worked that way. Not even when his debts were called in did Calvin Logan relent, leaving Vern to work out his own problems.

Vern was far from solving his dilemma when he had met a Kiowa half-breed named Whiskey Joe in the saloon one day. Joe sported a broken leg and lamented loud and clear that he could neither sit a horse properly nor move about easily. More than half drunk and feeling sorry for the half-breed, Vern proceeded to tell Joe his own tale of woe. When he finished, a sly smile lit up Joe's swarthy features.

Vern soon learned that Whiskey Joe was a gun smuggler, carrying guns and ammunition, ill-gotten, of course, to the Kiowa. The deal had been made, guns for prime pelts, but then Joe had the rare bad fortune of falling down the stairs after a night of sporting with a whore and drinking. The result was a leg broken in two places. And the guns the Kiowa expected to arrive shortly remained hidden in crates in Joe's one-room shack at the edge of town. If they weren't delivered on time, Spotted Pony and his braves would never trust him again. Joe sensed a desperation in Vern Logan that could be worked to his own advantage.

Vern's life had already been threatened by those

to whom he owed money, and he was at his wit's end. Just because his daddy was rich didn't mean he had unlimited funds available. Just the opposite, in fact. But professional gamblers are a hard lot, and when they wanted what was due them, they could be ruthless. When Vern expressed interest in Whiskey Joe's problem, Joe grew enthusiastic.

"I need a man to drive the wagon to Kiowa territory," Joe confided in a low voice. "Someone I can trust. Are you interested?"

"To Kiowa territory? You're loco."

"You'll be safe," Joe insisted, "as long as I'm with you. I may not be able to sit a horse but I can ride in the wagon. I've already got a buyer for the pelts and I'll split the take with you."

The deal was too good for Vern to refuse. He drove the wagon loaded with weapons and Whiskey Joe. All went well, Spotted Pony was pleased with the guns, bestowing honorary membership into his tribe on Vern Logan.

After the adventure, Vern had breathed a sigh of relief, for he could have been apprehended at any time by both the Texas Rangers and the Army. Not to mention killed by the fierce Kiowa. Vern had earned enough money to pay his debts, but his cowardly nature prevented him from attempting the foolish feat again. In any event, Whiskey Joe was killed shortly afterwards in a barroom brawl.

As he rode north with Sam, Vern fervently prayed that Spotted Pony would still remember him, and perhaps offer him more prime pelts for Samantha. If not, he would offer her to the squat, ugly chief as a gift for allowing him safe passage through Kiowa territory. Then he might continue north to Colorado and try his luck panning for gold. Once he acquired enough money, he intended to hire a lawyer to break his father's will.

Vern did not stop for their noon meal, calling a halt only when his mount began to tire near dusk. Sliding to the ground, he pulled Sam from the saddle, allowed her a few minutes privacy, then left her sitting against a rock while he prepared a makeshift meal. Once they had eaten, Sam was bound hand and foot and was left to spend the night in abject misery. Vern made no attempt to molest her in any way, and she thanked God for that. In fact, once he learned she carried Colt's child he had acted as if touching her made his skin crawl, so great was his hatred for the Ranger.

By the time the sun made its appearance in the eastern sky they were mounted once again. Sam knew this part of the country well, and familiar landmarks led her to believe they weren't too far from Karlsburg. Perhaps even close to the Circle H, for occasionally she saw a stray cow or two bearing the Circle H brand. She prayed mightily for one of the ranch hands to appear, but to her despair, no one did.

Though Sam struggled to stay awake in the saddle, her pregnancy as well as Vern's careless abuse drained her utterly, and she dozed fitfully. Her discomfort during the night and worry over the child she carried had kept her awake until nearly dawn. Keeping her baby safe until Colt came for her became her primary concern. Sam drew comfort from the belief that Colt would find her, somehow, some way, as long as she could survive.

Vern's sudden intake of breath and his hands sawing on the reins revived her instantly. They slid to a halt as one word exploded from Vern's throat. "Comanches!"

Vern's eyes registered stark fear as he watched a small band of Comanche braves ride down from the hills. For a moment he thought he was a dead man, until he remembered Sam and his reason for being here. What earthly difference did it make whether he gave Samantha to Kiowas or Comanches as long as it saved his skin? he thought, relief sweeping through him. Why not offer Samantha to these Comanches in return for his safe passage? No doubt they would be grateful to him for such an extraordinary gift, though she didn't look like much now with her lank hair straggling down her back and filth covering her clothes and exposed parts of her body. Still, she was white and the savages would enjoy her. Stilling his pounding heart, Vern forced himself to wait calmly as the Indians surrounded him and Sam.

Brave Eagle had led his small band out of the hills to confront the White Eyes riding across the land owned by Lion Heart and Violet Eyes, land set aside for Black Bear and his people. From a distance he could see that two people shared one mount, a man and woman. Closer inspection revealed that the woman appeared to be a prisoner of the White Eyes, for her hands were tightly bound to the saddle horn.

Glistening black hair concealed the woman's face, and her clothes were stained and covered with trail dust. Her body was that of a young woman, though her slumped position led Brave Eagle to believe she was suffering from exhaustion as well as great stress.

Riding his pony to within inches of Vern, Brave Eagle knew instinctively that this was a man few would call friend. Though he tried to pretend otherwise, Vern's light-colored eyes revealed all the fear he harbored in his cowardly heart. Brave Eagle motioned for Vern to dismount, and he obeyed instantly, spouting words Brave Eagle pretended not to understand, though he understood far more of the white man's tongue than he spoke.

"Let me go and the woman is yours," Vern babbled, motioning to Sam as he spoke. "She was intended for my friend, Spotted Pony of the Kiowa tribe, but if you want her she's yours. She has known Indians before and will make a satisfactory whore for your braves."

Making little sense of Vern's inane chatter, Brave Eagle was nevertheless curious. For some unexplained reason the White Eyes was offering his woman to them for their whore. Was this man truly a friend of Spotted Pony, the Kiowa chief? Brave Eagle conferred briefly with his men before stripping the knife from the sheath at his waist and slashing the ropes binding Sam's wrists to the saddle horn.

Too weary to care, Sam paid little heed to what was taking place around her. She knew that Vern spoke of giving her to Indians but had no idea it was the Kiowa to whom she was intended. She had hoped it would be Comanches, for she spoke the language and could claim kinship with Black Bear's tribe.

Only when the Indians spoke among themselves did Sam's hopes soar, for she realized the braves were speaking Comanche. She looked up just as Brave Eagle freed her hands, her violet eyes wide and pleading as she gazed at the tall brave. Brave Eagle's sharp intake of breath told Sam he recognized her instantly, and she managed a weak smile before sliding sideways from the saddle into Brave Eagle's waiting arms.

Riddled with pain, every movement agony, Colt left San Antonio at dawn the next morning, his torso bound tight as a mummy and his head pounding.

"Dammit, Colt, you're a ornery cuss," Jim had spouted as he helped Colt mount his horse. "You should be in bed. Does your head hurt?"

"Hurts like hell," Colt admitted grimly, "but it'll take more than a busted head and cracked ribs to stop me. I gotta find Logan before he harms Sam and our baby. Christ! She could already be dead." That terrifying thought provided the strength necessary to spur him on.

They rode to Twin Butte, where Colt carefully studied the tracks, confirming Jim's earlier suspicions that Logan traveled in a northwestern direction. After a few minutes, Colt said, "They're ridin' double, we should overtake them easy enough. C'mon."

A few hours later they arrived at the place where Logan had made camp for the night. A thorough inspection yielded nothing new, so they continued on, eating in the saddle, stopping only briefly for necessities' sake.

"We're gainin' on them," Jim opined. "Logan doesn't expect to be followed, so he's travelin' slow to accommodate his horse who's carryin' a double burden." They rode on.

Suddenly Colt reined in sharply, frowning.

"What's wrong, Colt?"

"Look around, Jim. You worked on the Circle H a spell. Do you recognize anythin'?"

Jim took careful note of his surroundings. "We're not far from Karlsburg," he said, astounded.

"Look again."

"Jesus, we're on . . ."

". . . Circle H property," Colt finished.

"You don't suppose Logan's takin' Sam to Karlsburg, do you?"

"Don't reckon he's that stupid. No, Logan has somethin' devious in mind for Sam."

"If he continues north he'll reach Kiowa territory," mused Jim thoughtfully.

Colt's face paled. "Christ, you don't think . . ." His words trailed off and the two men exchanged worried glances that spoke volumes.

"Colt, we could stop by the ranch and get Jake and the boys. We're not so far that it would delay us overlong."

Colt considered Jim's words. It was a good suggestion, but Colt hated the thought of wasting one second. "I can't risk it, Jim," he said. "I gotta intercept Logan before he reaches Kiowa territory."

"But, Colt . . ."

"You go, Jim," Colt urged. "I'm goin' on."

Indecision worried Jim's features. On one hand he didn't want to leave Colt, but on the other he was smart enough to know that one or two men had little chance against the Kiowa. Coming to a swift decision, Jim nodded. "We'll be right behind you, Colt. Be careful and don't do anythin' foolish till we catch up."

Colt continued on alone, his head pounding, pain a living flame within him. It was inconceivable that Logan had brazenly ridden across Circle H property. Granted it was a remote area, mostly hills and woods that Colt had set aside for Black Bear and his people, but . . . Christ! Black Bear! He had nearly forgotten. Were they still camped nearby? Had they seen Logan and Sam? If they were still in the area they would be camped in a valley by the stream, Colt reckoned, turning slightly west.

Fighting for survival, Sam struggled against the arms holding her down. Consciousness returned slowly, exhaustion and hardship draining her strength. "No!" she cried, flailing wildly in an attempt to free herself. "My baby!"

The woman's voice that answered was soft and comforting. "You are safe, Violet Eyes. Your child rests easily beneath your heart." The Comanche words sounded strange to her ears, but Sam understood them perfectly and relaxed, fear leaving her. She was safe among Black Bear's people.

Sam opened her eyes, smiling at Singing Wind who bent over her, clucking in concern. Black Bear's wife was a kindly woman Sam had come to respect. She had treated Laura as her own daughter and was much loved by the People. Sam realized she was lying on a mat inside a tipi, probably Black

Bear's, with Singing Wind and Spirit Dancer kneeling over her, a gourd of dark liquid in the shaman's hands.

"Drink," Spirit Dancer said, holding the gourd to Sam's lips. Sam did not hesitate, drinking deeply as Spirit Dancer nodded in obvious satisfaction. "You will sleep now." He left, taking Singing Wind with him.

Sam's eyes grew heavy, her body seemed to be floating in space. When she would have succumbed gratefully to sleep's healing balm, Brave Eagle slipped inside the tipi and knelt beside her. A scowl furrowed his noble brow though his black eyes regarded her with tenderness.

"Who is the man who mistreated you, Violet Eyes? Why did Lion Heart allow this? If you were my woman I would keep you safe." His voice was harsh and accusing.

"It's not Lion Heart's fault, Brave Eagle," Sam explained. "This man, Vern Logan, carried me away while Lion Heart was involved in business. He . . . he lost much wealth and blames me and Lion Heart for his loss, though he has no one to blame but himself. He's greedy, selfish, and cowardly. He shot Lion Heart and left him for dead, but I know he's alive and will come for me."

Brave Eagle nodded, his noble features grim with determination. "The White Eyes will soon know the meaning of Comanche justice. Sleep, Violet Eyes, for when you awaken you will be avenged." His superbly agile body moved gracefully as he rose and slipped through the tent flap as silently as he entered.

"Brave Eagle, wait! What are you going to do?"

But it was too late. Vern Logan's fate was already sealed. Then Sam succumbed to the healing drug administered to her by Spirit Dancer and knew no more.

Chapter Twenty-One

Something terrible was taking place—some unnamed horror that dragged Sam unwillingly from
her drugged slumber and finally penetrated her
befuddled brain. The animalistic scream that awakened her was a long wail of despair and agony. As
she noted the narrow strips of light filtering around
the edges of the tent flap, Sam's first thought was
that she couldn't have slept long for it was still
daylight.

The next drawn-out scream sounded less than
human, and Sam clapped her hands over her ears.
An odd, indefinable smell assailed her nostrils, like
roasting meat, yet different. Then the screams came
in quick succession, one after another until there
seemed to be no end to one and the beginning of
another. Then silence. Absolute, profound silence.
The tent flap opened and Brave Eagle entered, his
body vividly painted with yellow, white, and black

stripes. He spoke only three words but their meaning did not escape Sam.

"He died badly." Never had Sam seen anyone as fierce-looking as Brave Eagle at that moment.

Having no desire to confront what lay outside, not yet anyway, Sam remained inside the safe haven of the tipi. It was cowardly of her, she knew, but Comanches were known for their brutality. She was not yet up to facing what remained of Vern Logan. She lay back, forcing her mind to more pleasant thoughts, wondering how long it would take for Colt to come for her. She loved him so desperately she refused to countenance the notion that Colt might be dead. He would come. Somehow, some way, Colt would find her.

Dazed by what her mind refused to accept about Vern Logan's death and still affected by the drug administered by Spirit Dancer, Sam drifted once again into an uneasy sleep.

Colt's search for Black Bear's camp was rewarded when he came upon a group of tipis clustered beside the stream that cut through his land.

His body tense, mind alert and watchful, Colt rode into the camp. And then he saw it. The charred lump that once was flesh and blood tied to a stake in the center of the camp. Vomit roiled in Colt's stomach and threatened to spew forth but for his stringent control.

"Your woman is safe." Brave Eagle's words dripped with contempt. "If Violet Eyes were mine I would protect her better than you have done."

An angry flush crept up Colt's neck. "Has my wife been harmed?"

Brave Eagle's words cut deeply into Colt's heart. Lord knows he already blamed himself for not protecting Sam. He should have rushed out immediately to warn her the moment he learned Vern Logan was loose in San Antonio. His failure to do so had provided Logan with the opportunity to hurt Sam.

"Violet Eyes sleeps. Spirit Dancer gave her a healing draught. She is bruised and exhausted but otherwise unharmed. Violet Eyes is a brave woman, Lion Heart. She would have made me a fine mate. She will bear strong sons and beautiful daughters."

"They will be *my* sons and daughters," Colt gritted from between clenched teeth.

The truth of Colt's words seemed to deflate Brave Eagle, yet he could not resist a final taunt. "Be warned, Lion Heart, I will take Violet Eyes from you if you fail to protect her."

"She carries my son."

"He will become my son."

"Violet Eyes loves me."

"Are you certain? She has suffered much because of you."

"Did she tell you that?"

Brave Eagle's silence provided Colt with the answer he hoped for. The Comanche wanted Sam but would do nothing dishonorable—unless Sam expressed a desire to dissolve their union. And she hadn't. The longing and unrequited love visible in Brave Eagle's dark eyes healed all Colt's doubts.

"Where is my wife?"

"She rests in the tipi of Black Bear."

Colt's eyes searched the cluster of tipis until he located the brightly painted and distinctive abode of the chief. Grunting in obvious pain, Colt slid from his horse.

Brave Eagle's eyes narrowed astutely. "You are hurt."

"I'll live."

"Spirit Dancer will see to your wounds."

"No! I've already seen a doctor. I want to see my wife."

Reluctantly Brave Eagle stepped aside. But before Colt could move past the tall brave, Black Bear and Spirit Dancer appeared. The old chief greeted Colt more warmly than his son had done.

"Welcome, Lion Heart, we expected you."

"Once again you have come to my aid, Black Bear, and I'm obliged," Colt said solemnly. "Please feel free to camp on my land as long as you like. You will not be bothered here as long as you don't raid my neighbors. Your beeves will arrive as soon as I return to the ranch."

Black Bear nodded. "We will winter here. It is good land. Your beeves will provide the People with food so there will be no need to raid. Go to your woman now, she is anxious to see you."

Moving stiffly, his body rigid with pain, Colt strode past the three Indians.

"You are wounded," Spirit Dancer observed, his words more a statement than a question. His keen eyes easily found the bloody track in Colt's head and his hands probed for further injuries hidden beneath Colt's clothing.

"It's nothin'," Colt declared, hastening toward the tipi where Sam awaited. Before entering, he paused briefly, turned, and said, "Send word to my

425

sister. Jim is on his way to the ranch to gather a posse."

"It has already been done, Lion Heart," Black Bear said. "Fawn will prevent your men from riding in needless pursuit of a man already dead."

Noiselessly Colt entered the tipi, dropping to his knees beside Sam. With shaking hands he lifted the edge of the robe covering her slim form. She had been stripped and washed and lay nude beneath the cover. Someone had kept a fire going in the center of the tipi, and Colt's eyes glistened when he saw the slight bulge of her stomach. It amazed him that throughout Sam's ordeal she hadn't lost their child. His soft expression turned to one of anger when he noted the bruises on her face and bloody grooves girding her wrists and ankles. When Colt first saw Vern Logan's mutilated corpse he felt a smidgeon of pity, but now, seeing the results of his abuse, he wished he had arrived in time to watch.

With one finger Colt gently touched Sam's face, worshiping her with his eyes and fingertips. She stirred beneath his tender caress, smiling in her sleep as he slowly ran the back of his hand over her cheek, past her chin to the slender column of her neck. It astounded Colt to realize how much he loved Sam. If he had lost her his life would have no meaning. Who would have thought a hard-nosed drifter like himself would experience a love so profound, so all-consuming and intense it would change the entire fabric of his life? Not even his violent hatred of Indians had destroyed that love, though at times it came close.

Sam stirred restlessly as she started to awaken. "Violet Eyes, I love you."

Sam's eyes flew open. "Colt?"

"I'm here, darlin'."

"Oh, Colt, I knew you'd come!" Her arms circled his neck in exuberant welcome. He winced but gave no other indication of his discomfort. "I was so afraid you were hurt badly when Vern shot you. I nearly lost my mind when you tumbled over the ledge. And later I saw blood. Did Vern's bullet miss you?"

"Relax, darlin', the bullet just grazed my head. I'm alive because of you."

"Me?" squeaked Sam.

"Your warnin' caused a reflexive action in me that saved my life. My head jerked in answer to your cry, and the bullet merely scraped a path along my scalp."

Instinctively Sam's fingers flew to Colt's head, where she traced the groove put there by the bullet. Her concerned gaze dropped to his face, frowning when she noted the bruises and scrapes.

"It's a miracle you survived the fall down the hill."

"I'm okay, darlin', honest. I've been hurt worse."

As if to prove his words he scooped her into his arms, his lips proclaiming her his for all time. Their kiss deepened, held as Sam's mouth opened, inviting a more intimate caress, and Colt happily complied. His tongue slipped inside, discovering once again all the sweetness she had to offer, all the sweetness that was his alone to enjoy for the rest of his days. He focused on her lips as if they were the first pair he had ever seen. He held her suspended with those intriguing tawny eyes and Sam melted inside.

"Will it always be this way with us, my love?" Sam asked, her eyes luminous pools of amethyst.

"Always," Colt promised.

Sam's response was to wrap her arms around Colt's waist and squeeze tightly. Colt cried out, his face paling.

"You're hurt!" Sam exclaimed, tearing at the buttons on his shirt. "Where?"

"It's nothin', darlin', just some cracked ribs." Sam sucked in her breath when she saw the tight wrapping that covered him from armpits to waist.

"Hellfire and damnation, how did you ride wrapped up like that?"

Colt grinned cheekily. "Very carefully." Abruptly he grew serious. "Let's go home, darlin'. I want to make love to you in a real bed tonight."

"You shouldn't be making love at all until you're healed."

"What about you? Did Logan harm you in any way? It drove me frantic thinkin' of all the ways he could have hurt you." Lovingly he placed his hand on the slight swell of her stomach. "Our son is safe?"

"Spirit Dancer says he is strong and suffered no ill effects. As for me, other than being tied up for long periods and slapped when I angered Vern, he didn't hurt me. Spirit Dancer's medicine has greatly revived me. Take me home, Colt."

Sam watched Colt undress, his hard-muscled body fit and virile despite the bandage that bound his ribcage. Never would she tire of looking at him, of wanting him, of loving him.

It was full dark when they arrived home, escorted

by Brave Eagle and three other braves. Recalling Brave Eagle's parting words brought a flush to Sam's cheeks and she was glad Colt was too busy undressing to notice.

"If Lion Heart cannot protect what is his, Violet Eyes, I will gladly accept the responsibility. I will always want you."

Though Colt wasn't close enough to hear his words, he had stared at them warily, as if surmising what Brave Eagle said. Sam made light of the brave's words, expressing gratitude for all he had done for her and reiterating her love for Colt. For a fraction of a second Brave Eagle's impassive features betrayed his innermost feelings, and Sam was deeply moved by the look of love and longing that flitted across his noble face. Then the look disappeared so quickly Sam might have imagined it. Thinking back, she was surprised that Colt had allowed Brave Eagle that moment alone with her, for he had never made a secret of his jealousy over Brave Eagle's attention to her.

Homecoming had been a happy event shared by everyone on the ranch. Will had been beside himself with joy. The last he had seen of his sister was the day she rode off to Laredo. In the weeks she had been gone Will seemed to have grown up. In Sam's absence he celebrated his fifteenth birthday and was well on his way to manhood. A pang of sadness struck Sam at the thought that the Circle H was no longer Will's inheritance as their father intended.

Before Will, Jake, Jim, and Phil, who had returned to accept Colt's offer of employment, trooped out to the bunkhouse for the night, Sam had managed a few private words with her brother.

It was not easy telling Will that she was half-Comanche, or that they had different mothers. But she wanted him to know before he inadvertently found out from someone else. Will looked at her strangely, not speaking for several minutes after the telling.

Would Will hate her? Sam had wondered, tears springing to her eyes. Or hate their father for keeping her ancestry a secret? She needn't have worried. Will had matured in the past few months, thanks to Colt, who had insisted that Will be treated like one of the men and not a child. It mattered little to Will who Sam's mother had been, she was still his beloved sister, the only relative he had left in the world. His arms went around Sam's neck and he hugged her tightly.

"You're still my sister, Sam, and that won't ever change. I love you."

Returning the hug, Sam had said on a sob, "And I love you, Will. I want you to be the first to know that Colt and I intend to marry very soon."

Will grinned. "I'm glad. I like Colt. I was certain you didn't hate him. In a way he saved the ranch by buyin' it. At least it will stay in the family."

"You're not bitter about Colt owning the Circle H? Pop meant it for you."

"Maybe, at first," Will had admitted, "but only for a little while. The ranch is thrivin' under Colt's direction. We would have lost it in any event. You have to admit that stagecoach robbery was a scatter-brained scheme."

Sam had had to agree, though if it hadn't been for their crazy prank that day she would have never met Colt.

"What are you thinkin'?" Colt asked, sliding beneath the sheet. "Are you unhappy that our marriage was posponed? Don't fret, darlin', you have my word we'll have that ceremony soon. When you're rested enough to ride into Karlsburg."

Sam's mouth curved into a beguiling smile. "Actually, I was thinking about Will. He's more of a man than I gave him credit for."

"You told him?"

"Everything. He took it very well."

"I'm sorry, darlin'."

"For what?"

"For not acceptin' your mixed blood with the same good grace as Will. I must have put you through hell."

"I forgive you. But if you ever act like a bullheaded jackass again, you'll sleep in the bunkhouse," Sam promised sternly. Her eyes sparkled impishly, belying her words.

"I'm glad you didn't insist I sleep out there tonight."

"Why would I do that?"

"Because we're not married yet."

"Spirit Dancer joined us weeks ago," Sam reminded him. "A preacher's words could bind us no closer than that simple Indian ceremony. A second wedding will serve only to satisfy the society we live in."

Colt's tawny eyes turned to pure gold as he lowered his head to capture Sam's lips. He knew he didn't deserve this special woman, and he vowed to spend the rest of his life proving his love. "I want to make love to you," he whispered against her lips. "But I don't want to hurt you or our baby."

"Your ribs! You'll hurt yourself."

"It will hurt far worse if I don't love you."

"Then love me, for I can't bear to see you hurt."

Slowly, sensuously, she removed her nightgown, and Colt's eyes widened at the sheer beauty of her.

Colt had touched her before but never with such patient tenderness as he did tonight, leaving hundreds of tiny fires in the wake of his touch. He wasn't just making love to her but worshiping her. His hands stroked her back and hips as his head lowered to drop soft kisses over her shoulders and the swell of her breasts, nuzzling their velvety softness. Shifting upwards, he lowered his lips to hers and kissed her hungrily, thoroughly. Trickles of excitement slithered down Sam's spine as Colt's tongue-tip danced along the sensitive line where her lips met, then probed hotly between them. Colt groaned. Sam was all woman—sweet, wild woman, coming vibrantly alive under his caresses—and all his.

His mouth left her lips, dancing over cheeks, throat, to her breasts, where he greedily licked her nipples until they rose against his heated mouth, taut and jutting with pleasure. A soft moan left Sam's throat as her whole body began to tremble and vibrate. She dragged in a shaky breath as Colt's hand sought and found the satiny folds of tender flesh between her thighs. The silken lips of her gently swelling mound felt slick and wet as he slipped a finger inside her.

"I want to make you happy, darlin'. I want to taste your sweetness on my lips." He slid downwards, replacing his finger with his mouth, the warmth of his breath disturbing the nest of dark curls at the joining of her thighs.

His hands lifting her to him and separating the satiny folds of her femininity, Colt captured the heart of her desire with his lips, bringing her to immediate and unexpected climax with his erotic tonguing. His loving torment continued until Sam grew quiet, then stilled. When Colt would have filled her with his throbbing strength, Sam pushed him back, rising to her knees above him.

"No, let me. I . . . I want to make you happy, too."

Then she bent forward and pressed kisses to his most sensitive region, stroking his towering length with her hands. When she opened her lips to love him, she felt him stiffen and cry out. "Christ!"

Suddenly Sam found herself on her back, Colt looming over her, his face taut with passion. "I'm only human, darlin'," he rasped harshly. "You drive me crazy, Violet Eyes."

He flexed his tight-muscled buttocks to fill her again and again. She felt her body expanding with his hugeness as he lifted her hips, driving even deeper within her. Sam absorbed all of him, urging him on, his every thrust taking her far beyond any place he had ever taken her before. And then the sweet desperation began, growing with the thrust and withdrawal of each stroke until Sam knew nothing but the warmth, the taste, and the smell of the man she loved beyond all reason.

A ball of fire burst within Sam's stomach and spread flames to all parts of her body as ecstasy exploded. Only seconds behind her, Colt soared to his own reward, crying out sharply, then dropping his tawny head to rest on her breasts. The pain in his ribs brought Colt abruptly back to earth, and gingerly he lifted himself, rolling onto his back.

Immediately aware of his distress, Sam teased impulsively, "I hope it was worth it."

A slow grin curved Colt's lips. "Give me a few minutes and I'll prove how little pain bothers me when I'm makin' love to you. It's nothin' compared to the pleasure you give me. I can't seem to get enough of you, darlin'. I thought a lifetime of lovin' you would be enough, but now I know even that won't be enough."

"A few minutes, Lion Heart?" Sam taunted saucily. "Is my tawny lion growing old?"

"Old? Never!" Colt growled, baring his teeth in a feral grin that made him greatly resemble the fierce golden beast whose name he bore.

"Then love me, Lion Heart, love me and never let me go."

"Forever, Violet Eyes, forever and beyond."

Epilogue

The small church in Karlsburg was crowded. A beaming Ida Scheuer sat in the front row beside a smitten Phil Smith, who had fallen under the attractive widow's spell the moment they met. Mayor Mohler, Sanchez, and the men from the ranch were there, and surprisingly, Sheriff Bauer and Deputy Lender. Even Captain Rip Ford had altered his schedule to attend the wedding.

Dolly Douglas, owner of the Palace Saloon, and bartender Dirk Faulkner sat near the rear of the church. In fact, the entire town had been invited to share in this happy occasion.

It was to be a double wedding. Samantha Howard was marrying ex-Texas Ranger Steven "Colt" Colter while Colt's petite sister, Laura, was taking Jake Hobbs, foreman of the Circle H, for a husband. Will Howard, the bride's brother, and their friend Jim Blake acted as witnesses.

The whole town reverberated with gossip involving Sam and her Ranger. Though Colt was generally hailed as a hero by the townspeople, it came as quite a shock to learn he was the new owner of the Circle H. Of course no one knew the entire story of Samantha Howard's involvement with the handsome rogue; talk had her bedding him long before the wedding and already with child. Not that it really mattered—he was marrying her, wasn't he?

The talk concerning Laura Colter and Jake Hobbs was not so clear. Little was known about either of them, though it was obvious to all that the couple were deeply in love. A grand reception was planned following the ceremony at the Palace Saloon, of all places. Dolly Douglas had been most generous to offer her place of business when it appeared that the entire town intended to turn out for the wedding and reception. The party was in full progress when Dolly managed to corner Sam while Colt was momentarily occupied elsewhere.

"You're a lucky lady, Mrs. Colter." Dolly smiled wistfully. "Colt's a good man. I knew he loved you from the first but he was too stubborn to realize it. I'm glad everything turned out well for you. When is the baby due?"

Sam blanched. "You know? How . . ."

"I guessed," Dolly admitted. "You're radiant. Lovelier than a bride has a right to be. I suspected there was a reason for such happiness besides the wedding. And I couldn't help but notice how careful Colt is of you. Imagine, Colt a father. He must be thrilled."

"He . . . is." Sam blushed, too happy to be angry

with Dolly. "I'd appreciate it if you kept it to yourself."

"Colt and I are old friends and I'd do nothing to hurt him, or his wife. I sincerely wish you nothing but the best."

Looking into Dolly's wide blue eyes, Sam realized she meant every word. "Thank you, Miss Douglas."

Later Dolly found the opportunity to return the letter and will that Colt had left in her keeping. "I'm damn glad I didn't have to deliver this on the occasion of your death, Colt," she declared flippantly. "I'd much rather attend your wedding than your funeral."

"You mean that, don't you, Dolly?"

"Every blessed word. Now go to your bride, and be happy." She squeezed his hand, blinking back the moisture gathering at the corners of her eyes. If she didn't know better, Dolly reflected, she'd think she was getting soft.

Shortly afterwards, a glowing Laura and beaming Jake left for New Orleans to begin their honeymoon. Phil Smith was named overseer in Jake's place, and upon their return the couple planned to settle on their own land which Jake had recently purchased. Colt and Sam were happy just to return home and be alone at the ranch. They had had enough traveling for awhile. Besides, with a baby on the way Sam wanted no more excitement for a good long spell.

Sam hugged Laura exuberantly before she boarded the stage. "Take care of my brother, Sam," Laura said and laughed happily. "And my little nephew-to-be." Sam had already told Laura about the baby, just as Colt had told Jake. Of course Will also had been informed. "Perhaps when I come back I'll have some good news also."

Sam and Colt returned to the ranch that night, making love tenderly and with great passion in the privacy of their own bedroom, not once, but twice. Then, just before dawn, Colt kissed her awake.

"Ummm," Sam protested mildly, "again, my love? Greedy varmint, aren't you?"

"I am where you're concerned. Besides, I haven't given you your weddin' present."

"Wedding present?" wailed Sam, distraught. "But I haven't a thing for you."

"You're givin' me my child." He said it with such overwhelming tenderness it brought tears to Sam's eyes. "I wanted to do somethin' for you even though nothin' could compare with your gift."

His enthusiasm was infectious as he leaped from bed and padded over to the chair where he had carelessly draped his clothes the night before. A lamp left burning provided sufficient light to guide his steps in the early dawn. Sam experienced a delicious naughtiness as she watched the muscles of his taut buttocks flex and unflex. She thought his legs superb, strong and lithe, as sturdy as twin oaks. Corded tendons rippled beneath the smooth skin of his back, and Sam was amazed that such perfection existed in one man. Abruptly he turned, and her eyes were drawn to his manhood, impressive even at rest. Colt was fully aware of the effect he had on her as he approached the bed, his lips curved in a crooked grin.

"If you keep lookin' at me like that, darlin', you'll never get your present."

Sam flushed, reluctantly raising her eyes. Vaguely she wondered if all men were so magnificently endowed. Somehow she doubted it.

A puzzled frown furrowed Sam's brow when Colt placed a folded sheet of paper in her hand.

"What's this?"

"Your gift. Read it."

Holding it close to the light, Sam scanned the contents. Exhaling softly, she said, "It's the deed to the Circle H made out to Will." The heavy lashes that shadowed her cheeks flew up. Then she began to cry.

"I hoped you'd be pleased," Colt said, his lips pursed in a pout. "I knew how much you wanted your brother to inherit the ranch. We'll hold it in trust for him and continue to live here until he's old enough to manage on his own. I've purchased several hundred acres just west of here. It's prime land, darlin', and we can build a house to your specifications. I . . . I wanted to make you happy."

"Make me happy? Oh, my love, you've made me deliriously happy. I love this ranch, but I wanted to keep it intact mainly for Will. I'll be happy anywhere as long as we're together. We'll found a new dynasty for our children, and the Circle H will be preserved for Will. Thank you, Colt. But how did you manage it? Where did you get the money to buy land?"

"I still had money left in the bank, and the land was bein' offered dirt cheap. It's damned ironic that the railroad people decided on a more northerly route and all the land Calvin Logan acquired is bein' offered for a song by the bank. I approached the trustees and bought the best of the lot."

Sam sighed wistfully. "The Logans' underhanded dealings earned them nothing but painful death. Greed is a terrible thing. It spawns ruination and destruction."

"But love brings peace and joy," Colt countered, his eyes pools of golden flame. "And new life."

"Colt, I never knew you were poetic," Sam exclaimed, delighted.

"I've been many things, Sam, but never a poet," Colt said and grinned, taking her in his arms. "I'd like to be remembered as a lover, and the best damn husband and father in the state of Texas. Now hush up and let me love you again."

She did—and he did—and in six months Sam fulfilled Spirit Dancer's prophecy. She gave birth to her first son.

Dear Readers,

I hope you enjoyed WILD IS MY HEART. I would love to hear from you and answer all letters. Write to me in care of my publisher. Your response to BOLD LAND, BOLD LOVE was most gratifying.

Sincerely,
Connie Mason

SHADOW WALKER
CONNIE MASON

Bestselling Author of *Flame*!

"Why did you do that?"

"Kiss you?" Cole shrugged. "Because you wanted me to, I suppose. Why else would a man kiss a woman?"

But Dawn knows lots of other reasons, especially if the woman is nothing but half-breed whose father has sold her to the first interested male. Defenseless and exquisitely lovely, Dawn is overjoyed when Cole Webster kills the ruthless outlaw who is her husband in name only. But now she has a very different sort of man to contend with. A man of unquestionable virility, a man who prizes justice and honors the Native American traditions that have been lost to her. Most intriguing of all, he is obviously a man who knows exactly how to bring a woman to soaring heights of pleasure. And yes, she does want his kiss...and maybe a whole lot more.

_4260-6   **$5.99 US/$6.99 CAN**